It may be cold ou
inside these

It is going to
Regency Christmas!

One Snowy REGENCY *Christmas*

Two gorgeous, glittering and seasonal Regency romances from favourite authors Christine Merrill and Sarah Mallory

One Snowy REGENCY *Christmas*

CHRISTINE MERRILL

SARAH MALLORY

MILLS & BOON

First published in Great Britain 2011
by Mills & Boon, an imprint of Harlequin (UK) Limited, Eton House,
18-24 Paradise Road, Richmond, Surrey TW9 1SR

ISBN: 978 0 263 89055 6

013-1111

Harlequin (UK) policy is to use papers that are natural, renewable and recyclable products and made from wood grown in sustainable forests. The logging and manufacturing processes conform to the legal environmental regulations of the country of origin.

Printed in the UK
by CPI Mackays, Chatham, ME5 8TD

A Regency Christmas Carol

CHRISTINE MERRILL

Christine Merrill lives on a farm in Wisconsin, USA, with her husband, two sons, and too many pets—all of whom would like her to get off the computer so they can check their e-mail. She has worked by turns in theatre costuming, where she was paid to play with period ballgowns, and as a librarian, where she spent the day surrounded by books. Writing historical romance combines her love of good stories and fancy dress with her ability to stare out of the window and make stuff up.

Look for more great novels from Christine Merrill in Mills & Boon's Historical romances.

Dear Reader,

It is always a challenge to write Christmas stories in the Regency. It's a historical period where the holiday is defined as much by what they didn't have as what they did. Many of the trappings we consider traditional are actually Victorian. Without carols, cards, trees and Santa, a Regency Christmas looks more like a big house party. And that can end up looking like any other Regency house party, but with the addition of bad weather.

When I began studying the problems in the North during 1811, the task became even harder. The workers were in revolt. At one point there were more British troops there than there were fighting Napoleon. Mill owners were hamstrung by embargoes that kept them from selling their cloth to countries allied with France. That included America, which had been a major source of income. There was an anti-war sentiment that is rarely mentioned in our largely patriotic stories.

The problems I was finding as I researched resonate today as much as they did then. There was a desperate need for compassion and understanding between labour and management.

And that thought led me to a story which was completely out of period, but the best primer anyone can hope for on the reflection, redemption, and charity that can be found at the heart of the Christmas season.

I hope you enjoy it.

Christine Merrill

With thanks and apologies to Charles Dickens.
And a question. Why did the spirits do it "all in one night"
when Marley is so specific about needing three?
That's always confused me.

CHAPTER ONE

December 1811

BARBARA Lampett ran down the lane at the edge of the village of Fiddleton, feeling the crunch of icy mud beneath her feet and the stitch in her side from the cold air in her lungs. Lately it seemed that she was always running after something or other. She wondered if the lack of decorum on her part was the first sign of a life spun out of control.

It was really no fault of her own. Had she the choice, she'd have been in a seat by the parlour fire, staring out at the changing weather and pitying those forced to go about in it. But Father paid little heed to his own discomfort when he was in one of his moods, much less that of others.

And she could hardly expect her mother to go. Mother's volatile nature would add warmth to the day, but it would do nothing to cool her father's zeal. Nor was Mother young and strong enough to face the crowd that surrounded him when he spoke, or to extricate him from the hubbub he created.

The new mill lay almost two miles from the centre of the village. It was too short a distance to harness a carriage, but longer than a pleasant walk—especially on such a chill December day as this. Barbara found some consolation that the ground was frozen. She had decided to forgo pattens in favour of speed, but she did not wish to ruin the soft boots she wore by walking through mud.

And much mud there would have been if not for the cold. Ground that had once been green and lush was now worn down to the soil, with the comings and goings of wagons and goods, and the tramp of growing mobs that came to protest at the gates of the new buildings of Mr Joseph Stratford.

A crowd gathered here now. Another of the demonstrations that had been occurring almost daily thanks to her father's speeches. Mixed amongst the angry weavers were the curious townsfolk. They did not seem to care either way for the plight of the workers, but they enjoyed a good row and came to the gatherings as a form of entertainment.

There was a sudden blast of wind and she wrapped her shawl more tightly about her, unable to fight the feeling of dread that came with the exhilaration. While it pleased her to see the people attracted to her father's words, the path he was leading them down was a dangerous one and his actions dangerously unwise. With each passing day he seemed to grow more reckless, speaking from the heart and not the head. He could not seem to understand what his comments would do to the local populous.

But she could feel them, caught in the crowd as she was, buffeted by the bodies of angry and fearful men. There was a growing energy in the mob. Some day a chance word or a particularly virulent speech would push them too far. Then they would boil over into real violence.

When the wind blew from the east you could still smell the burned-out wreckage of the old mill, where so many of these men had been employed. That owner had paid dearly for his plans at renovation, seeing his livelihood destroyed and his family threatened until he had given up and quit the area. That had left the protestors with no work at all, and even angrier than they had been before.

It seemed the new master would be cagier. When he'd built his new mill, like the pig in the old story, he had used bricks. It loomed before her, a blight on the horizon. Every element was an insult to the community and proof that the person who had built it lacked sensitivity for his neighbours. It was large and squat and altogether too new. He had not built in the wreckage of Mackay's Mill, which might have given the people hope of a return to normality. Instead he'd placed it closer to the grand old house where he currently lived. It was not exactly in the front park of the manor, but plainly on the estate, and in a place by the river that the Clairemonts had allowed all in the village to use as common greensward when they'd lived there. It was obvious that Mr Stratford had thought of nothing but his own convenience in choosing this site.

Though he showed no signs of recognising the impropriety of the location, he'd built a fence around a place that had once been the home of picnics and fêtes, trampling the freshness to hard-packed mud. Barbara was convinced it demonstrated on some deep and silent level that the master of it knew he was in the wrong and expected to receive trouble for it. The wrought-iron border surrounding the yard separated it from the people most likely to be angry: the ones whose jobs had been taken by the new mechanised looms.

She pushed her way through the crowd to the place where her father stood at the foot of the stone gatepost, rallying the men to action. Though recent misfortune had addled his wits, it had done nothing to dull the fire in his eye or the clarity in his voice. While his sentiments might be unwise, there was nothing incoherent in the nature of his words.

'The Orders in Council have already depressed your trade to the point where there is no living to be made by an honest man—no way to sell your cloth to America and other friends of France.'

'Aye!'

There were shouts and mutters, and the brandishing of torches and axe handles in the crowd. Barbara's heart gave an uneasy skip at the thought of what might happen should any man think to bring a firearm into the already volatile situation. She was sure that the mill owner towards whom the ire was directed sat in the closed black carriage just behind the gates. From there he could listen to every word. Perhaps he was even noting the name of the speaker and any others preparing to act against him.

But her father cared nothing for it, and went on with his speech. 'The new looms mean less work for those of you left and more jobs falling to inexperienced girls, while their fathers and brothers sit idle, dreaming of days past when a respectable trade could be plied in this country.'

The mutterings in answer were louder now, and punctuated with shouts and a forward surge of bodies, making the gates rattle in response to the weight of the crowd.

'Will you allow the change that will take the bread from your children's mouths? Or will you stand?'

She waved her arms furiously at her father, trying to stall what was likely to occur. The government had been willing to use troops to put down such small rebellions, treating their own people as they would Boney's army. If her father incited the men to frame-breaking and violence they would be answered with violence in return. Mr Stratford might be as bad as her father claimed, but he was not the timid man Mackay had been. He would meet strife with strife, and send for a battalion to shoot the organisers.

'Father!' she shouted, trying to catch his attention. But the workers towered around her, and her voice was swallowed up by the din. Before she could speak a calming word the first shot rang out—not from the crowd, but from the door of the carriage in front of them. Even though it was fired into the air, the mob drew back a pace like a great animal, startled and cringing. Barbara was carried along with it, relieved all were safe and yet further from her goal.

The carriage door opened and Stratford appeared, leaping to the ground before his worried footman could help him and springing to the same stone post where her father stood. He climbed easily up the back of it until he stood at the top and towered over her father and the other men. He held what looked like a duelling pistol in his right hand. With his left he drew back his coat, so the crowd could see its mate was tucked into his belt. He looked like a corsair—nimble, fearless and ready for battle. Barbara could easily imagine him with a blade between his teeth, rushing the crowd.

She was just as sure that he would be the sort to take no prisoners. Though he was a handsome man, in a dark and hungry sort of way, there was nothing in his sharp features that bespoke a merciful nature. His grey eyes were hard and observant. His mouth, which might be capable of a sensual smile, was twisted in a sneer.

Her father thought him the very devil, set upon the ruin of all around them.

But if devil he was then he was a handsome devil as well. Although she could think of a hundred reasons she should not notice it, she thought him a most attractive man. She schooled herself not to stare up with admiration, as she had caught herself doing on those few times she'd seen him in the village.

Perhaps she should have found him less impressive, for that sneer on his face quite spoiled the evenness of his features. While she had thought the position he took on the wall made him look taller than average, he hardly needed the advantage. He stood well over six feet. Today he was a fearsome thing, and nothing for a young lady to gawk at.

To match his physical presence he had the sort of forceful personality that seemed to incite strong emotion in friends as well as enemies. And, frightening though he might be, Barbara was sure that once she was focused on him she would not be able to look away.

'Who will be the first through the fence, then?' Stratford shouted down at the crowd. 'I swear to you, that man will lose his life along with his livelihood.'

The workers shrank back another pace, huddling against each other as though seeking warmth in the cold.

The man on the post laughed down at them. 'I thought as much. All bluff and bluster when there is no risk to you, and cowardice when there is.'

Her father turned, shouting up at him. 'It is you who are the coward, sir. Vain and proud as well. You hide behind your gates with your idle threats, unwilling to walk among the common man and feel his pain, his hunger, his desperation.'

Stratford glared back at him. 'I do not have to walk among you to know about you. I can go to the ruins of Mackay's place—a mill that you destroyed—to see the reason for your poverty. If you could, you would burn my factory as well—before I've even managed to open it. And then you'd complain that I'd treated you unjustly. I tell you now, since you have so conveniently gathered here, that I will not listen to your complaints until you begin making sense.'

It was unfair of him to compare this gathering to the burning of Mackay's place. Most of the men here had taken no part in that, rushing to save their workplace and not destroy it. The matter was much more complicated than Stratford made out. He was too new here to know and unwilling to listen, just as her father had said. Barbara pushed against the men around her, trying to work her way to the front again so that she might be heard.

Just as she thought she might reach her objective a man's boot caught in the hem of her gown and she started to fall forwards under the crush. She felt a rush of panic as she realised that no one around her was noticing as she fell. They had forgotten their fear of the second gun and were advancing to disprove Stratford's claims of cowardice.

She called out again, hoping that her father might hear and help her. But his back was to her as he shook a fist to threaten Stratford. He was too preoccupied to notice what was happening. In a moment she would be knocked to her knees. Then she would be dragged under, as though sinking beneath a human wave, and stamped into the mud in the trample of hobnailed boots.

'Ay-up!' She felt a sudden change, and the crowd parted around her. A hand caught her by the shoulder and yanked her to her feet with a rip of cloth. There was a shout as loud and ringing as her father's. But it came from close at her side, easily besting the noise of the crowd. 'Mind what you are doing, you great oafs. You may say what you like to me, but mind that there is a lady present. Have a care for her, at least. Perhaps I judge you unworthy of employment because you behave no better than animals.'

Then she was back on her feet, and the support was gone from her arm. She felt the crowd swirl around her again as her rescuer retreated. But for a moment there was a subdued quality to the actions of the mob, as though their frenzy had been defused by shame.

And the man who had saved her was back at the front of the group again, pushing past her father and climbing back onto the pillar that held the gate. She had thought Mr Stratford an intimidating figure even while behind the gates. But it was even more startling to have been so close to him, even for a moment. He had used his strength to force others out of the way, and his agility to be down to the ground and back up the fence before the mob had realised that he had been in their grasp. He was staring down at them again, his expression more disgusted than angry, as though they had proved to him that he was correct in his scorn.

'Go home to your families, if you care so much about them. A new year is coming, and a new age with it. You had best get used to it. When Stratford Mill is open in a month there will be work for those of you willing to put aside this nonsense and tend to your shuttles again. But if you rise against me I will see the lot of you transported and run it with your daughters. They will cost me less and have the sense to keep their tongues.' He reached towards his belt, and the group before him gasped. He withdrew not a pistol, but a purse, showering the coins into the crowd.

'A Merry Christmas to you all!' he shouted, his laugh both triumphant and bitter as he watched the threat dissolve as the crowd scrambled for the money. 'Do not bother to come here again. As long as I breathe, I will not be stopped. If you destroy the machinery I will get more, until you wear yourselves out with breaking it. Take my money and go back to your homes. I have summoned the constable. If you are here when he arrives you will spend Christmas Day in a cell, longing for your families. Now, be off.'

It shamed her to watch the men of the village too

busy on the ground to notice this new threat. They were a proud bunch. In better times they would have thrown the coins back in the face of this stranger rather than accept his charity and his scorn. But the recent economic troubles had left most of the village without work and in need of any money they might find to make any kind of a Christmas—merry or otherwise—for their families.

Her father's rallying cries were lost in the scuffle as men scrabbled in the dirt for pennies. Barbara pushed through them easily this time, until she could lay her hand upon her father's arm. 'Come away,' she whispered. 'Now. Before this goes any further. You can speak another day.'

It seemed the mood had left him, passing out of his body like a possessing spirit, leaving him quiet and somewhat puzzled, as though he did not quite know how he had come to be standing here in front of so many people. He would come away with little struggle, and she would have him home before the law arrived. All would be well. Until the next time.

Directly above her, and removed from the chaos, Joseph Stratford observed—distant and passionless, as though he did not know or care for the pain he was causing. When she looked at him all her father's anger and frustration seemed to rush into her. If the Lord had bothered to imbue her with reason, then why could he have not made her a man, so that other men might listen to her?

She turned and shouted up at the dark man who thought himself so superior to his fellows. 'You blame the men around me. But you should be ashamed of yourself as well. You stand over us, thinking yourself a god. You are mocking a level of hardship that you cannot possibly understand. You act as if you are made of the same rough wood and cold metal gears that fill your factory. If I could see the contents of your heart it would be nothing but clockwork, and fuelled by the coal running in your veins.'

Just for a moment she thought she saw a change in his face, a slight widening of the eyes as though her words had struck home. And then he gave a mirthless, soundless laugh, little more than a lifting and dropping of the shoulders. 'And a Merry Christmas to you as well, my dear.' Then he turned and stepped easily from his perch, dropping to the ground, though it must have been nearly eight feet, and strolling back to his carriage and his nervous grooms and coachman. They came cautiously forwards to open the gates so that the carriage could get through. They needn't have worried, for the men who had blocked the way had turned for home in embarrassed silence as soon as the money on the ground had been collected.

She pulled her father to the side of the road so that the horses could pass. But there was the signalling tap of a cane against the side of the box as the vehicle drew abreast of them, and the driver brought it to a stop so that Stratford could lean out of the window and look at them.

'This is not the end of it, Stratford,' her father said in a quieter voice. Now that the crowd was gone he sounded capable of lucid argument, and quite his old self.

'I did not think it was, Lampett,' Stratford replied, smiling coldly down at her father, staring into his eyes like a fighter measuring the reach of his opponent before striking.

'I will not let you treat these people—my people—like so many strings on your loom. They are men, not goods. They should be respected as such.'

'When they behave like men I will give them respect. And not before. Now, go. You have lost your audience, and your child is shivering in the cold.'

I am not a child. She was full four and twenty. Not that it mattered. But she *was* shivering—both from fear and the weather. The slight made her stand a little straighter, and fight the shudders until she could appear as collected and unmoved as her enemy was.

It did not seem to bother Joseph Stratford in the least that the weight of the entire town was against him. They had broken his frames once already and sabotaged the building of the mill at every turn. Still he persevered. Barbara wished she could respond in kind with that careless, untouchable indifference.

The envy bothered her. Perhaps—just a little—she appreciated the man's sense of purpose. However misguided it might be. When she looked at him she had no doubt that he would succeed. While her father was all fire, he flared and burned out quickly. But Stratford was like stone, unchanging and unmoved. It would take more than a flash of anger to move a man like him once he had set himself to a goal.

She looked again at him and reminded herself that he was proud as well. That sin would be his downfall if nothing else was. He could not succeed if he reduced all men to enemies and herself to a faceless, valueless child.

As she watched the two men, locked eye to eye in a silent battle, she was relieved that her father did not own a firearm. Though she thought she could trust Mr Stratford—just barely—not to shoot without provocation, there was no telling what her father might do when his blood was up and his thinking even less clear than usual. She reached out for her father's arm again, ready to guide him home. 'Come. Let us go back. There is nothing more that you can do today. If he has truly called for the constable, I do not wish to see you caught up in it.'

He shook off the embrace with a grunt and stepped back, giving an angry shrug as the carriage moved again, travelling up the road to the manor house. 'It would serve him right if I was arrested. Then the world would see him for the sort of man he is: one who would throw an old man into jail to prove himself in the right.'

There was no point in explaining that the only lesson

anyone was likely to see was that Stratford sat in a mansion at a fine dinner, while Lampett sat hungry in a cell. 'But it would make me most unhappy, Father,' she said as sweetly as possible. 'And Mother as well. If we can have nothing else for Christmas, can we not have a few days of peace?'

'I will be peaceful when there is reason to be,' her father acceded. 'I doubt, as long as that man breathes, we will see that state again.'

CHAPTER TWO

Joseph Stratford rode home alone in comfortable, if somewhat pensive, silence. The conclusion to today's outing had been satisfactory, at least for now. The crowd had dispersed without any real violence. But if Bernard Lampett continued stirring, the town was likely to rise against him. Before that happened sterner measures would need to be taken.

In his mind, he composed the letter he would send to the commander of the troops garrisoned in York. It was drastic, but necessary. If one or two of them were hauled off in chains it might convince the rest of the error of their ways.

His carriage pulled up the circular drive of Clairemont Manor and deposited him at the door—so close that the chill of the season barely touched him on his way into the house. He smiled. How different this was from his past. Until last year he'd frequently had to make do on foot. But in the twelve months his investments had turned. Even with the money he'd laid out for the new mill he was living in a luxury that he would not have dreamed possible in his wildest Christmas wishes.

Joseph handed hat, gloves and overcoat to the nearest footman and strode into the parlour to take the cup of tea waiting for him by the second-best chair near the fire. As he passed the closest seat he gave a gentle kick at the boot of the man occupying it, to get Robert Breton to shift his feet out of the way.

Breton opened a sleepy eye and sat up. 'Trouble at the mill?'

'When is there not?' He lifted his cup in a mock salute and Breton accepted it graciously, as though *he* owned the house and the right to the chair he usurped. While Joe might aspire to knock away at his own rough edges, affect the indolent slouch and copy the London accent and the facile gestures, he would never be more than false coin compared to this second son of an earl. Bob had been born to play lord of the manor, just as Joe had been born to work. He might own the house, but it was Bob's birthright to be at ease there.

And that was what made him so damned useful—both as a friend and an investor. The Honourable Robert Breton opened doors that the name Joseph Stratford never would, and his presence in negotiations removed some of the stink of trade when Joseph was trying to prise capital from the hands of his rich and idle friends.

Joseph took another sip of his tea. 'Lampett has been

giving mad speeches again—raising the population to violence. Lord knows why Mackay did not run him off before now, instead of allowing himself to be scared away. He might have nipped the insurrection in the bud, and his business would still be standing.'

Breton shrugged. 'Anne tells me that Lampett was not always thus. There was some accident when the men fought the mill fire. He has not been right in the head since.'

'More's the pity for him and his family,' Joe replied. 'If he does not leave off harassing me he will be the maddest man in Australia by spring.'

'Anne seems quite fond of him,' Breton said. 'Until they closed the school he was a teacher in the village and a respected member of the community.'

Joseph reminded himself to speak to Anne on the subject himself, if only so that he might say he had. It did not seem right that one's best friend got on better with one's prospective fiancée than one did oneself. But Bob and Anne enjoyed each other's company—perhaps because Bob was able to converse comfortably on subjects other than the price of yard goods and the man hours needed to produce them.

'If Anne respects him, then she has not seen him lately. From what I have observed he is not fit company for a lady. There was a girl at the riot today who must have been his daughter, trying to drag him home and out of trouble. She came near to being trampled by the crowd and Lampett did not notice the danger to her. I rescued her myself, and did not get so much as a thank-you from either of them.'

'Was this before or after you threatened to have the father arrested?' Breton asked dryly.

'In between threats, I think.' Stratford grinned.

Breton shook his head. 'And you wonder why you are not loved.'

'They will all love me well enough once the mill is open and they are back to work.'

'If there is work to be had,' Breton said. 'The Orders in Council limit the places you can sell your wares. As long as America is a friend of France, there is little you can do.'

'They will be repealed,' Joseph said firmly.

'And what if they are not?'

'They will be. They must be. The merchants are near at breaking point now. The law must change or we are all ruined.' Joseph smiled with reassurance, trying to imbue confidence in his faint-hearted friend. 'It will not do to hesitate. We cannot err on the side of caution in this darkest time. If we wish for great profit we must be more sure, more daring, more active than the others. A busy mill and a full warehouse are the way to greatest success. When the moment comes it will come on us suddenly. Like the handmaidens at the wedding, we must be ready for change.'

Breton shook his head in wonder. 'When you tell me this I have no trouble believing.'

'Then take the message to heart and share it with

your friends.' Joseph glanced out of the window at weather that was slate grey and yet lacking the snow he wished for. 'When we have them here for Christmas I will wrap them tight in a web of good wine and good cheer. Then you shall explain the situation, as I have to you. Once they are persuaded, I will stick my hand into their pockets and remove the money needed for expansion.'

Breton laughed. 'You make me feel like a spider, waiting for so many fat flies to ride up from London.'

'But that is not the case at all, my dear fellow. I am the spider. You are the bait—if spiders use such a thing. Without you, they will not come.'

'We will be lucky if they come at all. Here in Yorkshire you are quite far out of the common way, Stratford.'

'And you are the son of the Earl of Lepford. There must be a few in London, particularly those with eligible daughters, who would be eager to spend a holiday in your august presence.'

'Second son,' Breton corrected. 'No title to offer them. But I am rich, at least. In much part I can thank you for that.'

'Be sure to inform your guests of the fact, should the opportunity present itself.'

Breton made a face. 'Talking of money at a Christmas house party is just not done. They will not like it if they get wind of your scheme, Joe.'

'That is why you will do it subtly—as you always do,

Bob. They will hardly know what has happened. You may apologise to them for my lack of manners and let them plunder my cellars to the last bottle. Talk behind your hand about me, if you wish. Dance the pretty girls around the parlour while I am left to their fathers. They will think me common at the start. But by the time I leave I will have their cheques in my pocket. To one in business, Christmas must be a day like any other. If your friends wish to invest in this new venture they will see a substantial return to make their next Christmas a jolly one.'

The door opened, and the housekeeper, Mrs Davy, entered, with an apology for the interruption and a footman carrying a large armful of greenery. As he began swagging bows from the mantel, Joseph stood and quizzed the woman, ticking things off the list in his head as he was satisfied that they had been taken care of.

'Everything must be in perfect order,' he said firmly. 'While nearly every mill owner in the district has had some problems with frame-breakers and followers of Ludd, it would reflect poorly on me if my guests see a lack of control over my own household. I cannot fault the cleaning you have done, for I would swear you've scrubbed the house with diamonds it sparkles so.'

The housekeeper bobbed her head in thanks, and showed a bit of a blush. But his praise was no less than the truth. Everywhere he went he could smell the beeswax that had been worked into the oak panelling 'til it reflected the light from multitudes of candles and fires with a soft golden glow.

'And the larder has been stocked as well, I trust?'

'It was difficult,' Mrs Davy said modestly. 'There was little to be had in the shops.'

'You sent to London, as I requested?'

She nodded.

'There is no shortage of food in the city, nor shortage of people with money to buy it. My friends from the South will not understand the problems here, and nor do they wish to be enlightened of them. If they come all this way to visit me, I mean to see that their bellies are filled and their hearts light.' He grinned in anticipation. 'And their purses emptier at the end of the trip.'

The housekeeper's smile was firm, if somewhat disapproving. 'They shall eat like lords.' She passed him the menus she had prepared. 'If you will but select the meals, Mr Stratford.'

Given the bounty she presented, it was impossible to make a choice. He frowned. 'There must be goose, of course, for those who favour it. But I would prefer roast beef—and lots of it. With pudding to sop up the gravy. Swedes, peas, sprouts.' He pointed from one paper to the other. 'Roasted potatoes. Chestnuts to roast beside the Yule Log. And plum pudding, Christmas cake, cheese…'

'But which, sir?' the housekeeper asked.

'All of them, I should think. Enough so that no one

will want, no matter what their preference. It is better to have too much than too little, is it not?'

'If we have too much, sir, it will go to waste.' From the way she pursed her lips he could tell that he was offending her to the bottom of her frugal Northern heart.

'If it does, I can afford the loss. A show of economy in front of these investors will be seen as a lack of confidence. And that is something I will not be thought guilty of.' He paced past her, down the great hall, watching the servants tidying, examining ceilings and frames with a critical eye and nodding with approval when he found not a speck of dust. 'All is in order. And, as just demonstrated, you have seen to the greenery.'

'There are still several rooms to be decorated,' she admitted. 'But some must be saved for the kissing boughs.'

'Tear down some of the ivy on the south wall. There is still some green left in it, and the windows are choked to point that I can barely see without lighting candles at noon. With that, you should be able to deck the whole of the inside of the house. Clip the holly hedge as well. Trim it back and bring it in.' He gave a vague sweep of his hand. 'Have them search the woods for mistletoe. I want it all. Every last bit of the house smelling of fir and fresh air. Guests will begin to arrive tomorrow, and we must be all in readiness for them.'

'Yes, sir.'

From behind him, Breton laughed. 'You are quite the

taskmaster, Stratford. Lord help the workers in your mill if this is the way you behave towards them.'

'I mean to master you as well, Bob. I will expect you to get up from your chair to help lead the games.'

Breton looked stricken at the prospect. 'Me, Stratford?'

'Of course. They are your friends. You will know what it takes to entertain them.'

'I don't think it is my place.' The man was almost physically backing away from the task. 'You are the host, after all.'

'I am that in name only,' Joseph insisted. 'I can manage to pay the piper, of course. But in God's name, man, do not expect me to dance to the tune. There has been little time for that in my life, and I never got the knack of it. I fear I am much better with machines than with people.'

'But I…' Breton shook his head. 'I am not the best person to stand at the head of the set for you.'

'At best, all they want from me is a hearty meal and a full punchbowl. At worst, they are coming to gawk at what a common mess I am likely to make of a grand old house. They would do without me if they could. For I am—' he made a pious face '—*in trade*. Too humble by half for the people who have invested in me. But the money draws them like flies. Everyone wants their little bit of sugar, Bob. We will provide it for them. Though they sneer into their cups as they drink my wine, they will not be too proud to swallow it.'

'But must I be a part of it? If they do not want you, then surely…?'

'You are one of them,' Joe said firmly. 'I will never be. I am lucky to have won over Clairemont, and will have his daughter to dance with, of course. If she means to accept my suit then she had best get used to being seen with me. The rest of the ladies I leave to you.'

'And what am I to do with them?' For all his town bronze, Bob could be obtuse when he wished to be.

'Smile at them. Flatter them. Keep their glasses filled. You could do worse than following my example and taking a wife, you know. Oaksley has three daughters, from what I understand. Perhaps one of them will do for you.'

There was also the daughter of that firebrand in the village. She had not been invited to the festivities. It would show a considerable lack of wisdom to have that man and his family here, to undermine his success. But she would be a fine match for Bob. She was both pretty and intelligent, and a gentleman's daughter as well. She was more respectable than he himself would have aspired to be just a few short years ago. Miss Lampett would be perfect for his friend in every way. Although now that the opportunity presented itself to suggest a meeting, Joseph found himself strangely unwilling to voice his thoughts.

'I have no intention of marrying,' Bob said firmly. 'Not now. Not ever.'

'Then take advantage of some more earthly pleasures,'

Joseph said, oddly relieved. 'There will be enough of that as well, I am sure. I've heard that Lindhurst's wife rarely finds her own room after a night of revels. I hope I do not have to explain the rest for you. Avail yourself of my hospitality as well. Eat, drink and be merry.'

For tomorrow we die.

Joseph shuddered. He was sure he had not finished the quote. But he'd heard the words so clearly in his head that he'd have sworn they'd been intoned aloud, and in a voice that was not his.

'Stratford?' Bob was staring at him as though worried.

'Nothing. A funny turn, that's all.' He smiled in reassurance for, though he liked the idea of socialising with strangers no better than Bob, he could not let his nerve fail him. 'As I was saying. I expect you here and making merry for the whole of the week. I mean to keep my nose to the grindstone, of course. But we have made a success of this venture, and you should be allowed to take some pleasure in it. There is more to come in the New Year. Now is the time to play.'

CHAPTER THREE

THAT evening, as ever, Joseph's trip to his own bedroom was a little disquieting. Much as he knew that he owned the house, he did not really feel it suited him. It was beautiful, of course. But at night, when the servants had settled in their quarters and it was mostly him alone, he walked the wide corridors to reassure himself that it existed outside of his boyhood fantasies of success.

The place was too large, too strange and too old. It would not do to let anyone—not even Breton—know how ill at ease he was, or that this late-night walk was a continual reminder of how far from his birth and true station he had come.

It was not as if a pile of stones could come to life and cast him out. It was his, from cellar to attic. He had paid for it and had got a good price. But when it was dark and quiet, like this, Clairemont Manor felt—for want of a better word—haunted. Not that he believed in such things. In an age of machines there was hardly room for spirits. Clinging to childish notions and common superstition bespoke a lack of confidence that he would not allow himself.

With a wife and children in it, the house would fill with life and he would have no time for foolish fancies. But since the wife he was in the process of acquiring rightly belonged here, it sometimes felt as though he was trying to appease them rather than banish them. Setting Anne Clairemont at the foot of the table would restore the balance that had been lost. It had been her father's house, whether he'd been able to afford to keep it or not. Returning a member of the family to the estate, even if it *was* a female, might pacify some of the ill feelings he had created in the area. It fell in nicely with his plans for the business. There was nothing superstitious about it.

It was a pity the girl was so pale and lifeless. Had he the freedom to choose a woman to suit himself, it would certainly not be her. He'd have sought someone with a bit more spirit, not some brainless thing willing to auction herself to the highest bidder just to please her father.

He'd have wanted—

He stopped in his tracks, smiling to himself at the memory. He'd have wanted one more like the girl he'd seen in the crowd today. Fearless, that one was. Just like her father, that barmy Bernard Lampett who led the rebellion against him. What was the girl's name? Barbara, he thought, making a note to enquire and be sure. She did not seem totally in sympathy with her father, from the way she'd tried to drag him away. But neither did she support Joseph, having made it quite clear that she disapproved of him. Barbara Lampett knew her own mind, that was certain. And she had no fear of showing the world what she thought of it.

But it wasn't her sharp tongue that fascinated him. She was shorter than Anne, curved where Anne was straight, and pink where his prospective fiancée was pale. When he'd been close to her, he'd seen a few freckles on her turned-up nose, and handfuls of brown curls trying to escape from her plain bonnet.

But it was her eyes that had drawn him in. Her gaze had been cool and direct, like blue ice, cutting into him in a way that simple anger could not. She judged him. It made him doubt himself. For could any cause be wholly in the right if it might result in harm to such a lovely thing as a Barbara Lampett, tramping her casually into the dirt? While he was sure he bore a greater share of the right than the men who stood against him, the truth of what might have happened to her, had he not intervened, weighed heavy on his conscience.

And so tonight he walked the halls more slowly than usual, thinking dark thoughts and counting the many rooms as though they were rosary beads. If the servants had noticed this ritual, they were too polite or well trained to comment. But he found himself taking the same path each night before retiring, as though he were touring someone else's great house and marvelling at their wealth. Reception room the first, library, breakfast room, dining room, private salon, stairs, reception room the second, card room, music room, ballroom. And then a climb to the second floor: red bedroom, blue bedroom, master bedroom… There was a third floor as well, and servants' rooms, larders, kitchens and possibly some small and useful places he had not bothered to investigate.

It was a sharp contrast to his childhood. When it had been but one room they'd lived in there had been no reason to count. As his father's business had grown, so had the rooms. A three-room flat. A five-room cottage. A house. They had risen from poverty in the days long before the war, when trade was unobstructed and money easier. But the successes had been small, and the work hard and unpleasant. He had hated it.

He had broken from it, rebuilt the work in his own image. And now he lived in the grandest house in the county—and was not happy here either. Perhaps that was his curse: to hurry through life reaching for the next great thing, whether it be invention or business. Each time he succeeded he would be sure that this time he had gained enough to please himself. Then the success would pale and he would seek more.

The thought left him chilled, and he felt the unease that seemed to stalk him through these halls. He remembered again the eyes of Barbara Lampett, who could see through him to his clockwork heart. It made him want to grab her and prove that his blood flowed just as hot as other men's, and perhaps a little warmer for the sight of her. If the girl were the daughter of any other man in the village he'd have at least attempted a flirtation. But she was too young and too much of a lady to understand the discreet dalliance he had in mind. Even if she was of a more liberal nature it would not do to have her thinking that sharing her charms might lead him to show mercy on her father.

While he might consider offering a bijou, or some other bit of shiny to a pretty girl, something about Barbara Lampett's freckled nose and the sweet stubbornness of her jaw convinced him that she was likely to bargain for the one thing that he was not willing to share: clemency for the man who plotted his undoing.

He shook his head, rejecting the notion of her as the long-case clock in the hall struck twelve and he opened the door to his room. To be sure he would not weaken, it was best to leave all thoughts of her here in the corridor, far away from his cold and empty bed.

'Boy.'

Joseph started at the sound of a voice where there should have been nothing but the crackle of the fire and perhaps the sounds of his valet laying out a nightshirt. The opulence of the room, the richness of its hangings and upholstery, always seemed to mute even the most raucous sound.

But the current voice cut through the tranquillity and grated on the nerves. The familiar Yorkshire accent managed to both soothe and annoy. The volume of it was so loud that it echoed in the space and pressed against him—like a hand on his shoulder that could at any moment change from a caress to a shove.

He looked for the only possible if extremely unlikely source, and found it at the end of the bed. For there stood a man he'd thought of frequently but had not seen for seven years. Not since the man's death.

'Hello, Father.' It was foolish to speak to a figment of his imagination, but the figure in the corner of his bedroom seemed so real that it felt rude not to address it.

It must be his distracted mind playing this trick. Death had not changed his da in the least. Joseph had assumed that going on to his divine reward would have softened him in some way. But it appeared that the afterlife was as difficult as life had been. Jacob Stratford was just as grim and sullen as he'd been when he walked the earth.

'What brings you back? As if I have to ask myself… It was that second glass of brandy, on top of the hubbub at the mill.' When he'd rescued the Lampett girl he'd been literally rubbing shoulders with the same sort of man as the one who had raised him. The brutal commonality of them had attached itself to his person like dust, sticking in his mind and appearing now, as he neared sleep.

'That's what you think, is it?' The ghost gave a disapproving grunt. 'I see you have not changed a bit from the time you were a boy.' Then he ladled his speech thick with the burr that Joseph had heard when he was in the midst of the crowd around his mill. 'Th'art daft as a brush, though th' live like a lord.'

'And I will say worse of you,' Joseph replied, careful to let none of his old accent creep back into his speech. No matter what his father might say of him, he had changed for the better and he would not go back. 'You are a stubborn, ignorant dictator. Two drinks is hardly a sign of debauchery. And I live in a great house because I can afford to. It is not as if I am become some noble who has a line of unpaid credit with the vintner. I pay cash.' He'd been told by Bob that the habit was horribly unfashionable, and a sign of his base birth, but he could not seem to break himself of it. It felt good to lie down knowing that, though he might need investors for the business, he had no personal debts.

Although why his rest was now uneasy he could not tell. The bad dream staring him down from the end of the bed must be a sign that all was not right in his world.

His father snorted in disgust. 'No matter what I tried to teach, you've proved that buying and selling is all you learned. You know nothing of art, of craft or the men behind the work.'

'If the men behind the work are anything like you, then I think I've had enough of a lesson, thank you. You may go as well.' He made an effort to wake and cast off the dream. To be having this conversation at all was proof that he was sleeping. To rouse from slumber would divest the vision of the last of its power.

His father gave a tug on his spectral forelock. 'Well, then, Your Lordship, I am put in my place. I hope by now you know that you don't fit with the posh sort that you suck up to. You are as much of a dog to be kicked from their path as I am to you.'

'Probably true,' Joseph admitted. There was no point in lying about that, even to himself. Though the gentry might be forced to mix with those in trade, there was nothing to make them enjoy it. 'But if I am a dog, then I am a young pup with many years ahead of me. Their time is ending, just as yours did. In the day that is coming men of vision will be rewarded.'

'At the expense of others,' his father replied.

'Others can seize this opportunity and profit as well, if they wish to,' Joe snapped back. 'It is not my responsibility to see to the welfare of every man on the planet. They had best look out for themselves.'

'That is no better than I expected from you,' his father replied. 'And not good enough. Believe me, boy, I can see from this side of the veil that it is not nearly enough. It is no pleasant thing to die with regrets, to have unfinished business when your life is spent and to know that you have failed in the one thing you should have profited at: the care of another human life.'

The statement made the speaker uncomfortably real. It was most unlike anything in Joseph's own mind. It sounded almost like an apology. And never would he have put those words in his father's mouth—no matter how much he might have wished to hear them. If things went as planned Joseph would be a father soon enough. It would not take much effort on his part to do a better job of it than his father had done with him.

'You would know better than I on that, I am sure. As of this time, I have no one under my care. I answer only to myself, and I am happy with that.' Surreptitiously he made a fist and dug his nails into his palm, pinching the skin to let the pain start him awake.

'Boy, you are wrong.'

'So you always told me, Father. Although why I should dream of your voice now, I do not know. I have only to wake up and look around me to prove that I am doing quite well for myself.' Although, thinking on it, he could not seem to recall having fallen asleep in the first place. But it was the only explanation for this. He was not in the habit of conversing with ghosts.

He was sound asleep in this bed and having a dream. No. He was having a nightmare. If he could not manage to wake, he must try to go to a deep, untroubled rest where his father would not follow. To encourage the change he sat upon the edge of the bed and began to undress himself. While it seemed strange to do so during a dream, he could think of no other way to set things right.

As he leaned forwards to pull off his boots his father stepped closer and brought with him the smell of the grave—damp earth, a faint whiff of decomposition and the chill of a cold and lifeless thing made even colder by the season. 'Do not think to ignore me. You do so at your peril.'

'Do I, now?' Joseph could not help it and stole a glance up at the spirit—if that was what it was. And he wondered when he had ever had a dream this real. He could smell and feel, as well as hear and see. He had to struggle to keep himself from reaching out to touch the shroud that the man in front of him carried like a mantle draped over his bony arm. He stared at the ghost, willing it to disappear. 'I ignored you in life as best I could. Because of it I gave you enough money to die in comfort, instead of bent over a loom. But that was years ago. Go back to where you have been and leave me in peace.'

'You do not have peace, if you would be honest and see the truth. Just as it always was when you were a boy, you are careless. You have not attended to both the warp and the weft. The tension is uneven. You have done much, and done it quickly with your fancy machines. But your work is without shape.'

Joseph glared into the hollow eyes before him, too angry at the slight to stay silent. 'I bore enough of that needless criticism from you when you lived—trying to teach me to weave when it was clear I had no skill for it. The last piece of work you will ever see me make on an old-fashioned loom was the shroud I buried you in. I wove it on your old machine with my own hands. I made it out of wool in respect for custom and your trade. If you have come to me to complain of the quality, then go back to your grave without it. As for my current life—there is no basis for this criticism. I can measure my success by my surroundings. This Christmas I will have a house full to the brim with guests and a table creaking with bounty. I have a new mill. When it opens I will be able to afford to fill the warehouse with goods, ready to ship when the sanctions are lifted.'

The ghost shook his head, as though all the achievement was nothing, and waved the shroud before him. 'Shapeless. Tear it out. Tear it out before it is too late. Your grain is off, boy.'

Joseph finished with his undressing and pulled a nightshirt over his head. Then he lay down on the bed with his arms stiff at his sides, fighting to keep from stuffing his fingers in his ears. He could hear the old man's death rattle of a breath, along with the same repeated criticisms that had tortured him all through his failed apprenticeship.

Then he thought of the girl who had been clinging to Bernard Lampett's arm in front of the mill. Her difficulties with her father had raised these memories in him. He felt a sympathy with her. And, for all his convictions that there could be no mercy shown, he would not rest easy until he had found a peaceful solution.

He looked at the shade of his father again, half hoping that it had evaporated now that he'd found the probable cause. But it was still there, as stern and disapproving as ever he had been. 'If you are my own guilty conscience, the least you could have done,' Joseph said, 'was come to me in the form of Barbara Lampett. And I'd be much more likely to listen if you told me plainly what you wanted.'

The ghost looked at him as though he was both stupid and a disappointment. It was a familiar look. 'It will not go well for you if you persist in talking nonsense. I came here hoping to spare you what is soon to come. My time is wasted, for you are as stubborn as you were right up 'til the day I died.'

'You? Spare me?' Joseph laughed. 'When did you ever wish to spare me anything? It was I who saved myself, and none other. I used my own brain and my own hands to make sure that I did not live as you did. And I succeeded at it.'

The ghost looked troubled, but only briefly. 'My goal is not to make you into myself. I was a hard man in life. A good craftsman, but a poor father.'

'Thank you for admitting the fact now that it is years too late,' Joseph snapped, annoyed that his mind would choose his precious free hours to remind him of things he preferred to forget.

'I bear the punishment of my errors even now. But my goal was to make you something more.' The ghost pointed with a pale, long-fingered hand that in life had been nimble with a shuttle. 'Here you are—proof that my job was not done. You are less than you should be. You are certainly less than you must be. That is why you must tear out what you have done. Tear out the work and start again, while you are able. It is not too late to go back. Find the mistake and fix it. Start again, before tomorrow night, or face another visitor.'

'I have no intention of destroying the work of a lifetime to please some niggling voice in my own mind that will be gone in the morning.' He pulled up the coverlet and waved a hand. 'Now, go, sir. Come again as some more interesting dream. You do not frighten me, though I will be glad to see you gone. Bring the girl instead.'

He smiled at the thought. If he could choose a bedtime fantasy, she was better than most. Then he pulled the sheet over his head and rolled away from the figure, trying to ignore the strange green glow that seemed to seep through his closed eyelids. What sort of dream remained even after one ceased to look at it?

One that could still speak, apparently. His father's voice came from just above him, unbothered by his ignoring of it. It was louder now, and Joseph had his first moment's fright, thinking if he pulled the blankets away he might find himself inches away from a corpse—close enough to choke on the smell of rotting flesh and see the waxy vacancy of a dead man's eyes.

'Very well, then. It is as was feared. You will not listen to me. Be warned, boy. If you have a brain, you will heed before Christmas Eve. From here, I can see what is coming, and I would not wish that—even on you.'

'Thank you so much, Father, for such a cold comfort.' Joseph snuggled down into the pillow.

'There will be three before Christmas. Look for the

first when the clock chimes one tomorrow. If you have any sense you will heed them, before it is too late.'

Joseph laughed into the bedclothes. 'You mean to ruin my sleep between here and Christmas, I suppose? And destroy every last pleasure I take in this holiday. Only *you* would be trying to visit me with dire predictions on this of all weeks. Come back after Twelfth Night and perhaps I shall care.'

'Sir?'

Joseph opened his eyes.

The voice was not that of his father but of his valet, who sounded rather worried. 'Were you speaking to me, Mr Stratford? For I did not quite catch…'

When he pulled back the covers the candles were still lit and there was no sign of the eldritch glow he had been trying to shut out, nor the figure that had cast it. 'No, Hobson. It was only a dream. I was talking in my sleep, I think.' It must have been that. He had come back to his room and dozed, spinning a wild fancy without even bothering to blow out the light.

His valet was standing in a litter of clothes, looking around him with disapproval. 'If you were tired, you had but to ring and I would have come immediately to assist you.' Hobson picked the jacquard waistcoat from off the floor, smoothing the wrinkles from it and hanging it in the wardrobe.

'I was not tired,' Joseph insisted. Although he must have been. Why had he been dreaming? Though he could remember each piece of clothing as he'd dropped it on the floor, he could not seem to manage to remember falling asleep at any point—dressed or otherwise.

'Then might I bring you a warm drink before bed? A brandy? A posset? In keeping with the season, Cook has mulled some wine.'

'No, thank you. No spirits before bed, I think.' At least not like the one he'd had already.

There will be three.

He looked to the valet. 'Did you say something just now?'

'I offered wine…' The man was looking at him as though he was drunk.

'Because I thought I heard…' Of course he was sure that he had not heard Hobson speak. It had been his father's voice for certain, come back to repeat his warning. Although, looking around the room, he could see no sign of a spectre. 'Did you hear a voice?'

The valet was looking behind him, about the empty room. Then he looked back at his master, struggling to keep the worry from his face. 'No, sir. Just the two of us conversing.'

Joseph gave a laugh to mask the awkward moment. 'I must be more tired than I thought. Pay me no mind. And no wine tonight, please. A few hours' untroubled rest is all I need.'

But if there were to be another evening such as this one he doubted that serenity would be a quality it possessed.

CHAPTER FOUR

IN THE little corner of the Lampett kitchen set aside as a still room, Barbara inhaled deeply and sighed. After the ruckus of yesterday it was comforting to be home again, immersed in the sights and scents and sounds of Christmas preparation. There were mince pies cooling on a shelf beside the pudding bowl, and the makings for a good bowl of punch set aside against any guests they might have between now and Twelfth Night. Before her she'd arranged what fragrant ingredients she could find—dried rose petals and lavender, cloves, the saved rinds of the year's oranges and handfuls of pine needles to refill pomanders and refresh sachets in recently tidied closets and drawers.

She glanced down at her apron, pleased to see that there were few marks on it to reveal the labours of the day. Everything spoke of order, cleanliness and control. She smiled. All was as it should be, and as she liked it.

Suddenly the back door burst open and her mother rushed into the room, dropping the empty market basket and looking hurriedly around her.

Barbara stood, fearing the worst. 'What has happened?'

'Your father? Is he here with you?'

'No. He was in the parlour, reading his paper. I've heard nothing unusual.' Barbara rushed to the kitchen door, opening it and staring into the empty front room.

'On the way to the village I passed Mrs Betts. She had seen him heading towards the mill. He was carrying the axe.'

Barbara stripped off her apron, pushing past her mother to grab a shawl and bonnet from pegs by the door. 'I will go. You stay here. Do not worry. Whatever he is up to, I will put a stop to it before any real damage is done.'

There could be little question as to what he meant to do if he had taken a tool of destruction. The papers were full of reports from other villages of the frame-breakers—followers of Ned Ludd got out of hand—destroying machinery. And of mill owners dead in their beds or at their factories by violence. While there was much that annoyed her about Mr Stratford, he hardly deserved death.

It might go hard for her family if her father was left unchecked. He could well lose his freedom over this—or his life. She thought of the pistol in Stratford's hand the previous day. His first shot had been fired into the air. If he felt himself sufficiently threatened he might aim lower, and her father would be the one to suffer for it.

She ran down the path from the Lampett cottage, forgoing the road and heading cross-country over the patch of moor that separated the mill from the village. She splashed through the shallow stream, feeling the icy water seeping into her shoes and chilling her feet near to freezing, making her stumble as she came up the bank. The thorns in the thicket tore at her skirts and her hem was muddy, the dress practically ruined.

It was a risky journey. But if she wished to catch her father before he did harm she must trust that the ground was solid enough that she would not be sucked down into the peat before she reached her destination. Even the smallest delay might cost her dearly.

When she reached the front gate to Stratford's mill she found it chained and locked. She wondered if Mr Stratford had left it thus, or if her father had gone through and then locked it behind him, the better to do his mischief in privacy. For a moment she imagined Joseph Stratford, working unawares in the office as an assailant crept stealthily up behind him, axe raised…

She threw herself at the wrought-iron bars, crying out a warning, shaking them and feeling no movement under her hands. And then she was climbing, using the crossbars and the masonry of the wall to help her up. Mr Stratford had made it look simple when he had climbed to face the crowd. But he had not done so in a sodden dress and petticoats. She struggled under the weight of them, stumbling as she reached the top. What she'd hoped would be a leap to the ground on the inside was more of a stagger and a fall, and she felt something in her ankle twist and give as she landed.

It slowed her, but she did not stop, limping the last of the way to the wide back entrance. She passed through the open dock, where the vans and carts would bring materials and take away the finished goods, through the high-ceilinged storeroom waiting to hold the finished bolts of cloth. She passed the boiler room and the office and counting house, which were quiet and empty, and continued on to the floor of the factory proper, with its row upon row of orderly machinery, still new and smelling of green wood and machine oil.

From the far side of the big room she heard voices. Her father's was raised in threat. Mr Stratford's firm baritone answered him. The two men stood facing each other by the wreckage of a loom. Her father's axe was raised, and the look in his eyes was wild.

Stratford must have been disturbed in working with the machinery. He was coatless, the collar of his shirt open and its sleeves rolled up and out of the way, with a leather apron tied around his waist and smudged with grease. In one hand he held a hammer. Though his arm was lowered, Barbara could see the tensed muscles that told her he would use it in defence when her father rushed him.

'Hello?' she called out. 'What are you doing, Father? I have come to take you home for dinner.'

'Go home yourself, gel, for you do not need to see what is like to occur.' Father's voice was coarse, half-mad and dismissive. There was nothing left of the soft, rather pedantic tone she knew and loved.

'Your father is right, Miss Lampett. It is unnecessary for you to remain. Let we gentlemen work this out between us.' Stratford sounded calm and reassuring, though the smile he shot in her direction was tight with worry. His eyes never left the man in front of him. 'You will see your father directly.'

'Perhaps I will,' she answered. 'In jail or at his funeral. That is how this is likely to end if I allow it to continue.' She hobbled forwards and stepped between them. And between axe and hammer as well, trusting that neither was so angry as to try and strike around her.

'Miss Lampett,' Stratford said sharply. 'What have you done to yourself? Observe, sir, she is limping. Assist me and we will help her to a chair.' He sounded sincerely worried. But she detected another note in his voice as well, as though he was seizing on a welcome distraction.

'My Lord, Barbara, he is right. What have you done to yourself now?'

Her father dropped his axe immediately, forgetting his plans, and came to take her arm. Sometimes these violent spells passed as quickly as they came. This one had faded the moment he had recognised her injury.

Stratford had her other elbow, but she noticed the handle of his hammer protruding from an apron pocket, still close by should he need a weapon.

'I fell when climbing down from the gate. I am sure it is nothing serious.' Though the pain was not bad, and she could easily have managed for herself, she exaggerated the limp and let the two men work together to bear her forwards towards a chair.

'The front gate?' Stratford said in surprise. 'That is nearly eight feet tall.'

Her father laughed, as though lost in a happier time. 'My Barb always was a spirited one as a youngster. Constantly climbing into trees and taking the short way back to the ground. It is a good thing that the Lampett heads are hard, or we'd have lost her by now. Sit down, Barbara, and let me have a look at your foot.'

She took the seat they had pressed her to, and her father knelt at her feet and pulled off her muddy boot, probing gently at the foot to search for breaks.

She sat patiently and watched as Stratford's expression changed from concern to interest at the sight of her stocking-clad leg. Then he hurriedly looked away, embarrassed that he'd been caught staring. He gave her a rueful smile and a half-shrug, as if to say he could hardly be blamed for looking at something so attractive, and then offered a benign, 'I hope it is nothing serious.'

'A mild sprain, nothing more,' her father assured him.

For a change, his tone was as placid as it had ever been. He was the simple schoolmaster, the kind father she remembered and still knew, but a man the world rarely saw. She wanted to shout into the face of the mill owner to make him notice the change.

This is who he is. This is who we all are. We are not your enemies. We need you, just as you need us. If only you were to listen you might know us. You might like us.

'Would it help for her to sit with her foot on a cushion for a bit?' Mr Stratford responded as he was addressed, behaving as though she had twisted an ankle during a picnic, and not while haring to her father's rescue. 'My carriage is waiting at the back gate, just around the corner of the building.'

'That will not be necessary,' she said. This had hardly begun as a social call, though both men now seemed ready to treat it as such. While she doubted her father capable of guile, she did not know if this new and gentler Stratford was the truth. What proof did she have that they were not being led into a trap so that he could call the authorities? Even if he did not, at any time her father might recollect who had made the offer and turn again to the wild man she had found a few moments ago.

'A ride would be most welcome,' her father said, loud enough to drown out her objections. His axe still lay, forgotten, on the floor behind them. For now he was willing to accept the hospitality of a man he'd been angry enough to threaten only a moment ago.

'Then, with your permission, Mr Lampett, and with apologies to you, miss, for the liberty…' Joseph Stratford pulled off his apron, tossed it aside, then reached around her and lifted her easily off the stool and into his arms.

While it was a relief to see how easily he'd managed her father, it was rather annoying to see how easily he could manage her as well. He was carrying her through the factory as though she weighed nothing. And she was allowing him to do it—without protest. The worst of it was, she rather liked the sensation. She could feel far too much of his body through the fabric of his shirt, and her face was close enough to his bare skin to smell the blending of soap and sweat and cologne that was unique to him. Such overt masculinity should have repelled her. Instead she found herself wishing she could press her face into the hollow of his throat. At least she might lay her head against his shoulder, feigning a swoon.

That would be utter nonsense. She was not the sort to swoon under any circumstances, and she would not play at it now. Though she *did* allow herself to slip an arm around his neck under the guise of steadying herself. His arms were wrapped tightly, protectively, around her already, and such extra support was not really necessary. But it gave her the opportunity to feel more of him, and to bring her body even closer to his as he moved.

'It seems I am always to be rescuing you, Miss

Lampett,' he said into her ear, so quietly that her father could not overhear.

'You needn't have bothered,' she whispered back. 'I am shamming.'

'As you were when the crowd knocked you down yesterday?'

Then he spoke louder, and directly to her father. 'If you would precede us, sir? I do not wish to risk upsetting the lady with too rough a gait. Tell the coachman of our difficulties. Perhaps he can find an extra cushion and a lap robe so that Miss Lampett will be comfortable on the journey.'

'Very good.'

As her father hurried ahead, Stratford stopped to kick the axe he had been wielding into a darkened corner. 'Though you may not want my help, I think it is quite necessary today, for the safety of all concerned, that we play this to the very hilt.' He started again towards the carriage at a stately pace, stopping only long enough at the door to lean against it and push it shut behind him. 'Do you really wish to protest good health and risk your father remembering and using his weapon?'

She shifted a little in his grasp, feeling quite ridiculous to be treated as some sort of porcelain doll. 'Of course not. But I do not wish you to make a habit of swooping in to care for me when I am quite capable of seeing to my own needs.'

'Your independence is duly noted and admired,' he said. Then he dipped his head a little, so he could catch her scent. 'Though I find your infirmity has advantages as well.'

She slapped hard at his arm. 'You are incorrigible.'

'You are not the first to have told me so. And here we are.' He said the last louder, for the benefit of her father, to signal that their intimate conversation was at an end.

She frowned. Stratford could easily have ridden the distance between the manor and here, or perhaps even walked. To bring a full equipage and servants to wait after him while he worked was just the sort of excess she had come to expect from him—and just the sort of thing that was angering the locals. Or it could mean that he had a sensible fear of being set upon, should he travel alone and vulnerable along a road that might be lined with enemies.

He set her down briefly, only to lift her again, up into the body of the carriage, settling her beside her father on a totally unnecessary mound of cushions, her injured ankle stretched out before her to rest on the seat at Stratford's side.

The carriage was new, as was everything he owned, and practically shining with it. The upholstery was a deep burgundy leather, soft and well padded. There were heavy robes for her legs to keep out the cold, and a pan of coals to warm the foot that still rested on the floor. The other was tucked up securely, the stocking-clad toes dangerously close to the gentleman there. The foot was chilled, and she resisted the urge to press it against his leg to steal some warmth.

Stratford had noticed it. He stared down for a moment, and then, as unobtrusively as possible, he tossed the tail of his coat over it and shifted his weight to be nearer.

Barbara warmed instantly—from the contact with his body and the embarrassment accompanying it. It was a practical solution, of course. But she would be the talk of the town if anyone heard of it. And by the smug smile on his face Joseph Stratford knew it, and was enjoying her discomfiture.

Then he signalled the driver and they set off, with barely a sway to tell her of the moment. It was by far the richest and most comfortable trip she'd taken, and she had to struggle not to enjoy it. Her subdued pleasure turned to suspicion, for at another signal to the driver they proceeded through the unlocked gates down the road towards Clairemont Manor.

'This is not the way to our home,' she said, stating the obvious.

'My house is nearer. You can both come for tea. I will send you home once I am assured that you are warmed and refreshed, and that no harm has come to you while on my property.'

'That is most kind of you,' her father said.

It was not at all kind. It was annoying. And she was sure that there must be some sort of ulterior motive to his sudden solicitousness.

But when she opened her mouth to say so, her father went on. 'There are not many who are such good neighbours. And are you new here, Mr…?' He struggled for a name. 'I am sorry. My memory is not what it once was.'

Barbara coloured, part relieved and part ashamed. She needn't worry that her father was likely to turn violent again, for it was clear that he had lost the thread of things and forgotten all about Mr Stratford while concerned for her ankle. But what was she to do now? Should she remind him that his host was the same man who, according to her father's own words, treated his workers 'like chattel to be cast off in pursuit of Mammon'? Or should she continue to let him display his mental confusion in front of his enemy and become an object of scorn and pity?

Stratford seemed unbothered, and responded with the barest of pauses. 'We have met only briefly, and I do not fault you for not recalling. I am Joseph Stratford, and I have taken residence of Clairemont Manor now that the family has relocated closer to the village.'

Her father gave a nod in response, still not associating the man across from them with the evil mill owner he despised.

'Would you do me the honour of an introduction to your daughter, sir?'

As her father presented her to this supposed stranger with all necessary formality, she thought she detected a slight twitch at the corners of Stratford's mouth. If he meant to make sport at the expense of her father's failed memory she would find a way to pay him out. But, after the briefest lapse, he was straight-faced and respectful again, enquiring after her father's work and commiserating with him on the closing of the little school where he had taught, and his recent difficulties in finding another occupation.

Mr Stratford had changed much since the last time she'd seen him brandishing a pistol and taunting the crowd. Though she could not say she liked him, she'd felt an illogical thrill at the power of him then, and the masterful way he had come to her aid. Now she was left with time to admire him as he conversed with her father, displaying intelligence and a thoughtful nature that had not been in evidence before. She found herself wishing that things could be different from the way they were and that this might be their first meeting. If she could look on him with fresh eyes, knowing none of his behaviour in the recent past, it might be possible to trust him. But she could not help thinking that this display of good manners was as false as her sprained ankle.

He had let the groom help him on with his coat again before they had taken off, and she could see that it was the height of London fashion, tailored to perfection and designed to give a gentlemanly outline to the work-broadened shoulders she had felt as he carried her. He was clean-shaven. But his hair was a trifle too long, as though he could not be bothered to spare the few extra minutes that the cutting of it would take. A lock of it fell into his eyes as he nodded at something her father had said, and he brushed it out of his face with an impatient flick of his hand. Though she could not call them graceful, his movements were precise. She could imagine that these were hands better at tending machinery than creating art, more efficient than gentle.

He made conversation with her father in an accent carefully smoothed to remind the listener of London, though she doubted that his tongue had been born to it. He spoke nothing of himself or his own past. But in the questions that drew her father to conversation Barbara heard the occasional lilt or drawl that was the true Joseph Stratford. He was a Northerner. But for some reason he did not like to show it.

She looked away before he could catch her staring. Even if he was nothing more than a tradesman masquerading as gentry, he deserved more courtesy than she was giving him. They were drawing up the long drive towards the great house where she had played as a child. That was before Mary had died, of course, and before her sister Anne had grown into such a great and unapproachable lady. Had the manor changed as well? she wondered. Were the places she'd hidden under chairs and behind statues the same or different? Although she wished the circumstances had been different, she very much wanted to see the place—just once more.

She could feel the eyes of the other man on her, watching her reaction to the house. So she worked to relax her posture and not stare so, or appear eager for a visit to it. It was little better than staring directly at him to admire his property as though she coveted or desired the luxury he took for granted.

'I had a friend who lived here once,' she blurted, to explain her interest.

'And perhaps you will again,' he replied easily.

She looked up sharply into a face that was all bland innocence. The carriage pulled up before the great front entry, and as it stopped he signalled for the door to be opened, allowing her father to exit first so that he might help her on the steps.

For a moment they were alone again, and he touched her hand and smiled. 'There is no reason for us to be enemies,' he said.

'Nor any particular reason for friendship,' she reminded him, drawing her hand away.

'I think it is too soon for either of us to tell,' he announced, ignoring her animosity.

The process of entering the house was much the same as their setting off from the mill had been, with him carrying her while she protested, her shoeless foot waving in the air. There was a flurry of alarm amongst the servants, many of whom recognised her and her father.

'Put me down now,' she insisted. 'Talk of this will reach the village. It will be the ruin of me.'

'If it is, your father is right here to set them straight.' He was smiling again, as though he knew how likely it was that her father would have no real memory of the event, for good or ill.

'I would prefer that no explanation be needed,' she said.

'And I would prefer that people think me less of an ogre,' Stratford replied. 'I will not have you limping about my house while I offer no assistance. Then it will get round that I let you suffer as a punishment to your father.'

For her own sake, and to preserve her reputation, he explained in a loud voice for the benefit of the staff that Miss Lampett had fallen, and he did not wish to risk further injury until she had rested her foot. But as he did so his hands tightened on her body, to prove to Barbara that he was enjoying the experience at her expense.

'You may put me down, and I will take my chances,' she said, glancing at a parlour maid who stood, wide-eyed, taking in the sight. 'I feel quite all right now.'

He pretended that he had not heard, and called for tea to be brought to the library, carrying her down the wide hall and depositing her on a couch by the fire.

How had Mr Stratford known, she wondered, the calming effect that the presence of books had on her father? Though he seemed to have more difficulty with people since the accident, the printed word still gave him great comfort. The Clairemont Manor library was the largest in the area and the best possible place to cement her father's recovery.

As the servants prepared tea, her father stood and ran a hand along the rows of leather-bound volumes. Stratford studied the behaviour and then invited him to help himself to whatever he liked, lamenting that business gave him little time to enjoy the books there.

Her father gave a grateful nod and fell quickly to silence, ignoring the cup that had been poured for him, and the plate of sandwiches, in favour of the Roman history in his hand.

Stratford gave her a wry smile. 'While your father is preoccupied, would you enjoy a brief walk down the corridor? If your ankle is better, as you claim, a spot of exercise will assure me that it is safe to send you home.'

She wanted to snap that she did not need him seeing to her safety. She had not wanted to come here at all. And now that she was here she would go home when she was ready, and not at his bidding. But it would be shaming to discuss her father's rude behaviour while she shared a room with him, so it was best that she allow herself to be drawn away.

'That would be lovely,' she lied.

He went to fetch her boot and helped her with the lacing of it, commenting that the lack of swelling was an encouraging sign. Behind a placid smile, she gritted her teeth against the contact of his fingers against her foot and ankle. He was very gentle, as though he cared enough not to cause injury to a weakened joint. But she suspected the occasional fleeting touches she felt against her stocking were not the least bit accidental. He was touching her for his own pleasure. Much as she did not wish to, she found it wickedly exciting.

Then he rose and went ahead to open the door for her,

standing respectfully to the side so that she might pass. She forced herself to stifle the unquiet feeling that it gave her to have him at her back—even for a moment.

It was possible that this latest offer masked something much darker. Perhaps he had designs upon her virtue. For, this close, she could not deny the virile air that he seemed to carry about with him, and the sense that he had a man's needs and would not scruple to act upon them. She gave a small shudder, barely enough to be noticeable.

'Is the house too cold for you?' he prompted. 'If so, I could have a servant build up the fire, or perhaps bring you a wrap...'

'No, I am fine. I suspect that I took a slight chill on the moors.'

'Your clothing is still damp from the fall. And I took you away from the tea I had promised.' He frowned. 'But I wished to speak alone with you for a moment, so that you might know I bear you no ill will because of recent events.' He rubbed his brow, as though tired. 'One can hardly be held responsible for the actions of one's parent. I myself have a troublesome father.'

He stopped.

'Had,' he corrected. 'I *had* a difficult father. He is dead now. For a moment I had quite forgotten.'

'I am sorry for your loss,' she said politely. 'I assume the passing is a recent one, if you still forget it?'

He looked away, as though embarrassed. 'Almost

seven years, actually. It is just that he has been on my mind of late. He was a weaver, you see.'

'You are the son of a weaver?' she said.

'Is that so surprising?' There was a cant to his head, a jutting of the chin as though he were ready to respond to a challenge. 'With all your father's fine talk of supporting the workers, I did not think to find you snobbish, Miss Lampett.'

'I am not snobbish,' she retorted. 'It merely surprises me that my father would need to tell a weaver's son the damage automation does to the livelihoods of the men here.'

'What you call damage, Miss Lampett, I call freedom. The ability to do more work in less time means the workers do not need to toil from first light to last. Perhaps they will have time for education, and those books your father finds so precious.'

'The workers who are put from their places by these machines will have more time as well. And no money. Time is no blessing when there is no food on the table.'

He snorted. 'The reason they are without work this Christmas has nothing to do with me. Was it not they and their like who burned the last mill to the ground and ran off the mill owner and his family? Now they complain that they have no source of income.'

'When men are desperate enough, they resort to desperate actions,' she said. 'The owner, Mr Mackay, was a harsh man who cared little for those he employed, taking them on and casting them off like chattel. It is little wonder that their spirits broke.'

'And I am sure that it did not help to have your father raising the rabble and inciting them to mischief.' He looked at her with narrowed eyes.

'That is a lie,' she snapped. 'He had nothing to do with that argument. He did not support either side, and worked to moderate the cruelty of the one with the need of the other.'

Stratford scoffed. 'He saves his rage for me, then, who has not been here long enough to prove myself cruel or kind?'

'He was not always as you see him,' she argued. 'A recent accident has addled his wits. Until that night he was the mildest of gentlemen, much as you see him now. But of late, when he takes an idea into his head, he can become quite agitated.' When he recalled the scene she had come upon at the mill, just a short time ago, he must know that 'agitated' was an understatement. 'Mother and I do not know what to do about it.'

'You had best do something,' Stratford said. 'He appears to be getting worse and not better. If you had not come along today...' He paused. 'Your arrival prevented anyone from coming to harm, at least for now.'

From his tone, it did not seem that he feared for his own life. 'Are you threatening my father, Mr Stratford?'

'Not without cause, I assure you. He is a violent man. If necessary I will call in the law to stop him. That would be a shame if it is as you say—that the rage in him is a thing which he cannot control. But you must see that the results are likely to be all the same whether they proceed from malice, madness or politics.'

'Just what do you propose we do? Lock him up?'

'If necessary,' Stratford said, with no real feeling. 'At least that will prevent me from having him transported.'

'You would do that, wouldn't you?' With his understanding behaviour, and his offers of tea and books, she had allowed herself to believe—just for a moment—that he was capable of understanding. And that if she confided in him he might use his ingenuity to come up with a solution to her family's problems. But he was proving to be just as hard as she'd thought him when she'd seen him taunting the mob of weavers. 'You have no heart at all to make such threats at Christmas.'

Joseph Stratford shrugged. 'I fail to see what the date on the calendar has to do with it. The mill will open in January, whether your father likes it or not. But there is much work I must do, and plans that must be secured between then and now. I will not allow him to ruin the schemes already in progress with his wild accusations and threats of violence. Is that understood, Miss Lampett?'

'You do not wish our coarseness and our poverty to offend the fancy guests you are inviting from London,' she said with scorn. Everyone in the village had heard the rumours of strangers coming to the manor for the holiday, and would be speculating about their feasting and dancing while eating their meagre dinners in

Fiddleton. 'And you have the nerve to request that I chain my father in our cottage like a mad dog, so that he will not trouble you and your friends with the discomfort of your workers?' She was sounding like her father at the beginning of some rabble-rousing rant. And she was foolish enough to be doing it while alone with a man who solved his problems with a loaded pistol.

'There was a time when I was little better than they are now,' he snapped.

'Then you must have forgotten it, to let the people suffer so.'

'Forgotten?' He stepped closer, his eyes hard and angry. 'There is nothing romantic about the life of a labourer. Only a woman who has known no real work would struggle so hard to preserve the rights of others to die young from overwork.' He reached out suddenly and seized her hands, turning them over to rub his fingers over the palms. 'As I thought. Soft and smooth. A lady's hands.'

'There is no shame in being a lady,' she said, with as much dignity as she could manage. She did not try to pull away. He could easily manage to hold her if he wanted to. And if he did not respond to her struggle the slight fear she felt at the nearness of him would turn into panic.

His fingers closed on hers, and his eyes seemed to go dark. 'But neither is there any pride in being poor. It is nice, is it not, to go to a soft bed with a full belly? To have hands as smooth as silk?' His thumbs were stroking her, and the little roughness of them seemed to remind her just how soft she was. There was something both soothing and exciting about the feel of his fingers moving against hers, the way they twined, untwined and twined again.

'That does not mean that we should not feel sympathy for those less fortunate than ourselves.' He was standing a little too close to be proper, and her protest sounded breathless and excited.

'Less fortunate, eh? Less in some ways, more in others. Without the machines they are fighting I would be no different than they are now—scrabbling to make a living instead of holding the hands of a beautiful lady in my own great house.'

It was not his house at all. He had taken it—just as he had taken her hands. 'I did not give you leave to do so,' she reminded him.

'You gave me no leave to carry you before either,' he said. 'But I wanted to, and so I did. You felt very good in my arms.' He pulled her even closer, until her skirts were brushing against the legs of his trousers. She did not move, even though he had freed her hands. 'It is fortunate for me that you are prone to pity a poor working man. Perhaps you will share some of that sweet sympathy with me.' He ran a finger down her cheek, as though to measure its softness.

She stood very still indeed, not wishing him to see how near she was to trembling. If she cried out it would draw the house down upon them and bring this meeting to a sudden end. But her words had failed her, and she could manage no clever quip that would make him think her sophisticated. Nor could she raise a maidenly insistence that he revolted her. He did not. His touch was gentle, and it made her forget all that had come before.

He seemed to forget as well, for his voice was softer, deeper and slower. 'Your father broke one of my looms today. But it will be replaced, and I will say nothing of how the destruction happened.'

'Thank you,' she whispered, wetting her lips.

'If you wish to make a proper apology, I would like something more.' His head dipped forwards, slowly, and his lips were nearing hers.

Although she knew what was about to happen she stayed still and closed her eyes. His lips were touching hers, moving lightly over them. It was as it had been when he had touched her ankle and held her hands. She could feel everything in the world in that single light touch. Her whole body felt warm and alive. Hairs rose on her arms and neck—not from the chill but as though they were eager to be soothed back to smoothness by roving hands.

She kissed him back, moving her lips on his as he had on hers. His mouth was rough, and imperfect. One corner of his smile was slightly higher than the other, and she touched it with the tip of her tongue, felt the dimple beside it deepen in surprise.

In response, he gave a playful lick against her upper

lip, daring her. Her body's response was an immediate tightening, and she pressed herself against him, opening her mouth. And what had been wonderful became amazing.

He encircled her, and his arms made a warm, safe place for their exploration—just as they had when he'd carried her. The slow stroking of hands and tongue seemed to open her to more sensations, and the tingling of her body assured her of the rightness of it, the perfection and the bliss. Although she knew all the places on her body that he must not touch, she was eager to feel his fingers there, and perhaps his tongue.

Just the idea made her tremble with eagerness, with embarrassment, and the knowledge that had seemed quite innocent was near to blazing out of control. And it was not only his doing. Even now she had taken his tongue into her mouth, and it was she who held it captive there, closing her lips upon it.

She could tell by his sigh of pleasure that he enjoyed what she'd done. But his only other response was to go still against her. His passivity coaxed her to experiment, raking his tongue with her teeth and circling it with her own, urging him to react.

He had trapped her into being the aggressor. At the realisation, she pulled away suddenly. He let her go, staring down at her in mock surprise, touching his own lips gingerly, as though they might be hot enough to burn his fingers.

'Stop that immediately,' she said.

He smiled. 'You have stopped it quickly enough for both of us. And now I suppose you wish me to apologise for the way *you* kissed *me*?'

'Only if you wish me to think you any sort of gentleman,' she said, feeling ridiculous.

'But I am not a gentleman,' he said with a shrug. 'Isn't that half the problem between us? I sit here, a trumped-up worker, in a house that should belong to my betters, had they not lost it through monetary foolishness. My presence in this house upsets the natural order of things. My touching you…'

'That is not the problem at all,' she snapped. 'I do not care who you are.'

'If you do not care who I am, it was highly indiscriminate of you to allow me the kiss. And even worse that you returned it.'

'You are twisting my words,' she said. 'I meant that it should not have happened at all. Not with any man. But especially not with you.'

'I don't know,' he said with an ironic laugh. 'I might be the best choice for such dalliance. If you complain to your father, I would be obligated to do right by you. Then my house and my fortune would be yours. You might trap me with your considerable charms and force me to marry you.'

'But to do that I would have to admit to Father that you had touched me, Mr Stratford. I think we can safely say that such a circumstance will never happen. Not for all the money in the world, and Clairemont Manor thrown into the mix. Now, please return me to the library.'

He smiled in triumph, as though that had been his end all along. 'Very well, then. Let us go back to your father, and both of you can be gone. I trust that now we have spoken on the subject I will see no more of you, or be forced to endure any more of your father's tirades? For, while I can see that there is more than a little madness to them, they cannot be allowed to continue. If arms are raised against me and the opening of the mill disrupted, or my equipment damaged further, I will be forced to take action. While I am sure that neither of us wants it, you must see that I do not intend to be displaced now that I am so near to success.'

He turned and led her back towards the library. As he opened the door he made idle comments about the furnishings and art, as though they had just returned from a tour of his home. It was all the more galling to know that some of the things he said were inaccurate, proving that he knew little more about the things he owned than how to pay for them. He really was no better than he had said: a man ignorant in all but one thing. He had made a fine profit by it. But what did that matter if it had left him coarse and cruel?

As they entered, her father looked up as though he had forgotten how he had come to be there. 'I think it is time that we were going, Father,' she said firmly. 'We have abused Mr Stratford's hospitality for quite long enough.'

Her father looked with longing at the book in his hands.

Joseph Stratford responded without missing a beat. 'I hate to take you from your reading, sir. Please accept the volume as my gift to you. You are welcome to come here whenever you like and avail yourself of these works. It pleases me greatly to see them in the hands of one who enjoys them.'

Because you have no use for them, you illiterate lout, she thought. She responded with a smile that was almost too bright, 'How thoughtful of you, Mr Stratford.'

Her father agreed. 'Books are a precious commodity in the area, and it is rare that we get anything new from London that is not a newspaper or a fashion plate.' He wrinkled his nose at the inadequacy of such fare to a man of letters.

Stratford nodded in sympathy. 'Then we will see what can be done to correct the deficiency. If there is anything you desire from my library, send word. I will have it delivered to you. And now it appears that your daughter is properly recovered. If I may offer you a ride back to the village?'

Her father stood, and the men chatted as they walked to the door as though they were old friends. In a scant hour Bernard Lampett had quite recovered from his fit of rage, and Mr Stratford was behaving as though the incidents in the mill and in the hall had not occurred. If he remembered them at all, he appeared untouched by them.

But in the space of that same hour Barbara felt irrevocably changed, and less sure of herself than she had ever been.

CHAPTER FIVE

LATER that evening the guests began to arrive, and Joseph was relieved to have no time to think of Barbara Lampett. Even when he should have focused his energy elsewhere, he could feel the memory of her and her sweet lips always in the background. It had been madness to take her out into the hall. He had known that he could not fully trust himself around her. When they were alone he should have limited himself to urging her to moderate her father's actions. But he'd had the foolish urge to show her his house, so that she might see the extent of his success. There might even have been some notion of catching her under a kissing bough and stealing one small and quite harmless kiss. He had been eager to impress her, and had behaved in a way that was both foolish and immature.

All of it had got tangled together in an argument, ending with a brief and heated display of shared emotion. It had been as pleasant as it had inappropriate. While such little indiscretions happened all the time, ladies like Barbara Lampett did not like to think themselves capable of them. She would not wish to be reminded, nor to risk a repeat display. He would not see her again.

And that was that.

He turned his attention to more important matters. After the rejections in today's post, it appeared that his house would be barely half-full for Christmas. There had been several frosty refusals to the offer of a trumped-up tradesman's hospitality. But it would not matter. Even one or two would be plenty—if they were rich enough and could be interested in his plans.

As promised, he let Bob take the lead in introductions and in the planning of activities, doing his best to respond in a way that was not rough or gauche. His casual offer that tomorrow's skating on the millpond might end with cakes and punch served in the empty warehouse was accepted graciously—once the ladies were assured that it was quite clean and that no actual work was being done. While they were there he would arrange a tour of the tidy rows of machinery. Breton would make mention of the successes they'd shared with the production and sale of such looms to others. The seed would be planted.

Before they returned to London one or two of the men would come to Bob, as they always did after such gatherings, making offhand remarks about risk and reward. A discreet parlay would be arranged in which no money would change hands. There would be merely a vague promise of it, for such people did not carry chequebooks with them. They carried cards and wrote letters of introduction to bankers, who stayed in the background where they belonged. But if they offered, they would deliver. Honour was involved. A true gentleman's word was as good as a banknote.

He frowned as the last of his guests took themselves off to bed, leaving him free for a few hours of rest. He was tired tonight, after last night's uneasy rest. Dinner had tired him as well. It was like speaking another language, dealing with the gentry and their need to seem idle even while doing business. So much easier to deal with the likes of mad Lampett. Though he was of a changeable nature, he would at least speak what was left of his mind.

For plain speaking, Lampett's lovely daughter was better than ten of the milk-and-water misses he was likely to see this week. Even Anne Clairemont, whose family had put in a brief appearance this evening, had looked puzzled by the conversation, and nervous at the prospect of a little skating on a properly frozen pond. He would not have faulted her if she had politely excused herself from it. But she had looked from her father to him, blinked twice and then forced a smile and declared it a wonderful notion.

Miss Lampett, in a similar situation, would have likely announced to the assembly that the whole trip was a thinly disguised attempt at business and refused to take any part in it. For some reason the imagined scene did not bother him. He could just as easily imagine drawing her out in the hall to remonstrate with her, only to have the conversation degenerate into another heated kiss.

When his valet had left him for the night he settled back into the pillows and pulled the blankets up to his chin, closing his eyes and thinking of that kiss. He really shouldn't have taken it. It had been improper and unfair of him to take advantage of her innocence. But he would do it again if he had the chance. That and more…

He awoke hungry. It made no sense. The clock was only striking one, and dinner had been a feast, stretching late into the evening. He had partaken of it with enthusiasm. But it was gone from him now, leaving his guts empty and gnawing on themselves in the darkness.

He had not known want like this since he'd become master of his own life. This was the kind of nagging hunger he'd felt as a child, going to bed with an empty belly and knowing that there would be nothing to fill it again tomorrow. It was a kind of bleak want that existed in the body like an arm or a leg: something that one carried with one from moment to moment, place to place, always there and impossible to cast off.

But it was easily rectified now. He had but to sit up in bed and ring for a footman. He would explain the need and have it filled. It would mean getting some poor maid out of her bed to do for him. But what was the point of having servants if one could not make unreasonable demands upon them?

When he opened his eyes, the room was strange. Not his own bedroom at all, but a different, emptier room, filled with a strange, directionless golden haze.

From the corner of the room there was a sigh.

Joseph sat bolt upright now, searching for the source of the sound. And with it he found the origin of the glow. A man sat in the corner—a Cavalier, in a long well-curled wig and heavy-skirted coat. The light seemed to rise from the gold braid upon it, diffusing into a corona around him.

This man was a stranger, and yet strangely familiar. He looked around the room and sighed again. He glanced across at Joseph and gave a pitying shake of his head. 'When I was summoned here, I must admit I expected better. These are not the surroundings to which I am accustomed. But I suppose if there is no problem, then there is no need…' The Cavalier gave another heavy sigh.

'Just what do you mean by that?' snapped Joseph, rubbing his eyes. 'I grew up in a room not unlike this one, and…'

As a matter of fact he'd grown up in a room exactly like this one. Its appearance was softened somewhat, by the glow of the phantom and by his own fading memories, but it was the same room. It was where he'd felt the hunger that plagued him now, which was still as sharp and real as ever it had been.

'I belong at the manor and have been sent to fetch you back to it,' the man said bluntly. 'Although even that is no treat. For I must tell you the place under your governance is not as nice as it once was.'

'Now, see here,' Joseph said, sitting up in his bed only to realise that it was not the thing he'd lain down on but a narrow bunk, with a rush mattress and thin blankets that could not keep the cold from his feet. 'You need not take me back, for I did not go anywhere. I am still there, fast asleep and dreaming.' This time he gave himself a hard pinch on the back of the hand, not caring if the spirit before him saw it.

'I was told that this had been explained to you. Three visitors would come. We would show you your errors. You would learn or not learn, as was your nature…' He droned in an uninterested way that said he did not care what Joseph learned, so long as he did it quickly and with as little bother as possible.

Joseph glared at the spirit, annoyed that it was still before him. 'I was told by my father. Who is dead and therefore should not be telling me anything. While he said there would be three, he did not say three of what. If there was any truth in it he might as well have said four, thus counting himself.'

'Do not think you can reason like a Jesuit to get yourself out of a situation that you yourself have created.' The Cavalier sighed again, and flicked a lace handkerchief in front of his nose as though offended by the stench of such humble surroundings. 'Be silent and I will explain. And then we might be done with this vision and go back to the house.'

'But you are not real,' Joseph argued. It was most annoying to be lectured at by one's own imagination. And then he placed the identity of the thing sitting before him. 'You are Sir Cedric Clairemont, and nothing more than a portrait hanging in the gallery on the second floor. This room is the place where I was born. I am blending memories in a dream.'

Sir Cedric gave a resigned glare in his direction, and sighed again as though facing a difficult child. 'Let me put this plainly, so that you might understand it. I would say I am as real as you, but that would lack truth. I was real. Now I am a spirit, as is your father. As are the two that will come after. By the end of it you will know where you were, where you are and what you will become.'

'I know all these things for myself, without your help. I will not be frightened into a change of plans by some notion created out of a second helping of trifle after a roast pork dinner.'

'Touch me,' commanded the spirit.

He did look almost real enough to touch, and just the same as he did in his portrait. But from what memory had Joseph created the man's voice, which was a slightly nasal tenor? Or his mannerisms as he swaggered forwards with his stick and looked down at Joseph with amused superiority? This man was not some ghost from a painting, but so real that he felt he could reach out and…

Joseph drew his hand back quickly, suddenly aware of the gesture he'd been making—which had looked almost like supplication.

The ghost stared at him with impatience. Then he brought the swagger stick down upon Joseph's head with a thud.

'Ow!'

'Is that real enough for you, Stratford? Or must I hit you again? Now, get out of the bed and take my hand—or I will give you a thumping you will remember in the morning.'

The idea was ludicrous. It was one thing to have a vivid dream. Quite another for that nightmare to fetch you a knock to the nob then demand that you get out of bed and walk into it.

'Certainly not.' Joseph rubbed at the spot where he'd been struck. 'Raise that stick to me again and, dream or not, I will answer you blow for blow.'

Sir Cedric smiled ironically. 'Very well, then. If you wish to remain here I can show you images of your childhood. Although why you would wish to see them, I am unsure. They are most unpleasant.'

As though a candle had been lit, a corner of the room brightened and Joseph felt increasing dread. It was the corner that had held the loom.

'Tighten the warp.' He heard the slap and felt the

impact of it on the side of his head, even though it had landed some many years before on the ear of the young boy who sat there.

'S…sorry, Father.' The young Joseph fumbled with the shuttle.

The man who stood over him could barely contain his impatience. 'Sorry will not do when there is an order as big as this one. I cannot work the night through to finish it. You must do your share. Sloppy work that must be unravelled again the next day is no help at all. It is worse than useless. Not only must I do my own part, I must stand over you and see to it that you do yours. You are worse than useless.'

'I was too small,' Joseph retorted, springing from the bed and flexing his muscles with a longing to strike back. 'My arms were too short to do the job. All the bullying in the world would have made no difference.'

'He cannot hear you,' the ghost said calmly. 'For the moment you live in my world, as much a spectre to him as he is to you.'

'It was Christmas. And it was not fair,' Joseph said, trying to keep the childish petulance from his voice.

'Life seldom is.'

'I made it fair,' Joseph argued. 'My new loom is wider, but so simple that a child can manage it.' The weavers of Fiddleton and all the other places that employed a Stratford loom would not be beating their children at Christmas over unfinished work.

But the ghost at his side said nothing, as though

Joseph had done no kindness with the improvement. He held out his hand again. 'Do you need further reminders of your past?'

Without thinking, Joseph shook his head. The past was clear enough in his own mind without them. It had been hard and hungry and he was glad to be rid of it. 'I made my father eat his words before the end,' Joseph said coldly. 'He died in warmth and comfort, in a bed I bought for him, and *not* slaving in someone else's mill.'

'Take my hand and come away.' Sir Cedric sounded almost sympathetic, his voice softer, gently prodding Joseph to action.

Joseph turned his back on the vision and reached for the arm of the spectre, laying his hand beside the ghostly white one on the stick he held. The fingers were unearthly cold, and smooth as marble, but very definitely real to him in a way that the man and boy in the corner were not. 'Very well, then. Whatever you are, take me back to the manor and my own bed.'

There was a feeling of rushing, and of fog upon his face, the sound of the howling winds upon the moors. Then he was back in his own home, walking down the main corridor towards the receiving rooms in bare feet and a nightshirt.

'What the devil?' He yanked upon Sir Cedric's arm, trying to turn him towards the stairs. 'I said my bedroom, you lunatic. If my guests see me wandering the house in my nightclothes, they will think I've gone mad. All my plans will be undone.'

If this was a ghost that escorted him, the least it could do was to be insubstantial. But Sir Cedric was as cold and immovable as stone. Now that they were joined Joseph could not seem to pull his hand away. He was being forced to follow into the busiest part of the house, which was brightly lit and brimming with activity, though it had been empty when he'd retired.

'Don't be an idiot, Stratford. Did I not tell you that I am a spirit of the past, and that you might pass unseen through it?' The ghost sniffed the air. 'This is the Christmas of 1800, if I have led us right. It is the same night when we saw you clouted on the ear. Well past my time, but the holiday is much as I remember it from my own days as lord here, and celebrated as it has always been. The doors are open to the people of Fiddleton. Tenants and villagers, noble friends and neighbours mix here to the joy of all.'

The ghost gave a single tap of his stick and the ballroom doors before them opened wide. The same golden glow Joseph had seen before spilled through them and out into the hall, as if to welcome them in.

This is how it should be.

The thought caught him almost off guard, as though the sight of this long-past Christmas was the missing piece in a puzzle. The rooms were the same, the smells of Christmas food very nearly so. But it was the people that made the difference.

Even in mirth, his current guests were polite and guarded. The men considering business looked at him as though calculating gain and loss. Anne's family treated him with an awkward combination of deference and contempt. A few others avoided him, acting as though the wrong kind of mirth on their part would admit that they did not mind his company and would result in some life-changing social disaster.

But the very air was different in this place. It was not simply the quaint fashion of the clothes or the courtliness of the dancing. There was a look in their eyes: a confidence in the future, a joyful twinkle. As though there was no question that the future would be as happy as the past had been. But they were not bending, more than ten years on, under the weight of a never-ending war, or the feeling that their very livelihood might slip from their fingers because of the decisions made by men of power and wealth. They were dancing, singing and drinking together, unabashed. The spirit was infectious, and Joseph could not help but smile in response to the sight.

There was a pause in the music and he heard the laughter of young girls—saw a pair, still in the schoolroom, winding about the furniture in a game of tag.

'Do you not wish they would stop?' the ghost prodded gently. 'It is most tiresome, is it not? All the noise and the bustle?'

'No. It is wonderful.' For all the quiet dignity of the party he was throwing, there was something lost. It lacked the life of this odd gathering so bent on merriment. He could see village folk amongst them—the grocer, the miller and younger versions of the same weavers who had threatened only yesterday to break the frames in his factory. But now they danced with the rest, as though they were a part of the household.

He cast a questioning glance at the ghost.

'It is the annual Tenants' Ball,' Sir Cedric supplied. 'Held each Christmas night—until the last owner could no longer keep the spirit of the season or afford the house.'

'Perhaps if he had been a wiser steward of his money and not spent it on frivolities such as this he would still reside here.' But his own conscience told him that was an unfair charge. The celebration *he* was throwing was far more elaborate than this, and not a tenth as happy.

'He seems successful enough there, doesn't he?' Sir Cedric raised his stick and pointed towards the corner, where stood Anne's father, Mr Clairemont, looking happier and less careworn than he had done since Joseph had known him. And there was Mrs Clairemont, who showed a change even more drastic. Eleven years ago she had been a gracefully aging beauty. Now she was grey, pinched and nervous.

'Whatever the reason, the Clairemonts are gone from here and none of your concern. I hear the house is held by a harsher master now.' The ghost gave him a look one part disappointment and one part disapproval, followed by another heavy sigh.

'I am harsh because I did not invite the whole village for Christmas dinner?' Joseph waved a hand at the assembly. 'How was I expected to know of this? It is not as if I was born of this area. The cottage we began the night in was miles from here. Clairemont said nothing of this responsibility when he sold me the house.'

'And you are so tragically robbed of speech that you could not enquire.' The ghost nodded in mock sympathy.

Now the lord of the manor was offering baskets to the families that had come, shaking hands and slapping backs as though every last man was an old friend. If the Clairemonts were still in the house, it must mean that the woman he now meant to marry was somewhere in the throng—and no older than the girls at play. He searched for the pair he had seen and dismissed earlier, but there were so many children, and they seemed to swarm out of doorways and hiding places, tearing down the halls, heedless of the other guests.

Then he spied Anne. Even now he could not quite manage to think of her as 'his' Anne. The unfamiliarity of her youth made it no easier. This little girl was as unlike her in manner as she was like in face. In childhood there had been none of the sombre grace that the woman carried now. She was a mischievous imp who did not care that her hair ribbons had come untied so long as she was not caught by the one who followed.

And the other, following close on her heels, was just alike. A twin? Or very nearly so? For the girls were very similar in looks. If they were not birthed together, then no more than a year could have separated them.

'Mary! Anne! Wait for me.' A third girl appeared, as though out of nowhere, seemingly forgotten as the game of hide-and-seek went on without her. When he turned to the sound of her voice he saw a hanging on the wall that had concealed her still rustling back into place.

Focused as she was on the two who had passed, she did not see him until it was too late, striking his legs with a surprisingly solid thump. 'Excuse me, sir.'

As he reached out a hand to steady her, her little face turned up to his. Barbara Lampett. It must be her. For there was the same turned-up nose. And those were her blue eyes, as bright and searching as a beacon, with the curiosity of unvarnished youth. No one had told her not to stare, or taught her to cloak the energy of her spirit in courtesies and false manners.

He felt the same connection he had at the riot, and again in this very hall. But this was different. Tonight she knew nothing about him. She'd had no chance to form an opinion, no reason to think him anything less than a gentleman. She had no cause to dislike him. She was smiling at him with those same pursed lips that had shown such disapproval this afternoon.

The thought staggered him. Seeing her here, as she had been, he very much wished that he might have met the girl full-grown tonight, and had even the smallest opportunity to let the woman she had become see him as anything else than an enemy.

He steadied her, and stepped out of her way. 'No harm done, Miss Lampett. Go and find your friends.'

But the other girls had come back for her, grabbing her hands and pulling her away, paying no heed to him.

'Barbara, what are you waiting for? Come.'

Then she was gone from him, with one passing look and a tip of her head, as though she could not quite make out his purpose in standing in the hall, staring.

'Who is the man in the nightshirt?' she said to the nearest girl, looking back at him again.

'What man?' Her friends looked back, through him.

'I… Never mind.' Barbara smiled and looked away again, as though the memory of him was already fading.

'She saw me?' he said in wonder, looking down at his own hand as though he could still feel the muslin of her gown under his fingers.

'It seems so,' said the ghost, barely interested. 'There are those who see the world around them plainly, and those who don't. Miss Lampett is more perceptive than most.'

Joseph thought again of her ill opinion of him. That was hardly a sign of keen perception. Her animosity seemed to be shared by most of the community.

'And some others can learn to see properly if they are shown,' the ghost added.

'You are speaking of me, I suppose?' Joseph answered.

'You do seem to be most singularly blind to your surroundings.'

'I see it more as an ability to avoid distractions and to focus on the future.'

'Really?' It was more a question than a statement. 'The future is not my purview. There is another…' The ghost stopped for a moment and gave a slight shudder. 'You will see soon enough how clear a view of the future you hold. But for now I bring you to the past so that you might learn from it. Do not forget it, my boy.'

'Stratford! What the devil? Joseph, get up immediately. What are you about, sleeping in a common hallway?'

Joseph started awake, focusing in confusion for a moment on a man's legs, before looking up into the worried face of Breton. 'Hallway?' he echoed in puzzlement, struggling to remember the details of the previous evening. It had begun normally enough. But now…

He looked around him. He was slumped on the floor in the hall, in front of the ballroom, still clad in his nightclothes. He stood up quickly, glancing around to make sure they were alone. 'Did anyone…?'

'See you? Dear God, I hope not. I am sure we will hear of it if they have. But you must consider yourself fortunate that I am an early riser and can help you out of this fix. What happened?'

'I am not sure. I must have roamed in my sleep. I had a very vivid dream.' And vivid it must have been. He could see the bruise on his hand where he had pinched himself. And feel a small knot on his skull where he had been rapped by the Cavalier's beribboned walking stick.

'Well, you look like the very devil. Grey as a paving stone and just as cold.'

Joseph turned behind him to the curtain that hung on the wall and swept it aside, to reveal a small alcove with a stone bench just large enough to hide a pair of lovers. Or a girl playing at hide-and-seek.

'I did not know of this before now,' he said numbly to his friend. 'But I dreamed it was here.'

Breton was staring at him as though he were as barmy as Bernard Lampett. 'If you wish to search the house for priests' holes, it might be best to continue when fully dressed.'

'Perhaps so.' He frowned. 'But I am surprised I had not noticed this before.'

His friend took him by the arm, tugging him towards the back stairs. 'That is little shock to me. It has nothing to do with the running of the mill. That is all you seem to care about lately.'

'Unfair,' Joseph charged. 'I care about many things. It is not as if I am made of clockwork, you know.' Who had told him he was?

They mounted the steps and Breton hurried him towards his room, his valet and his clothing. 'Sometimes I wonder. But, if you have them, tell me of these other interests. I defy you to name one.'

Now that he was pressed, Joseph could not seem to think of any. Unless he could count Lampett's fractious daughter as an interest. If the spirit of Sir Cedric had taught him anything, it was of his desire to see another of the smiles she had worn as a child.

In response to his silence Bob gave a snort of disgust. When he spoke, the amusement in his voice had been replaced with sincere annoyance. 'That was where you should have announced your excitement at your impending engagement. Have you forgotten that as well?'

'Of course I have not forgotten.' But he had responded too late to be believable.

'I might just as well have included it as part of your business. It is little more than that to you, isn't it?'

'Little more to her as well,' Joseph said, a little defensively. 'Her father wishes her back living in this house. This is the most efficient way to accomplish it.'

Breton pushed him towards his room. 'Once she is here, you will notice her as little as you do your own furnishings—or that hole in the wall you found so fascinating. And that is a pity. Anne is a lovely girl, and deserving of better.'

There was that prickling of his conscience again, and the echoing warning of his father to unravel his plans and start fresh. Perhaps that was what he'd meant. His other business plans were sensible enough. He hardly needed a wife to cement his place. But he could think of no honourable way to back out of the arrangement he had made with Clairemont.

'There is nothing to be done about it now,' Joseph said with exasperation. 'We are as good as promised to each other. Everyone knows I mean to make the announcement on Christmas Eve. I cannot cry off, even if I might like to. The scandal to the girl would be greater than any that might befall me.'

'Then the least you can do,' Breton said more softly, 'is to recognise that you have won a prize, and treat the girl as such. For if I find that you are neglecting her, or making her unhappy, I will be forced to act.'

Joseph looked at his friend as if for the first time. Bob, who had been ever loyal, friendly and trusting, was acting as strangely as though he had been receiving nightly revelations as well. He looked angry. It was disquieting.

'Very well, then,' Joseph answered, searching his friend's expression for some understandable reason for this change. 'I will take your words to heart. Although it will not be a love match, I will make sure that she does not suffer for my neglect.'

His friend sighed. 'I suppose it is as much as I can expect from you. But see that you remember your words.'

And mine as well.

The echo of a voice from the portrait gallery caused him to start nervously.

His friend gave him another suspicious look. 'Is there something wrong, Joe?'

'Nothing,' he said hurriedly. 'You are right. I have been working too hard. I have not slept well for two nights. And I am neglecting Anne. Today I will change. I promise. But for now I must dress. I will see you in the breakfast room shortly.' He backed hurriedly into his bedroom and shut the door before the conversation could grow any more awkward.

He would make a change—if only to avoid another night like the one he'd just had. Although, with the minimal direction his nightly ghosts had given him, God only knew what that change was supposed to be.

CHAPTER SIX

'WILL that be all, Miss Lampett?'

Barbara checked carefully through the list she'd set for herself to finish the Christmas shopping. A matching skein of wool to complete the warm socks she was knitting for Father, and the new fashion plates that her mother would enjoy, along with enough lace to make her a collar. 'I can think of nothing more.'

'Do you want this sent round to the house, Miss Lampett?' The girl behind the counter looked at her expectantly.

There was plenty of space left in her market basket on top of the groceries: three oranges, one for each of them, and a pound of wheat for her father's favourite frumenty. The roast she'd got from the butcher sat in the bottom of the basket, wrapped tightly in brown paper so that it would not spoil the rest. The poor bit of meat was leaner than she'd wished for. But then so was the butcher. What with the war, and the general poverty of the area, Christmas itself would be sparse for many people, and she had best be grateful that her family had the money to purchase a feast.

Barbara counted the remaining coins in her purse, calculating the pennies needed to reward the boy at the end of his journey. 'No, thank you. It is a fine day, and not far. I will carry this myself.'

The shop girl gave her a doubtful look and wrapped the package carefully, placing it on top of the others.

Barbara hefted the basket off the counter, feeling the weight shift. It was heavy now. In a mile it would be like lead on the end of her arm. Her muscles would ache with carrying it. But she smiled in gratitude, to show the girl that it was all right, and pulled it to her side, turning to go.

'Allow me, Miss Lampett.' Without warning, Joseph Stratford was there at her side, as suddenly as he had been two days past in front of the mill. He had a grip on the basket handle, and had pulled it from her without waiting for her to give him leave.

'That will not be necessary,' she said, trying not to sound breathless from the shock of the sudden contact. It was strange enough to see him in the village, shopping amongst the peasants in the middle of a work day. But it was doubly disconcerting to have him here, close to her again, after the intimacy of yesterday.

'Perhaps you do not think it necessary,' he agreed. 'But I would not be able to stand aside and watch you struggle with it. You had best take my assistance, for both our sakes.'

'I would prefer not.'

'But I would not be able to sleep, knowing I had left a lady to carry such a burden.' He smiled at her in a way that might have been charming had she not known so much of the source. 'I can hardly sleep as it is.'

The charm faded for a moment, and she saw shadows under his eyes that had not been there two days ago. Maybe her father was weakening him, after all. She reminded herself that he deserved any suffering he felt, and gave him a false smile in return. 'Heaven forefend that you are uneasy in your rest, sir.' She reached again for the basket, but he pulled it just out of reach.

'Come. You and your packages will have a ride home in my carriage.'

'It is a short distance,' she argued.

'The weather is turning. Come with me, and you will stay warm and dry.'

'My reputation…'

'Will be unharmed,' he finished, glancing at the people around him for confirmation. 'I mean you no mischief. I will take you directly home. It is on my way.' He looked around with a glare, cowing the shop girl and the other customers. 'No one will cast aspersions if I attempt to do you good. They can see plain enough that you are resisting, but I am giving no quarter. Come along, Miss Lampett.'

Then he and her basket were ahead of her, out of the

door and walking towards the large and entirely unnecessary carriage. She had no choice but to trail after.

As she passed, his groom jumped to attention, rushing to take the basket, get the stair down and hold the door as he helped her up. Across from her, Joseph Stratford leaned back into the seats as though he was ascending to a throne.

Then he smiled at her, satisfied. 'There. As you can see, you are perfectly safe, and still in clear view of those in the street. I am all the way over here—properly out of reach of you. There will be no such incident as there was the last time we were alone together.'

'I had no doubt of that, Mr Stratford. I would die first.'

He laughed at her for her primness. 'You are a most ungrateful chit, Miss Lampett. One kiss did you no permanent harm. And, if you will remember the altercation outside the mill two days past, you must admit I have shown concern for your welfare. If I was as awful as you pretend, I would have let the mob trample you.'

'You would not have.' He'd moved with such speed to get to her side that she was sure it had been all but involuntary.

He looked surprised. 'You give me credit for that much compassion, at least. Thank you for it.'

The silence that came after served to remind her just how unequal things had become, and just how unfair she was being to him—even if she did not particularly like the man. 'I deserve no thanks, Mr Stratford. I owe them to you. At least for that day. I am perfectly aware that if you did not save my life, you at least spared me serious injury.'

'You're welcome.' He seemed almost embarrassed that she had noticed the debt she owed.

'But now you are giving me a ride, when I told you I did not wish one. After yesterday...'

'Can you not accept this in the spirit with which it was given?' he asked with a smile. 'It is foul outside, but it appeared that you wished to forgo even the help of a delivery boy and struggle home by yourself. There was no reason for it.'

He looked at her sideways for a moment, and then out of the window, as though his next comment was of no consequence.

'Perhaps I remember what it was like to count pennies as though they were pounds, and do without the smallest luxuries.'

He had guessed her reason for walking? 'Then I also apologise for the comment I made in our last conversation, accusing you of being unsympathetic to those in need.'

He was frowning now, and hardly seemed to speak to her. 'You were right in part, at least. I had meant, when that time passed, to remember it better. I pledged to myself that I would be of aid to those who were impoverished, as I had been while growing up. It seems I have forgotten.'

'Do not think to make my family an object of pity to

salve your stinging conscience,' she snapped. 'If you wish to offer charity, there are others that need more of it.' Then she looked out of the window as well. She felt bad to have spoken thus, for it was very ungrateful of her. He seemed able to put her in the worst temper with the slightest comment. But then, he could arouse other emotions as well.

Her cheeks coloured as she thought again of the kiss. When she'd accepted this ride, had there been some small part of her that had hoped he would attempt to do it again? Was that what made her angry now? She was a fool if she thought that his offer had been anything other than common courtesy. She meant nothing to him. Nor did the kiss.

'It is hardly charity to offer another person a ride on a cold and rainy day,' he said gently. 'I'll wager you'd have accepted if the offer had come from Anne Clairemont or her mother.'

'That would not have been likely,' she said.

'Why not? You were friends with the Clairemont girls as a child, were you not?'

She turned and looked at him sharply. 'What gave you that idea?'

His gaze flicked away for a moment. 'You mentioned it as we were driving towards the house yesterday.'

'I said I'd had a friend there. But you said "girls" just now. I did not mention Mary.'

'Perhaps Anne did,' he said, still not looking at her. 'Mary was her sister, then?'

The idea that Anne might have mentioned her seemed highly unlikely. Something about the calculated way he spoke made her suspect he fished for information and was piecing the truth together with each slip Barbara made. 'Mary has been dead for quite some time,' she said, praying that would be the end of the conversation.

'What happened to her?'

'There was nothing mysterious about her death. She took ill, faded and died. If you wish to know more you had best ask your fiancée, Miss Clairemont.'

'I have not offered as of yet.'

'But you will. The whole village knows that the festivities you have organised are meant to celebrate your engagement to her.'

'Do they, now?' His voice had dropped briefly, as though he was talking to himself. 'I did not know that the world was sure of plans that I myself have not spoken.'

Were they not true? Anne seemed sure enough of them, as was her father. But Stratford's response gave Barbara reason to fear for them. It would be most embarrassing should they have misunderstood this man's intent so completely and allowed themselves to be used to further his business. 'I am sorry. Perhaps I was mistaken.'

'Perhaps you were.' He was looking at her rather intently now, as though trying to divine her opinion on the subject.

She reminded herself that she had none. Perhaps she

was a little relieved that he was not riding with her or kissing her while planning to marry Anne. She had no wish to hurt that family again by seeming too interested in Mr Stratford. Nor did she want to do anything that might encourage him to become interested in her if he was otherwise engaged.

But his eyes, when seen this close, were the stormy shade of grey that presaged a violent change in the weather. The slight stubble on his chin only emphasised the squareness of his jaw. Now that she had noticed it she found it hard to look away.

He broke the gaze. 'Then again, perhaps you were not mistaken about my engagement. I have not yet made a decision regarding my future, or that of Miss Anne Clairemont.'

She looked down at her feet, embarrassed for having thought anything at all other than cursory gratitude that she was not walking in the rain. 'Either way, it is rude of you to discuss it with me. And, I might add, it does not concern me whatever you do. You might marry whoever you like and it will not matter to me in the slightest.'

'It is good to know that. Not that I planned to seek your approval.' This was more playful than censorious, and delivered with a strangely seductive smile, as if to say it was in his power to make it matter, should he so choose. 'But why do you say that the Clairemonts would not offer you a ride if you needed one? They seem like nice enough people, from what I know of them.'

Perhaps enough time had passed that they were better. Barbara was not sure of the mood in the Clairemont household. But she would rather cut her tongue out than ask Anne, for fear the answer she might receive would open old hurts afresh. She gave a firm smile. 'It is an old family quarrel, and nothing of importance. I would not seek to bother them if I did not have to.'

'But I would like to hear of it, all the same.'

'You will not hear it from me,' she said, shifting uncomfortably in her seat. 'You are new to Fiddleton, Mr Stratford, and might not know the ways of small villages. When one lives one's life with the same people from birth, it sometimes happens that one makes a mistake that cannot be corrected and that will follow one almost to the grave.'

'Are you speaking of the Clairemonts, then? What mistakes could you have made to render you less than perfect in the eyes of this village? From where I sit, I see a most charming young woman—and well mannered.' He smiled. 'Although not always so to me.'

'You do not always deserve it, sir.'

'True enough,' he agreed. 'But you are kind to others, modest, clearly devoted to your family. And beautiful as well.'

'Though too old to be still unmarried,' she finished for him, sure he must be thinking it. 'The verdict has already been rendered as to my worth in that regard. I have learned to accept it.'

'Then we are of a kind,' he said. 'Although I am the

worse of the two of us. I have just got here, and I have made myself universally hated. But I do not let it bother me. I do not care a whit for the opinions of the locals. I am who I am, and they had best get used to it.' He looked her up and down again. 'If they think less of you, for some foolish reason or other, I cannot give their views much credence.'

Between the kiss they had shared and the look he gave her now, she suspected he had got quite the wrong idea about it all. He was hoping that there had been a man involved in her downfall. But their trip was almost over, and he had offered no further insult, so it was hardly worth correcting him. As long as they were not alone again he would give her no trouble.

But his disregard for his own reputation bothered her. 'Perhaps you *should* care what people think. There are worse things than social ostracism, you know. Mill owners have been accosted in their own homes and on their ways to and from the factories they own.'

'That is why I carry this,' he said, patting the bulge in his pocket and reaching in to draw out the handle of a pistol.

'Are you really going to use it?'

'Do you doubt my bravery?'

'I do not doubt your foolhardiness,' she said. 'It has but one bullet in it. If there is trouble, there will likely be a gang behind it.'

'Then I will be forced to appeal to the garrison for aid, and it will not go well with them,' he said, as though that settled the matter. 'I do not seek violence, Miss Lampett. But if I feel myself threatened I will resort to it. You need have no doubt of that.'

She imagined the possible consequences with a sinking heart. 'Since the violence you describe is likely to be turned against my father, I believe we have nothing more to say to each other. It is fortunate that we have arrived at my home.'

Stratford glanced out of the window. 'So we have.' He turned and tapped on the door to signal the driver. 'Another turn around the high street, Benjamin. The lady and I are not finished with our discussion.'

'And I have just said we are.' She reached for the door handle, only to fall back into her seat as she felt the carriage turning. 'This is most high-handed of you, Mr Stratford.'

'But, knowing me as you do, you must expect nothing less of me, Miss Lampett.' He smiled again, as though they were doing nothing more serious than dancing around a ballroom. 'The subject we discuss is a serious one. I think I may have found an agreeable solution to several dilemmas at once. But it requires your co-operation, and the chance for us to speak privately for a little while longer—as we are doing now.'

Which explained the ride, she supposed. She should be relieved that he had not sought her out of any deeper desire for her company. But, strangely, she was not. 'Very well, then. Speak.'

'As you say, in a small village news travels fast. You

say that you know of my plans for the Christmas holidays?'

'You are entertaining guests from London. The only people of the village who will be in attendance are the Clairemonts. If it is not an engagement, then I suspect the gathering has something to do with the opening of the mill.'

'Why would you think that?' he asked, surprised.

'Because you are the host of it. Having met you, Mr Stratford, it seems unlikely that the people coming are old friends.'

'Ha!' Rather than being angered by her insult, he seemed amused by it.

She continued. 'Everything you do has to do with your business in some way or other. This Christmas party is like to be the same.' Then she allowed her true feeling of distaste to show. 'It is vulgar in the extreme to use the Lord's birth as a time for doing business, if that is what you mean to do.'

'Whether you have reached your conclusion from local gossip or shrewd deduction, you are correct, Miss Lampett. I am entertaining investors from London.' He gave a slight frown. 'Because, apparently, I think of nothing but business.' He paused for a moment, as though he had forgotten what it was he meant to say. 'I do not have quite so many guests as I had hoped. There were more negative replies in today's post.'

'Probably from gentlemen who understand the impropriety of it,' she said.

He shrugged. 'Or perhaps they do not wish to associate with one who is in trade, even though he offers them the opportunity to do it far from the prying eyes of the *ton*. It does not matter, really. As you have pointed out, they are not my friends. But I need only one—perhaps two—to come, agree and invest. Then, for me, this Christmas will be a happy one.'

It appeared that her father was right about the man, if that was how he measured his happiness. 'There would be far more joy for all should you choose to spend that time in meeting your neighbours, sir. If you could not manage that, then perhaps you could release the Clairemonts from their obligation to attend? For I suspect it will pain them greatly to see their home treated as the London Exchange.'

'It is no longer their home, Miss Lampett. It is mine to do with as I please.'

'But I do not see why you wish to tell me of it. It is no business of mine,' she said, almost leaning out of the window in an effort to put space between them.

'On the contrary. I mean to make it your business. I understand that there has traditionally been a gathering of villagers at the house for Christmas. You have been in attendance at it, with Miss Anne Clairemont and her sister.'

'But that was years ago,' she admitted. 'Not since…' Not since Mary died and the Clairemonts shut up the house at Christmas. But the circumstances were no business of Stratford's.

'You and your family will honour me with your attendance this year as well,' he said. 'I am short of ladies, and there are likely to be several young bucks who would prefer an eligible young partner to dancing with their sisters.'

'On our limited acquaintance, you expect me to sit in attendance on your guests? That is rude beyond measure, sir.'

'Nothing of the kind. I invite you to be one of my guests. There would be no obligation to dance if you did not wish to do so. Though should you meet someone and form an attachment to him it would solve the question of your unmarried state quite nicely. Between your father's trouble, and the problem you have hinted at with local society, it must be difficult for you to be so removed from the company of equals.'

It was. Though she tried to control it, a wistful longing arose in her at the prospect of a chance to put on her nicest gown and dance. 'I do not need your help in that situation,' she said primly. 'I am quite fine on my own.'

'So you keep telling me. But I need *your* help, Miss Lampett,' he said, his hands open before him. 'My business negotiations, whether they are improper or no, are at a delicate juncture. I dare not risk your father giving another angry speech while the investors are here to see it. Nor do I wish to call the law down on him with Christmas dinner.'

'Then I think you would want us quiet at home for the holiday, and not dancing at the manor.'

'On the contrary. I have seen your father's interactions with you. When he is concerned about your welfare, all thoughts of violence go quite out of his head. If you told him that you wished to come to my party he would not disrupt it for fear of spoiling your enjoyment.'

'Even so, I would not trust him for any length of time in the company of strangers.'

'Then I shall send him a selection of books from the library. Old favourites of mine that are sure to occupy his mind for the duration of the week.'

'Old favourites of yours?' she said in surprise. 'You gave me to understand that you had no time for books.'

'Not now, perhaps. But I'd read most of the volumes in the Clairemont library long before my arrival here. In the coming year, when the mill is employed, I hope to have some evenings to myself and might read them again.'

'You said you were a weaver's son,' she said, thinking of her father's recalcitrant students and wondering if she had misunderstood him.

'I did not say I was clever at the trade. I was a horrible weaver, and no amount of teaching could make me better. I was more interested in books than the loom. When Father did allow me to go to school I taught myself, in whatever way I could manage.' He smiled bitterly. 'I fear I was a grave disappointment to him.'

'But why did you remain involved in the trade? Surely there might have been another occupation more suited to your tastes?'

'The life I wanted was forever closed to me, for I was not born a gentleman, Miss Lampett. It appeared that, no matter my lack of skill, I was destined to weave. So I redesigned the loom to make it easier for my clumsy fingers to manage. The machines to be used at the factory are of my own invention.'

Somehow she had imagined him purchasing the frames he used with little knowledge of their workings. But there was real passion in him as he talked of cold and unfeeling machines, and an energy that drew her in like a lodestone. It was only with effort that she noticed the fact that there was no mention of anyone other than himself.

'Is that why the talk of frame-breaking bothers you so? It must be difficult to see your work destroyed.'

He shrugged. 'Not really. Before coming here, my business was mostly in the supplying of other mills. When their looms were damaged by vandals, I made additional money in the repair and replacing of their machinery. While the production of cloth is a risky business, there can be no surer trade right now than the making of a thing that is useful, and very much in demand, but needs to be purchased multiple times when it is ruined. That business was the source of my wealth. Though your father and his friends might seek to see the end of me, like men have been my making.'

'You view the misfortune of others as the source of your success?' she said, amazed at how far removed he was from the people around him.

'So it has been. But enough of me and my business. Tell me what your response to my offer is likely to be.'

'It would be most improper for a single lady to accept an invitation from a gentleman if there is no understanding between them,' she said, wondering what he could be thinking to ask her in this way.

'Of *course*.' He pounded his fist against his leg once, in irritation. Then he gathered himself a little straighter. 'Please accept my apologies. It was forward of me. I will extend a formal invitation, in writing, for your whole family to join in whatever activities take place. There will be nothing to upset your father, I assure you. There will be dinners, dancing, games. I expect that it will be a very jolly time. If your parents do not wish to come, you must come alone—in the company of Miss Anne Clairemont and her family.' He gave her a firm look. 'There will be no trouble on that front. The doors of my house are open to you.'

There was a faint emphasis on the word 'my' to remind her that things had changed. She wondered if he would put the situation to the Clairemonts in the same blunt tone. It almost made her pity them.

But, no matter what he did, it would not be as it had once been. The merriment would not touch the community that it bordered. 'No, thank you,' she said. 'It hardly seems appropriate to celebrate when so many people are unhappy.' They had reached the gate of the cottage again, and she looked longingly in the direction of her home.

'How very pious of you.' He had noticed their destination as well, and tapped to signal the driver. 'It is a lovely day. Let us make another pass of the high street, shall we?'

'Do you mean to hold me prisoner in this carriage until I agree to your scheme?'

He held his hands up in a symbolic gesture of release. 'The thought had occurred to me. But I will let you go home to consider this and see if you do not think it a temporary respite from our troubles. Either way, the mill will open in January. Change is coming and there will be no avoiding it. Once it is open, and at least some of the locals are employed in it, we will find them less likely to raise a hand against me. Until then we must find together a way to stall your father from upsetting my plans—or I will take steps that are pleasant to neither of us.'

The carriage drew smoothly to a stop, and when the door opened he went before her, offering his hand to help her to the ground. Then he signalled for a footman to carry her basket to the house and returned to his seat, closing the shiny black door behind him.

CHAPTER SEVEN

WHEN she was through the door of the cottage she saw her father waiting in the front room, arms folded across his chest. Today she did not fear him so much as dread the weight of his displeasure.

'Well?' There was so much disappointment in the one word that Barbara glanced behind her, out of the open door and down the road, thinking that the burden of carrying the weight of her loaded basket could not possibly have equalled this.

She turned back, squared her shoulders and explained. 'Mr Stratford offered me a ride from the shops because the weather was changing.' She gave a little shake of her cloak to show the patter of icy drops that had hit her in the short walk from the carriage to the house. 'He was quite insistent. It seemed that I was likely to create more of a scene by refusing than accepting. So I relented.'

'There was time enough for someone to come from the village and inform me of the fact and be gone again,' her father said suspiciously. 'One would think that a man on foot could not best a team of horses in traversing the distance.'

She cleared her throat. 'Mr Stratford was deep in conversation with me as we neared the house. To continue it, he turned the carriage and we travelled once more around the village.'

'Thus it became a social drive.' Her father shook his head. 'That is a demonstration of the perfidy of the man. It is much like the mill—offered as an olive branch to the people of this community, only so he can snatch it away as they draw near. He took you, just as he took their jobs, and he dangles you like a bauble, just out of reach, and plays with you at his leisure.'

'Hardly, Father. We talked for but a few moments. The carriage remained on the high street and I sat in the window of it. I am sure that many in the community could see me and know that nothing untoward was happening.'

The argument seemed to have no effect on him, for he went on with increasing anger. 'The man is the very devil, Barb. I swear. The *devil.* He is here to ruin the village and all the people in it with his new ideas and his cheap goods. Nothing can come of cheapening the quality of the work, I am sure. It is the veritable road to hell.'

'And nothing to do with the matter at hand,' her

mother added firmly from behind him. She looked past him at her daughter. 'You say that you were seen the whole time? The carriage took no side trips, nor left the sight of the high street?'

'Not at all, Mama.'

'You could not have waited until the rain had passed? Or hurried home before it?'

'I did not want to spare the penny for the boy if I did not have to. The basket was heavy. And Mr Stratford would not take no for an answer.'

Her mother nodded. 'The offer of transport was fortuitous, even if there was an ulterior motive. What did you speak of?'

'His business.' And Mary, of course. They had spoken of her. But it was hardly worth mentioning.

'Then it had nothing to do with you?'

'Just as I suspected. It was an effort to turn you against me, and the village against us. The man is the devil,' her father insisted.

'Enough!' her mother snapped, ignoring her husband again and turning back to Barbara. 'We must deal with the more important matter first. And that should be the honour of our only child, which has not been harmed in the least by the trip, whether it was social or practical.'

'He invited us to the manor for Christmas,' Barbara added. 'He suggested that there might be gentlemen there, and dancing.' She tried to sound matter-of-fact about it, as though it did not matter one way or the other. She did not particularly wish to meet gentlemen.

There was one in particular that she might like to know better, but her father was probably right to call him a persuasive devil who was best avoided.

Still, it had been a long time since she'd danced—with or without demons. Would it really do any harm?

'Dancing at the manor? Of course you should go, then.' Her father's sudden change caught them unawares, as it often did. Though he had been angry only a few moments before, now he was smiling at her. 'You have not been since last Christmas, and you always enjoy it so. Visiting Anne and Mary will do you a world of good.'

She shot a worried glance over his shoulder to her mother, and then said, 'Father, Mary is dead. The Clairemonts no longer live at the manor. There has not been a Christmas celebration there in six years.'

'I know that,' he said quickly, embarrassed at his lapse. 'I only meant that you would be better off dancing at the manor than driving on the high street with Lucifer in a silk waistcoat.' He darkened again, as suddenly as he had brightened. 'A silk waistcoat made by hands that slaved for pennies so that he might ride high and mighty like a prince.' His eyes lit at the sound of his own words. 'I must write this down. It will be the basis of my next speech.'

'You do that, Father.' Barbara hurried to the little desk in the corner, setting out paper, uncapping the ink and trimming the nib of the pen. Then she pulled out his chair and took time to settle him there. It seemed to give him comfort, for he sat down and began writing industriously, staring out of the window before him into the sleet-streaked sky as though the next words were written on it and he could pluck them from the air.

'Come into the kitchen, Barbara. Let us see what you have brought back from the market.' Her mother turned quickly, but not before Barbara could see the trembling of her lip that was the beginning of tears.

'A moment, Mama.' She hurried to the sewing basket, to conceal her mother's Christmas gift. Then she followed her out of the room.

By the time she had reached her in the kitchen her mother was more composed, though clearly worried.

'What are we to do, Mama?' she whispered. 'He is like this more and more.'

'There is little for us *to* do. There is no changing him.' Her mother gave a brief, bitter laugh. 'He changes often enough on his own. Like the tides, he goes to extremes at both ends.'

If he continued thus there would be no chance of him returning to employment, and they would end their days living off the dwindling inheritance her mother had received from her own family. Barbara thought of the pennies in her purse again, and gave quiet thanks to Mr Stratford. Even if he was the devil, he had saved her the bother of a wet walk.

Her mother seemed to be thinking of him as well. 'Tell me about this Christmas invitation you have received. It does seem to be a lone bright spot in the day.'

'I told him it was improper,' Barbara said, frowning. 'For I did not think Father would approve.'

'Your father is lucky to remember from one minute to the next why he hates the man. We will tell him that you are gone to see Mary. For if there are gentlemen there, as he said...' Her mother was thinking forward, hoping for a bright future in which a wealthy stranger would appear with an offer and solve all their problems.

'But I refused,' Barbara said, dashing her hopes.

'Oh,' said her mother, properly disappointed.

'He offered again—including the family. When I told him that there was no way Father could manage such a gathering, he offered a selection of books as Christmas gifts—to keep him home and quiet over the holiday. He said he would send something written, so that I would know he spoke with sincerity.'

'A written invitation to the manor?' Her mother positively glowed with the prospect.

'I doubt he will remember,' Barbara said hurriedly. 'I am sure it was said only in passing, to make conversation. It was just an effort to be social.'

'A most curious effort, then.' Her mother was looking closely at her, trying to determine what she might be concealing. 'He has made no attempts at civility to the rest of the village. And yet he singles you out. A gentleman would know better than to make promises he cannot keep—especially when he is courting another.'

'One can hardly call him a gentleman, Mother. He is in trade. He admitted to me that he was a weaver's son.'

'Really?' Her mother's eyebrows arched. 'You speak like your father, my dear. It is idealistic to set men of business firmly below us and to act as though birth is all. Perhaps realism would be a better path, considering our circumstances. It is possible to be a gentleman and poor as a church mouse, while the weaver's son dines and dances in a manor. The world is changing. While we might not approve of all the changes, we must make the best of them. Let us hope that Mr Stratford is as good as his word.'

And his offer proved true. A short time later, while her father still pondered his latest diatribe, there was a knock on the door. Outside, the same coach that had deposited her waited for the liveried servant who held a properly sealed and decorated invitation and a package of books.

Before her father could say otherwise, her mother had snatched it from the poor man's hand and instructed him to wait upon the response. Then she pushed her husband's work aside and reached for paper and pen.

'As usual, Satan sends his handmaidens in fine garments to tempt the unwary,' her father barked.

The footman looked rather alarmed and peered behind him, unaware that he was the handmaiden in question.

'Nonsense, dear. It is an invitation to the manor. Nothing more. It can do us no harm to accept, surely?'

'Well, then.' Her father beamed. Then he waved a hand at the man who waited. 'My regards to Lord

Clairemont, his wife and his daughters. Tell them to be wary, just as they are merry.' Then he opened the first of the books and immediately forgot the source of his discomfiture.

The man gave a hesitant nod, and waited upon the hurriedly scribbled response from her mother before returning to the carriage.

Mother and daughter returned to the kitchen.

'You cannot mean for us to go, Mama,' Barbara whispered. 'Look at Father. There is no way for us to keep the pretence that it will be as it was. And no way to predict, once he is there, what he will say in front of Mr Stratford and his guests. It would be better if we refused politely and stayed home.'

'It would be better if your father and I stayed away. But there is no reason why you cannot go,' her mother said firmly. 'While I like dinner and a ball as well as the next person, I am content to sit here with your father and allow you to get the benefit of an invitation. He said there might be gentlemen?'

'Friends from London.'

'Stratford means to marry Anne. She and her parents will be there to recommend and chaperone you. I am sure, if you wrote to her, she would offer you a space in their carriage so that you needn't walk to the manor.'

'That was what Mr Stratford suggested as well. He said he would speak to them. But I do not think they would like it very much. Perhaps there is another way.' Although Barbara could think of none.

'I will not let you walk to the manor in dancing slippers. Nor will I allow you to refuse this invitation,' her mother said, giving her a stern look. 'I will write to the Clairemonts about it. I will choose my words with care. Perhaps, after six years, you should not blame yourself for something that was no fault of your own, and they should find it in their hearts to forgive you.'

It was not nearly enough time, Barbara was sure. It had been just this morning that she'd met Lady Clairemont walking down the street and seen the way the lady looked sharply in her direction, and then through her. 'Please, Mother, do not.'

'There is no other way. This is an opportunity that you dare not turn down. If there were other suitable men anywhere in the area I might think twice. But if there is a chance of a match amongst Mr Stratford's guests we must seek it out for you. One of your old gowns will have to do. But we can trim it up with the lace you bought this morning and I am sure it will look quite nice.'

'Mother!' Despite her best efforts, her mother had seen into the shopping basket. 'That was intended as a gift.'

'For someone who has less need of it than you,' her mother said, laying a hand on hers, 'it would do my heart good to know that you are out in society again—even if it is only for a day or two. I will write the letters, and then we will see what can be done with the gown. You must go where you are invited, Barbara, and dance as though your future depended on it. For it very well might.'

CHAPTER EIGHT

JOSEPH went to his bed that night in the knowledge that his rest would be well and truly settled. He had managed his guests—impressing the men with his plans for the mill, and charming the ladies without appearing ill-mannered or common. He had skated Miss Anne Clairemont twice around the millpond without falling or precipitating a fall in her. Then he had gone into the village, located Miss Lampett and presented his proposition.

If the ghost, or whatever it had been, had meant to upbraid him on the fate of that poor girl, he had done his best to return her to the society to which she was accustomed. Although why her fate should fall to him, he had no idea.

Perhaps it was because he was the one with the most power to change it. When his future mother-in-law had protested that she would not be seen in the company of 'that girl', he had explained tersely that it would be so because he wished it so, and that was that.

He wondered for a moment what Barbara had done to deserve such frigid and permanent rejection, but concluded it was nothing more than the usual fall from grace involving some young man—possibly a suitor of Anne or the departed Mary. If that was the case Miss Lampett had well and truly atoned for it, after years of modest dress and behaviour.

And more was the pity for it. If the kiss they'd shared had been any indication of her capability for passion, he'd have liked her better had she *not* found her way back to the straight and narrow. He smiled, imagining a more wanton Barbara, and the sort of fun he might have had with her.

The clock in the hall struck two.

'Leave off having impure thoughts about the poor girl, for your work is far from finished.'

Joseph sat bolt upright in bed at the sound of another unfamiliar voice, booming in the confines of the chamber. He had not even risked wine with supper, and had shocked his valet with a request for warm milk before bed. But now he wondered if perhaps it might have been better to forgo the milk and return to a double brandy in an effort to gain a sound and dreamless sleep. 'Who might you be, and what makes you think you can read the contents of my mind?'

'You are young enough, and healthy enough, and smiling at bedtime. If you are not thinking of a young lady then I do not wish to know what it is you *do* think on.'

This night's ghost wore a scarlet coat of a modern cut trimmed in gold braid. His buff trousers pulled tight across his ample belly as he laughed at his own joke. The brass of his buttons was gleaming as bright as the gold leaf upon the coach he must drive. But tonight it seemed to be even brighter than was natural, as was the coachguard's horn he carried in his right hand as further indication of his job.

'As to who I am, you may call me Old Tom, and know that I departed this life just a year ago, along the Great North Road. You would not have had to ask my name had you lived any great time in this country. All know me here. At least those who are not so high and mighty as to have no need of public conveyance.'

Joseph snorted. 'Although I have no real memory of you, I've heard of you—driving drunk and taking your passengers with you to the next life when you upset the coach. I must be running out of ideas. I am reduced to populating my own dreams with little scraps of facts that do not even concern me.'

The driver laughed again. 'You give yourself far too much credit, Joseph Stratford. Even if you think yourself clever with machines, you are rather a dull sort for all that, and not given to colourful imaginings.'

'Dull, indeed.' Joseph rather hoped the ghost was real. If it was not, it was proof that his own imagination was prone to self-loathing and insult. 'If I refuse to believe in spirits it is a sign of a rational mind, not a slow one. For ghosts do not exist.'

'If you do not believe in ghosts, then why are you sleeping in your clothing?' asked the shade, drawing back the bedclothes to reveal Joseph still in shirt, trousers and boots.

'Because I woke this morning near naked in a downstairs hallway. Ghost or not, the situation will not be repeated.'

'Very well, then. You are not dull. More like you are so sharp you'll cut yourself. You are willing to believe anything, no matter how unlikely, so that you don't have to accept what is right before your eyes.' Old Tom glared. 'For your information, I was not drunk on the night I crashed. I did sometimes partake, when a glass was offered. Who would not, with the night air being chill and damp? But that night I was sober as a judge and hurrying to make up time. A biddy at the Cock and Bull had dawdled over her supper and left us to run late.' He leaned closer and added in a conspiratorial tone, 'And she will not leave off nagging and lamenting about the time, even now on the other side. Some people never learn, as you well know.'

The ghost looked him up and down and laid a finger to the side of his nose, as though Joseph should learn something from the comment. Then he went on. 'I was late, and pushing the horses to their limit, when a rabbit darted out from the hedge and right under 'em. It spooked the leader and he got away from me. Just for a moment. And that was that.'

Joseph swung his feet out of bed and sat up to face the ghost. 'An interesting tale, certainly. But there is no way to prove it, and nor am I likely to try.'

'You would not believe it even if you found the truth,' Old Tom replied in disgust. 'You are cold as ice, Joseph Stratford, and just as solidly set. I gave you too much credit when I arrived. It is just as likely I found you warming your thoughts not with some beautiful lady but with fantasies of machinery and ledger books.'

'So I have been told,' Joseph said with bitterness. 'Yet I have spent a portion of this day seeing to the wants of others, with no chance of personal gain likely to come of it.'

'No gain at all?'

He remembered the way he had phrased his offer to Barbara, as an effort to keep her father safely at home. 'Very little gain. The majority of the good done will benefit others. After last night's visitor, I made a change in my plans and invited Miss Barbara Lampett back to the manor house. There is my proof that I have learned something and rendered tonight's lesson unnecessary. I am making an effort to help the daughter of my enemy.' He gave a wave of his hand. 'And so you may depart.'

'Well, thank you, Yer Lordship,' the ghost said with a sarcastic bob of his head. 'But for your information it is I who will set the time of my departure, and not you. Before I can complete my final journey I have been called back for one task alone to make up for the carelessness of my end. I mean to do the job properly. When I leave here you will be well and rightly schooled.'

The ghost shuddered for a moment, as though uncomfortable in his surroundings. 'I'd have thought that if called to haunt I could have taken to the road, just as I did in life. Instead they sent me to *this* dreary place, colder than a moor in December.'

Again Joseph was annoyed that his spiritual visitor seemed less than satisfied with surroundings it had taken him half a lifetime to afford. 'This is the finest house in twenty miles, as you should know. The fire is lit, as are the candles. There is tea on the hob and brandy in the flask. Or perhaps you would like a shawl, like an old woman?'

Tom snorted. 'As if I could take pleasure in such, here on the other side. I am quite beyond feelings such as that.' He shuddered again. 'But I can see things you cannot. There is a cold coming off you like mist from a bog.'

He raised a finger to point at Joseph. In an instant the friendly driver was gone, and before him Joseph saw only a tormented spirit with a dire warning.

Then Tom smiled. 'But I have been set to warm you up a bit. A hopeless task that is like to be. Now, come on. We haven't got all night.' The ghost reached out a hand. 'Tonight you will walk with me, and if you are lucky you will learn to see the world as others do. At the least you will see what you are missing when you cannot take your nose from the account books and your feet from the factory floor. You will learn what people think of you. It should do you a world of good. Now, take my hand.'

Joseph's mind warred with itself, but the battle was shorter than it had been on the previous two nights. Whether real or imagined, Tom would not leave until he was ready to. And Joseph did not like being afraid of men—in this world or the next. So he reached out and grabbed the hand that was offered to him.

To touch it was even worse than touching Sir Cedric the previous night. Old Tom's hand was large and doughy, and thick with calluses from handling the reins. But it was freezing cold—like iron lying on the ground in December. The instant Joseph touched it his own fingers went as numb as if they'd died on his hand. And this, more than anything else, made him believe. His father might have been a memory, and Sir Cedric a walking dream. But in his wildest imaginings, he'd have conjured nothing like the feel of this.

He withdrew quickly, and after a stern look from the ghost adjusted his grip to take the spectre by the coat-sleeve instead. That was cold as well, but not unbearably so.

'The first stop is not far,' the ghost assured him, as though aware of his discomfort. 'Just beneath you, as a matter of fact.' Then they seemed to sink through the floorboards until they stood in the first parlour.

Though he'd thought that she had gone home with her

parents, he found Anne sitting in a chair by the fire and weeping as though her heart would break.

'There, there,' he said awkwardly, reaching out a hand to comfort her.

'Have you not yet learned what a pointless gesture that would be?' Old Tom asked. 'While you are with me she will not notice you.'

'Perhaps she will.' Joseph reached out to pat her shoulder, only to feel his hand pass through her as though she was smoke. He looked helplessly at the ghost. 'Last night, it was not always so,' Joseph argued, remembering the young Barbara.

'And tonight it is,' Old Tom said.

Behind them, the door opened. Though he needn't have bothered, Joseph stepped to the side to allow a man to enter the room.

Robert Breton glanced into the hall, as though eager to know that he was not observed, and then shut the door behind him and went quickly to the seated woman and took her hand.

'Bob?' Joseph knew then that he must indeed be invisible, for never had he seen such a look on his friend's face—nor was he likely to. The gaze he favoured Anne with was more than one of sympathy to her plight. It had tenderness, frustration and—dared he think it?—love.

On seeing him there, Anne let her tears burst fresh, like a sudden shower, and her shoulders shook with the effort of silence.

'Tell him,' Breton said. 'I have confronted him on the subject. He will not break off at this late date for your sake. He fears for your reputation even more than you do. If you do not end it for yourself, it is quite hopeless. I will not speak if you say nothing, no matter how much I might wish to. I have said more than enough already. You must be the strong one, Anne.'

'And I never was,' she answered, not looking up. 'Perhaps if Mary was here…'

'Then the lot would have fallen to her. Or it might never have occurred at all. But it does not matter,' Breton said firmly. 'She is dead and gone, much as no one wishes to acknowledge the fact. You cannot rely on her for help. You must be the one to speak, Anne.'

'Speak what? And to whom? To your father? To me?' Joseph took his place on her other side, as though he could make himself heard to the woman through proximity. But she said no more and, realising the futility of it, he looked up at the ghost. 'What do you want? I will give it to you, if I can. I am not totally without a heart, you know.'

'I think you can guess what she wants,' the ghost said. 'And why she does nothing about it.'

'It is not as if I am forcing the union on her. She agreed to it. And what does Bob have to do with any of it?'

'Not a thing, I expect, if it all goes according to your plan. He is a gentleman, is he not?'

'But he is a man first,' Joseph said. 'If he wants the girl for himself, then why does he not say something?'

The coachman laughed in response. 'You make it all sound quite simple. I envy you, living in a world as you do—where there are no doubts and everyone speaks their mind. The woman he loves has chosen another. He has been bested by a richer man. He will step out of the way like a gentleman.'

'But not before warning me to care for her,' Joseph said glumly. Their conversation in the hall that morning made more sense to him now. 'I cannot cry off now that there is an understanding. Unless she finds the courage to speak, we must all make the best of it.' But now that he knew the mind of his would-be fiancée it would be dashed hard to pretend a respect where none existed.

'Is this all, then?' he asked of the ghost.

The ghost smiled in a way that was hard and quite out of character with his jolly demeanour. 'Did you think it was likely to be? Your sins, when added together, total more than just heartlessness to this poor, foolish girl.'

'If you mean to brand me sinner, show me the proof of it so that I may go back to my bed. Take me away from here, for I have seen all you intended me to in this place.' He did not wish to follow the ghostly coachman, and this might still be little more than an unsettling dream, but the sight of his friend and Anne together felt like a violation. If he could not find a way to change things, then the least he could do was allow the two who were suffering a moment's privacy.

'Very well.'

Old Tom stepped forwards, and Joseph along with him. There was a rushing of wind, and in the time it took for his foot to fall he was stepping into another room, in another house. This place reminded him of his visit to his childhood home the previous night, though it was not so grim. It was sparsely furnished, and bare of ornament, but the kitchen where they stood was kept with the sort of earnest tidiness he expected of a home with a living wife and mother. A woman was busy at the hob. Her husband sat at the table, shoulders slumped and head bowed as though in prayer.

'Who might this be?' Joseph asked, for though the man's face was familiar he could not attach a name to it.

'If you had bothered to speak to him, or any other in this community, you would know him already.'

'I know that he was waving a sledgehammer at me when last I saw him, just two days ago,' Joseph said testily. 'It did not put me in the mood for gaining a proper introduction.'

'His name is Jonas Jordan,' replied Old Tom, ignoring his retort. 'He is the most skilled worker in the area, and might be your foreman should you and your mill survive long enough to hire him. And this is his family, preparing for the Christmas you and your kind have made for him.'

The man had not moved from his place, though his wife now gathered the children for their meal, overseeing the washing of hands and the setting of places. There were five of them. The youngest was a babe that was likely still at breast, and the oldest was too young to work.

In this little house, on a narrow side road just off the high street, there were none of the smells he had come to associate with the season—neither burning Yule Log nor sizzling fat and fresh bread. The fire in the grate burned low with the meagre handful of coal that made it, so that the cold crept out into the corners of the room, and the children, who should have been boisterous, huddled together as though they had little energy to do else.

'Mama,' said the second youngest, 'I am hungry.'

Without a word, the woman brought out bowls and set them around the table. The children gathered to take their places. Then she ladled some thin porridge from the pot that sat by the fire, and reached for the jug that sat upon the table. She poured out water rather than milk. The children took it in silence and she looked on, worried. When she reached to set a bowl before her husband he pushed it away, without a sound, until it sat before her.

She watched, her own supper untouched, as the children finished what they had. Then she shared the contents of the last bowl between them. She sat hungry, as did her man.

'It would be more nourishing for the children to have a bowl with a good dollop of cream in it,' Joseph said stupidly, knowing that there would be none of that in this house.

'Perhaps if the lord of the manor had not sold off the herd that once grazed where the new mill stands they might have. It has been the nature, these many years, of the Clairemonts to keep the dairy and to graze the herd. All those who wished might come with jugs and buckets to take their share. But now they must send for milk from the next village. It is one more thing, along with all the rest, that this family cannot afford.'

'So they are starving?' Joseph said, doing his best to harden his heart. 'They were just so before I arrived. It might well be because this very man stood up against the last master and burned his place to the ground.'

'When men are pushed to the edge of reason by circumstances they act without thinking!' The ghost shouted the words at him, as though even a spirit could be pushed beyond endurance. 'Jordan and his family were hungry before. But they ate. He stayed at home with his babes the night the old mill burned. What has happened was no fault of his.'

'Then when the new mill opens he shall have work,' Joseph promised. 'If that is the only reason you visit me, you have no reason to fear. I am bringing employment to the area.'

'For some,' the coachman said.

'For as many as I need,' Joseph answered him. 'If it means so much to them, I will enquire with Clairemont about the dispersal of the herd and decide what can be done to reopen the dairy on different ground. It was never my intention to cut people out of their places or make their children suffer.'

'But neither did you make enquiries into their needs when you came here. I am sure if I asked you to quote figures about your building and your products you would know them, chapter and verse, without even opening a ledger. Yet this man, who will be your good right hand if you let him, might starve and die as a stranger to you.' The ghost's brow furrowed as though he were working a puzzle. 'It is a wonder that the only way you can be made to look clearly at the suffering right before your eyes is to be dragged from your bed by a supernatural emissary.'

The ghost was hauling him forwards, through a closed door towards God only knew what fresh nightmare, and Joseph pulled back, struggling in futility against his grip.

'Very well, then. I see my present clearly,' Joseph shouted back. 'The people I need to work in my mill are starved to the point of hatred. My best friend betrays me. The woman who I would take to wife cannot be bothered to speak a word of truth to my face and set me free of the promise I made to her family. I have seen enough. I will do what I can. Take me back to my room.'

'Not just yet. There is one more you must see.'

Now they were in the home of his nemesis: Lampett.

'Not here,' he said to the ghost. 'I get quite enough of

what I am likely to find here without a ghostly visitation.'

'And what is that?'

'Abuse heaped upon abuse. Violence from the father, and scorn from the daughter.' He thought of the previous evening. 'It is likely she will see me, as she did last night. How will I explain myself to her?'

The ghost crooked a smile. 'She is grown into the sort of woman who is much too sensible to see ghosts. And she has given you more than abuse, if I have heard correctly.'

'You mean the kiss?' Joseph scoffed. 'It was hardly a gift freely given. I took it from her, and then I tricked her into responding.'

'Did she enjoy it?'

'I expect that Eve enjoyed her taste of the apple. But that hardly made hers a wise decision.'

The coachman laughed all the harder. 'You think yourself the devil?'

'They do.'

'Let us see, shall we?'

Just in case, Joseph huddled inside the brassy glow of Old Tom's shadow, thinking that the light would render him invisible if nothing else could. Perhaps this Barbara *was* too sensible for ghosts. But she could see through him easily enough if she chose to do so—just as he could see more of her heart than he wished to.

More of her life as well. He should not want to spy upon her. Her life, her family, her thoughts and words when she was not with him should be no concern of his. But there was a dark undercurrent growing in the curiosity he felt tonight—a possessiveness that was stronger than anything he felt for Anne, or even for his business. Suddenly he was hungry for any detail he might learn of her. Secretly he was glad that the spirit had brought him to her again. Once he had married there would be little chance for any conversation with her. For now, he would rather hear a bitter truth from her lips than the silence he deserved.

To hide his confusion, he examined his surroundings. The Lampett house was nicely though simply kept, and too small to need a servant. There was no sign of strife or need except for the worried look in the eyes of the pretty girl as she stood at the shoulder of the man sitting at a desk by the window.

'Please, Father, take some stew. It is supper, and you must not go without eating.' She set the dinner on his desk, nudging it in the direction of the paper he had been writing upon. Unlike in the last house, there was meat in the bowl she offered, and Joseph could smell fresh bread and mince pies cooling in the kitchen. His mouth watered.

But her father seemed unaffected by the sight and smell of the food. 'Don't want it. There is work to be done. I must stop Stratford before this goes any further.' The man pushed the bowl to the side, and his daughter shot a worried glance in the direction of her mother, who sat by the fire, stitching a piece of blond lace on to a blue muslin gown.

Joseph wished he could offer some reassurance—prove that they had nothing to fear from him, or his mill. When it had opened, and the men were back to work, he might be able to sit at their table as a guest, talking about books with her father and offering polite compliments about the housekeeping of the mother and the prettiness of the daughter. Despite the tension in the air there was a feeling of love and family that was lacking in the manor, just as it had been missing from his childhood.

Then he remembered that he was in the last house in Fiddleton where he might be welcomed as a friend. The disappointment he felt was sharpest when he looked at Barbara. While he was used to hearing her father rail against him, she had much more personal reasons to despise him and he deserved every scornful word.

'Go on, then,' Joseph said, bracing himself. 'Give your opinion of me. When I am with you, you do not have a word of kindness for me other than the few thank-yous I have forced out of you. What do you say when we are apart?' It would hardly be a surprise. She was quite plain about it when they were together. She did not like him in the least. But all the same he tensed, waiting for her words.

'While many of the things he has been doing are wrong, they are not so much evil as they are misguided,' she said, as slowly and carefully as possible. 'I am sure, with time, he will come closer to your way of thinking.'

'Defending him, are you now?' Her father was staring at her, hurt, betrayed and sullen. She was clearly torn by the sight of his agitation.

'Go ahead,' Joseph said softly to her, putting aside his bitterness at the sight of her distress. 'Say what makes this the easiest. It is not as if one more harsh word will hurt me. His mood upsets you. Agreeing with him will calm him down.'

'Yes,' she said suddenly. 'I *will* defend him against your more unreasonable charges. The men in the district need work, Father. You must see that. There must be a mill of some sort, and Mr Stratford has built one where there was nothing. He has done it at great expense and risk to himself. Do the papers not say that it is a bad time to be doing business? He could just as easily have tried his hand at something more profitable. He could have stayed in London. Or built elsewhere.'

'So he brings a few jobs to the Riding?' her father said dismissively. 'He will find another way to make the men starve once it is opened.'

'Perhaps,' Barbara admitted. 'But perhaps not. If we show him reason and kindness and make him feel welcome here he might respond in kind. He does not have to be like Mr Mackay. He might provide a safe and clean work place, and be a benefit to the community. He is an extremely clever man. In talking to him, I find that he is well read and ingenious. If there is anyone who can help the people here, I believe it might be him. You will like him when you know him better. Do you remember the books he sent to you?'

'Yes,' her father said grudgingly, like a child forced to be mannerly.

'They are his favourites, and you like them as well. Might that not be a sign of a kindred spirit? But he must be given a chance to prove it to you.'

Joseph sank to the bench in the corner, quite taken aback by the flood of warmth he heard from her. 'You listened to me, didn't you?' He grinned at the ghost, his own spirit much lighter than it had been. 'It was not all anger on her part. Her chiding had some bluster in it. Perhaps there is some hope for me, after all.'

Old Tom laughed. 'I wonder how your wife will feel about your success with this girl. Since she does not care for you, she will likely be relieved that you seek the affections of another. And you will have this one talked around in no time. If you wished to get her into bed—'

Joseph jumped to his feet, fists balled. 'Do not say another word, sir, about the honour of that lady, or you will answer to me at dawn.'

The ghost observed him with a deathly expression. And, coming from one with such an intimate experience with that state, it was a truly fearsome thing. 'You are a year too late to threaten me, Mr Stratford. Being from beyond the grave gives one the ability to say what one likes without fear of repercussion. So I will tell you that you're only pretending to be a gentleman towards her. You care little enough for people unless they can be of benefit to you. You would bed this girl in a heartbeat if you saw the chance to do it. You would do it even faster if you thought it would give you an advantage over her father.'

Joseph opened his mouth to defend himself, and then closed it again as he realised he had considered doing just that. The fact that he had not acted on the impulse was hardly a point in his favour. As the ghost pointed out, he'd had no opportunity.

Old Tom held up a hand to silence him, for the Lampetts were speaking again.

'Let us talk of something more pleasant.' Her mother interrupted the argument between father and daughter. 'It is almost Christmas, after all.'

'And a time for gifts,' said Barbara, seizing upon the subject. 'Although I do not know how I shall surprise you, Mama, if you keep rummaging through my sewing basket and stealing the contents for other purposes.'

'Never mind what we want. What are we to get for you, my dear?' her father asked, turning back into the doting parent that Joseph had seen the other day. 'You still have not said. And it is too late to send to London for anything special.'

'You know that is not necessary,' the girl said, dropping her head.

'We wish to get you something,' her mother insisted. 'It gives us pleasure to know that you are happy.'

'You should know by now that I am happy just to

have the days pass,' Barbara said, staring into the fire. 'It is never an easy time for me.'

'But by now it should be. It has been years, Barbara,' her mother said firmly.

'Almost six,' Barbara said absently.

'It is not as if we expect you to forget.'

'Very good. Because I shall not.'

'Only that it is time to cease punishing yourself for a thing which was none of your fault.'

'There are still those that blame me,' she said, without looking up.

'Fools,' her father grumbled.

'Let us not talk of them, or of the past,' Barbara said quickly, as though eager to avert another dark mood. 'Let us simply say that I am not overly fond of Christmas. I would prefer to celebrate it by knowing that those I love are safe and happy, and not by focusing on my own wants and needs.'

The scene seemed to fade from view again. Joseph could see the players in it, but could no longer hear their words, though he strained to catch some whisper of them. He turned back to Old Tom, frustrated. 'Very well, then. You are right. I have been base and callous in regard to the people of Fiddleton, and this family in particular. But it would help me to understand them better if they were more open about the truth. Six years,' Joseph said, counting on his fingers. 'She would have been eighteen then.' He stared at the ghost of the coachman. 'You were still alive. What happened?'

'I am here to show you the present, not explain the past to you,' the ghost said, a little impatiently. 'If the information is important to you, then you should talk to the girl before you.'

'Did you not just hear her?' Joseph retorted. 'Whatever it is, she will not speak of in front of her own family. How likely is it that she will reveal all when I question her?'

The ghost gave him another sidelong glance. 'I expect it will depend on how you ask her.'

'Stop tormenting me with the idea that I will seduce her,' Joseph said, setting his jaw against the idea. 'It is clear that she has unhappy memories associated with Christmas time. I do not mean to be another of them. If that is what you wished me to learn this night, then let me go.'

In the blink of an eye he was in his bedroom again, standing alone and fully dressed before the fire, and lecturing the mantel clock as it struck three.

'I will not forget,' he said, just in case some wisp of the spirit remained. 'I will be better. You will see. Let this be the last of these nightly visits. For I have had quite enough of them.'

He changed for bed, then—cautiously, as though at any moment he might be interrupted and dragged away again. It was nearly dawn before he closed his eyes.

CHAPTER NINE

The next evening found Barbara packed as an unwelcome fourth into the Clairemont carriage, trundling through the sodden streets towards the road that led to the manor. The drizzle had continued for most of the day, as though trying to decide minute to minute whether it would be rain or snow. Barbara felt in sympathy with it. Her own heart was as changeable as the weather, still unsure whether it wished to run towards this evening and its host, or away from it.

But Anne seemed unbothered. 'I am sure it will be a delightful time,' she said, with a wan smile. 'There is to be dancing. And cases of champagne. Cook is preparing a fine buffet, and a cold supper at midnight. Joseph has promised a celebration to rival anything in London.'

'Hmmmf,' said her father, and scowled out of the window.

Her mother said nothing at all, unwilling to acknowledge either their destination or the extra passenger they had accrued for the short journey. The Clairemont family had moved to the largest house in Fiddleton proper, with five servants and room enough to keep both a carriage and horses, but it was nothing compared to the manor. Returning to it as guests was obviously a source of irritation that they would conceal only when absolutely necessary.

But Anne seemed to feel less of it, looking from one to the other of them with a kind of desperate enthusiasm, as though she could imagine nothing better than visiting her old home only to leave it again at the end of the evening. 'Joseph says the chestnuts are particularly good this year. He has sampled them already.'

'I imagine he would have,' her father retorted. 'He goes to excess in all other things. If he is not careful he will be prone to gluttony.'

'I doubt it will come to that,' Anne assured him. 'He will not sit still long enough to grow soft. It is more likely that when he is in the throes of work he will need to be reminded to eat.'

Her father muttered something barely audible beyond the word 'trade'.

Anne fell to silence again, and Barbara could almost hear her thoughts. She was wishing that she had not brought up the subject of her prospective fiancé having an occupation at all. It was clearly another sore spot in the conversation.

She looked desperately to Barbara, who said gamely,

'He seems a most solicitous gentleman. When I was struggling in the shop yesterday he offered to transport myself and my basket in his carriage.'

Anne gave an approving nod, as if to say she would not have thought any less of him.

Her mother responded, 'That might just as easily show a fickle nature. What is he doing, offering courtesies to others when he is promised elsewhere?' She narrowed her eyes at Barbara. 'Unless you were angling after a ride?'

Anne sucked in her breath, but Barbara managed to keep her reaction invisible to the other passengers. She knew Lady Clairemont's opinion of her. But she'd hoped to see no obvious demonstration of it tonight.

'Mother,' Anne said quickly, 'I am sure it was nothing of the kind. Though you might not think it so, Joseph has a kind and generous heart. I am not the least bit surprised that he should offer to aid Miss Lampett.'

'Until his ring is on your finger you had best be less generous and more sensible,' her mother informed her. 'This party would be an excellent time to finalise the arrangement between you.'

'I cannot very well demand that he make the announcement,' Anne said, obviously embarrassed by her mother's bluntness.

'But his inviting other young ladies to this ball does not bode well.'

'I think there is someone he wishes me to meet,'

Barbara said hurriedly. 'He was quite clear about there being eligible gentlemen in attendance.'

'Probably that Breton fellow,' Anne's father grunted. 'He's a bit high in the instep for you, my dear. But a bit low… Second son…' His comment trailed off into inaudibility again.

'You have not even met him, Father.' Anne gave Barbara another silent apology. 'He is really very nice. A true gentleman—neither too high nor too low.'

'And no concern of yours, no matter what his birth. He will do for Barbara, here, if that is what Stratford intends for them. But he cannot be much of a man if he lets a business associate make such decisions for him.'

Anne stared out of the window, as though searching for another topic of conversation. 'I hope the weather favours us this evening. It seems likely that the rain will turn to snow.'

'Then we shall be forced to remain at the manor,' her mother said, showing the first signs of cheerfulness. 'I assume that Stratford has taken the master bedroom. But we shall make do in the next best suite, and you shall have your old room back, Anne.'

'Then I hope that travel is not made difficult,' Barbara said, considering the awkwardness of the situation. 'I am quite unprepared to stay the night.'

'Oh.' Lady Clairemont gave a sad little moue that ended in a smile. 'Do not worry upon it, my dear. I am sure there is a maid that can lend you a nightdress, should we be stranded.'

When they had arrived at the manor, the Clairemonts' behaviour grew no warmer. Lord and Lady Clairemont swept into the ballroom as if they still owned it, greeting other guests as though they were old friends. Anne trailed along in their wake, polite and silent.

When Barbara made to follow, Lady Clairemont turned, giving her a cold and very deliberate look. The direct stare seemed to change as she held it, to look past Barbara and then through her, as though she did not exist at all. The cut was so beautifully made that for a moment Barbara longed for a mirror, convinced that it was she who had faded to transparency. With a single look, Lady Clairemont had made it clear to her that, whatever Joseph Stratford might think, Barbara Lampett was an unwelcome guest here. If there were introductions to be made, he had best appear and make them himself, for the Clairemonts planned to pretend she did not exist.

She had to admire the perfection of the revenge Lady Clairemont had devised. The room was full of strangers. And, if she wished to be thought a well-mannered young lady, Barbara could hardly introduce herself to any of them. She would spend her first night in ages as a sort of social ghost, separated by a glass wall of propriety from the merrymaking.

Nor would Anne come to her aid. Though she did not hold the deep animosity for Barbara that her parents did, she lacked the spine to stand against them.

She was sure that Joseph Stratford would help her, if

she could find him. But there was no sign of him, and she assumed that he must be in a card room somewhere, talking business. She could expect little else. To him, that was the only purpose for the gathering. Even if he had meant to be a proper host, it should be Anne standing at his side and not her.

But it was just as well Mr Stratford did not see her. Having taken a moment to admire the other women, she could see that she did not belong amongst them. While her dress had seemed quite nice in the cheval glass at home, it looked dowdy compared to the pale silks and fine embroidered shawls she saw tonight. And the loveliest amongst them was Anne Clairemont. Her net gown was trimmed with tiny pearls, her hair held in place with diamond pins. She glided through the room like a swan: pure white, slender and graceful.

In comparison, Barbara's retrimmed blue gown managed to be both too bright and too plain. Her neck was bare. Her hair was dressed simply, with no jewels to ornament it. Even if Joseph were to see her he would look on her with pity rather than desire. She was little better than a charity case here—just as she had been the last time she saw him. She must learn to face the reality of it and not let the disappointment show. Invited or not, she did not belong here.

She must remember not to call him Joseph—to his face or to others. Anne Clairemont had that right of intimacy. She did not. But she quite liked the sound of the name in her head. After receiving a secret kiss from him, and being alone with him on two occasions, in the privacy of her thoughts she did not need to think of him as Mr Stratford.

To save herself the embarrassment of another cut, Barbara withdrew, pretending to admire the hangings in the ballroom nearest the door and then easing through it to stroll towards the portrait gallery, as though engrossed in the quality of the art. She considered herself fortunate that the manor was so large, and she so familiar with it. She would steal her share of the refreshments and then wander away by herself to relive happier times in her mind.

When she went home she would concoct a story for her mother about the fine food and the dancing, and the courtly gentlemen who had paid her attention. None so specific as to make her expect a call, but she would claim that it had been a delightful night, and that she had enjoyed herself most thoroughly.

A group of gentlemen passed her in the hall, carrying heaped plates of cakes and sandwiches, clearly on the lookout for a quiet place to sit. Lord Clairemont was amongst them. To avoid further awkwardness she withdrew to one of the many hiding places she'd known as a girl—a chair behind a statue of Mars, which had been decorated in a most undignified manner with garlands of holly.

'Has anyone seen our esteemed host this evening?' asked the first, a rather large man with a lurid pink waistcoat.

'Still trying to do business,' the next remarked. 'He would not let me alone before. Stratford is a most persistent fellow.'

'Little else can be expected of his sort,' the other responded pityingly. 'In trade, you know. It seems they can think of nothing else.'

Unlike some, who thought of nothing but filling their bellies. Barbara looked hurriedly down at her empty glass and the plate of crumbs beside it. Of all the sins of which Joseph was guilty, she could not fault his hospitality to his guests. The portions were generous, and any whim would be indulged for one so fortunate to have been invited into his home.

It made the absence of the villagers more keenly felt. She was sure, had he bothered to include them, that he would have rewarded any stranger from the village with the same casual generosity.

It seemed Lord Clairemont viewed the abundance with less charity. 'There is too much of everything here.' He picked a leaf from Mars and flicked it to the floor. 'When Anne is mistress, I trust she will teach him manners. He is rich, of course, but quite common. Did you see what he has done to the ivy on the south side of the house? He has stripped away great patches of it and brought it here.'

'Decorations, man!' Pink Waistcoat laughed. 'It is hardly Christmas without the stuff.'

'But there is a time and a place,' Lord Clairemont said primly. 'One does not go about denuding houses.'

Barbara was in two minds about that. The rooms looked very nice with the fresh greens. And now that some of the troublesome vines had been removed from around the windows she suspected there would be daylight in the library and the ballroom. Both had been gloomy places even by day, and she recalled being quite frightened of them.

'Stratford and your daughter do make a lovely couple,' one of the men remarked grudgingly. 'It seems that birth does not show on one's face.'

'But it is plain enough in his conversation,' Lord Clairemont remarked. 'He goes to the best tailor in London, but he tells people that the fabric for his coat was woven by himself—on his own modern loom.'

'Perhaps we will find him in the parlour, knitting a muffler?' said Pink Waistcoat. The men around him laughed, moving on.

Barbara leaned back against the wall, eyes closed, wishing she had stopped her ears, before hearing a word of that conversation. She was ashamed of herself for eavesdropping, and embarrassed for Joseph as well. How awful must it be for him to be an object of ridicule amongst his guests and a source of amusement in his own home. She felt a rush of kinship with him. Of all the people in the manor tonight, maybe neither of them belonged.

'Playing at hide-and-seek, Miss Lampett? I understand it is a common game here at Christmas.'

Her eyes flew open to find her host, leaning against

the wall at her side, scant inches away, smiling down at her.

'I was doing nothing of the kind. I was simply—' she searched for a plausible explanation '—resting for a moment. The dancing is most strenuous.'

'It must be, for you to grow tired just by watching it. But you have not even done that, have you? I have been in and out of the ballroom all evening, and have not seen you there at all. Explain yourself.'

'Before I stand up to dance I must be asked,' she said. 'And before that there must be introductions.' She smiled politely. 'But I am having a lovely time, reacquainting myself with the house. It is beautiful—especially done up for Christmas. I thank you for your invitation.'

'Rubbish,' he said sharply. 'You came with the Clairemonts, did you not?'

'They were kind enough to give me a ride in their carriage.'

'But they did not make you known to the other guests?'

She could think of no proper answer for this, so she remained silent.

'And I was negligent in my duties as host and let you wander, alone and abandoned.' He swore then, a short colourful vulgarity that she had never heard before. She supposed she should be shocked by it, make some comment about his low birth and stalk off. But he had had enough of that reaction, she was sure, and she did not have the heart to add her censure to the rest.

He collected himself quickly, and gave a curt bow of apology. 'Come, Miss Lampett. We are going back to the ballroom so that you might dance with me.'

'Really, that is not necessary,' she whispered.

'There you are again, trying to tell me what is needed and what is not.' He grabbed her by the arm and pulled her out from behind the statue. 'You must know by now that it is quite hopeless to stop me once I have an idea in my head.'

'But I must try,' she said, pulling her arm from his grasp, and permitting him to escort her properly. 'I know that your invitation here was little more than a sop to gain my father's silence. But if we dance the Clairemonts are likely to think it was something more.'

'Do not ascribe such dark motives to me,' he said. 'Perhaps I merely thought that you would enjoy the opportunity of socialising and devised an excuse so that you would not refuse my invitation. Instead I see you are wedded to the wall because my future in-laws are unable to behave like the lady and gentleman they purport to be. I do not know what the gripe is between you. But it ends now.'

'This is a waltz,' she said, tripping along at his side as he stalked into the ballroom. 'And I do not know how. Perhaps if we waited…' But it was hopeless. He was tugging her very gently towards the dance floor.

'It is the simplest of all dances, and you will learn

it as we go,' he said, swinging her about to face him. 'People will call me rude and brash and inappropriate. But I am quite used to that already and will not be bothered.'

'And if people think ill of *me* because of it? Dancing so intimately with a man I barely know?' Although she quite liked the sound of the music and the feel of his hand on her waist. She liked even better the look of shock she saw on Lady Clairemont's face as she spun past her.

'I am your host,' he said, giving a gentle push on her hand to guide her. 'You can hardly refuse me. It is Christmas, which is traditionally a time for small latitudes. No one will say a word.'

'Even if they do, they are all from London and I will never see them again.' She sighed in satisfaction.

With his hand upon her ribs, he noticed. 'That was a happy sigh, I trust?'

She gave a hesitant nod. 'I have not had many opportunities to dance. Sometimes it seems as though I went directly from the schoolroom to the shelf, with no stopping between.'

He snorted. 'You? On the shelf? I should say not.'

'I am twenty-four years old,' she said, with a purse of the lips. 'There are few gentlemen in the area. And girls who are younger, prettier, more biddable...'

He laughed again. 'You make those sound like virtues.'

'Are they not?'

'Young and biddable is often synonymous with naive and without a fully moulded character. Easier at first, perhaps. But it would make for a most dull union to marry such a girl.'

Which was strange. Because it was exactly how she would have described the object of his own matrimonial plans, had she been called to compare with her. 'And beauty?' she asked. 'Surely you have no problems with that?'

'At your worst, you are quite pretty enough to suit even the most discriminating men,' he said, looking down at her with an appraising eye. 'Tonight you are looking most charming indeed. If you hear any complaints on the subject you must send the offenders to me.' His fingers flexed on her waist and his hand squeezed hers. Just for a moment his face dipped closer to hers, sharing a conspiratorial smile.

And she thought, with a sudden flash of insight, *If I allow it, he is likely to kiss me again. Right here on the dance floor. Or in a dark corner, when we can be alone.*

She knew, if the opportunity presented itself, that she would let him. She stumbled and broke the moment of intimacy.

He concentrated on the steps, easing her gently back onto the beat until they were steady again, pretending that the mistake was his to put her at her ease.

It made her feel quite awful. She had accused him of all manner of horrible things, directly to his face. She had thought even worse about him. But it was becoming plain that, though his nature seemed brusque, he was quite capable of behaving like a gentleman when he wished to. It was a shame that he was not being treated as such.

Though it was the height of bad manners to repeat what she had heard, neither did she feel right about keeping the truth from him. 'They are all laughing at you, you know. The other guests. Even Anne's family.' Then she realised that it might sound as if she was sabotaging a rival. 'Not Anne, of course. She is much too good for that.'

'Oh, of course not,' he answered back with sarcasm. 'But she and the rest are not too good to accept bread and board from likes of Mr Joseph Stratford. They lack the strength of their convictions. Some of the people I'd hoped to see tonight refused me outright. I have more respect for them. They are incapable of pretence.' There was no tension as he said the words, sweeping her further out on the dance floor, twirling her effortlessly with the other dancers.

'You realise what they are saying about you?'

'Of course,' he said, with a wry smile. 'You did not honestly worry I'd be hurt, did you? What a sensitive creature you must think me, Miss Lampett. I do not shrink from their displeasure, nor do I acknowledge their gossiping. I am willing to stand against your father and his armed mob, my dear. But to my knowledge no one has ever bled to death from the cut direct.'

'Maybe people would not act that way to you if only

you were not so...' She could not seem to find a word to describe it.

He sighed and smiled at her. 'I am too much of everything, I fear. But it is hard to explain the novelty of a full larder to one that has always had their fill.' He looked out of the window at the snow falling in the gardens, as though he could see past it into his own future. 'This is nothing compared to what it will some day be. Two years ago it was a few machines. Now it will be a factory. And before I am through? An empire.' He waved a hand towards the hall they had left. 'They may laugh behind their hands, if they like. But the gentleman in the horrid pink waistcoat has promised me ten thousand pounds. And the gentleman beside him another five. Both will see a good rate of return on their investments. Neither of them need fear that I will reveal our association or bother them with my presence in London. It will work well for all of us.'

'That is all that concerns you?'

He nodded. 'If I had chosen to behave properly and stay where I was born I would be on the other side of the gates right now, looking in at the people dancing. Tomorrow I would be standing outside another man's mill, threatening the master with violence, living in fear that the last crust of bread would be ripped from my hand.'

'You have a very grim view of the world, Mr Stratford.'

'And a very accurate one. I was once poor, Miss

Lampett. Now I am rich. But I will never clear the stink of poverty from my skin. I accept that.' He grinned. 'But, all the same, I cannot help but revel in the change.'

The dance ended and he walked her to the edge of the floor. As they approached the people standing there she hesitated, laying a hand on his arm to halt him. 'If they think so little of you, then what will they say to me, in last season's gown retrimmed in borrowed lace?'

'They will treat you with the utmost courtesy, I am sure. I will introduce you to Robert Breton, who is a true gentleman with impeccable manners. He will shepherd you about the room to the others. I recommend that once I am gone you comment at my boorish behaviour in forcing you to dance. Your future will be secure.'

She could not help it, and gave a short laugh. 'I would never...'

'I know you would not.' He was looking into her eyes again, and she felt the warmth, the pull. 'Although I am sure you have thought it.'

'No.'

'Do not lie,' he said, giving her hand a squeeze. 'But do not feel that I fault you. You cannot be blamed. My manners are rough. Considering our circumstances, I appreciate that yours are not, and thank you for it.'

Then he led her across the room to his friend, making another formal bow and as proper a presentation as she could have hoped for. In truth, it was a bit too formal, but that was better than the alternative of being forgotten.

In turn, Mr Breton made polite and much more polished conversation, then took her around the room to his friends and acquaintances, making sure that she was properly introduced to each of them. Her dance card for the evening was quickly filled with gentlemen of the *ton*—younger brothers and married men, who had been rousted from the card room to make up for the lack of dancers.

It was pleasant. She relaxed and remembered what it had been like to attend similar parties, before the house had been shut up in mourning and she'd felt the sting of rejection. But this night was different in that she longed to turn and find the eyes of a particular gentleman following her about the room, even though they had danced only once.

Joseph had taken a personal interest in her. It was to be expected, she supposed. He wished her to be at ease, just as he did the other guests. That was all it was. If there had been any proprietorial interest it was a fabrication on her part. His effusive compliments were another sign of his lack of social grace, not a partiality unique to her.

When she looked for him, as she found herself frequently doing, he was giving his attention to Anne, just as he should. The man was engaged to her, or near to it. He wanted nothing more than to see Barbara similarly happy.

As another dance ended, her partner returned her to Mr Breton, who offered her escort on a trip to the refreshment room. As they passed Joseph Stratford, Breton caught her gaze and looked back at his friend with a mixture of frustration and admiration. 'If you foster hopes in that direction you must know that there is an understanding with another young lady.'

'I know that,' she said, trying not to blush at how obvious he must think her. 'I am merely surprised at how kind he has been to me—though he barely knows me, except through Father. And that is…difficult.'

'So I understand,' said Breton. 'You must go home and explain to your father, if you can, that all is not as simple as it seems.' He looked across the room at his friend. 'For all his faults, Stratford is a visionary. We must trust him to know what is right.'

'I cannot say that I approve of his vision,' Barbara said, shaking her head. 'To the villagers, it seems to be nothing more than wanton destruction and change that benefits one man more than any other.'

'Not at all,' Breton insisted. 'I was there when he made the decision to come here. He was poring over a pile of maps, gazettes and indexes. He chose and then rejected several sites. Then he showed me this place. "Here," he said, "is the land, and here are the workers. Here is the river that will bring the finished goods to London and to the ports. Here are the fields, already full of the sheep to give us supplies, and the roads that will bring the coal."' Breton grinned with pride. 'He sees it all as though it were a pile of loose links, waiting to become a chain. Some men can come up with an idea for improvement, but he is one of the few that understands enough to put that change to work.'

'You are a gentleman,' she argued. 'I would think you knew better than to get so closely involved in trade.'

He shrugged. 'At one time, perhaps. I am a second son, and must make the best of my inheritance. I was dubious when he came to me with the idea for an improved loom. But he is very persistent. He would not leave. So I made one quiet investment. He turned my modest income into a fortune. When he suggested an expansion, I decided I would be a fool to refuse him.'

He glanced around at the largely empty dining hall. 'He expected there to be more speculators, since the chance to do business far outside the eyes of the *ton* would be a pleasant one. Joe's cellar is good, and his table groans. The house is as nice as any one might see in London. The beds are soft enough for a lord, certainly. I have no complaints.'

Barbara pursed her lips. 'He spoke to me of this, and he does not seem disappointed. But I wonder what the Clairemonts think of it all.'

'It hardly matters,' Breton supplied with finality. 'It has been demonstrated to me on several occasions that the God-given right to property does not automatically assume the wisdom or skill to keep it. While your friends the Clairemonts could not maintain their position, I am sure you will find Mr Stratford to be more than able. This is the first such fortune he will make in his lifetime, and the first house he shall purchase. While he continues to advance, the Clairemonts of the world shall be left with nothing more than the honour of their names. Genteel poverty is poverty nonetheless, Miss Lampett. Surely you must know that by now?'

The man they had been discussing rounded the corner, coming upon them without warning. He stopped suddenly and stared at the two of them in surprise, and then offered a hurried apology before turning back the way he had come.

'Whatever does he mean by that?' Barbara said in confusion.

Breton glanced up. 'He thinks he has caught us under a kissing bough. Although how we could manage to avoid them I am not sure. Stratford has them hung in nearly every room and doorway, despite the decidedly unromantic nature of this gathering.'

'Surely if there is an engagement to be announced, there must be a trace of romance in the air.' The thought did nothing to lift her spirits, and Mr Breton seemed equally pensive. He was looking up at the garland of mistletoe and ribbons and around at the empty room. 'I suppose we had best make use of it while we are here.' He hardly sounded enthused about the prospect.

Barbara did not wish to show her own lack of desire. 'If you wish, sir. It is Christmas, after all.' She closed her eyes and raised her face to his.

She had hoped it would be the briefest buss—over

quickly and forgotten. But it appeared that he wished for something more memorable, and did not immediately withdraw. Neither did he advance, or show any real enthusiasm for it. It was not exactly unpleasant, but it was most definitely awkward.

There was a gasp of surprise from the doorway, a stifled sob and then the pattering of lady's slippers down the hall. Breton jerked away from her and muttered a curse. 'If you will excuse me, Miss Lampett?' He gave a hurried bow and raced from the room, leaving her alone again.

CHAPTER TEN

JOSEPH Stratford practised the words of his proposal quietly to himself in the silence of the library. If he meant to do the deed he had best do it tonight, while there were guests to celebrate it. It was a culmination of sorts—a final proof to his investors of the confidence that the Clairemonts placed in him. It was another step in his entry into society.

In all ways it was an excellent choice. He had selected Anne with clinical precision, just as he had the household decorations. There was no question that she was a beauty, and her manners and breeding were impeccable. Though her father might be cold and abrupt to him, Anne paid just the correct amount of interest, making it clear without seeming inappropriately eager that when he chose to offer the answer would be yes.

His heart was not engaged, of course. Neither was hers. That was for the best. If he sought affection elsewhere she would likely be more relieved than upset. Though he would make every effort to see her happy, as he had promised Bob, he would expend nothing more to try to win a love that was not likely to appear. And if she sought comfort with another? As long as the first son looked like him, what right did he have to care?

He thought of the brief and unpleasant scene he had witnessed a few moments ago: Breton and Barbara standing awkwardly under the kissing bough. That had been his plan when he'd invited her. She should find someone who valued her, and he could think of no better choice than Bob.

But Joseph did not find his success nearly as enjoyable as the one dance he'd shared with her, or the heroic feeling of rescuing her from her hiding place in the portrait gallery. If he was not careful he'd destroy plans that had been months in the making in trying to interpret a few mysterious dreams and appease spirits that were entirely the makings of his own overtired brain. If he was lucky, the girl was even now getting on well with Breton, and he would never have to think of her again.

Anne was her superior in every way, he reminded himself firmly. Barbara's face was as far from patrician as one could imagine. To call her complexion ruddy was unfair, but it had a healthy glow about it—as though she partook freely of the northern air. She was not short, nor stout, though she appeared stunted next to the tall and slender Anne. In all ways she seemed less refined, less delicate, less of a lady.

And his body did not seem to mind that a bit. While Anne might be as lovely as a china doll, china dolls were made to be admired more than touched. They were expensive things, to be cherished, set upon a shelf and forgotten.

Other toys were meant to be played with. When he looked at Barbara Lampett, oh, how he wished for playtime. She made him think of Christmas morning, with gifts waiting to be unwrapped, games to be won, and nights full of pleasant surprises. The likelihood that she would spend her adult life as a spinster caring for her mad father seemed vastly unfair. He wondered yet again what the truth was in her disgrace and banishment from local society. If there was a stain already on her character, perhaps in time…

The door opened suddenly, and he was face to face with his intended. 'Anne,' he said dumbly, taking a moment to wipe his mind clear of its recent speculation.

'Joseph.' She seemed to need a moment's composure as well. He pretended not to notice the deep breath she took, and the fading flush on her cheeks. 'I am sorry. I did not mean to disturb you.'

'It is quite all right. I meant to seek you out just now. If you have a moment…?'

'Of course.'

Now that the time was upon him, he was unsure what the correct emotion was to suit it. Whatever was expected, he was sure that he was not feeling it. There was no tingle of nerves, no pleasant sense of anticipation, no triumph and no relief. He was certainly not feeling the desire he might wish for as she stepped into the room, closing the door behind her and leaving them alone together for the first time in their acquaintance.

She was totally composed again, staring at him with a pleasant, neutral smile, waiting for him to speak. He wondered if he should begin with some inane comment like, *I suppose you wonder why I've asked you here.*

But they both knew damn well the reason. To pretend there was doubt as to the question and its inevitable answer was an annoying ceremony that he could not quite manage.

So he waited until the click of the door latch no longer echoed in the still air of the room, took the few steps to her side, went down on one knee and said, 'Miss Anne Clairemont, would you do me the honour of becoming my wife?'

The words, though they were only a formality, were surprisingly hard to say.

'Thank you. I would be honoured in return.' It was good that he had not expected her to go into raptures. Her expression had not changed one iota from the one she had worn in the ballroom.

He rose. 'I have no ring to offer at this time. After Christmas I will take you to London, where you may choose something suitable that is to your taste.' It would save her being embarrassed at his lack of style, should he choose incorrectly.

'That will not be necessary,' she said, with the same

unfailing smile. 'I am sure Mother will have something appropriate in her jewel case.'

Apparently when he had purchased the house and its contents he had purchased the bride and her ring as well. He stifled a sudden and totally inappropriate desire to laugh.

'Very well, then. Let us meet in the ballroom at—' he checked his watch '—midnight exactly, to make the announcement. Until then…' They had almost three quarters of an hour. If he was wise, he would use the time to get to know his bride in a way that was more physical than social.

He leaned forwards and she closed her eyes, preparing herself to be kissed. He reminded himself to be gentle, though there was hardly a need. She did not seem frightened of him. Their lips met.

She was warm and pliable, and with a small amount of pressure her lips opened and she responded. It was clear that she knew what was expected of her, but she did not behave like a strumpet so much as a woman reconciled to the prospect of intimacy with a stranger. He had the sudden horrible feeling that now the words had been spoken she would permit whatever he might dare, greeting it with the same polite and placid smile.

To say that it was like kissing a statue was unfair. It was more like *being* a statue. Though he could feel the pressure and taste her tongue against his, it was little different from the walks with his ghosts had been, when he had been near the action but not really a part of it.

He broke the kiss. 'Until then I will allow you to refresh yourself. Now, if you will excuse me…?' He gave a brief bow and left her.

He was not fleeing the room, he told himself firmly. Merely returning with alacrity to the ballroom—to see to his other guests, prepare the musicians for the announcement and await his fiancée so that he could take her hand and make the biggest mistake of his life.

She would smile demurely, like the wooden poppet she was. She would colour with the faint blush of excitement that he assumed she was even now painting on her face in the ladies' retiring room. And he would smile, to prove himself aware of his good fortune, and accept the hearty congratulations that he would receive and the endless toasts drunk in their honour.

The very idea made him want to choke.

From the moment that he had kissed her—really kissed her, hoping to feel something of their impending life together—he had known it was a mistake. But by then the words were already spoken and it was too late to call them back.

In an act of supreme cowardice he swerved as he passed the little alcove in the hall, and ducked behind the curtain. He could not hide for ever. But even five minutes of privacy would be a welcome thing.

'Joseph!' Her voice was a hissing whisper that stirred his blood.

He turned in the tight, confining space and found Barbara Lampett hiding there as well. He put his hands to her waist, drawing her close, and though his mind roiled his body forgot that there was anything or anyone outside of this small niche and responded.

'Miss Barbara Lampett. Hiding again? And now, I assume, we are playing sardines?'

'Nothing of the sort,' she snapped.

'Then apparently you do not know what you are playing at,' he said suddenly, jerking her body until it rested against his, and relishing the feeling of being once again in control. Then he took her mouth, because he could not stand to be without her for another moment. She responded as he'd known she would, massaging his tongue with her own, urging him on. The taste of her sent the life rushing back into his body, and a joy so reckless that he knew it must be dangerous. He pulled away.

'Release me and exit from here immediately, or I swear I shall scream.'

Her words were the correct ones for any offended maiden. They had to be said, if only to be ignored. But as she spoke she made no struggle to escape him. Nor was there any fear in her voice. Instead she gripped his arms and leaned into him.

'Scream, then,' he said, half wishing she would. It would solve many of his problems. Anne would surely hear of it, and his engagement would be over before it had begun. But it seemed whatever indiscretion she had taken part in six years ago had left her devoid of outrage, and he was damned glad of the fact.

She took a deep breath, and for a moment he almost thought she might make good on her threat. Then she sighed, as though defeated. 'Just once, will you not do the proper thing? Why must you make this so difficult?'

'Perhaps it is because I do not wish to let you go,' he replied.

'And I lack the strength to resist you.'

'I doubt that very much,' he whispered, touching her lips with his. 'You are stronger than you know. Strong enough to break my will.' Then he brought his mouth back down to hers to give her the kisses he should have given another. And he felt her burst into flame again.

She took a breath, and he took it away again, letting the smell and the taste of her soak in, until it became a part of him to his very bones. His future might be as cold as a northern winter, but if he could have nothing else he would have a woman like this to remember. He thrust his tongue deep into her mouth and she raked it with her teeth, biting almost hard enough to draw blood, pushing her breasts eagerly against his waistcoat and swaying to excite herself.

He broke the kiss and pushed her away, stroking his fingers once down the front of her gown, making her tremble. 'I suppose you will now offer me some needless objections about how things must be between us,' he told her, making a half-hearted offer to let her leave.

And leave she should—rushing from the little alcove

after giving him a sharp word and a slap for his insolence. He deserved nothing less for behaving in a way that was everything despicable, everything he despised about himself and other men who would abuse their power over those in their debt.

But as he said it he reached around her and his fingers tightened on her bottom, flexed and then tightened again. She was round and lush, and he could imagine the feel of her naked flesh, cradling her in his lap as he pushed into her. His body gave a jump of desire in response.

With that little encouragement, she pulled him close again, and he felt another tremble as her body gave an answering surge.

He buried his face in her hair. 'No objections, then. Very good.' He forced her back with him, further into the darkness of the alcove and of his own soul.

He could hear the faint murmuring of couples in the refreshment room and a low moan from his partner, her quickening of breath and the shift of her gown against his coat. 'Someone might hear us,' she whispered.

He touched a finger to her lips. 'Then we will be careful.' He bent to kiss the slope of her breast, then tugged gently at the neckline of her gown, pushing the lace out of the way and probing beneath it to where her chemise had been tucked low and her breasts forced high to the top of her stays. At last his fingers found a nipple and coaxed it upwards to rest just outside her dress, so that he could latch upon it with a sigh.

She should be fighting for her virtue, or at least pretending to resist. He should be racked with guilt at his easy betrayal of Anne. But it felt so good to touch, and to feel a response. This was no mannequin but a living, breathing woman. The sort that a man could make a future with, have a house full of life and love and children.

She gave another gasp at the sudden shock of delight when his teeth closed upon the tip of her breast, and he swirled his tongue as he nipped and sucked. It was tender and sweet, and along with lust he felt the power of bringing her to life. And the bitterness of knowing that he had no right to this—that he was stealing it for his own pleasure, just as the villagers accused him of stealing their livelihoods.

'Tell me to stop,' he said, into her skin. For a moment he did, and looked up at her, admiring the fine line of her chin and cheekbones, for her head was thrown back as she panted in excitement.

'No.' She gasped, her face twisted as though it was agony to feel what he was making her feel. 'I want more.'

'I thought you did. When I saw you at the factory that first day I knew.' Even then her energy, her passion and her anger had shown, in that dull crowd, like a jewel in dross. She deserved more than this little village could offer her. She needed someone who could match her heat for heat. 'I want more as well. I want everything. I want to give you that as well. Everything you ever dreamt of. Let me set you free.' He dropped his head to her breast again.

He could feel that the intensity of his words frightened her. For a moment she seemed almost frozen by them, her frame stiff and rigid, neither welcoming nor resisting. But as he sucked rhythmically upon her he drew a greater response with each pull. Her hands rose to his shoulders, clutching, and then digging in with the sort of hard, painful, rhythmic massage that he might have expected from a cat that didn't know the power of its own claws. He cupped his hands beneath her breasts, holding them to his face before smoothing his fingers down over her skirts, outlining hips and thighs, and reaching behind one of her knees to urge her foot up on the bench beside him.

And she allowed him to do it. Her legs fell open to his touch. Her raised knee pressed encouragingly into his side as he stepped between them. His hand hovered at the fastenings of his trousers for only a moment before rejecting his own pleasure. There was not time, and this was not the place. She deserved more than a selfish coupling against a wall in a common passageway.

He pressed his lips to her ear and whispered, 'Relax for me. Trust me. Let me touch you.'

His hand went to her ankle, then slid up the silk of her stocking and higher, to the silk of her skin. He was teasing her gently, with playful strokes, between her legs, and he felt her surprised intake of breath cut short in an effort to keep quiet. Then he kissed her, and delved his fingers into the wonderfully warm, wet softness at their apex, circling and then pressing, pushing against the opening and then into it, gently, and then with more force. He deepened into a slow slide and thrust that matched the rhythm of his mouth.

She stifled her cry of surprise inside their kiss. There were people passing in the hall, barely feet from where they were. Discovery was inevitable if she could not keep silent, and she knew it.

He did not care. It would mean ruin for both of them. Anne and her family would leave in shame. The schemes he had built, largely from air, would collapse around him, leaving him with nothing but the woman in his arms.

But that would be more than enough. More than he deserved. He withdrew his hand and dropped to his knees before her, pleasuring her body with his mouth, first coaxing and then demanding a response from her. The harder she fought to keep silent, the more he teased, sucking the petals of her into his mouth and nursing upon them as he had at her breast. She bucked her hips against his tongue until he trapped them with his hands, held them still and had his way with her as her fingers twined in his hair, holding him close. Her trembling increased and he reached up again and gave a single hard thrust of his fingers. Her world unravelled, leaving her body throbbing and shaking, totally in his control.

He relaxed, letting his head loll against her thigh,

planting gentle kisses on the skin above her garter as he fought for mastery of his own body.

Above him, his lover turned her head and laid her cheek against the stone wall, as though trying to cool the heat in her blood. But her hands still played in his hair and stroked his temples, and her legs were still spread wide in welcome. She breathed slowly, deeply, in and out, waiting for him to accept the final gift she could offer.

In the silence he felt reality pressing against him, as it had when he'd come here to hide. He had thought only yesterday that he knew what he wanted. Wealth, power, respect, success. A moment ago he had been willing to risk it all—playing games with a woman who had been a stranger to him a week ago.

He reached with one hand to disentangle himself from her arms, and rose to his feet. But for a moment his other hand remained just where it was, fingers buried deep within her clenching body, to remind her who was controlling and who controlled, who was possessed and who possessed.

As though to confirm the truth, her body tightened on his fingers.

His gave an answering lurch of pleasure, even while he tried to regret what had happened. Then he withdrew his hand and stared silently into her eyes, which glittered in the darkness. He could not trust himself to speak. He dared not offer words of comfort or love. But neither could he dismiss her.

She read what she wished to into that silence and pulled away from him, as far into the corner of the little space as she could. She gave a snap of her skirt, to let it drop back into place, and straightened her bodice—which was in sore disarray and barely covering her luscious body.

'You are despicable. You know that, don't you?' she whispered, making sure that her voice was cold and controlled, even if it was the only part of her that was. 'You were trying to make me cry out just when the risk would have been greatest. You wanted discovery.'

'And you love me for it,' he said. 'The risk excited you. You climaxed. No harm was done. If I was as bad as you claim, I'd have taken the same pleasure. I could, even now, take the step that you could not retreat from, and you would go to whatever cold marriage bed fate has planned for you thinking not of your husband but of me.' It was an idle threat. For he would be damned before he'd let another man touch her from this night on.

'You flatter yourself, Mr Stratford.' She raised her chin, arrogant even in confusion.

'Frequently,' he admitted. 'But I am honest about it. I was born low, and not graced with connections or education. I would never call myself a handsome man. But I am the cleverest man in the room, and rich as Croesus. And I know that you want me.'

'That is quite different from loving you,' she said.

'Perhaps. But not for you. It is all of a thing to you.

For you could not love a man without wanting him, and you would never want a man that you did not love. At least a little,' he qualified, allowing her some pride.

'We have barely met, and yet you think you know me well.'

'I think I do,' he said. 'And I like what I know. I wish to know more of you. Come to my room tonight.' There would be no more ghosts with her at his side, and no fears of a cold and passionless future.

She shook her head and turned her face from his. 'After this shameful incident there is little left for you to learn of me. You must allow me to keep some secrets for myself, Mr Stratford. Now, if you will ascertain that we are alone so that I may exit, I will go to the retiring room. And you, sir, should return to your fiancée. While she will be too polite to notice your absence, I suspect that you will find others in the community less forgiving of it.' She pushed past him, not bothering to check the emptiness of the hall, and ran.

He sank to the bench behind him, frustrated and confused. What the devil was he doing? Her set-down stung, but he had no right to complain of it. Even if there was a secret in her past that tainted her virtue, it gave him no right to treat her like an experienced London widow. He had been planning, just now, to set her up and keep her for his pleasure, forgetting who she was and who her father was. To take a mistress while taking a wife was not unheard of. But he could not have picked a worse one than Barbara Lampett.

He was lucky that she had not raised a cry that would end his hopes with Anne. Or burst into tears and aroused some guilt in him for the way he had treated her, forcing him to cry off and offer properly. Even if he had sought, in a careless moment, to ruin himself, he had no right to do it at her expense. To finish by demanding entrance to her bed proved he was as uncouth and deserving of scorn as she seemed to think him. He was a base, simple creature, who answered with an enthusiastic affirmative to any temptation that called to him, and he had demanded that she be the same.

But even then she had not rejected him. She had merely refused to confirm the truth. While he suspected that Anne would be just as content to be a widow as a bride, Barbara could not keep her body from responding to his—though she clearly wished to.

She deserved better. And he deserved exactly what he was getting: a big house, a successful business and a wife who neither loved nor wanted him. It should have been enough. More than enough. It was certainly more than he had expected out of life. He had no right to complain.

He felt the desire in him dying, and realised that Barbara had been wrong on that first day. It could not be coal in his veins, for coal was never this cold. He stood, straightened his coat and brushed the dust from the knees of his breeches. Then he drew back the curtain enough to let in a ray of light by which he could check his watch. There was still a quarter of an hour left before midnight. If he applied himself in that time, he suspected he could get quite drunk and still be in the ballroom before the clock chimed twelve.

CHAPTER ELEVEN

FOR the third time tonight Barbara was hiding. At least this time she had chosen the ladies' retiring room, which seemed a bit more dignified than returning to her childhood haunts in a stranger's home.

The alcove had seemed like a clever idea when she'd wanted to think undisturbed about what she was sure she'd discovered. That had been Anne in the doorway, gasping and crying over an innocent Christmas kiss. The reaction might have been appropriate had she come upon Barbara a few days earlier, in the arms of Joseph Stratford. But she had seemed unusually distraught that Robert Breton might kiss another.

It was interesting. And it had given her a flutter of hope. Despite what everyone might say was the future, there were other forces at work tonight. If Joseph asked, and Anne refused… Or if Breton asked first, as his reaction to Anne's tears said he might…

She had sat alone behind the curtain, thinking the most delicious thoughts, smiling to herself and imagining Joseph, either stunned or relieved, turning to her for comfort. Despite her father's feelings on the subject, she would give that comfort gladly. Not tonight, of course. They were still almost strangers. But in the coming months they might grow closer, while her father grew used to the idea.

Then the man she'd been imagining had burst in upon her and everything had changed.

She looked at herself in the mirror, watching the blood rushing to her cheeks and wondering what to think of what had occurred. Maybe it was not as significant as she made it out to be. She'd kept her maidenhead, after all. But it would be a lie to think of herself as innocent. Another shudder went through her body at the memory, and she gripped the edge of the little table before her until her knuckles went white, trying to regain control.

His words after had been harsh and hurtful—but exciting as well. She had tried to respond in kind, aloof and yet passionate, not wanting to reveal her heart lest this all be a game to him. But she hoped it was not. She could not help but love Joseph. His passion and enthusiasm for his work drew her, and they were tempered with a kindness and generosity that few had seen but her. Given time, he could be made to see the errors he was making. Or perhaps it was he who was right, and her father in the wrong. There had to be a compromise of some kind to avert disaster. And she might be the only one who could bring it about.

The door opened behind her. When she glanced into the mirror she saw Anne Clairemont enter. Just for a moment the other girl shot a look of unvarnished loathing at the back of her head. Then she seemed to realise that it had been observed. Her features softened and her expression reformed into the placid mask that she so often wore. She went to a little bench on the opposite side of the room and began straightening hairpins, dabbing lightly at her eyes in an effort to disguise the tears she'd shed earlier, powdering her cheeks until the face in her own mirror was a deathly white.

'Here, let me help you.' Barbara turned and went to her, smoothing the loose curls at the back of her head and rubbing gently at the other girl's cheeks to get some colour back into them.

'Thank you,' Anne said, a little coldly. 'I fear this evening you are not seeing me at my best.'

'What you saw in the refreshment room was nothing,' Barbara said, wondering even now if she was apologising for the correct offence. 'Mr Breton was attempting to be kind to me, I think. I am grateful, of course. But that is all.'

'It does not matter,' Anne said quickly, but there was a flash of spirit in her eyes that quickly died again.

'I think it might,' Barbara said. 'Perhaps we could call the carriage and return home rather than going back to the party. If it would help, I could pretend an indisposition and you could pretend to help me.'

'No,' Anne said hurriedly. 'The snow has come, and I will be staying the night. You as well. Do not worry. Arrangements are being made. I will be quite all right—really. I must return to the ballroom. Father will be expecting me. And Joseph.'

'But what do *you* wish, Anne?' It was maddening to watch the girl, so obviously miserable, headed in lock-step towards the altar, unwilling to consider another option.

'I wish for everyone to be happy this Christmas,' the other girl said firmly. 'It does not matter what I want. That will not be possible. I think we can only hope to do as little harm as possible.' She lifted her chin, inspecting herself in the mirror. 'That is much better. Thank you, Barbara. Now, if you would be so kind, I would like to return to the ballroom, and I do not wish to walk alone.'

They linked arms and proceeded down the corridor towards the ballroom, chatting amiably of nothing in particular. And if Barbara felt Anne's arm tensing as they passed the kissing bough in the doorway of the refreshment room, then she ignored it—just as Anne needed to ignore Barbara's flinch as they passed the alcove.

Then they were back in the ballroom, and little knots of people glanced in their direction, Anne's father giving an approving look. There was Joseph, standing near the musicians, holding out a welcoming hand.

For a single, foolish instant Barbara thought that he was looking to *her*, offering that friendly gesture to coax her near. Then the moment passed and she realised that it was intended for the woman at her side.

Anne stiffened in a way that was imperceptible to any but Barbara. Then she fixed the serene smile more firmly in her lips and stepped forwards to take the offered hand and her proper place at Joseph Stratford's side.

He gave a nod of approval and cleared his throat. Although the noise was not particularly loud, it caught the attention of everyone in the room. They turned to look at him expectantly, and Barbara watched in admiration at his easy mastery of the crowd.

But in horror as well. For, despite all his vague words, and his actions towards her, and Anne's obvious penchant for another, Barbara could see what was about to happen—just as everyone else could.

'My pleasure to announce…done me…honour…hand in marriage.'

The words seemed to fade in and out of her hearing. It was clear that the others had no problem, for they smiled and clapped politely. Champagne was pressed into her hand by a ready servant. Barbara accepted it with a numb nod. All around her glasses were raised and toasts made to the happy couple—for that was what they appeared to be.

Just before her knees gave way she took a half-step back to the little chair against the wall, so that it would seem she sat rather than collapsed. As the music began again she shrank back, pulling it behind a pot of ivy, and sipped wine that seemed like vinegar on her tongue.

CHAPTER TWELVE

Too late, too late, too late.

It should have been a triumph. Joseph had acquitted himself as well as could be expected amongst the gentry who had accepted his invitation. He'd secured financing for his business plans, he had found himself a wife to secure his position in the area, and his truce with Lampett had lasted long enough to avoid embarrassment.

That he was well on the way to making the man's daughter into his mistress was a point that did not bear close observation. Nothing must come of that—no more than the extremely pleasant dalliance they had experienced in the hall. Surely she knew it was no more than that.

But he had seen the stricken look in her eyes even through the brandy-soaked haze he'd created to steel his nerves for the announcement. Even if she had done similar things before, she had allowed him to do what he had done because she loved him—or thought she did. He had taunted her with his knowledge of her feelings, cheapening them to hurt her. Then he had publicly pledged himself to someone else minutes after leaving her.

So he was marrying the wrong woman for the right reasons. What of it? The move was very like unto himself. He always seemed to be turning a good idea into a bad one. Though they suited perfectly, Bob and Anne would be parted so that he might advance in society and in business. After her brief visit to the manor he would pack Barbara Lampett back off to the village. She would stay as a virtuous spinster, so long as he kept his hands off her.

He remembered the vague promises he had made to the ghostly coachman of how things would change now that he knew of the problems. But for the life of him, he could not think what he might have done to make any difference. If the visions he had seen the previous evening were true, they would all be the sadder for what had occurred tonight, and he was to blame for that misery.

Too late. Too late.

His valet laid out his things and prepared him for bed. All the while Joseph listened to the ticking of the clock, which seemed to chant the words to him as each second passed. It was a wonder that man had invented such a clear measure of the passage of time—one that could be felt almost to the bone on silent nights like this.

It was not as if he needed a further reminder of his mortality. Lord knew, his father had seen to that in recent nights. And tonight's visitor would be the worst of all. For why would this charade have been needed if the future was a happy one? And it was almost three o'clock.

Too late.

The edges of the room seemed to darken and chill. Though it was well stocked with coal, the fire burned low in the grate. It was the spirit coming for him, he was sure. And he did not wish to see what it foretold.

He had made a mistake. Nothing unusual. He'd made many over the course of twenty-five years. But the mistakes of late were irrevocable. He was marrying a woman he did not love. Toying with one he did. Upending an already fragile community with the arrogant assurance that his plans would set everything right, given time.

But now it seemed that only his own death could call a halt to what had begun. He was unsure whether he was likely to be taken by the night's spirit, or simply driven to make his own end by the grim future that lay ahead.

Too. Late.

His valet withdrew in silence, leaving him alone.

Joseph sat on the edge of the bed, waiting for the end, disgusted with his cowardice. Perhaps his father's real plan had been that he meekly accept judgement on this last night. But there had to be something he could do. There must be some fact he was missing that might explain the village and the women in it, for they were a mystery to him. When Lady Clairemont had announced that they would be staying tonight, rather than fighting the weather, he had asked if it was her intention that Miss Lampett stay as well. He had been greeted with a look of such cold hostility that he could not believe it had risen from a simple indiscretion.

If tonight was to be his end, he would never know the truth. Nor would he know the woman who was sleeping just down the hall from him, in the smallest of the guest bedrooms. He could wait in his own room for the angel of death or the very devil himself to take him. Or he could go to her, demand the truth and love her—just once.

There would never be a better time for it, he was sure. If he was already damned, one more sin was not likely to make things any worse. He dared not miss the chance and leave her thinking he felt nothing.

He stood and threw off the nightshirt, grabbing a dressing gown and wrapping it about his naked body. Then he threw open the door and walked down the hall to seal his fate.

CHAPTER THIRTEEN

IT HAD been a miserable evening, and one that Barbara would repeat in memory for the rest of her life. Each time she saw the happy couple who were lord and lady of Clairemont Manor her stomach would twist as she wondered how much Joseph remembered, and how much Anne knew of it. And if that brief interlude in the alcove had meant anything at all.

Then there was Robert Breton, who had been too cowardly to seize the opportunity when he'd had his chance. She hoped he would fade into obscurity rather than continue to haunt the area. If he stayed, she rather feared that they would become friends and spend long days brooding jealously over the lives they might have had. Perhaps they might marry, and have the same kind of dreary and passionless union that Joseph and Anne shared.

Why could she not just go back to her loneliness of a day ago? It had been so much simpler.

There was a knock at the door.

She sat up in bed and pulled the covers up to her chin. This was not the scratch of a servant, nor the polite tap of Anne, come to share a quiet conversation before bed. This was the firm rapping of the master of the house. He was standing in front of her door, probably one more knock away from calling out to her, which might wake a neighbour or alert a servant. The resultant scene would be almost as bad for him as for her.

She pushed aside the covers, hurried across the room and threw open the door before the night could become any worse. 'What are you doing here?' she whispered, not wanting to draw further attention.

'I have come for answers,' Joseph said, in a voice that was loud and unembarrassed.

'As if you are the one who needs them. Talk to me tomorrow over breakfast, if you must.' Preferably in the presence of chaperones, to ensure that she did not do anything more foolish than she already had.

'I don't have tomorrow.' As usual, he could think of no further than himself.

'Be quiet,' she whispered. 'Someone will hear.'

'If you do not wish to draw attention, you had best let me in,' he said, with a strange tight smile.

She grabbed him by the lapel and pulled him into the room, closing the door quickly, silently, regretting that she had touched him at all, for her hand seemed to burn with the contact. And now he was in front of her, blocking her way into her own room, and she was planted, shoulders to the door panel, in a way that half reminded her of those scandalous moments in the alcove. Except now she was wearing nothing but her chemise—not that there was much of her body he had not seen.

'What do you want?'

She tried not to squirm at the memory, and the traitorous desire to step forwards, to relax and to go to him. But perhaps that was not what he wanted. He did not reach for her. He was frowning, as though deep in thought.

'Tell me what has happened here.'

'I beg your pardon?'

'Here. In this community. Before I arrived. I need to know about the people right now, before I can go another step.'

She laughed, for it was so far outside what she had expected to hear that she could hardly credit it. 'You wish to know now—after moving here, building here and spending untold sums of money to achieve your ends—what the people might think of it?'

'I know what they think of it,' he said dismissively. 'They hate it—as they would hate any change. That is not what I mean and you know it. Tell me about Mary. Tell me about the mill fire. And your father's accident. Help me make sense of it all.'

'Help you to make sense of it?' She pushed past him to return to her bed. 'There is nothing to make sense of.

No blame to assess. Accidents happen. People are hurt. They die. Time passes. The survivors are changed, but they live on. For what else is there to do?' She turned back to face him. 'If that is all you have come here to say, then you are wrong. It *can* wait until morning, and a setting not so completely inappropriate. Goodnight, Mr Stratford.' She climbed into bed, turning away from him and pulling up the covers. He could make his retreat in anger or embarrassment. She did not care. But she should not be forced to watch it.

But he did not leave. She felt the weight of him, sitting on the edge of her bed, not touching, just out of reach of her. 'Tell me.'

'You are selfish and horrible to come and remind me of these things, tonight of all nights.' Even knowing the stupidity of it, after their time in the alcove she had cherished some small fantasy that he would come to her, attempting to continue what they had begun. Perhaps he would speak of love, and even though she would recognise the words for lies, it would be better than nothing.

'Barbara.' He laid his hand on her shoulder, and through the covers the weight of it was warm, heavy and soothing—as was the sound of her name on his lips. 'Tell me the truth. You have held things back from me. I would have no more secrets with you.'

'Like the fact that your engagement to Anne was in place even as you fondled me?' she shot back, the humiliation still fresh. 'Go to her, if you want a bed partner. Let me have some peace.'

'That is not what I mean. Not at all. Or at least that is not all.' He fumbled with his words, as though he could make no sense to her or himself. 'I need to know everything. I need to know about *you*.' He said it with such curious emphasis that for a moment she believed that he really cared. 'Why are the Clairemonts so cold to you? Tell me.'

He stretched out behind her on the mattress, the covers separating them, and the hand that had shaken her shoulder was wrapped about her waist, drawing her close as he buried his face in her hair. He would not leave until she spoke. She was sure of it. If she must give him the truth, it would be easier while lying in his arms, pretending that his strength was her own.

'Because I killed their daughter, six years ago at Christmas time. It is my fault that Mary is dead. They hate me for it, and I do not blame them.'

He did not move away from her, not even to breathe. If anything, his arms held her tighter, and his lips pressed to the back of her throat, close to her ear. 'You said she was ill.'

She sighed. 'And so she was—because of me. My friend Mary Clairemont died of influenza. There is no story. Many of us were sick that season. But none so bad as her,' Barbara admitted. 'We were the best of friends and spent all our time together. When I sickened she brought me broth and calf's-foot jelly. She read to me to pass the time. Her mother came as well. They took the illness back to their own home. Mary died of it.'

'You blamed yourself?'

'Not at first. But Mr Clairemont came and argued with Father. I heard them. He said that I should have been the one to die. It was horrible. After that, we were no longer welcome at the manor.'

'That was unfair,' Joseph said from behind her. 'But from what I have seen of Mr Clairemont it is not so very surprising.'

'Mrs Clairemont was distraught, and still weak from her own illness. It was a cold winter, and she did not recover until nearly spring. Christmas, which had been such a merry time at the manor, was silent.'

'I understand there were parties here?'

'Like this one. But bigger.' She could not help but smile at the memory. 'Not for years, now. Their sadness cut the heart out of them. They could not celebrate without thinking of Mary.'

'Time to move on, then,' Joseph said. His voice was gruff, as though it were possible to reject the softer emotions.

'One cannot just push away grief when everything about the Christmas holiday is a reminder,' she informed him, rolling to face him and leaning on her elbow. 'You must show more compassion for Mrs Clairemont. The family was forced to strip the greenery from the house and use the feasting foods for a funeral. It was a great shock to them.'

'But wrong to blame you for it,' he said, touching her hair with his hand.

'And Mr Clairemont lost his grip on his business. The war took its toll as well. Mr Mackay leased the land from him, but was not able to sell his goods. He bought the new looms to save money at the expense of the workers.'

'If Clairemont had been smart, he would have noticed before things got bad,' Joseph said, reasoning like a machine even while looking at her like a lover and lying near naked at her side. 'He lost a building because of it. A valuable tenant as well. That allowed me to capitalise…'

'Always business,' she said with a sigh. 'Father tried to help him at the last. Despite their differences, he ran to help save the mill with the rest of Mr Clairemont's friends. But he was the one who was struck down by a falling beam. He was unconscious for three days. We were sure he would die. And now…'

'His thoughts are addled,' Joseph finished. 'He blames the mill for it. He blames me as well.'

'But really it is my fault,' Barbara said. 'From the very first. If I had been the one to die, and not Mary…'

Before she could finish the sentence his arms had tightened upon her, drawing her into a breath-taking hug. 'Then things would have been different. But they would have been no better for the majority of people here.' His lips touched her cheek, kissing away a tear that she did not remember shedding. 'I have travelled the country, north and south, and seen what the war has done to trade, and what the new looms have done to tradesmen. It would have been uneasy here no matter what had happened. If your father had not been the one to speak against me then someone else would.'

She wanted to believe that almost as much as she wished that things could have been simpler—young and clean and pleasant, just as they had been a few years ago. 'There are a great many ifs,' she said. 'I think of them often. Sometimes it is only necessary to change the life of one person to set the world upon a different course.'

He stiffened. 'So I have been told. But I do not think that you are that person who must change.'

She laughed softly. 'And so I am put in my place, sir. It is good to know that you think me of so little importance in God's great scheme.'

'On the contrary. You are surprisingly important to...' He paused. 'To many people. But you are also blameless of anything that has happened here. Do not change. You are just right as you are. I would not alter an atom of you. But I owe you an apology. I assumed that the trouble was something quite different. A dispute over a suitor, perhaps.'

'There has never been anyone,' she admitted, then took a breath to gather courage. 'Other than you.'

He lay very still beside her. 'I never would have done what I did had I understood.'

'Did you think I was the village whore, then?' she

asked, struggling to escape his arms. 'It is a wonder you allowed me to associate with your guests.'

'No.' He said the word in a groan, and his arms were no longer gentle but holding her like iron as she fought against him. The lips that had been pressed softly to her cheek were taking her mouth, until she stilled and allowed his kiss, which was as rough and improper as he was. He filled her mouth with his tongue, making the rest of her body feel empty in comparison. The thin blanket that separated them was like a million miles of desert. And suddenly she was fighting not to get away but to be closer to him, praying that in total surrender he might finally admit what he felt for her.

'No,' he whispered, staying her hand and keeping the barrier between them. 'My guests are not worthy of you. Neither am I. I am a villain, a rogue, a debaucher. But I cannot seem to let you go. I only wanted to make things better, I swear. But with each turn I dig deeper. After tonight I will never get free.'

'If it is me you seek to be free from, then I hope you never succeed,' she whispered.

Perhaps it would have been better had he been right. If she had already fallen she would know how to proceed now, to find the thing that would make him happy, would make him stay. She pressed her lips to his earlobe and then his cheek, licking the dark stubble and following it to his jaw. He looked even more tired than he had before. She remembered that he complained he could not sleep. It must be true, for it was well past three and he was still awake and worrying about her.

Whatever he felt for her, he needed a comfort that only she could give him. She nestled her head against his throat and kissed the places that had been covered with his cravat. Then she found his fingers with hers and untangled them from the sheet he held, pushing the covers down so that they could be together.

He sighed and stopped resisting. Then he kicked away the last of the blankets and yanked at the tie of his robe, to be free of that as well. Suddenly she was sharing a bed with a naked man.

Though it was of her own choosing, she found that she was afraid to look on him. So she stared into his eyes, and found them to be infinitely sad, and perhaps a little frightened.

'No matter what happens, no matter how it appears,' he whispered, 'I am yours until I die. Do you understand that? And I am afraid of that. Because I know I will hurt you.'

'You never shall,' she said. It was another lie, of course. But she decided she would believe it, just for tonight. 'Would you help me to remove my chemise, please? For I think I would like to feel…'

His shoulders shook from laughing as he reached for the hem. 'Is that what it is like to make love to a lady? All "please" and "thank you"? I will give you a reason for those words.' He stripped her last garment from her and held her away from him for a moment, so that he could admire her body and kiss each of her peaking nipples.

'Cold?' he asked, smiling against her breast.

'A little,' she admitted, with a delicious shiver as he blew a cooling breath on her damp skin.

'I will take care of you.' He spread his robe over her shoulders and it was still warm with the heat of his body, the quilted silk arousing her body where it touched her. If she had been hoping for some deeper declaration she ought to be disappointed. But it felt good to be cared for, decadent and exciting.

Then he kissed her again. At first his lips pressed innocently to her forehead. Then they slipped down her face in a trail of small kisses on her eyelids and cheeks, coming to rest upon her mouth. It was not precisely chaste. But neither was it as unbridled as it had been a moment ago. His lips had lowered to hers in an almost leisurely fashion, brushing her face before settling, opening, deepening and taking her tongue into his mouth.

She kissed him back, as he had been kissing her, touching each feature of his face with her lips and tongue before settling on his mouth and losing herself in it. Being with Joseph was more than just passion. It was a solution, an answer, the opening of a locked door. It was right, no matter what her head should be telling her.

They parted for breath and he touched her cheek with his finger. 'May I stay with you until dawn?' he whispered. 'We do not have to lie together, if you do not wish…'

It was an odd thing to say. But she did not take the time to wonder at it, for there were far more interesting things to notice. 'It is what I wish,' she admitted. It was yet another point of no return—to say aloud that she wanted him. Before she could lose her nerve, she ran her hand once down the length of him, over his chest to rest near his sex, afraid to do more than that. She took a deep breath, and then spoke what was in her heart. 'Because I want to show you what I feel. Whatever happens tonight, tomorrow or in the distant future, you must know that I love you.'

'You have known me for such a short time that you cannot know the truth of your feelings.'

'I know that as well,' she said. 'And I know that you do not want my love. But I think it is important that you hear the truth. You do not love me. But I love you.'

'You should not,' he said, a little uneasily.

'I cannot help it.' She leaned back into the pillows and closed her eyes. With his body, he followed her, throwing a leg over her hip so that they could lie together, skin to skin.

She felt her body wakening as though it were newly born, every sensation a first. Despite the danger to her reputation, and to her heart, she felt warm and safe, and more sure of her love than ever. She must have been meant for him, and he for her. Why else would their bodies fit so well together? Why else would they respond so quickly? She could feel him, hard between her legs. And her hips gave an answering push against him, wet with invitation. The act of love, which had seemed most unusual when her mother explained it to her, now seemed like the most right and natural thing in the world.

Joseph understood, and gave a little shake of his head. 'Wait. There is more.'

'More?' After what had happened in the alcove this evening, what was left for them but to finish what they had started?

'I wish to know every inch of you.' His hands began to explore, smoothing down her shoulders and spine, and up the backs of her arms. His leg moved against hers, the hairs of it tingling as they brushed her. Then his mouth left hers to kiss her fingertips, her elbows and her ribs. He took one of her nipples into his mouth and gave it the softest of kisses. Then he rubbed his face gently between her breasts, so she could feel the roughness of his cheeks, grating ever so slightly against her skin. Then he turned his head to take the second breast less gently than the first, turning the soft kiss into a series of nips that made her cup his face in her hands, arch her back and press her body into his open mouth.

His fingers stroked her as his eagerness grew, gripping her thighs and parting them, and then giving one single touch of a fingertip in the place where they met. It hovered for a moment, and then slid down, and in.

She gasped. She had thought, after the sample he had

given her by the ballroom, that she understood what it must be like to make love. But though he touched her in the same way she felt different now, as though every part of her body burned.

He slid up her body again, so that he could kiss her on the lips, and the passage of his rougher skin against her body was maddening. She wanted to writhe against him, purring and winding herself about him like a kitten, demanding to be stroked.

'If I can do nothing else, I want to make you feel as you do me, when I look at you.' He smiled. 'I will make you want me to the point of madness. And together we will take the want away with having.'

'You have.' It seemed that now he was nude he was larger. Not just… She looked down and then hurriedly up at his face again. Not just the increase she had expected. It was the whole of him, as though the power and energy which had been hidden beneath his clothing was suddenly released. She was awash in it, tingling from the tips of her toes to the top of her head.

She looked down again, at the pair of them naked and side by side on the bed. For a moment she was more amazed than aroused. It was natural and right to be this way with him, just as it had from the first moment they'd been alone together, when he'd grabbed her by the arm and pulled her to safety. He reached for her now and caught her suddenly under the arms, rolling and pulling her close. Then he was on his back, and she was being pulled down, over and against him, sprawling over his body, covering him like a blanket.

It was his turn to lie back into the pillows, sighing contentedly. Then he pulled her head down to meet his and kissed her, with the tickle of his chest hair against her nipples and the stirrings of his erection between her legs. His hands were busy, adjusting, moulding, positioning, until his body was fitted to hers, his manhood nudging at her maidenhead.

Now she was waiting, fairly sure of what the next step would be, but unsure of how it would come about. 'Relax,' he murmured against her temple. 'We are still strangers, the pair of us. Touch me. Learn my body so that I may better know yours. I want to feel your hands.'

'Where?'

'Anywhere. You will know when it is time for more than that.'

How would she know anything of the sort? Perhaps he still thought she had some experience in the matter. If so, she was likely to embarrass herself soon enough. But all the same she ran her hands over his chest and felt the muscles move in response. She touched his arms and they moved to circle her, to stroke her, to hold her in place against him. She bit his shoulder and he clutched her bottom, grinding his hips into hers as she sucked upon his skin.

And so she dared to sit up, balancing on his thighs, and reached lower to touch the part of him that touched her. His hands slipped between her legs, spreading them wide, probing the opening of her body and taking it while she stroked him. He teased and thrust with his fingertips, leaving little spearings of pleasure that coalesced inside her, urging her to pull his sex, which had grown hard, towards her own. She hung there, on the edge of something, afraid to take the leap that would end in a flight or a fall.

And then she was sure. She wanted it. She wanted him. She wanted to be his, even if it was just for a night. She cried out to him, 'Help me. Please.'

'Barbara. Darling.' The hands that had been slow and gentle before moved lightning-quick, pulling her forwards and onto him. There was a lance of pain. Then he rolled so that she was beneath him.

When she looked up, into his face, the expression she saw was as surprising as anything else had been. It was as though he had changed, in a moment, to a different man. There was no trace of hardness in him, nothing frightening or aloof. The flaws had burned away in a burst of triumphant energy, leaving bliss, peace and desire.

Then he began to move in her. She felt a sense of connection to him that was beyond physical. They were working together towards some common goal, and she smoothed her hands over the muscles of his back, trying to go where he led her, sure that there would be pleasure enough for both of them when they arrived. Everything was alive in her—every inch of skin. The places that touched and rubbed were different from the bare places touched by night air and firelight. The place where their bodies met was the best of all. There was no feeling like this. No words to describe it. It was like springtime, full of promise, melting ice and birdsong, the stirrings of things that had been sleeping inside her.

Inside her body some part of him touched some part of her, and it was as though the whole world had lurched violently to one side and then righted itself. Then it happened again. She seemed to lose all control as her body turned upside down and inside out. And in all that confusion he was with her, holding her, feeling the same thing. He tensed, gasped and stilled.

He was lying on top of her. But it was not as she'd expected. Even though he was a large man, he seemed to weigh nothing, covering her like a shield, keeping her warm and safe. He was a part of her now, and would be even after they parted, as she was sure they must. He drew away from her, but only a little way, reaching towards the foot of the bed to pull the coverlet over the pair of them and then settling back at her side, wrapping his arms about her body and keeping her close.

'I should go,' he whispered.

She did not really wish him to. But it might be better for him to leave now, while they were both happy, than to stay too long, until that feeling changed.

'You should,' she agreed. 'But I do not mean to let you. Not just yet.' She held him close, and he turned her so her back was against his chest, wrapping himself around her in a different way, as though he wanted to know every inch of her body before he released it.

'I will see to it that I am back in my room before the house wakes in the morning. I will listen for the chiming of the clock. It is already well past four. I did not hear it strike at all. Perhaps that is late enough. Nothing has changed.' Then he relaxed, stroking her hair, his hand moving slower and slower as he lost consciousness.

And she dozed as well. But before she was lost to all she wondered what he had been expecting.

CHAPTER FOURTEEN

THE next morning was much as any other visit to the manor had been, even though another man was master. A round of sleepy guests gathered in the breakfast room for steaming plates of eggs, thick slices of ham, toast, marmalade and subdued chatter.

It was all familiar except for their host, who sat at the head of the table looking like death and subsisting on nothing more than black coffee. If he had slept at all, it did not show. His skin was grey and there were hollows in his cheeks that the razor had not touched. Barbara wanted to go to his side and cut the food on his plate, feeding him like an invalid before sending him to bed.

But that was not her job. It was Anne's.

There could be no acknowledgement of what had happened between them—not even to share the fatigue they had felt while lying in each other's arms waiting out the hour between the clock chiming four and five, wondering if each minute would be the last they'd share. She was as tired as he, though she had made an effort to look lively so that no one might ask her about it. But it was a happy exhaustion. She had come to the table and smiled down into her plate, trying not to show the world how wonderful she felt.

Then Joseph had arrived. And the longer she'd sat with him the worse she'd felt. She found herself listening to the ticking clock once more. Eating mechanically and longing for the moment she could escape.

Morning had come and everything had changed—in that it was much the same as it might have been had nothing happened at all. Joseph was there at breakfast, greeting his guests, helping himself to more coffee and making sure that all needs were met. But he showed her no special favour, enquiring politely if she had slept well without a wink or a nod.

She responded in kind. If she seemed awkward, or somewhat chilly, it would be taken for a sign of the estrangement between her family and him. Nothing more, nothing less.

Then he turned his attention to Anne. He could at least manage a smile for her, though it was little better than a death mask. His concern was more pointed. Her plate was heaped full and taken away just as quickly when she did not seem pleased with it.

Barbara felt her own food curdling in her stomach, and reached very deliberately for the teacup in front of her. As she lifted her gaze to stare fixedly across the table she caught the eyes of Robert Breton. His expression was similar. Just as bland and unflappable. He was just as stubbornly uninterested in the proceedings at the end of the table as she was.

But as he looked at her there was the slightest rise at one corner of his lip, and an equally slight salute as he raised his teacup, as though he were toasting their shared misery.

To kindred spirits, she thought, and responded in kind.

'Will you be participating in today's activities, Miss Lampett?' he asked politely. 'I understand that the skating on the pond is quite pleasant. There will be games in the parlour, and the lighting of the Yule Log.'

'I had not given it thought,' she answered. 'When I arrived I was hardly prepared for more than an evening. If there is a way to return to the village...with a servant, perhaps.' Even now she sat at the table wearing her ridiculously unfashionable ballgown, because it was all she had. Today it was just one more thing to single her out from the group as not quite belonging to it.

'Oh, please do stay,' Anne insisted. 'And do not give me any excuses about lack of preparation. Your skates are still here, you know, from when we were young together. Anything else needed you might borrow from me. Or there are Mary's old things...'

There was a sharp intake of breath from Lady Clairemont, who was seated beside Joseph. Anne fell silent again.

'Yes. Please. Stay. I will accept no excuses.' Joseph made the offer mechanically, without even looking up, and Barbara took another hurried sip of tea to stop the words on the tip of her tongue.

What do you mean by that? Are you in any way sincere? Or is that sarcasm I hear? Even if it is a bald-faced lie, could it not be delivered with a smile?

'No,' she said softly. 'I thank you for your gracious offer of hospitality, but I must be getting back to Mother and Father. Perhaps, after Christmas, I might return. It has all been quite lovely and I am very glad that you invited me.'

'Very well, then,' Joseph said, not even bothering with a token resistance. 'I will see that the carriage is brought round—or perhaps there is a sledge.'

A spirited discussion erupted as to the delightful nature of sleigh rides, and what fun it might be to make an outing into the village, which was declared 'quaint' by the visitors from the South. It was a relief when the attention turned to more cheerful topics than the fate of the dowdy young woman at the foot of the table, leaving Barbara to excuse herself unnoticed.

She fled to her bedroom, counting on the privacy of a locked door. There were no belongings to gather before departure. Hiding above stairs would spare her any more awkward conversations. She could sit in the window seat and watch for the carriage that would take her away from the disaster that this visit had become.

But even there she was not alone. When she entered,

she startled the maid who had come to make up the room. The girl was the youngest daughter of the Stock family, who lived a scant quarter-mile from Barbara's home, and she was staring at the tangle of sheets on the bed, and the bloody smudge in the midst of them. She offered a quick curtsey, and muttered an apology for the interruption. Then she smiled, as though she had been presented with a tidbit juicier than any she might see with Christmas dinner, and hurried from the room.

Barbara almost turned to go after her, with a lame story of her restless night and the sudden monthly imposition that would explain the spots of blood. But there was no way gossip could be avoided. To deny it would be as good as admitting the truth: a couple had been sporting here, and the lady involved was the formerly virginal Miss Barbara Lampett.

They had been careful, or so she'd thought. Between kisses Joseph had assured her that the walls were thick, and that no one would see him come or go. She had consoled herself that if she was lucky enough to avoid pregnancy—and she dared not think about any other possibility—the secret would go to her grave.

She had not counted on the maids. While a bit of gossip about Mr Stratford's London guests would be harmless, and gossip about Anne would be avoided for the sake of her family, there was no magical protection that extended to Miss Lampett. She was a lady and should know better.

She gave one last look around the room to remember

that, however briefly, she had been supremely happy here. She had belonged to someone, if only for a few hours. Now she must return to her home and put the happy memory away, as she had so many others. She would not return after Christmas, for she doubted she could bear another visit.

And so she wandered, avoiding the breakfast room, where so many people were still gathered, and the salons and reception rooms, where plans for the day were being made. Instead she went to say goodbye to the portrait gallery, and to the ballroom, stopping to touch the curtain that covered the little alcove and wondering, if she pulled it back suddenly, if she would find the ghost of her younger self hiding there. Or had all those old times been supplanted by memories of Joseph?

With a little smile, she drew aside the curtain—only to hear a gasp, and the rustle of clothing falling back into place as the couple inside sprang apart.

'I'm sorry,' she said, 'I had no idea…' She turned quickly, shielding her eyes.

Anne stumbled forwards into the hall. Mr Breton acted almost as quickly to thrust her back into the recess and step in front of her, as though it were possible to shield her from view. He cursed very softly, and ran his fingers through his hair in an effort to compose himself. Then he bowed. 'I am sorry you were a witness to my disgraceful behaviour, Miss Lampett.' He bowed again to Anne. 'And that you had to experience it, Miss

Clairemont. My actions were totally inappropriate, and no apology can be offered for them other than an excess of alcohol.'

He looked back at Barbara, knowing that she had seen him, sober as a judge, at the breakfast table, less than an hour ago.

He gave a helpless shrug. 'My fate is in your hands, miss, as is the honour of a lady. Though I would not wish what has occurred here to be known, I cannot demand that you keep my secret. Know that I will be leaving Mr Stratford's home early in the New Year and returning to London. There will be no further risk of another incident.' Then he walked hurriedly away from them, down the hall.

The moment he was gone Anne rushed forwards, seizing her hands. The polite pretence of soft, smiling apathy had disappeared. 'Please, Barbara. Please. I beg you. Say nothing to Joseph of this. I know that I have no reason to ask your help. My family has treated you horribly for a thing which was no fault of yours. But, please, say nothing.'

For a moment the frozen woman before her melted into the image of her lost sister, into something much more human than she had been: a woman with desires who was at least capable of making mistakes, if not yet able to admit to them.

There was so much that Barbara was not speaking of already. Why should there not be one more thing? 'I saw nothing, Anne. Nothing at all that I wish to remark upon to anyone. But just for a moment can you not be honest with me? Was this all his doing? Or is there feeling on both sides?'

And Anne, normally so reserved and in control, burst into tears in her arms.

Barbara glanced around, relieved to see that there was no one there to witness the outburst. Then she took a firmer grip on Anne's hands and dragged her back into the alcove, to sit on the bench, pinning back the curtain to allow some light into their sanctuary. 'Come, now. If you cannot get hold of yourself, then at least come where fewer people might see you. Now, tell me. Do you love him or not?'

Anne gave a hesitant nod. 'He is leaving. Even before you discovered us he was threatening. Now he will go for sure.'

Barbara stifled surprise. She had meant to ask about Joseph—the only man whose future mattered. She corrected herself. 'You will lose Mr Breton, if you do not cry off your engagement.'

'How can I?' Anne looked up at her from watery blue eyes. 'I am the only daughter left. Everyone is depending on me to do exactly what is needed. Joseph wishes a lady for the manor. My father wishes to get his foot back in the door. He would rather stay here as a doting father-in-law than learn to be comfortable in new surroundings.' For a moment there was uncharacteristic bitterness in the sweet voice. 'No one is particularly interested in what *I* want. I had thought, since I had no real objections to the character of the man, that it would be enough to be comfortable and back in my own home. But, Barbara. Oh, Barbara.' She smiled. 'That was before I met Robert. I did not know that I could feel like this. And now it will end.'

Then she was crying again, and Barbara could find nothing to do other than offer her shoulder and pat the girl ineffectually on the back. Would it do her any good to be assured that her future husband did not care about her either?

That could not possibly be a comfort. Though she did not seem to expect it of him, Barbara doubted that the girl in her arms wished to know the extent of his uninterest, or that an old friend was a co-conspirator in her betrayal. Love was not her reason for marrying. And there was nothing Barbara could say that would make the Clairemonts' desire to regain the manor any different than it was.

'There, there,' she said, and could not manage to sound the least bit enthusiastic about it. Success for Anne meant failure for her.

There was no way, in good conscience, that she could talk the girl into crying off. 'Would it help,' she asked cautiously, 'if I spoke to Mr Stratford for you? Perhaps if he understood how unhappy you are…'

'No.' Anne gripped her arm. 'You mustn't. He would be furious. So would my father.'

Barbara doubted that would be totally true. Though Lord Clairemont would be angry at having his plans thwarted, she'd seen no evidence that Joseph would be similarly affected at the loss of his impending marriage.

But then, she had seen no evidence to the contrary. In all that little time they'd spent together he'd said nothing about Anne, either positive or negative. She was sure that he'd said not a word about terminating the engagement.

'Very well, then. I will not expose you.'

Anne gave her a watery smile. 'I am sorry again for how my family has treated you. How I have treated you as well. You are good and kind. I will do anything I can to help you in the future if you will keep my secret.'

With secrets of her own, Barbara could feel nothing but sympathy for the sister of her dearest friend. 'I will do nothing to hurt you, I promise. And if I can find a way to help you, I will do so.'

'I can ask for nothing more than that,' Anne said, carefully drying her eyes with a handkerchief.

'Miss Lampett?' Mrs Davy the housekeeper called from the end of the hall. 'The carriage is ready to take you to the village. Dick says you had best leave soon, or the roads will turn to mud.'

Without another word Barbara dropped the curtain into place, pretending that she had been alone. 'Of course. I am ready.' She walked quickly to the front of the house, wondering if she was obligated to say a farewell to her host. She decided against it. He knew very well how she felt, and the reasons for her leave-taking. 'You will give my regards and my regrets to

Mr Stratford, of course,' she said politely to the housekeeper.

'That will not be necessary, miss. He is waiting to see you off.'

'Oh,' she said weakly, forcing her steps not to falter on the way to the door.

He was waiting there, just as the housekeeper had said, looking more like a professional mourner than a party host, a few flakes of snow lying unmelted in his dark hair.

She nodded at him, trying not to show the fear she felt that he would try to stop her. If he revealed even one moment of true feeling she was likely to turn back on her plan and go meekly to the room he had given her.

'I've come to see you off,' he said, without expression. 'I am your host. It is appropriate, I think, to wish you well and see you safely from the premises. People will wonder, otherwise.'

'And it is appropriate for me to thank you for your hospitality,' she answered back. But she said nothing further.

'Well, then. Go.' He said it gruffly, as though he could turn her decision into his own wish.

'There is no reason to stay,' she said firmly.

He sighed, his composure breaking. 'And yet I do not want you to leave.' That was at least said with some tenderness, as though he actually meant it.

'You know I must. There is nothing for me here.'

He reached out and touched her arm. 'There is always tonight.'

'You think that because of last night I will allow you to make a habit of coming to me in secret?'

'There could be no other way. I cannot cry off from Anne without disgracing her.'

There. He had finally said it. He could not hurt Anne, but he thought nothing of what he might do to Barbara Lampett, who had far less protection than the daughter of the most honourable family in the area.

'You are horrible,' she said. Despite how wonderful she had felt, his touch now was torture. It made her want to cry. She pulled her arm from his grasp.

'You said you loved me.' He said it softly, urgently.

'And you have never said the same to me. Not even as a lie. I was foolish to tell you. And foolish to feel it as well. For you are unworthy. Cruel and selfish, just as my father tried to tell me.'

'It is not as you think,' he said.

'But you offer no further explanation to tell me how it might *be*, if it is not exactly as it appears. You are using me, and you will marry another.'

'I did not intend to,' he admitted. 'But I could not sit alone in my room, waiting for the end.'

'The end? That is a tad melodramatic, Mr Stratford. I suppose next you will tell me that you are afraid of the dark.' She laughed scornfully, hoping that it might hurt him just a little, so that he might feel some part of what she felt whenever she looked at him.

His look in response was strange. A little blank, a little panicked. And clearly saying that she had discovered some part of the truth. 'That is it, isn't it? You are afraid to sleep alone in a darkened bedroom. You used me for a night to solve the problem.' She shuddered. 'That is all I was to you. A warmer for your bed and a candle on a dark night.'

'It was more than that,' he said. But still he would not say what.

'I ruined myself in the hope that there was some affection on your part. But I could have been anyone at all.' Without his help, she heaved herself into the body of the carriage and tried to close the door.

'Barbara. Wait.' He was just behind her, his shoulders blocking the entrance.

'I have waited too long already.'

'Do not leave me.' He sounded almost plaintive now, as though he were actually afraid of facing another night alone.

'Tonight you must go to Anne for your comfort. It would make more sense. I am sure you have much to talk about.' She bit her tongue then, to keep back the spiteful revelation that she had been almost ready to share. 'But of course you will not, will you? She is a lady, and deserves better than to be treated as a receptacle for your carnality. And I? I was a lady once. But no longer, now that you are through with me. Now I am through with you. Good day, sir.'

She sat facing carefully forwards, ignoring his presence, until with an oath he slammed the door and signalled for the coachman to drive.

CHAPTER FIFTEEN

How much had the coachman heard? she wondered, huddling beneath the coach robe and pulling her shawl around her shoulders. How much had the grooms guessed? Between the bunch of them they would piece together the bits of her argument with Joseph and their secret would be no secret at all. The tragedy involving Mary had been the talk of the village for a while. Then most had decided that it could not have been helped, and that even if the Lampetts should have known better than to allow company in a sickroom, they'd meant no harm by it.

But now she would be infamous. The people would expect no less of Joseph, for he was a man. He was an outsider, as well, and already reviled. But *she* should have known better, and society would punish her for her lapse in judgement. Women would cut her, and avoid her mother as well. Her father, if he could be made to understand, would be devastated.

She would have to leave. As soon as she was sure that there would be no child she would advertise for a position as a governess, or a lady's companion. Perhaps, if she threw herself on the mercy of the vicar, he would write a letter of reference for her, assuring the world that she was gently brought up and properly educated. Even Lord Clairemont might help, if it was understood that her goal was to get as far away from Fiddleton as she could, so that she could create no further trouble. Her parents would be heartbroken at her leaving, but once she had managed to explain Mother would likely agree.

The carriage had pulled up to her house now, and a groom helped her down, seeming at a loss that there was no package or bag that she might be helped with. She thanked him, and went up the walk alone, without turning back.

Her mother greeted her in the front room, eyes sharp, discerning, not willing to let her pass without a challenge. 'I have sent your father to the bakery to get us bread for supper,' she said. It was an obvious ruse so that they could be alone, for Barbara had seen to the baking only yesterday. 'Did you enjoy your visit to the great house, then?'

'Of course,' she said. 'We stayed the night because of the weather, but I was not feeling quite myself this morning, and thought it best…' She had dropped her head as she spoke, unable to meet her mother's gaze. That was her undoing. She showed her guilt plainly by hiding the expression that she could not let her mother read.

'One of the maids from Clairemont has been to the market and gone already. But on the way she visited her mother, Mrs Stock. The entire family is in service up at the house. And they do like to gossip.'

'I gave them no reason to talk.'

'Do not try to lie to me, Barbara. You cannot trick me with words, like your father and his speeches. The maid says that there was a man in your room last night, sharing your bed. Who was it?'

The plans she had made as she'd ridden towards the village had not included this first, most difficult conversation. If she was to manage any of the scandal it would not do to fight now, against another who would bear the shame of it. She sighed and collapsed onto the bench by the fire, hanging her head in embarrassment. 'It is as bad as you think. Probably worse. I love him.'

'You cannot,' her mother said firmly. 'In my opinion, if you meant to lie with the man before marriage, love is the worst reason for it.'

She stared up at her mother in surprise and wondered just what she might know of such things, and why she was not more shocked than she was.

Her mother gave her a candid look. 'You are not some fainting schoolgirl, Barbara. You are a young lady, well on your way to spinsterhood. Sometimes these things happen. If you were seventeen and in your first season it might ruin your chances. Now there are no opportunities left to spoil.' She sat down beside Barbara and said, more quietly, 'Who was he? I hope it was not some London dandy. If so, his words were likely false ones, and there is little hope that he will stay past the New Year. Was it that nice Mr Breton I have seen occasionally in the village? He might be persuaded to do the right thing for the sake of your reputation. Or we could write his father and demand a settlement.' She sounded almost hopeful at the thought, as though there were a way to make something good come from her daughter's mistake.

'Joseph Stratford,' Barbara said, with a sinking heart.

The older woman slumped beside her, as though her last hope had been dashed. 'I suppose now you will tell me that, while he claims to have feelings for you, he has no intention of crying off from Anne Clairemont.'

'He does not love her.' But that was no defence at all.

'Neither does he love you, or we would not be having this conversation.' Her mother stared down at her hands, which were trembling in her lap. 'Do you understand, even for a moment, the predicament we are in? Your father is failing.' The last words came in a harsh whisper that made them all the more terrible. 'When he is gone, there will be nothing to save us from our fate. My own inheritance is running out. I bore no sons. What little we have from your father will go to his brother. Even a bad marriage is quite out of the question for you once it gets round that you've been bedded by the most hated man in Fiddleton.'

'I thought to leave,' Barbara said hopefully. 'If I take a position, I might send what money I earn back home.'

Her mother said nothing to this for a time. When she finally spoke her voice was even quieter, as though she was afraid that the house itself might hear. 'There is another solution—if you are not too proud to take it.'

'I do not understand.' Until a moment ago Barbara had not thought of herself as hopeless. Now she was not sure what her mother saw as a last salvation.

'Joseph Stratford has no intention of marrying you—not while he can have the lady that belongs in the great house he's bought,' her mother said bitterly. 'He is little better than a child playing with a dolls' house. It does not matter if he cares for her. He will have Anne Clairemont because she belongs there.'

She had not thought of it. But her mother was right. It was a chilling idea that Anne would sit, just as she wanted, in the chair at the end of the great dining table, writing her letters in the morning room, lounging in the salon with the careless grace she had affected with so many years' practice. But she would be little better than an ornament.

'But Stratford has proven himself to be a greedy and licentious man. He cares nothing for the people here.'

'He's not like that,' Barbara said. But, though she believed him to be different, there was ample evidence that her mother was right.

'Of course he is,' her mother said, more firmly. 'And isn't that the argument of every foolish young girl whose head is turned by broad shoulders and a kind word? *"To me, he is different."*'

But to her, he was. It would do no good to repeat what she knew to be true. But she remembered what it had been like, the previous night, as he'd comforted her when she spoke of Mary. He had needed her as much as she had needed him.

'He's had you, and there's little more to it than that, I am sure. He'll do the same again, if you let him.'

And now what had felt so wonderful felt wrong and shameful. Her mother was right. Even as she'd tried to escape him he'd been trying to lure her back. She wanted to bathe herself, scrub at her skin until there was no memory of it left. 'It will not happen again.'

'Oh, yes, it will,' her mother said, with a sad frown. 'If you love him, you will go when he sends for you. You will not be able to help yourself. That is the nature of love, after all. In the face of it, my warnings will mean nothing to you.'

She put an arm around her daughter, drawing her close and untying her bonnet so that that Barbara could lay her head on a comforting shoulder.

Her mother smoothed her hair and whispered, 'We cannot take back the past. I will not stop you if you go to him. But if you do, make sure there is an arrangement. One time and people will call you a fool. Twice and they will call you a whore. If Mr Stratford cares for you at all, make him give you your due. There will be little use for fancy dresses and frippery. But we will have need of a steady income before too much longer.' Her mother choked back a tiny sob, and then said in a firm voice, 'We need to be practical about the future.'

Barbara sank down into a chair, waiting for the room to stop spinning around her. It had all come to that, had it? And so soon. She had wanted to believe there was a respectable future ahead of her, with forged references and a quick trip to a place where no one would know that she'd disgraced herself. But her mother, always the most practical woman, had dismissed that fantasy without another thought. There would be no concealing the truth. She was ruined, and now she must make the best of it.

And she could do that by being honest and admitting that she wished to go back to Joseph. She would be a mistress: a rich man's whore. But she could still love him, and be with him, even if she could not have him for her own.

Joseph would marry Anne, just as he'd planned to do. He would have his great house, and his pretty wife, and his woman, too. Perhaps that was what he'd planned all along. He had silenced the opposition to his mill as well. For she would now be forced to make Father understand how unwise it was to anger the man who put bread upon their table. If Joseph tired of her, for whatever reason…

Barbara's future would be secure and her family

would be safe as long as she pleased him. But when she did not? He would send her away. There were few men like him in this small backwater, but plenty would know her as a great man's cast-off. If she did not arrange for a settlement at the beginning she would have to find another protector.

One that she did not love.

Barbara searched her feelings, trying to remember the conversations they'd shared, the constant rescues, the way she had felt as they had danced, and as he'd held her last night. Perhaps it was not love on his part. But there was nothing to indicate a lack of generosity. If she was to be a fallen woman, she could do much worse than to fall for Joseph Stratford.

As long as she put her heart to one side and thought sensibly there was a way out of this. Her mother was right. But if she meant to survive she must remember that love had no part in it. And as she sat there, ridiculous in an out-of-fashion ballgown, though it was near to noon, she let that part of herself die. There would be no foolish tears over things that could not be changed. She would seize the opportunity that had presented itself, and work it to her best advantage.

Joseph would approve of that, she was sure. Was that not the way he did business as well? If nothing else, she would prove that they were more alike than he knew.

CHAPTER SIXTEEN

CHRISTMAS Eve dinner was excellent, with roast beef fair to melting from the bone, and a Yorkshire pudding to sop up the rich gravy. The Christmas pudding was so soaked in spirits that a man could feel drunk on the richness of it, his own soul licked with the blue flames that danced over the surface of it without consuming it.

To Joseph Stratford every bite tasted like sand.

The Yule Log was crackling in the grate, and beside it were pans of chestnuts. Tables were set with bowls of wine and currants ready for snapdragon. His guests lit the spirits and snatched at the little fruits, shrieking with laughter and shaking their singed fingers.

And yet Joseph was cold.

The music, though not as raucous as it had been the previous evening, was lively enough to satisfy. But all the songs in the world could not have chased the dullness from his own spirit. He had done nothing as the only person who could make a change in him had turned and left. He had not stopped her. And soon he would pay the price for that.

To avoid conversing with others, Joseph danced the better part of the evening with Anne. True to form, she had little to say to him, letting him stride through the patterns in silence. She wore the same serene smile she always did. But there was a slightly panicked look in her eyes, as though she was bearing up no better than he. In encouragement, he squeezed her hand.

She started. Then, her worried eyes darting to his, gave an answering squeeze as if to admit that, while they both might be trapped, there was some comfort in knowing she had his sympathy.

Not trapped for long, my dear, he wanted to say. He had his own suspicions on how this night was likely to end. Try as he might, he could not see a marriage—happy or otherwise—looming on his life's horizon. Though it had been his whole world just a few days ago, the opening of the mill now seemed a distant and unlikely thing that he would have no part in. He wondered if Breton had the nerve to take it on. But that would mean turning his back on his birth and taking on a real position. Perhaps he could find some man of business to run the place. More likely the whole of it would fall to ruin if Joseph was not alive to fight for it.

It made him wonder... Would it have seemed too fatalistic to draw a will? He had no heir. Perhaps the house could revert to the Clairemonts once he was out of the way. It would have been wise to leave some document stating that it was his wish, should the worst occur tonight.

Although he had thought to fear death, now that it was likely upon him he could not seem to care. Barbara was gone, and he felt the emptiness of it as he walked the corridors of the great house before bed. He should have said something to her when he'd had the chance.

But what? How did one find the words for something that came so suddenly, so illogically, so inappropriately into one's life, upsetting plans, breaking vows, subverting all sense and reason? If he had fallen in love with her a few short months ago it might have been difficult. Now that he had formalised the agreement with Anne and her family it was quite impossible.

But then, everything seemed impossible to him. Where once his head had been full of bright and ambitious plans, it was now totally empty. He could not have a future with Barbara Lampett. But neither was he able to imagine one without her.

After his valet left him, he lay in silent dread, waiting for the strike of the clock. His father had been unnecessarily vague about the purpose of these visits. But he had said there would be three of them.

If he had seen the past and the present, then there could be little doubt that next would be the future. What if he had no future? It was quite possible that there was no future to see. If death was coming to take him, then he would be an angry spirit for having been kept waiting a night longer than expected.

If vengeance was due, then it was little more than Joseph deserved. He thought of his recent treatment of those around him, and the way Barbara had turned from him in disgust after only one night. She was right. He had used her, clinging to her like a lifeline in a stormy sea, trying to postpone what he'd known was coming.

If the coming shadow was no more than his death, he had waited too long to tell her what she meant to him. He would go to his grave in silence, and she would never know. He had given her reason enough to hate him. Perhaps that would be easier. Then she would not grieve.

He opened his eyes, aware of a change in the room. There was movement, but none of the light that the other spirits had brought with them. This future, whatever it was, was darkness. And the greatest cold yet. The very air around him was as the touch of the previous spirits, and it froze the breath in his lungs and the soul at his core.

He reached out to the darkness in the corner. Tonight it suited his mood to embrace it. 'Whatever you are, come and be done with it. I deserve all the punishment you wish to deliver. But if this is the end, then I request a boon. Give me one more day to make right what needs mending. Do not take me to judgement, knowing what I have left undone.'

There was no answer.

'Very well, then.' He sighed. 'I suppose that all men facing this have regrets. And if you granted wishes then it would be one more day, and one more, in a never-ending string.'

A deeper silence was his only answer. He could sense nothing: no amusement, condescension or annoyance from the thing in the corner. Only a feeling of waiting.

He studied it. The dark thing was man-shaped, and yet not quite a man. As tall as he. Cloaked, perhaps, for the outline of the head had a hooded quality. But only that. It seemed the harder he tried to look at it the less he could see. This lack of definition made him uneasy, building a fear in him that was worse than anything he might have imagined. If it had simply been some horror, he would have catalogued the deformity and recovered from the shock of it.

But this nameless, faceless thing taunted him with the idea that, if he struggled for a while, he would know it for what it was. It drew the tension in him out like a fine wire, making him wait for the snap of recognition that would cause him to go mad.

He deliberately looked away and stood, walking towards it. 'Come on, then. Take me to wherever it is that you mean to, and let us end this.'

He touched its hand. Or thought he did. For when he looked down there was nothing there. Yet the feeling of cold dry bones in his hands remained. This time they did not fly. They walked slowly—out of the bedroom, down the stairs and into the front hall, marching towards the front door, which swung open before them, engulfing them in a chill mist. He could feel the December wind rattling the leafless trees until they scraped against the windows and rustled curtains. And high on the icy gusts he heard a cry that was not so much a wail as a low moan. It came not from outside, but within.

As they passed the door of the salon he heard voices, and turned to view the tableau. A couple wrestled on the couch in a passionate embrace, near to devouring each other with the intensity of their kisses.

Anne looked as he had never seen her, beautiful but dishevelled. Her hair was free, her bodice loosened and her expression hungry. 'We cannot. We must stop.' Even as she said it she tore at the neckcloth of the man who held her.

'So you have said, for ten long years. Yet we never do.' Robert Breton kissed her again, pushing her hands away to pull at his shirt collar. 'Some day he will discover us. He is not a man who takes lightly the violation of what he considers his.'

Joseph's wife laughed bitterly. 'I doubt he cares. He must know by now. There have been no children. Nor are there likely to be. But he barely even tries any more.'

'Do not speak of your time together. I cannot bear to think of it.' His oldest friend reached up to smooth the hair away from his wife's face. 'You never should have married him.'

'But I did. And now it is too late.'

'You are still young,' he assured her. 'And just as beautiful as the day I fell in love with you, so many Christmases ago. Leave him. Run away with me.'

Do it, you faithless harlot. I do not want you. The words sounded clear in his mind, and in his heart. He wanted to scream at the harshness of them, even if they were true.

'I cannot.' Anne sighed. 'I do not love him, nor does he love me. But without me he would be alone.'

'You know that is not true.'

'I do not wish to think of that,' Anne whispered, with a sad little laugh.

'Then think of his work. He has the mill to occupy him. It is his one true love.'

'He takes no more pleasure in that than he does in me. When he is at home he wanders the halls at night, counting the rooms.'

Had the habit never changed, then? Even ten years later, was he still so unsure of himself that he needed evidence of his wealth?

'He drinks far too much.'

'All the more reason to leave him,' Breton encouraged her.

She shook her head. 'It is likely to be the death of him soon enough. I have looked into his eyes. He is not well. What harm would it do to wait a month? Maybe two? I will be a widow then. None will think it odd that we find each other.'

His old friend's jaw tightened imperceptibly at the

thought of further inaction. 'I will wait, if I must, for the love of you. I know how difficult it would be for you to leave here, and to admit to the world what has been going on between us. But if he does not finish himself soon, then it is not the drink that will end him.'

Anne clung to his arm. 'You mustn't say such things.'

Bob Breton, who was the mildest and most pleasant man that Joseph could name, looked colder than December. 'I think them often enough. I find it difficult to stay silent, with the cancer of it eating me from the inside. I said I understand why you stay, and I cannot fault you for it. He is your husband, and can offer much beyond the legality of your union. But that does not mean that I like it.'

He kissed her again, until she was near to swooning with desire for him. Then he spoke. 'I love you, Anne. But I cannot wait much longer. If he does not let you go with his own timely death I will do what is necessary to achieve the end necessary so that you might be free.'

Joseph waited for the denial, the pleading from his wife that would spare his life. Instead she was silent, but worried. She leaned forwards into Breton's shoulder, as though her only fears were for him. Breton's arm went about her, offering her the support that a husband should have given her.

Strangely, he felt no real jealousy at the sight—only sadness that it had come to this, and that two people so obviously in love had been poisoned to desperation with it.

'Enough of this,' he said to the shadow at his side. 'They hate me. There is nothing more to see. I am a cuckold, but at least I am alive. Take me to the mill, for I wish to see how it fares.'

They continued down the hall and out through the front door, across the lawn and into a mist so thick that the walk might have been one mile or ten for all he knew of it. There was no landmark to show him the way. Nor did he feel the passage of time as he walked.

They were standing at the mill gates now. The silent spectre reached up, resting a wisp of a hand against the gatepost, tracing a divot where a bullet had struck brick.

'There was trouble here, then?' There was no other evidence of it. The mill still stood, even larger than it had been when he'd last seen it, a decade before. He released an awed breath. 'Let me go inside.'

They entered through the dock, to see goods rolled and stacked in neat rows along the wall, ready for delivery. The boilers chugged and rattled, letting off heat and clouds of steam and the stink of sizing and dye. On the factory floor the looms rattled and the shuttles clattered in and out of the warp in a sprightly rhythm—the deafening sound of industry.

Everywhere he looked he saw workers: silent, sullen women and children, operating as surely and mechanically as the machines he'd made for them. From time to time they looked up with quick, rat-like glances at the clock. Then they hurried back to their work with a nervous shudder, as though they did not want to be caught looking anywhere but at their assigned tasks. It was functioning exactly as he'd hoped. And the sight of it filled him with a misery he could not describe.

'Very well, then. All I have worked for, all my dreams, will be like a mouth full of ashes to me in ten years' time. Is there more? Or will you take me home to bed?'

The shadow moved on, out into the fog again. There was nothing he could do but follow.

They walked down the high street of the village, a little way behind a hunched figure that seemed strangely familiar. Joseph quickened his pace to catch the man and end the mystery. But then he watched the villagers look up from their daily doings, stiffen and turn away. 'They see me?' he asked the spirit. If they did, it was not a connection he welcomed. While he had not been well liked in his own time, their glares now held a level of animosity he was not prepared for. What had once been reserve and suspicion had hardened into cold hatred. And it was all the worse because it was mostly the women who stared at him—not just the men who had always been angry.

In fact there seemed to be an unusual number of females.

Then a woman stepped directly into the path of the man in front of him, blocking his way.

The man he was following stopped dead in his tracks. He did not push past the stranger, but neither did he say anything, either in apology or enquiry. It was as though this was a ritual that had occurred before.

'Merry Christmas, Mr Stratford,' she said to the man he followed. 'I hope you are glad of it.' Then she spat on the ground at his feet.

Without a word, this other, older him stepped around her and continued on his way to the edge of the village, past the church and into the little graveyard beside it.

Not so little any more, Joseph noticed. Not huge, by any means, but larger than he would have expected. Had there been an epidemic? Or some other disaster to account for the additional graves? With little warning, the spirit at his side turned in at the gate and walked through the headstones to the last row of stones.

They were all names he recognised, for he had seen the men gathered around him just a few days ago, with hammers and torches, eager to push through the gates and smash the frames on the mill floor. Wilkins, Mutter, Andrews—and the eponymous Weaver, whose family had been at the craft for so long that they shared its name. All dead. All on the same day.

Had he called the militia? Or some other branch of the law? It could have been hanging, or just as easily a pitched battle that the local men were overmatched to fight. But the arrival of troops would explain the crease a bullet had made in the stonework at the mill. No matter what it had been, the rebellion had been stopped. And he had been at the heart of it. Calling in the law to protect his rights, and wiping out families in the process.

'It seems I won the argument in the end,' he said to the spirit. 'But there is no joy in knowing it.'

He looked down at another grave, some way distant from the cluster, and found Jordan—the man whose family he had seen starving just two nights ago. This man's stone was flanked with two smaller ones, topped with stone lambs. Joseph felt a chill, and found he did not have the nerve to look closer, for he was already imagining that table of hungry children, and the likelihood that whatever food was offered there now did not have as far to stretch.

The spectre gestured that it was time to withdraw, but he shook his head. Joseph searched the gravestones for one name in particular, knowing that if these men were here Barbara's father had likely died at their side, a victim of violence. She might have been hurt or killed, and the fault would lie with him.

'Where is Bernard Lampett? He must be dead as well. Why does he not lie with his friends?'

The ghost led him back to a monument worthy of a lord: a marble tomb, with brass fittings and a weeping angel at the top that shone with gilt. It was just the sort of grand thing he'd have ordered, had he the choice. It was garish and horrible next to the sad simplicity he had visited, but at one time he would not have been able to resist this final display of wealth. He fingered the letters carved in the side.

'Lampett. Dead the same day as the rest. And his wife three months later.' Whether she had passed from poverty or grief, he did not know.

There was no sign here of what had happened to Barbara. But he could read the truth in the marble. Whatever had occurred, she had been there to see her father fall and to know that Joseph was to blame for it. The crypt he stood before was the product of his own guilty conscience. He had buried her parents properly, hoping to assuage whatever obligation he had incurred from the deaths.

He would only have done that if Barbara were still alive.

'Take me to her. I need to know what has happened,' he said, not bothering with a name. If the spirit knew to show him this, then it knew everything. He glanced helplessly as it raised a hand in the direction of the village, and they set off down the road together.

They would not be walking if there was nothing to see. He tensed, knowing that if the lessons held to form the spirit had likely saved the worst for last. But he had to know the truth, and so he set an eager pace.

'If you have something to show me, then be quick about it. I think you have managed to teach the lesson you wished. I must change. Although how I will do it I am not sure. There are expectations on me, you know. I cannot throw aside my engagement with the promise that she will be better off. Nor can I let the profits go hang and the equipment be destroyed. I cannot just walk away from it all.'

In response, the spirit said nothing.

'And now you will show me Barbara. What has become of her, then? Has she forgiven me? I seriously doubt it. Does she hate me? What misery am I likely to see? How will you lay it all at my door? Surely these people deserve some credit in their futures?' he said. 'She could just as easily have made a hash of things on her own, without my help. She was well on the way to that when I met her.'

He might as well have been arguing with the fog, for all he heard was the echo of his own empty words. But even he did not believe them. Even if he could convince himself that her misfortunes were her own doing, or her father's, it would pain him to see them.

At least they were going back to the village and not searching the graveyard for another stone. Surely that meant there was hope.

If he could just see her, it would be all right. What he saw—whatever its cause—could be changed for the better, even if he had to move heaven and earth—he glanced at the spectre beside him—or perhaps heaven and hell.

They were stopping at the same cottage she lived in now, as quietly cheerful as it had ever been, despite what he had just seen of her family. It held the same air of peace that he had seen just the other day, with the path swept of snow and the holly bushes by the door carefully trimmed. But it was as if, with the passage of time, the presence of the two others who had lived there had evaporated. If he searched, he would find no pipe ash in the garden, nor papers scattered on the writing desk. And there would be no Christmas dinner big enough for three and whatever guests might stop.

They drifted through the door as though it was nothing more than mist, and he was glad. He was sure that the cold tended to get in with each opening of the door, and it had a way of lingering like an unwanted guest. At least she should be warm and comfortable in her own home.

She was not in the front room, or the little kitchen, and he drifted with the spirit towards the bedrooms, feeling like a voyeur but unable to contain his curiosity.

He was right to be ashamed, for she was not alone. Though it was the middle of the day she was in bed, the sheet pooling around her waist as she stroked the back of the man lying beside her. She was older, as Anne had been, but still as beautiful as he remembered her from the previous night. Her breasts larger, heavier, her waist thickening. He wondered, if he passed through the cloth that hung over the doorframe of the other room, whether he would find a cradle in use, or a row of tiny cots. Were there children playing in the garden behind the cottage?

But there was no sound of laughter in the house or the garden.

He did not like to think that she had made no family for herself. But she was looking up at the man beside her with such warmth that perhaps the future was not so very grim. If he had nothing else, he would know that she was safe.

Then her lover turned, and Joseph saw his older self, rising from the bed.

Without thinking, Joseph ran his hands over his own body, seeking reassurance of sound mind and limbs. Was this really what he would look like? Or did he have some bit of that in him now? Vanity had made him sure that he was handsome, and ladies had done nothing to dissuade him from the belief. But this new him was a strange thing—pale, hair shot with grey, face hardened into a frown, body spider-thin and beginning to stoop.

The other him rose from the bed, not even looking down at the lovely woman who reached for him, pulling on trousers, tugging a shirt back into place and hurriedly tying his neckcloth.

'You cannot stay?' Barbara held out a hand to him, inviting.

'Why would I wish to? You could not even manage to heat the room, though you knew I would be coming.'

If the words hurt her, she gave no sign of it. 'It is warm enough in my bed, is it not?'

'It would be even warmer in a larger bed, with softer sheets. I have given you ample opportunity to move to more hospitable lodgings, and yet you insist on remaining in this hovel.'

'It is my home,' she said simply.

'It forces me to come into the village in the middle of the day. You know how the people treat me. And we both know what they think of you because of my visits.'

She smiled sadly. 'I cannot help how they treat you. What they think of me is no less than the truth. I fail to see, after all this time, how I can change that.'

Joseph felt a hint of dread. How had it come to this? Just this morning she had left him with her pride intact. Lying with her had been a mistake. But he had intended something different by it. Surely it meant more than this?

The older Stratford scowled. 'I do not like it.'

At last he was showing some compassion, and Joseph looked on anxiously.

'It reflects poorly on me. I will build you a house—a fine one—with servants and proper receiving rooms. I will place it closer to the mill so that it will be more convenient.'

Joseph winced, for he could guess the sharp rejoinder he would receive. Barbara would put him in his place, right enough. Then he would apologise for his foolishness.

'But it would not be as convenient for me,' Barbara said softly, with a lying smile that was close to the one he'd seen most often on Anne Clairemont. 'It would cost you nothing if I remained here and you came more often, rather than staying so long at the mill.'

'You know I cannot put aside my work for you.' His

own voice was deeper, rougher and annoyed. 'If I leave the floor even for a minute there is mischief. Thieves and ruffians, the lot of them.'

'You work too hard,' she chided gently. 'And you are hard on those who work for you. Perhaps if you showed compassion…'

'There is no place for compassion in business,' he barked. 'Since you know nothing about it, it would be better if you learned to keep silent, instead of parading your ignorance.'

Her smile faltered. 'Of course. But if I speak it is only because I care too much for you.'

Why do you bother? This man was hardly worthy of her affection. Suddenly, Joseph realised that he was thinking of himself as a stranger, and feeling jealous of and angered by the way that individual had squandered the trust that he was working so hard to earn. Apparently he had not even the courtesy to come to her in the night, to conceal what they did from the eyes of her neighbours.

And Barbara accepted it from him. She allowed him to treat her so after all the things he had done to hurt her, soaking up his cruelty like a sponge.

The other him looked down at her, eyes narrowed in suspicion, as though he had no reason to take her kindness for what it was. 'I give you no reason to care. But thank you.' He reached into his pocket and withdrew a jewel case. 'For you. A tiara to complete your parure.'

'Thank you,' she said, with a misery that the older Joseph Stratford did not seem to notice. She did not bother to open the box, merely set it on a table at the side of the bed.

'You idiot,' he said to his other self. 'I have no taste to speak of. But even I know that she would have no use for a crown. How could you? You are treating her…'

Like a whore.

'You're welcome,' said the other Stratford, and his response was as false as her thanks. 'And good day.' He turned to go.

Barbara's shoulders slumped in defeat, but she did not rise to see him out.

Joseph stepped forwards, unable to stand it any longer. He tried to catch the arm of the man at the door and his fingers passed through it. He swung again, in frustration, with enough force to bruise, and yet felt nothing but the passing of the air.

'Stay with her,' he demanded. 'Hear me, you bastard. I know you can. I am the sound of your own voice in your head. Listen to me.'

There was the slightest flinch in the shoulders of the man, as though he had felt a slap.

'Stay with her, damn you. Or at least take back that jewellery. You cheapen her with such a gift.'

The man he would become twitched again, as though he were throwing off a lead, and strode through the door and out of the cottage, letting the door slam behind him.

Slowly Barbara leaned back into the bed, as though it were an effort to stay upright and maintain the pretence of happiness when he was not there to see it. Without a word, or so much as a whimper, her tears began to fall. He knew the meaning of tears like that, shed in such utter silence. He had cried like that as a boy, when he had been convinced that there was no future for him.

He could bear it no longer, and reached out to touch her. But when his hand touched her face it seemed to glide through, leaving only a momentary warmth on his fingertips. There would be no comfort in this for either of them. He moved to sit on the edge of the bed, so close that he should have been able to feel the warmth of her body against his leg.

Apparently she felt the cold in him, for she shivered. 'It will be all right,' he said softly, hearing the trembling in his own voice. 'I will make it better. It will never come to this. I swear to you. You will not cry, damn me for each tear. You will not cry.'

He leaned closer, letting the shadow of himself fall onto the shadow of her until they were as one body. He felt the fear and pain and confusion that was in her as though it were his own. Worst of all, he felt her despair. She knew with certainty that it would never be better than it was at this moment, and would most likely be worse. He was slipping away a little more with each visit. She could sell the jewellery. She did not need it. She would never know want. But she would never know love. How had it come to this? He had sworn to take care of her.

He felt her own guilt at her weakness, and her shame at betraying her parents' memories each time she touched him. But she had loved him from the first. She still loved him. It had never meant more than money to him, but she had wanted to believe otherwise.

And Joseph realised with a shock that there was no blame here for anyone but him. He had done this to her—had changed every element of her life, had taken her family from her. And what he had put in the empty place was nothing more than cold comfort.

He could feel the increasing impatience of the silent spirit at his back, tugging him free. He fought, trying to stay with her, wishing she could feel some bit of him and take comfort in it, or that he could take away with him some small part of the burden she carried.

But he was gone with a wrench, being dragged back down the street towards the manor. He looked back at the haze of the spirit, feeling tears wet his own cheeks, and he said, 'I can change. Let me change.' He reached out to grab at the hood of the spirit, forcing it to face him as he had been afraid to before.

It turned to him then, reaching a thin, pale hand to uncover its face and stare at him.

It was his own face staring back. Not the one he saw in the mirror each morning, nor even the hardened man that was stalking through this unhappy future. This was him as he would be fifty years hence—still breathing, but near the end. He would be strong and healthy, but nearer to a century than to fifty.

And his eyes. At first he thought them soulless. But there was a flickering of pain, like a tormented thing racing about in his head, and a twitch at the corner of his mouth that he could not seem to control.

Joseph stared at him, into those familiar gray eyes, into the darkest part of his own soul. 'I have seen enough. Take me back. It will be different. As it should be. I promise.'

The ghost's shoulders slumped, as though relieved of a weight. The tension in his mouth relaxed. His eyes closed. And an empty cloak dropped to the floor.

It was a blanket. Nothing more than that. It had slipped from his own bed, in his own room. He had chased it to the rug and was sitting upon the floor and staring at it in the light of Christmas dawn as though he had never seen the thing before.

Joseph gave a nervous laugh and shook it, as though he expected to see some remnant of his vision. 'All over. Merry Christmas.' He said it almost as an oath more than a greeting. 'It is over, and I live to tell the tale.' Not that he could, lest he be thought mad. But he was indeed alive.

To the open and empty air, he said, 'And I will remember it all, whether it be dream or no.'

He reached for the bell-pull and rang for butler as well as valet, thinking it would be easier to rouse the housekeeper through an intermediary rather than directly. It would take more than one hand to set his plan in motion. The whole house might be needed, even though it was just past dawn on Christmas Day.

CHAPTER SEVENTEEN

JOSEPH stumbled down the stairs one step ahead of his valet, who was still holding his coat. The shave Hobson had given him had been haphazard at best. But there was much to do, and he could not wait any longer for the butler to deliver his message.

'Mrs Davy!' He stood in the centre of the main hall and shouted for the housekeeper. It felt as though he were taking his first deep breath in an age, after being deep underwater.

The poor woman hustled into the room, hurriedly tying her apron, a look of alarm on her rosy face.

He gasped again and grinned at her, amazed at the elation that seemed to rush in along with the plan. It made him feel as he had on the day he had first thought of the new loom—full of bright promise. Only this was better.

'Mrs Davy,' he said again. 'My dear Mrs Davy!' And then he laughed at the look on her face.

She took a step back. 'Sir?'

He had worried her now. Though he was not a cruel master, when had he ever taken the time to call anyone dear?

'I have more work for you. I take it the larders are still full, and ready to feed my non-existent guests?'

She gave a hesitant nod. 'There was much more than was needed, sir.'

'Then we need to do something with the bounty. Baskets. Baskets and boxes—and bags. Bowls, if you must. I want you to search the house and fill every container available with the excess. Enough to feed every family in the village. While you are about it make enough for a box for every servant here. Make sure that you and your helpers take enough for yourselves as well. Empty the pantry. I wish to give it away.'

'Sir?'

Had he really become so ungenerous as to cause this look of surprise? If so, it was all the more reason to change his ways—with or without the intervention of ghosts.

'I want,' he said, more slowly and with emphasis, 'everyone in the village to have as happy a New Year as I am likely to. It will not happen for any of us if I sit alone in a house that is barely half full, and they sit in the village with empty cupboards and fears for the future. I have broken a tradition. I mean to mend it now. As quickly as possible.'

'Oh, sir.' She was grinning at him now, as though he had fulfilled her fondest wish by forcing her to labour on Christmas Day.

'If you can fill the baskets, I will take the carriage into the village. And a wagon as well. I will see to it that they are delivered. And with them I will send an invitation for this evening. All who wish to come must dance and drink and be merry.'

'Yes, sir!' She was already bustling back towards the kitchen, disappearing as quickly as she had appeared, as though borne on a cloud of enthusiasm.

'What the devil is going on?' Breton was approaching from the stairs, still wiping the sleep from his eyes. 'Stop making such a racket, Stratford, or you will wake the whole house.'

Joseph grinned at him. Good old Robert. Loyal Bob, who must be sorely conflicted by his feelings of late. 'A Merry Christmas to you, Breton.' He seized the man's hand and shook it vigorously. 'And may I take this moment to say I never had a truer friend, nor a better partner?'

'I might say the same of you,' Breton said, looking quite miserable. Then he took a deep breath. 'That is why I must speak. I know it is not the time or place, but there is something I wish to discuss. I did not get a wink of sleep last night, and I do not think I can stand…'

'Not another word.' Joseph held up his hand to stop

the confession that he suspected was coming. 'I wish nothing more for this Christmas than that you save any difficult revelations for after New Year's Eve. If you feel the same way—'

'I doubt a few days will change my mind on what I wish to tell you,' the man interrupted. 'For I wish—'

'...after I break my engagement with Anne.'

'...to go back to London. I...' They'd spoken on top of each other. And now Breton looked as if he wished to suck his last words back into his mouth. 'I beg your pardon?'

'I am going to speak to Anne. We both know that she does not love me. I am quite sure I will not make her happy. No matter how much business sense it might make, it is wrong to catch her up in it and force a union which might be disagreeable to her.'

'There are certain expectations...' Breton said cautiously.

'And they are all about this house. Well, damn the house. I do not want it,' Joseph said firmly. 'I would be quite content with something smaller. With fewer rooms, and not so many ghosts.' He laughed again. 'Her father can have it off me for a breach of promise settlement. That is what he wants, after all. Unless...' He grinned at Breton. 'Unless you would be willing to take the thing off my hands? I expect you would be troubled endlessly by Clairemont, of course. He seems to have the daft idea that his daughter shall be mistress, no matter what she wants. You'll be in his sights for a husband then, I am sure. You'll likely have to take her with the deal.'

'How dare you speak of her in that way? As though she were property to be traded!' Breton was simmering with rage and quite missing the point.

'I cannot trade a thing I never possessed, Bob.' He gave his friend a significant look. 'I doubt that my leaving will create much heartache for Miss Anne Clairemont. But can there be any doubt that such a lovely girl will be married by spring? I should think there is some gentleman who would wish to fill the void I leave. If I knew of him, I would urge him to act quickly—use the disarray I'm likely to leave in the Clairemont household to good advantage and whatever bait might come to hand to clinch the deal.'

'I see.' But he did not seem to. Breton's face was still wary.

'If there is a man who loves her as she deserves, I would wish him well.' To finish, he gave Bob a hearty clap upon the back, as though to jolt the man out of his lethargy.

'I see. Yes, I think I do.' The grin spread slowly across his friend's face as his plans for the future came clear.

'I think you do.' Joseph grinned back at him. 'And a Merry Christmas to you, sir.'

'I think it shall be.'

'Now, what was it that you wished to say to me earlier? For I do not think I quite heard it.'

'Nothing,' Bob said, waving a hand to scrub the air of his words. 'Nothing at all other than to wish you well.'

'That is good. For this might be a trying day for you. What do you think our London friends are likely to say if I bring the whole of the village back with me for Christmas dinner?'

Breton thought for a moment. 'I expect they will be horrified.'

'Well, apparently, it is the custom in these parts. I cannot keep alienating the workers, or there shall be hell to pay.'

'You might lose some investors,' Breton warned. 'Feathers are likely to be ruffled on your fat pigeons.'

'Then I shall have to win them back another way. Or I shall find others. But let us see, shall we? I mean to visit Anne next. Perhaps I can enlist the aid of her father in smoothing the way with the Londoners. If he does not throw me bodily from his house first.'

Joseph's carriage pulled up to the door of the Clairemonts' new home and he wondered why he had not taken the place for himself. He had deemed it too far from the mill and rejected it out of hand. But, even with the addition of a wife and children, twelve rooms and a modest staff would be much closer to his needs than the monstrosity he now owned. How had he been so foolish?

He was admitted, and waited patiently in the parlour for Miss Anne, who was preparing for church, relieved that their current bond would make his appearance seem somewhat less alarming to the household. How they would feel about him in a quarter-hour was likely to be a different story. He wondered with a smile if he should have instructed his coachman to keep in his seat, whip in hand, for the hasty escape they would need to make.

There was a wild scrambling in the hall, followed by a sudden pause and the sedate entrance of Miss Anne Clairemont. The single curl out of place on her beautiful head and the lopsided bow of her sash were the only evidence that he had caught her unawares. She gave a graceful curtsey, as though allowing him the moment to admire her, and then asked sweetly, 'Did you want me, Mr Stratford?'

'I have come to ask you the same thing, Miss Clairemont.' It was a bold question, but his morning was a busy one, and there was no point in beating around the bush. He watched as her pretty face registered confusion. 'Come, let us sit down and talk awhile.' He sat. Bob would have been horrified, and reminded him that he could not go ordering young ladies about in their own homes, nor sitting when they stood.

But this one did not seem to notice his lapse, and perched nervously on the couch at his side, waiting for him to speak.

He took her hand. 'Before we go another step on life's road, Anne, I must know the truth. Do you want me?'

'I…I don't understand,' Anne said firmly. But the

truth of it was plain on her face—if only he could get her to admit it. 'In what way? Your visit is unexpected, of course, but not unwelcome.'

'I do not mean to ask if you want me now—this instant. I mean as a husband, and for life. Do you desire my company? I wish to know the reason for our upcoming union.'

'You wish to cry off?' Now her face was a mix of hope and dread, and a trembling that was the probable beginning of tears.

'I have asked and you have answered,' he said, as gently as possible. 'And that is how it will remain, if you truly wish it. Do not think I will cry off and leave you.' He paused and looked her clearly in the eye. 'If to have me is the thing that will truly make you happy.'

'Of course I am happy.' Her face fell.

If she persisted in this way he would have no choice but to marry her. Or perhaps he should arrange a match between her and the Aubusson. As she was making her heartfelt declaration she could not seem to take her eyes from the rug at their feet.

'You have honoured me with your proposal. My family stands to gain much by it. It will secure my future. Why would I not be happy?'

That sounded almost as if she asked herself the same question. It gave him reason to hope.

'Then now you must do something for me,' he said. 'Consider it a gift for our first Christmas.'

She looked up, quite terrified. 'I do not think… After

we are married…of course…but now? It is Christmas morning, Mr Stratford. And this is my parents' parlour.'

He laughed at her total misunderstanding of him, and at her obvious horror at the prospect of the conjugal act, wondering about how much she might have already learned from his friend about inappropriate acts of passion. If this was her view of him it was quite beyond a display of maidenly resistance, and much closer to active distaste. 'What I am requesting is nothing like what you expect. If we are to marry, we will be together for a long time. The rest of our lives, perhaps.'

He should not have said *perhaps*. He should have been more definite. That alone should have told him of his own heart. For once they were joined there would be no reprieve.

'And I should think, if we can give each other nothing else, we deserve mutual honesty—to be given without fear of recrimination. I have reason to suspect that you might be happier if you had been able to accept another. And that the primary goal in taking me is to help your family return to the place of social prominence it once held. If that is the truth, there is no shame in it. But would it not be better to state it outright, so that there can be no confusion?'

She blinked at him, unable to speak. But neither did she offer the quick denial that would have corrected a mistake.

'Now, tell me the truth. In one word. Do you love me?'

'It is not really expected, when one is of a certain

class, that one will marry for love,' she said, as though by rote.

'Nor is it expected that they will give a simple answer to a direct question,' he countered, but without any real irritation. 'But am I to assume, from your misdirection, that your answer is no?'

'I respect you, of course. You have many worthy and admirable qualities that would make a woman proud to be your wife.'

He sighed, for she was not making this easy. 'Then I am sure, since you have such respect for me, that you will be happy to hear that this morning I have taken the first step towards selling your old house to Mr Robert Breton.'

There was a moment of blankness on her face, a deliciously unattractive drop of her jaw and a sudden and complete lack of composure. It was the first sign of humanity he had seen in her. Then she spoke—not in the decorous half-whisper that he had grown accustomed to, but a full-throated, unladylike shout.

'Father!' She stood and shouted again. 'Father! Come downstairs immediately. I am about to break my engagement with Mr Stratford.'

Next, the carriage stopped at the first door in the village. His groom made to get down and take a package, but Joseph held up a hand. 'It must be me, I think. At least for the first few houses. Simply hand things to me, and I will be the one to knock.'

The first door was opened by a child. Before she could run for Mama, Joseph thrust the basket into her arms and shouted, 'Merry Christmas!' and then turned away to receive the next hamper and walked the few steps to the next door.

There. Not so bad, he told himself. He had half feared that there would be a punch upon the nose and a slammed door before he could get his gift across the threshold. At the next house he saw a wife. After that he found one of the weavers most vocal in opposition to him still in nightshirt and cap.

Joseph pushed the basket into his arms, with a hurried 'Season's Greetings!'

'I suppose this is to make up for the trouble you've caused?' the man said sceptically.

'It is mince pies,' Joseph answered, lifting the corner of the cloth. 'And a ham. While it lacks the supernatural power to mend our differences, it will at least be good with warm bread. I believe there is some wine as well. More concrete and useful than an apology, I should think. But you can have one of those as well. The rest can wait until Twelfth Night.' He turned away to get another basket.

With the man still standing dumbstruck in the open doorway, Joseph began to walk down the street. From the corner of his eye he saw the man turn as well, shouting back into his house. As Joseph walked he could see the man darting down a side street, and heard a pounding on a back door somewhere ahead of him.

He delivered his next basket, and the good wife who took it accepted it with a hesitant smile and a nod of confirmation—but none of the surprise that he had seen in the first houses. From then on he could almost hear the buzz as the news preceded him down the street with shouts, pounding footsteps and lads panting in kitchens to relay that the old dragon Stratford had gone mad and was giving away his hoard. A crowd was growing behind him as well, for just as the news ran ahead, out through back doors and down alleys, the consequences were trailing him like a parade.

At last he came to the Jordan house, and pushed a particularly large package into the man's hands as the door opened. 'Mr Jordan,' he said happily. 'A Merry Christmas to you. And—' he lifted the corner of the napkin that covered the gift '—a brace of partridge, cheese, oranges, sweets for the children, mince and a bottle of milk with the cream still floating on the top. Children need milk, Mr Jordan. And yours will not want for it once you have accepted the position of foreman at my mill.'

'Mr Stratford?' The man could not manage anything else, not even a thank-you.

'You needn't say more right now,' Joseph assured him. 'But you might help with the distribution of the rest of the packages in the wagon that is following my carriage. I have another important errand to run that will take me away from it. While you are about it, could you be so kind as to invite your neighbours to the manor this evening? The doors will be open, just as they always used to be.'

Jordan managed a weak nod.

'There's a good man. I will see you this evening, shall I?' Joseph looked at his watch.

Then he turned and ran.

The Lampett cottage was on the edge of the village, almost into the country, and set back at the end of a short drive. Joseph could feel the collective eyes of the people on him as he went. It was very near the same crowd as he had seen rioting at the mill. But where he had felt rage and distrust on that occasion he now felt a kind of wary encouragement pressing him forwards. The gifts he had offered had done much to disperse their ill will. But how they felt about him in the future would depend on his reception at this last and most vital of houses.

And none of it mattered, really. Not for the reasons they thought. While he might argue trade and tariffs until the last trump, he would have to agree to disagree with her father, and manage his troubled mind as well. But as long as they could be in agreement on one thing none of it would matter to him.

The winter air was sharp, and he ran until he could feel the pain of it in his lungs, in his side. Then he ran further, as he had when he was a boy and had no money for horses and no use for them either. It was good to be alive—to see the robins flitting in the bare branches of the few small trees in the garden, to kick the hoarfrost from the twigs and see it shower to the ground in a sparkle, and to hear the sound of the Christmas church bells growing louder as he neared the front gate and ran through it and up the drive towards the house. He did not stop even as he reached the door, but banged his body against it, striking knees and palms flat against the wood as he might have when playing tag as a child.

He peeled himself away to knock properly. Then he laughed and hammered on the door with his fists, heedless of the way it must look.

And then the door opened.

CHAPTER EIGHTEEN

FROM her bedroom, Barbara could hear the pounding on the door, and then her father arguing with someone in the parlour.

Why must he act up on Christmas morning? It did not help that she was already feeling quite fragile, nerving herself for the curious glances she was likely to receive in church today. She did not think she could stand a scene from him as well. Mixed in with his rising voice she could hear the chill tones of her mother, who was never able to soothe him.

She looked in the mirror, straightening her brown merino church dress with trembling hands. She could think of only one thing that would cause such strife and anger to both of her parents. But would anyone be cruel enough to tell tales about her on this of all days? If that was the problem, she had best go and face it herself, for neither parent was likely to be up to the task.

When she went into the parlour she saw her father standing in the doorway, his shirt collar open, neckcloth in hand. Mr Joseph Stratford was crumpling the linen of Father's cravat with a vigorous handshake. Her mother stood to the side, looking like nothing so much as an outraged hen when a cat was stalking in the chicken house.

Joseph glanced past her father to her, smiling as though he had not a care in the world. 'Good morning to you, Miss Lampett. And a Merry Christmas.'

'What are you doing here?' she asked, rooted to her spot in the doorway to the hall. Why could she not stop looking at him, cross the room, push him out of the house and shut the door? Why did he have to look so well, so handsome and so much more vital and alive than he had after their night together? Did he mean to show her how well he did without her? Surely he must know that she drank in every detail whenever she looked at him.

Joseph realised that he had not released her father, and let the hand drop suddenly, turning to her mother with a deep bow. 'And to you, Mrs Lampett. A Merry Christmas. I do not think we have been formally introduced.'

'I know just who you are.' Her mother said it in a way that would tell him where he stood with the whole of the family.

He grinned in her direction, as though to say, *Just you wait. Things are about to get interesting.*

Remembering how purposely obtuse he could be when he had a goal in sight, how utterly heedless of others, she gave a warning shake of her head.

'I suppose you are wondering why I have come here in this way, at this hour, on this day.'

'I am wondering if I shall have to put you out,' said her father. 'I assure you that I am quite capable of it, should you make any more trouble.'

Father was no more capable of success in that than in flying to the moon. But this was hardly the time to call attention to it, so Barbara put in, as meekly as possible, 'I certainly hope that will not be necessary.' She shot Joseph an evil glare. 'If I could just talk to you outside for a moment, Mr Stratford? We might settle whatever it is that brings you here, and continue our preparations for church.'

'But I did not come to speak to you, Miss Lampett. At least not just yet. I promise I will be brief.' He gave her the quickest of apologetic smiles, and then returned to her father. And, if she was not mistaken, she saw a twinkle in his eye.

He was making fun of her. After all that had happened he was amusing himself at her expense. She would be sure he was brief, indeed. The first time he stopped speaking to take a breath, she would haul him by the neck from the room.

'Then proceed, sir. Have you have come to threaten me with arrest again?'

Oh, dear. This would be one of the days when Father

was clear of memory and in a foul temper. Barbara's mind worked furiously to come up with a distraction that would separate the pair of them.

'On the contrary, Mr Lampett. I have come to ask for your help.'

This was so shocking a request that it reduced the whole Lampett family to silence.

Mr Stratford used the pause to his advantage. 'You know that I mean to reopen the mill in a few weeks, and that there are likely to be more workers than positions available? This concerns me greatly.'

'It does?' her father said, stupefied at this reversal of positions.

'You know the people better than I, for I am near to a stranger. I can think of no one better qualified to help me find other employment for them. I would compensate you, of course, for it would take a fair amount of your time. Then, if I can persuade Robert Breton to be its patron, we will likely be reopening the school. You would be needed there as well—either as a teacher, or in an advisory capacity.'

'I don't know what to say.' And clearly her father did not. The onslaught of new ideas had stopped his anger in its tracks.

'You need not make a decision now. Think on it for a time. I am opening Clairemont Manor this evening for the annual Tenants' Ball. Perhaps there will be time for us to discuss it then. But feel free to share my ideas with any in the village you might meet. They are in no way secret. I mean to find employment of some kind for all those who are willing to work.'

'I will. I will at that. Margaret!' He gestured to his wife. 'We must go to church immediately. We will see many of the men affected. I will broach the subject to the vicar as well.'

'You will broach it after the last hymn,' her mother said severely.

'Of course.'

But Barbara could see by the look in her father's eye that he was unlikely to hear much of what was preached, and would spend the next hour scribbling pencil notes in the back of his prayer book that would become a stirring and inspiring speech on the subject.

Father grabbed for his hat and opened the door, as though he'd quite forgotten that there was a guest present.

'One more thing before you go, sir.' Stratford touched his arm. 'Might I request your daughter's hand in marriage?'

'Certainly,' her father muttered. 'Margaret, what have I done with my muffler?'

But her mother could manage nothing more than a squeak of surprise.

'It is on your neck, Father,' Barbara said weakly.

'Very good, then. Let us go to church.'

Her mother recovered her composure and shot an exasperated look around the room. 'After we have tied your neckcloth, Bernard.' She struggled with his collar button and the rumpled linen. 'We shall go on ahead—and you, Barbara, shall meet us there. Mr Stratford, if we do not see the pair of you in the family pew before the end of the first hymn… Well, I do not know what we shall do. But I trust you to behave as a gentleman.'

'I do not know why you would, ma'am,' Joseph said with a smile. 'Perhaps you do not know me as well as the rest of your family does. But you can trust me in this, at least. I will take good care of your daughter.' He gave another respectful bow as Barbara's parents withdrew, leaving them alone.

Barbara shot a helpless look after them as the door shut. Then she turned to face Joseph. 'And just *what* is the meaning of this, Mr Stratford?'

'I should think that would be obvious,' he said, with another smile. But there was no mischief in it. He was looking at her as if he had never seen anything so wonderful.

'There is nothing obvious about it. Was it not just two days ago that you made public your betrothal to Anne Clairemont?'

'And this morning I broke it.' He reached out to take her hand, running a weather-roughened finger across the back of her knuckles.

'You did not,' she said, pulling her hand away from him. 'Anne will be heartbroken.'

'She most certainly will not,' he answered back. 'She is utterly besotted with my friend Robert, and thoroughly glad to be rid of me.'

'You knew?' She breathed a little deeper knowing that the dark secret she had uncovered was no secret at all.

'I concur with her. They are very well suited. But to make sure that there is no trouble with her father I am selling Bob the house. Lord Clairemont will have what he wants, and Anne will marry the son of an earl and the man she loves. And no one will be forced to marry into trade.' Then he looked at her more seriously. 'Not even you, if you do not wish to. Marry me, that is.'

'It might be the wisest thing,' she admitted quietly. 'After what happened the other night.'

'You could marry me because it is the wisest thing to do,' he agreed. 'But I would rather you didn't. If it is only out of concern for your reputation I would understand. But I was rather under the impression that you had strong feelings for me.'

Must I confess everything again? Though it is true that I love you, I am tired of being your plaything. She bit back the foolish words that she wanted to say, and fought the desire to throw herself into his arms quickly, before he found a way to ruin it all again. 'I would much rather hear your reason for wanting to marry me. What could I possibly have that you need, Mr Stratford?'

'My heart,' he said simply. 'I think you must have taken it with you when you left yesterday. It is not clockwork, as you said. If it was, I should be able to replace it.'

'You are clever with machines,' she admitted, doing her best to still the fluttering in her own breast.

'It turns out I am flesh and blood, after all. And likely to make quite a mess of things if I am allowed to go on like this. I have given up my fiancée and my manor. I have walked through the village handing over so much food that I am not sure there will be anything left for supper—nor money to buy more, now that I have promised to employ the whole village. And to top it off I will likely frighten my London investors by letting the rabble into the house this evening.' He held out his open arms. 'I am a disaster in the making, Miss Lampett. Someone should take me in hand while I still have a penny left in my pocket.'

'Not me, surely,' she said with a little smile. 'For I would not change a bit of you. It was a wonderful thing you just did for Father.'

'I doubt it will solve all his problems,' Joseph said, taking her hand again. 'But perhaps, if he has a purpose and a different direction for his energies, we might harness a portion of his madness and do some good with it.'

'That is a far cry from threatening him with a one-way trip to Australia,' Barbara noted. 'That was the tune you were singing to me just a few days ago.'

'I find I cannot stomach the idea of a father-in-law who is a convict,' he said, with a wry twist of his mouth. 'I might be in trade, Miss Lampett, but even I have some standards.'

'You seem quite sure I will accept you.'

'Because I will not take no for an answer.' He dropped to one knee then, and gave her hand a squeeze. 'I have seen the future, Barbara. While I cannot claim that I will die if you do not have me, I am quite certain that it would not be worth my living without you.' He dropped his head to plant a kiss on the back of her hand, humbled and at her feet.

'Oh, do get up.' She nudged at him with the toe of her shoe. For she'd had a sudden memory of what had occurred in the little alcove the last time he'd knelt before her. And she was sure her face was burning bright red.

'Not until you say yes.' He looked up hopefully. 'I have no ring to offer you, but you may have whatever you like. And I promise that I will not waste money on a gaudy parure with a tiara that you do not need.'

'That is the most outlandish thing I have ever heard,' she said. 'What sort of man gets down on his knees and swears that he will *not* buy his wife jewellery?'

'One who is so totally undone by love that he is no longer sure what he is saying.'

'You are undone by love?' She was not sure she believed him. But she quite liked the sound of it.

He nodded. 'And running out of time to plead my case. The church bells have stopped. Soon your mother will be coming back to box my ears.'

'Then I had best take you, hadn't I?' She stepped back and tried to tug him to his feet. 'For I rather like your ears just as they are.'

'Do you, now?' He stood and caught her around the waist, pulling her close for a kiss. 'I like yours as well. And your nose. And your eyes. And your fingertips.' He followed each revelation with a brief kiss to the honoured feature, and then put his mouth to her ear and whispered several other things that he appreciated, but that she was quite sure she should not let him see again until the banns had been read.

'It is Christmas,' she reminded him. 'And broad daylight. We are expected elsewhere, and already late.'

He sighed. 'Then put on your bonnet and we will be off.'

'I suppose you've brought your carriage again?' she said, tying up the ribbon on her new hat.

Then he proved to her that he had truly changed. For he reached into his pocket and tugged on his gloves, before setting his hat upon his head. 'Actually, no. It is not far, and such a nice day I did not bring it. We shall have to walk.'

'Together?' she said with a smile.

'I would have it no other way.'

* * * * *

Snowbound with the Notorious Rake

SARAH MALLORY

Sarah Mallory was born in Bristol and now lives in an old farmhouse on the edge of the Pennines with her husband and family. She left grammar school at sixteen, to work in companies as varied as stockbrokers, marine engineers, insurance brokers, biscuit manufacturers and even a quarrying company. Her first book was published shortly after the birth of her daughter. She has published more than a dozen books under the pen-name of Melinda Hammond, winning the Reviewers' Choice Award in 2005 from Singletitles.com for *Dance for a Diamond* and the Historical Novel Society's Editors' Choice in November 2006 for *Gentlemen in Question.*

Look for more fabulous novels from Sarah in Mills & Boon's Historical romances.

Dear Reader,

When writing a book, it is not unusual to be describing one sort of weather while living through something quite different. However, when I was writing *Snowbound with the Notorious Rake* I was experiencing just the same winter weather as my characters! Living high up on the Pennines we can have quite harsh weather and this winter we had a prolonged spell of ice and snow, turning the moors into a winter wonderland but making the roads impassable. Luckily I love this kind of weather and wrote most of this book curled up with my laptop before a roaring fire, with the snow flinging itself against the window—sheer heaven!

Being snowed in can be wonderful—as long as everyone is safe and there are sufficient supplies of food and fuel. There is a great sense of isolation; the rest of the world seems so distant that it no longer matters. This is what happens to my heroine, Rose, when she finds herself stranded at a lonely house on the moors. It is an escape from the tedium of her real life. Is it any wonder that Rose soon finds herself succumbing to the fairytale setting and the charms of the house's owner? It does help, of course, that Sir Lawrence is just the sort of man to melt a maiden's heart!

I was born in the West Country and it was such a pleasure to set this story on Exmoor. However, I decided not to use real places for the major settings of my story, preferring to let my imagination run wild—something that is very easy to do in such a wild and beautiful part of England. I do hope you enjoy *Snowbound with the Notorious Rake* and I wish you all the happiness of the season.

Sarah Mallory

To Marianne, Paul and Steven, who lived with a distracted mother and had to fend for themselves while I wrote this book.

CHAPTER ONE

THE drawing room of Knightscote Lodge was considered by many to be the ideal room for a cold winter's night, the beamed ceiling and polished oak panelling being declared perfect by the romantically minded. Certainly with a cheerful blaze in the huge fireplace and the golden glow of the candles, the room looked warm and welcoming. However, its present occupant was sunk low in his armchair, his booted feet resting on the hearth as he stared moodily into the fire, a half-filled wineglass held casually between the long, lean fingers of one hand.

It had started to snow earlier in the day and now it was swirling against the tiny diamond panes of the windows, driven by the howling wind. Sir Lawrence Daunton raised his head as a particularly fierce gust rattled the casements. It occurred to him that if the blizzard continued no one would be able to get along the lane for days.

'Good,' he muttered the word aloud as he drained his glass.

It was Christmas Eve. When he had ridden down to his hunting lodge on the edge of Exmoor a few days earlier he'd had two objects in mind. The first was to avoid all company during the festive season; the other was to get very, very drunk. With the second of these worthy aims in mind, he reached for the bottle standing on the table at his elbow. It was empty and he was making his way to the servants' quarters in search of another when he heard a loud hammering at the door. Lawrence stopped.

'Who the hell can that be?'

With great deliberation he put down the empty bottle and picked up a lantern. His footsteps rang on the flagstones as he walked to the door. It took him a moment to wrestle with the locks and the catch, but at last he flung the door open.

A blast of icy air took his breath away.

As did the vision standing in the shelter of the porch.

Before him was a young woman enveloped in a powder-blue-velvet travelling cloak. The hood was edged in white fur that framed a pale, delicate face with a straight nose, generous mouth and a pair of blue-grey eyes fringed with dark lashes.

All this Lawrence took in immediately, but even as he blinked to see if the vision would disappear, she stepped quickly into the hall, saying, 'Do not keep me standing in the snow! Pray tell your mistress that Mrs Westerhill would like to see her. Immediately.' This last word she added a little sharply, for Lawrence was still staring at her. She continued, 'And my groom is outside with the horses. Perhaps before you shut the door you could direct him to the stables.'

Lawrence blinked. A gust of wind sent another flurry of snow into the hall where it fell gently onto the dark flags and dissolved.

'Yes. Excuse me.' Quickly he stepped outside, pulling the door closed behind him, and ran across to where the hapless groom was holding the reins of two horses. A few words of instruction and Lawrence hurried back into the house. The hall was empty, but a trail of wet footprints led off towards the drawing room, where he found the lady warming her hands by the fire. She had discarded her cloak to reveal a high-necked gown of deep-blue wool, unrelieved by any ornament save a small edging of white lace at her throat and wrists. The severity of the gown was alleviated by her abundant honey-brown hair, which fell in soft ringlets to her shoulders.

'Well? Have you told Mrs Anstey that I am here?'

'Er…no.'

She straightened, fixing him with a frowning look.

'This *is* Knightshill Hall?'

'Alas, no,' he replied. 'This is Knights*cote* Lodge. Knightshill is on the Stoke Pero road.'

'Oh, heavens. Then this is *not* Mrs Anstey's house.'

'No. You must have missed the turning.'

Lawrence watched as her small white teeth momentarily gripped a bottom lip that was as full and red as a ripe cherry. Her eyes travelled about the room and for the first time she seemed aware of its untidy state.

'*Is* there a mistress in this house?'

Lawrence's eyes danced. 'Not at the moment.'

'Then perhaps you would inform your master…' She trailed off as she looked up and read the merriment in his face. 'Oh, heavens.' Her hands came up to her mouth, and her eyes with those ridiculously long lashes stared at him in horror. 'Oh, pray do not tell me *you* are master here.'

'Very well,' he said promptly, 'I won't.'

Her eyes twinkled, but she said severely, 'Pray do not be absurd. If you are the master, then tell me your name.'

'You do not know?'

She shook her head.

'I must appear dreadfully ignorant, sir, but I do not venture abroad often; we keep very much to ourselves.'

'I am Daunton,' he announced, watching her closely. 'Lawrence Daunton.'

Immediately the humour left her face and she retreated a step.

'*Rake* Daunton?'

He grinned, saying with some satisfaction, 'So you *do* know me.'

'I know of your *reputation*,' she retorted. 'When I said we keep to ourselves I did not mean we do not know what is going on in the world. I have an aunt in town who writes regularly and the society pages of the London newspapers provide a rich source of entertainment. Your name is never out of them!'

'All gossip and innuendo, I assure you.'

'Oh, heavens!' She put her hands to her cheeks. 'This is so dreadful!'

He folded his arms. 'More dreadful than it was five minutes ago? I thought we were getting along famously.'

Her eyes flashed.

'Not only am I stranded miles from my home, but my companion is one of the country's most notorious rakes.'

Lawrence spread his hands.

'I pray you will acquit me of planning this!' Some spirit of mischief made him add, 'I have never yet had to employ such base tactics with any woman.'

She did not appear to believe him and looked about her anxiously.

'Are there any other females here?'

'Not one.'

'Oh, good gracious!' She snatched up her gloves. 'Then I must go immediately.'

'Go where?'

'To Knightshill Hall. Coming here was a dreadful mistake. The snow was covering the sign at the gateway and only the first few letters were visible. I was sure this must be it.' She straightened her shoulders, put up her head and announced formally, 'I will take my leave now; I beg your pardon for disturbing you.'

She walked to the door, but Lawrence made no effort to open it for her.

'Oh, but I cannot let you go.' Her eyes widened with sudden alarm and he added, 'You cannot cut across the moor in this snow, and it is too far to travel by road; it is a good mile back to the crossroads and another few miles from there to Knightshill Hall.'

'Oh. Well, there must be another family close by who will give me shelter.'

She fixed her hopeful gaze upon him and for a moment Lawrence was almost sorry to disappoint her. Almost.

'I'm afraid not. This is a hunting lodge, you see. Designed to be away from all other habitation. We are in the middle of nowhere.'

She took the news very well, her dismay only showing in her eyes, which darkened a shade to slate grey.

'Well,' she said at length, 'then we must try to get home. If you will show me the way to the stables, I will talk to my groom.'

Lawrence shook his head.

'He has probably just finished settling the horses.'

'Then he must unsettle them,' she retorted. 'We must be on our way again, and as quickly as possible.'

Lawrence walked over to the window.

'Of course, but I do not think that will be tonight.' He held out his hand, inviting her to join him. 'Come here and look.'

She approached, but was careful not to stand too close to him as she peered out. It was still snowing heavily, the wind driving the flakes almost horizontally across the window.

'But we might get through it, at least back to Exford…'

'Out of the question.' He drew the curtains together, belatedly shutting out the night. 'There is no house or shelter within miles of here, and in this blizzard it would be madness to attempt it.'

'Then what am I going to do?'

For the first time Lawrence heard a note of uncertainty creep into her voice. He put his hand under her elbow and guided her back to the fire, gently pushing her down onto a chair.

'I am going to fetch a bottle and you are going to drink a glass of wine with me.'

As soon as she was alone, Rose jumped to her feet again. She walked back to the window and peeped out through the curtains. Perhaps she had been mistaken; perhaps it was not as bad as she had first thought.

If anything it was worse. The snow continued to fall in thick white flakes, tossed about by the wind that gusted and howled around the old house. Restlessly she picked up her cloak and spread it over a chair to dry, then she returned to her seat by the fire to consider her predicament. She was alone in this house with a libertine. No, not quite alone—Evans, her groom, was with her, although she had no idea exactly where he might be. Perhaps Sir Lawrence had overpowered him. Poor Evans might even now be languishing in a cellar! Quickly Rose dismissed such thoughts, scolding herself for being fanciful. So far Sir Lawrence had behaved with perfect decorum. True, he was dressed very informally, but then he had not been expecting visitors. A fierce gust of wind rattled the window and whined down the chimney, reminding her of the tempest raging outside. She had not taken much notice of the house as they rode up, too thankful to see the welcome light shining from the window. It was similar to other old manor houses in the area, a low, rambling building with a gabled roof. Inside, it was furnished for comfort rather than fashion: heavy dark furniture and panelling was alleviated by richly coloured cushions and wall hangings as well as quantities of gleaming brass and copper. She looked about her. The room was clean enough but it had an air of untidiness, cushions disturbed, empty glasses on the mantelpiece, as if there was no one to clear up after the master.

The master.

Rose found her thoughts turning to that disturbing individual. Really, it was no wonder that she had thought him a servant, appearing in topboots and breeches, with his waistcoat undone and his shirt open at the neck to display a very improper view of his chest with its smattering of crisp, black hair. And that dark shadow on his jaw, too, signalling the fact he had not shaved today. When he'd opened the door to her she'd had the impression of a giant, his black hair brushing the lintel and his wide shoulders filling the doorway. Standing together in the narrow hallway, she had found him quite overpowering. That was why she had made her way to this room, preferring to have a little more space between them. Of course, now she knew just who he was, she realised she was right to feel nervous.

She jumped as the door opened and her host came in carrying a bottle. He went to a sideboard and proceeded to fill two glasses. His hand was steady enough, but it occurred to her that he might be drunk—that would account for the glitter she had noticed in his blue eyes. It was more of a glint, really, a twinkle, inviting her to share his amusement. She found it both alarming and attractive, which was extremely worrying. She would need to keep her wits about her and resolved to take no more than one glass of wine with him.

'Where is my groom?' she asked as he handed her the wine.

'In the kitchen. I told him to make himself comfortable there. And if he keeps the fire going it is one less task for me.'

'You have no servants here?'

'No. I sent them away to enjoy Christmas with their families.'

'Why—?'

He shook his head, lowering himself into a chair on the opposite side of the hearth.

'I have answered enough questions. I think you should tell me what you are doing abroad on such a wild night.'

Was there anything she could say that would not add to her vulnerability? Playing for time, Rose took a sip of the wine. It was rich and fruity and surprisingly comforting.

'I have been taking flowers to my husband,' she said at last. 'I am a widow, you see. My husband died on this day four years ago, and since that time I have visited Exford twice a year: on his birthday, and every Christmas Eve, to place flowers on his grave.'

'But that is not where you live now?'

'No. I live at Mersecombe.'

'Mersecombe! It must be all of ten miles from there to Exford.'

'No more than eight, surely. And it was not snowing when I left home.'

'And of course one expects perfectly sunny weather in December.'

'I have made the journey quite safely for the past three years!'

'Only a ninnyhammer would set out on such a journey at this time of the year.'

'Then I am a ninnyhammer,' she said, sitting up very straight.

For a moment he stared at her and she tensed herself, expecting another sharp response. Instead he said quietly, 'I beg your pardon. To make the journey to Exford in the middle of winter—I admire your devotion.'

Almost without realising it Rose fluttered her hand, dismissing his comment. It wasn't devotion that had drawn her away from Mersecombe that morning. A touch of guilt, perhaps, that her husband was so rarely in her thoughts these days, combined with a restlessness that was increasingly hard to bear. Riding to Exford with just her groom for company gave her a temporary freedom from the ties of duty and responsibility. Not that she resented those ties, they were forged out of love, but when she had left home that morning she had been aware of a longing to be free to do just as she wished, even for a short while.

Seeing the gesture, Lawrence smiled.

'At least accept that you have great determination.'

'Thank you, but it does not help my predicament. There is no getting away from the fact that I am in the most horrendous fix, being here, alone, with you.'

'Many women would envy you.'

'And I would gladly exchange places with them!'

Her candour made him laugh.

'Point taken, madam—by the bye, what is your name?'

She shook her head at him.

'I do not think I should tell you. It is not fitting that we should know one another.'

'Dash it all, I cannot call you "ma'am" for ever! Besides, I have only to ask your groom.'

Rose imagined an undignified race to the kitchen, where she would order Evans not to disclose her name. It would be too foolish.

'I…am Rose Westerhill.'

'Very well, Mrs Westerhill, let me assure you that I have no designs upon your virtue. I came here to get away from the world.'

'Why?'

'That, madam, is no concern of yours.'

He sounded irritated, which suited Rose very well—

surely there was less chance of him becoming amorous if he disliked her? She replied with great cordiality, 'No, thankfully it is not. Well, there is no hope of going anywhere until the morning.' She slanted a challenging look at him. 'Is there a spare bedroom, or shall I be obliged to sit up here all night?'

'Oh, there are plenty of bedchambers, but none is prepared.'

'If that is all, I am sure I can manage to put sheets on my bed.'

'Yes, but it's where to *find* the sheets.'

A smile tugged at her mouth.

'If you will show me your housekeeper's quarters, I will endeavour to locate them.'

'Very well.' He emptied his glass and jumped up. 'Shall we go and look now?'

She put a hand to her rumbling stomach.

'I would rather find something to eat first.'

He nodded.

'To the kitchen, then!'

Rose followed her host through the dark, chilly passages to the kitchen, where they found Evans sitting in a chair beside the hob-grate. He took off his cap and rose as they came in.

'So you have banked up the fire here—good man.' Lawrence nodded. 'You found all you needed in the stables?'

'Aye, sir. I shall check the 'orses again before bedtime, but they are snug as bugs out there.'

'You will need somewhere to sleep,' said Rose, casting an enquiring glance at Sir Lawrence.

'There's plenty of space above the stables, but the scullery boy has a bed in the small room off the kitchen—behind the fireplace. You might be more comfortable there.' Lawrence paused as another icy blast spattered against the window. 'You would certainly be warmer.'

'Aye, I spotted the bed.' Evans nodded. 'I'll settle down there, if you've no objection.'

'Just make sure you take your boots off before you climb between the sheets,' Rose warned him and earned a pained look.

'I's lived in a gennleman's 'ouse for long enough to know *that*,' the groom retorted.

Lawrence strode across the room and lifted the lid of a small black cooking pot balanced on the hob. An appetising aroma filled the room.

'I guessed this was for your supper, sir,' remarked Evans, 'so I put it in the flames to heat up.'

'Yes, my housekeeper, Mrs Brendon, said she had left something for me. Hmm. Not much for three of us.' He went into the larder and began to investigate the pots and tubs kept there. 'There's a little bread, and a ham—plenty of rice and flour—and a basket of vegetables. Oh, and lemons.'

Rose had found an apron and tied it over her gown. She picked up a wooden spoon and gave the soup a stir.

'Is there a hen house?'

'Why, yes,' said Lawrence, backing out of the larder. 'I believe there is, on the far side of the yard.'

'Then there may be an egg or two, even at this time of the year. Perhaps you would go and fetch them.'

Sir Lawrence's black brows went up.

'Me?'

Rose gave him an innocent smile. 'I would ask Evans, or course, but I need him to fetch in more peat for the kitchen fire.' She held out a small basket. 'You may need this.'

Without a word Sir Lawrence took the basket and slouched out of the room.

'I could've done that *and* fetched in the peat, Miss Rose,' opined Evans, when the door had closed again.

'I am sure you could,' murmured Rose, stirring the soup. 'But it will do Sir Lawrence no harm to cool his—er—head out of doors for a while.'

Lawrence pulled his hat a little lower over his face and tucked his chin into his muffler as he bent into the wind that howled across the yard, throwing icy needles of snow against his cheeks. Damnation, he had been looking forward to a quiet evening, drinking copious amounts of wine and perhaps helping himself to a little soup and bread before he went to bed. Now all that had changed and he was obliged to find enough food for his visitors.

He wished it had been a man at the door; then they might have enjoyed a drink together, perhaps played at cards and made do with the ham and cheese from the larder. Or even a lightskirt—that would have been entertaining! Instead he was saddled with a respectable widow who looked set to take over his kitchen. One, moreover, who expected him to work for his supper! A laugh shook him. This was *not* how he had envisaged spending his Christmas!

Half an hour later Sir Lawrence was back in the kitchen, shrugging himself out of his greatcoat.

Rose counted the eggs in the basket.

'Half a dozen, how clever of you to find so many, and in the dark, too!'

'Thank you, ma'am.'

She glanced up at him, her eyes alight with laughter.

'Oh dear, do I sound as if I am talking to a child? Forgive me, but you remind me very much of my own little boy.'

Lawrence almost winced. A masterly set-down, designed to put him firmly in his place! He looked around the kitchen.

'Where is Evans?'

'I sent him to the drawing room with more logs. I thought we should eat there; I had a quick peep in your dining room, but it is so cold it would take for ever to warm up.'

'You are willing to risk dining alone with me?'

'It cannot be helped. Poor Evans would not eat a thing if we imposed ourselves upon him here in the kitchen. I shall have to trust you to behave yourself.'

Again that minatory tone.

'I believe I can remember how to act as a gentleman.'

'I do hope so. It will be much more comfortable for

us all if you do.' She treated him to a smile. 'Perhaps you will be good enough to set the table? It will take me but a moment to cook the eggs.'

'I take it you know *how* to cook?' he challenged her.

'But of course. My mother thought it very important that I should learn something of the art. I am going to make a pancake of the eggs and add a little ham. We will follow it with the soup.'

'Excellent.' Lawrence realised how hungry he was. 'I will fetch out a bottle of good wine to enjoy with our feast!'

Sir Lawrence said nothing untoward during dinner, but Rose could not forget his fearsome reputation. Since her husband's death she had not dined alone with any man and sitting at the small dining table with Sir Lawrence seemed almost indecently intimate. She was disturbingly aware of her companion. With his tall, athletic form and darkly handsome features she could understand why he was so successful with women; even his informal dress and the dark shadow of a beard on his chin did not detract from his charm—if anything, it was enhanced by the element of danger. She sipped at her wine, determined to have no more than one glass: Sir Lawrence might be a model of propriety now, but there were many long hours to go before morning.

As the evening wore on and his behaviour towards her remained perfectly correct, Rose began to relax and their conversation became more natural. He asked her about her life and she found herself telling him about the home she shared at Mersecombe with her mother and her young son.

'Why did you not stay in Exford, if your husband is buried there?'

She made no comment as he filled her glass again. Should she tell him the truth—that she had wanted to escape from the pitying looks and whispers? That she had found the memories just too painful?

'I was obliged to sell up to pay his debts.' That was also the truth. Suddenly it was a relief to talk to someone. 'Harry was a dreamer. When we moved to Exford he thought the farm would provide a living, but he would not listen to advice.' She sighed. 'He sacked his manager, who was a local man, and brought in another who knew nothing of the land. By the time Harry died there was nothing left but debts and the deeds to Hades Cove, a worthless mine. I sold the house and the farm, but by the time I had paid off the creditors there was precious little left. I took Samuel back to Mersecombe, where my mother has a neat little house. We manage very well and I supplement our income by running the church school.'

'Ah.' His eyes glinted as he smiled at her. 'You are a schoolteacher. That explains your managing ways.'

His smile robbed the words of offence and she found herself smiling back at him, fascinated by the way the candlelight gleamed in his blue eyes. It really was very attractive. A tiny wisp of desire stirred deep inside. She looked away, conscious of the need to maintain her defences.

'You should be thankful for my managing ways,' she replied crisply. 'Heaven knows what would have happened if I had not taken charge of the kitchen this evening.'

'I would not have been sent off like a lowly scullery boy to collect eggs!'

'Oh dear, did you really object to that?' She turned back to him, a laugh gurgling in her throat. 'But you did it so *well*!'

'Do not try to turn me up sweet with your flattery, madam.'

The glinting smile in his eyes reassured her.

'Well, if you had not been such a ninnyhammer as to send all your staff away...'

He laughed at that, a real, full laugh, and Rose thought how much younger he looked. How carefree. Again she felt that little tingle of desire and quickly repressed it. The man was a rake; she must keep her distance.

Their meal over, Evans came in to collect the dishes and carry them away to the kitchen. Rose would have followed, but he shook his head.

'You prepared the meal, madam, 'tis only right that you should rest awhile.'

She sat back, glancing across the table at Sir Lawrence, who said, 'I am in your debt, Mrs Westerhill, I do not know when I have dined so well. Since the rest of the house is so chill, I cannot suggest that you withdraw, so instead I will invite you to join me in a glass of brandy.'

It was tempting—the glowing candlelight, the wine, the roaring fire—but Rose dared not relax her guard.

'That is very kind, sir, but there is more work to do. We have yet to prepare a room for me.' She spoke as if it was the most natural thing in the world for her to be sleeping in his house. Not by a blush or the flicker of an eyelid would she betray her nervousness. 'Perhaps we could seek out the linen cupboard?'

She tensed, half-expecting a knowing look or *risqué* comment, but Sir Lawrence merely nodded and pushed back his chair.

'Come along, then. I am not familiar with Mrs Brendon's part of the house, but I am sure we shall find something.'

The house was cold, dark and full of echoes. Rose kept close to Sir Lawrence, who was carrying the lamp. Too close. When he stopped suddenly she cannoned into him. His hand shot out to steady her, but his warm touch through the thin sleeve of her gown made her tremble even more.

'I—I beg your pardon.' Her voice was little more than a croak. 'I stumbled. The uneven floor…'

'Ah.' His hand slid down her arm and he caught her fingers. 'Then let me help you.'

She did not pull away. It was only sensible to accept his support. And she felt so much safer with her hand tucked into his large, comforting grasp.

They walked on in the little pool of lamplight until they reached a corridor with a series of cupboards built along one side. Lawrence began pulling open the doors. One was crammed with pewter dishes and an old dinner service, another held neatly folded suits of servants' livery. A heady scent of summer herbs wafted over them as he opened a third door.

'This is it,' murmured Rose.

Sir Lawrence stood to one side, holding up the lamp to display orderly stacks of white linen.

'Very well, madam. Help yourself.'

Rose stepped up. Soon she had a pile of sheets, pillowcases and bolster covers in her arms.

'Let me carry those for you.'

Rose shook her head at him.

'No, no, they are not heavy. If you will just show me the way to the bedroom?'

He placed his hand under her elbow and guided her back along the corridors.

'I think you would be most comfortable in the Blue Room,' he told her. 'It is one of the smaller chambers, but that will make it easier to keep warm.' He threw open a door. 'Here we are.'

Rose did not move from the doorway as he went around the room lighting the candles in the wall sconces. A large tester bed took up most of the floor, the mattress shrouded in a plain white cover.

'It has no hangings, I'm afraid,' remarked Lawrence, twitching off the dust sheet. 'But there are plenty of blankets and an elegant cover, embroidered by some previous lady of the house, no doubt. And the mattress is very comfortable.'

Rose found herself wondering how he knew that—what sort of guests had he entertained here before?

Best not to think of that. She put down the pile of linen.

'Thank you,' she said briskly. 'Now, if you will excuse me, I will get to work.'

'Can you manage on your own?'

'Perfectly well, thank you. I am not such a lady that I cannot make my own bed.'

'Very well. Then I will light the fire for you.'

'Oh, there is no need. Evans can—'

'Evans will have plenty to do checking on the horses before he retires.' He added, 'I am not such a gentleman that I cannot light a fire.'

'No. Of course.' She smiled at him. 'Very well, then, thank you.'

In a remarkably short time the bed was made and a fire was burning steadily in the hearth. Sir Lawrence stood to admire his handiwork for a few moments.

'It is still early,' he said, turning to her. 'Will you join me in the drawing room for a little while and give the fire a chance to warm the room?' When she hesitated he shook his head at her. 'I have nothing more sinister in mind than conversation, madam.'

'I thought you had sent your servants away because you wanted to be alone.'

'I did, but your presence in my house precludes me from carrying out my original plan, which was to drown my sorrows in a bottle.'

He spoke lightly, but Rose heard the underlying

bitterness in his voice. She caught the fleeting shadow of pain in his eyes.

'Perhaps you would like me to prepare some coffee?'

'No, we will save that for the morning.' He was smiling again. '*I* shall make us some hot punch!'

CHAPTER TWO

THE fragrant aroma of lemons and cloves greeted Rose when she returned to the drawing room a short time later. A small iron pot was suspended over the fire and Sir Lawrence was leaning over it, thoughtfully stirring the contents. He did not look up immediately and she took the opportunity to watch him, noting the way the dark coat strained across his broad shoulders, admiring the long, powerful legs encased in buckskins and top-boots. The firelight glinted on his black hair and heightened the strong lines of his handsome face.

Many women would envy you. His earlier words flitted through her mind.

He looked up and smiled as she approached.

'I thought you might have fallen asleep.'

'I went to speak to Evans.'

'And is he comfortable?'

She chuckled.

'Very. Especially so since you gave him leave to help himself to the cider!'

'I hope he will not regret it in the morning.'

'I trust Evans not to drink too much; he knows we will need to be on our way as soon as may be once it is light.' She sat down in one of the two armchairs he had pulled close to the fire. 'You are shaking your head, sir. Do you think I am too optimistic?'

'If the snow continues, then the roads may well be blocked.'

She shrugged. 'Then we will ride across the fields. I have done that before.'

Lawrence filled a rummer with hot punch and handed it to her.

'What a resourceful woman you are, Mrs Westerhill.'

'I am a widow, sir, and needs must be resourceful.'

Rose settled back in her chair, savouring the hot, sweet punch. What had happened to her resolution not to drink more than one glass of wine? She pushed the thought aside.

The wind had dropped and the only sounds in the room were the steady tick of the clock and the crackle of the fire. Lawrence occupied the chair opposite, his booted feet resting on the hearth. His gaze was fixed on the leaping flames, but Rose sensed that his thoughts were far away. The drooping curve of his mouth reminded her of his earlier words.

'What did you mean, sir, when you said you wanted to drown your sorrows?'

She thought for a moment that he would not answer

or would change the subject with a careless word. She was about to offer him an apology for her impertinence when he spoke.

'Some fourteen months ago, my fiancée died of a fever.'

'Fiancée!' She flushed as his scorching glance swept over her. Her incredulous exclamation was insulting. After all, she knew nothing about the man, except gossip. 'I b-beg your pardon,' she stammered. 'I thought—I did not know—'

'How should you? It was never announced. The betrothal was of very long standing. Even her death was accorded no more than a line in the society pages, easily missed. Our betrothal was not a secret, but it was unremarkable.' He held up his glass and stared at the dark liquid. 'It has always amazed me that my indiscretions are emblazoned throughout the society news sheets, but my sweet Annabelle, whose short life was so full of kindness and charitable acts, was not considered worthy of a paragraph.'

'You say it was a private arrangement, sir. Were her parents against the marriage?'

'Oh, no. Why should they be, when it would mean the combining of our two estates? It had been arranged between the families when we were children. We are neighbours, you see, and it was always understood that a marriage between the Cravens and the Dauntons would be most advantageous.' His lip curled. 'But I was not to be constrained. I would go to London, sow my wild oats, then return to Hampshire to the family seat and marry my childhood sweetheart. Only before I could do so, she caught a fever and…died.'

'I am very sorry.'

'So, too, am I. Last Christmas I returned to Daunton House. It had become the custom, you see, for both families to be in Hampshire during the winter season. My parents died some years ago, but there are the aunts, uncles and cousins, as well as the whole Craven family. They descend upon Daunton and the Craven estate to spend Christmas together. But with Annabelle gone—' He broke off, giving his attention to refilling his glass. 'It was the condolences,' he said harshly. 'Everyone was so dam—dashed sympathetic. What had I ever done to deserve their compassion? Instead of commiserating with me on my loss they should have berated me for neglecting poor Annabelle, condemning her to her quiet life with her charities and her good works while I scorched my way through society like a—a comet, bent upon my own destruction. That is why this year I determined I would not go back. I would come here and—'

'Wallow in self-pity.'

His head shot up.

'Why should I not?'

'No reason at all.' Rose held out her rummer, not speaking again until he had refilled it. 'What was she like?'

'Annabelle? An angel. Patient, forgiving—'

'She sounds more like a saint,' observed Rose. 'To sit at home year after year while you spent your time on routs and revels! Good heavens, if *we* could read about your…exploits here, so far from London, surely she must have done the same?'

'Of course.'

'And she never once took you to task over your wild ways?'

'Never.' His black brows snapped together. 'And just what does that look mean?'

'I beg your pardon. It is none of my business.'

He pushed himself upright in his chair.

'You are quite right, of course,' he said, fixing his hard eyes upon her, 'but since we have come this far, pray do not stop now. Explain yourself.'

Rose hesitated.

'I do not understand why her family—or yours—did not express their disapproval at your excesses. I admit they make very entertaining reading—my mother is an avid follower of the crim. con. and the latest *on dit*—as is my aunt and most of her friends!—but I think they would feel very differently if it was anyone connected to us. The lady's family must have been aware of the damage you were doing to yourself.'

'Of course they were. Annabelle's brother George spends his time in town and he knew exactly what I was about. But as long as I did not damage my *fortune*, they were all happy to turn a blind eye.'

Again she heard the bitterness behind his words. Pity stirred, but instinct told her it would not do to show it. Instead she said thoughtfully, 'Well, I think it is a very good thing that you did not marry her.'

The silence that followed Rose's announcement was as brittle as glass. She sipped at her punch, trying to look unconcerned while a pair of piercing blue eyes bored into her.

'Would you care to explain?'

His voice was dangerously quiet. She had the impression of sitting opposite a tiger who was ready to spring and she had to steel herself to continue.

'I cannot see that you would have been happy. Unless, of course, you intended to live apart.'

'That is not at all what I intended.'

'So you planned to settle down with a woman of whom you knew nothing—'

'I beg your pardon! I told you we were neighbours. The families had known each other for years.'

'Truly? Did you grow up together, like brother and sister?'

'Of course not. I was sent off to school before Annabelle came out of the nursery.'

'Perhaps you played together during the holidays?'

'Well, no. George and I were friends, but Annabelle did not enjoy good health…'

'And once you had reached your…*understanding*, she was quite happy to let you go off and…sow your wild oats.'

'By heaven, ma'am, I am no worse than her brother, or most of the men in town!'

'Pardon me, sir, but if only half the reports I have read are true then you are *much* worse than most!'

He gave a savage bark of laughter.

'Only because I do not hide my peccadilloes. In actual fact, they are not so very bad—my worst crime is that I enjoy the company of beautiful women and they seem to enjoy mine. But I will not pay to have my name kept out of the news. I am not such a hypocrite.'

'That, of course, is to your credit, sir.'

Rose returned his furious gaze with one of limpid innocence, but she noted how those long, lean fingers whitened around his glass. She thought it just possible that he might strangle her.

He drew a deep breath, as if containing his anger. 'I never lied to Annabelle. She knew what I was.'

'It seems you made no effort to conceal it.'

'She also knew I would change when we were wed.'

'Hah!'

'The devil, madam! You dare to dispute with me?'

'Well, there has certainly been no shortage of news about you this past year, sir.'

'With Annabelle gone I have had no reason to change my way of living.' When she said nothing he put his rummer down with a snap. 'Do you think a man cannot change?'

She fixed her eyes upon him.

'A snake may shed its skin, Sir Lawrence, but it is still a snake! If you had married this poor woman, then one of two things would have occurred: you would have been heartily bored within a month or you would have continued your wild career and broken her heart. You might even have managed both.'

With a smothered curse he leapt out of his chair.

'Confound it, how dare you say such things to me!'

'Well, it is about time someone said them,' Rose retorted. 'It seems to me the poor girl was to be married without any consideration for her happiness, or yours. Do you honestly believe she was content living her solitary life, waiting for you to decide when it was time to settle down?'

'Yes! Yes, she was. In fact…' She waited, watching him as he strode about the room. After a while he stopped and rubbed a hand across his eyes. 'I admit I was surprised that she was so content with her lot. I sometimes wondered if she really *wanted* to marry me.'

'Perhaps she did not.' She added drily, 'Charming as you may be, a libertine does not make a good husband.'

He came back to his chair and threw himself down again, slanting a quick glance towards her. 'You really do not think very much of me, do you?'

Rose looked away.

'You do not think enough of yourself, sir.' She finished her punch. 'It is getting late, I should retire.'

Immediately he was on his feet.

'I will escort you.'

'Oh, no, that is not necessary—'

He was already at the door, holding the lamp. He tilted his head, listening as the long-case clock chimed the hour.

'I remember how nervous you were earlier. How much more so will you be now it is midnight?'

His kindness surprised her. She had angered him, criticised his way of living, yet still he could consider her comfort. She did not argue, merely took the proffered bedroom candle and allowed him to lead her up the stairs. Their conversation rattled around in her head. Perhaps she had been too outspoken, but he was a rake and she despised rakes. But it was no business of hers how he chose to conduct himself. Still, she was a guest in his house and she did not like to think that she had been impolite. A fleeting glance at his face told her nothing.

'This is your room.' He stopped. 'Goodnight, Mrs Westerhill. Let us hope the snow has eased by the morning and you can continue your journey.'

'Sir Lawrence! What I said earlier—if I offended you, I am most sorry.' The look he bent upon her was unfathomable, but the flickering shadows made his features seem harsh and uncompromising. She hurried on, 'I was taught never to let the sun set upon a quarrel.'

'I thought what you said to me was more in the nature of…home truths.'

She dragged up a smile.

'You are regretting your kindness in giving me shelter.'

The harsh look fled from his eyes. He said with a touch of humour, 'I cannot recall I had any choice in the matter.' He reached for her hand and raised it to his lips. 'Goodnight, Rose Westerhill. Content yourself with the fact that you have given me much to think on.'

Rose stepped into her room and leaned her back against the closed door. She was trembling, but not with cold, or the effects of their harsh words. It was shock at the bolt of wanton lust that had shot through her when he had pressed that final kiss upon her hand.

Lawrence opened his eyes and lay very still, watching the play of light upon the ceiling. Something was amiss. He was at his hunting lodge, it was Christmas Day, but his head was unusually clear.

Then he remembered.

He slid out of bed and reached for his dressing gown. He had a visitor. A respectable schoolteacher who dared to lecture him—him!—upon how he should grieve for Annabelle. Well, the sooner Rose Westerhill was on her way and out of his life the better.

It took only a glance out of the window for him to know she would not be going anywhere today. The snow had fallen heavily all night, covering the ground with a thick white blanket and piling heavy drifts against the walls. There was a knock at the door.

'Come in!'

Evans entered.

'The mistress's compliments, sir. She sent up hot water. Said as how you would want to wash and shave before you came down to breakfast.'

'Did she, now?'

'Aye, sir.' The groom fixed his eyes somewhere over Lawrence's shoulder. 'She also said you shouldn't dress too fine, even though 'tis Christmas Day. She said there's work to be done!'

The clock was chiming ten when Sir Lawrence strode into the kitchen. Rose heard his impatient tread and turned towards the door. Her heart, which had become very unreliable recently, leapt to her throat and then began to hammer against her ribs.

I knew it. I knew he would be unbearably handsome!

When she had seen him last night with his hair untidy, clothes dishevelled and a day's growth of beard upon his cheek she had thought him a rogue, albeit one with kind eyes and a blinding smile. Now he appeared before her clean-shaven, his hair brushed until it gleamed glossy as a raven's wing and she was sure the snowy whiteness of his starched neckcloth would not have looked out of place in a London salon. His brown jacket appeared to be moulded to his frame, but no more so than the tight buckskins that clung to his thighs. She had heard that some gentlemen deliberately shrunk their breeches to make them fit so tightly. His certainly left little to the imagination. Her mouth was so dry she could not speak.

'Well—' his deep voice was rich with laughter '—do I pass muster?'

She blushed vividly.

'I asked Evans to tell you not to dress up today.'

He glanced down.

'This is my usual country wear. Nothing special. The coffee smells good. May I have some?'

'What? Oh—oh, yes. Of course.'

With a supreme effort Rose pulled herself together.

'I found some muffins that your housekeeper had left for you. And there's honey and butter…'

'Excellent. Have you eaten yet?'

She shook her head.

'Then we shall break our fast together.'

They sat down at one end of the big table and toasted the muffins before the fire. Rose found herself relaxing, enjoying the companionship—there could be no false airs when one was licking butter from one's fingers. Sir Lawrence was watching her over the rim of his coffee cup. She smiled.

'Oh dear, have I made a terrible mess? There is no dainty way to eat these things!' She picked up her napkin and wiped her lips.

He put down his cup.

'You have butter on your cheek. Here—let me.' He took the napkin from her fingers and leaned closer.

Rose held her breath. His hand was on her cheek, but his face was just inches from hers, so close she could see the tiny laughter lines around his eyes, follow the curl of each dark lash, study in detail those incredibly blue eyes. When she breathed in she was aware of the clean, fresh scent of him. She had heard that the Prince Regent used a perfume water scented with roses. Whatever fragrance Lawrence favoured it was not roses, but a much more subtle blend of herbs—lavender, perhaps. His hand stilled on her cheek and he looked down, exposing her to the full force of his gaze. Rose knew she must say something, and quickly.

'Wh-what is that fragrance you are wearing, sir?'

The blue eyes never wavered from her face.

'It is from France. Eau de cologne.' The corners of his mouth twitched. 'I am sorry to say Bonaparte's endorsement has made it rather unpopular in England. Do you not approve?'

Oh, yes, she thought, her senses swimming as she breathed in the heady fragrance.

She cleared her throat.

'It is not for me to approve or disapprove, sir.'

He was still hovering over her, tantalisingly close. 'Most ladies seem to like it.'

The words were provocative. She should give him a set-down, but it was impossible. He was still staring at her and she could not tear herself away. But then, she did not wish to. All her virtuous resolutions had deserted her. She was drowning in a pair of blue eyes.

'By gum, 'tis a cold 'un.'

A blast of icy air enveloped them as Evans came in, knocking the snow from his boots before shutting the door. The groom's entrance had freed Rose from her inertia. Heavens, how close she had come to disaster! She rose quickly and began to gather up the dishes, clattering them angrily together.

'Bad, is it?' Sir Lawrence asked him, unperturbed.

'Aye, sir. Nothin's travelling today, that's for sure. Miss Rose asked me to go down as far as where I guessed the main track should be, but the drifts are terrible deep. Once the packhorses have pushed through, then we can follow their trail, but I don't expect to see 'em today. 'Tis Christmas Day, after all.'

'So it is!' Sir Lawrence turned back to Rose. 'Let me be the first to wish you a Merry Christmas, madam.'

'Do you mean to say we will be stranded here for another day?' she demanded.

Sir Lawrence grinned.

'At least.'

It occurred to Rose that her host was not at all upset by the news.

'When do you expect your staff to return?'

He shrugged.

'I had told them to come back tomorrow. However, if it snows again that may change. If we cannot get out, *they* will not be able to get in.'

'You do not seem very put out by the prospect.'

'Why should I be? Mrs Brendon has left the larder well stocked with ham and cheese, probably biscuits, too.'

'Enough for you alone, perhaps. But…cold meats on Christmas Day?' She rose, brushing down her apron. He had accused her of being a managing female—she would prove him right! She said briskly, 'Very well, then, we must get to work. Evans, have you checked the stables yet?'

'No, ma'am. There's a gert snowdrift across the door.'

'Well, I think you should dig it away and look after the horses.'

Sir Lawrence stood up.

'I'll give you a hand—'

'No, sir, I have another job for you.' Rose gave him her sweetest smile. 'I am afraid, Sir Lawrence, that the occasion calls for a sacrifice.'

Sir Lawrence scowled. 'This is a damned unusual Christmas!'

Rose chuckled.

'I know, Sir Lawrence, but needs must, as they say.'

They were in one of the outhouses, surrounded by feathers.

'I only hope these birds were not the best layers,' he muttered. 'Mrs Brendon will have something to say when she returns.'

'But, my dear sir, we must have something to eat today.'

He cast a fulminating glance in her direction.

'My requirements were quite minimal. A slice of ham, a bottle of wine…'

'But it is so cold I am sure your housekeeper will be pleased to know you are going to eat a proper meal,' replied Rose, trying not to smile. 'I have almost finished plucking my bird, Sir Lawrence. You do not seem to be making much progress with yours. But I acquit you, since you were the one who had to despatch the poor things.' She looked up and laughed. 'Fie, Sir Lawrence! I do believe that, at this moment, you wish it had been my neck that you had wrung!'

His mouth curled in a reluctant grin.

'I admit I was sorely tempted, ma'am, when you told me what you wanted me to do.'

'But you will enjoy your meal, sir, I promise you.' She put aside her own bird and reached for his. 'Let me finish that for you, Sir Lawrence.'

He looked at her, his brows raised.

'Why do I have this suspicion that you will find me something equally onerous to do now?'

'No, no, not at all.' She laughed at him. 'I only want you to go and make sure the fires are banked up! Evans has fetched in more peat, but you might wish to refill the wood basket.' She added, in the way of a treat, 'When you have done that and I have prepared these birds for the spit, perhaps we should step out and see for ourselves just how bad the roads are.'

The blizzards of the previous evening and the overnight snow had given way to a gloriously clear blue sky. The glistening white world shone just outside the door. Rose was dazzled by its brightness. She longed to go out and explore it, but she had spent years teaching her pupils that leisure time was much more enjoyable when it was earned, so she carried the two hens to the kitchen and set everything in readiness for dinner before she allowed herself even to think about going out of doors.

When she ran upstairs to collect her cloak she stopped for a moment to gaze out of the window. The world was transformed by a blanket of white. She thought of her family back at Mersecombe. They would have realised how impossible it was for her to get home. She hoped they would not be too anxious; little Sam would not worry at all, he would be much too excited by the first real snow of the winter, but Mama—she knew Rose had Evans with her and would surely believe her daughter was sensible enough to take shelter. Rose gave a little laugh. Sensible! If her mother could see her now she would think her anything but sensible, stranded in a large old house with a man whose licentious reputation was known countrywide! But, in truth, what else could she do? The sensible thing had been to remain at Knightscote and it was eminently sensible to make sure they had a good meal. Humour bubbled in her throat again. Perhaps she could have fainted off, or had hysterics when she realised just who her companion was, but Rose could not see that such behaviour would have benefited her at all. No, she would just have to make the most of it. Her family would be at church now, so she uttered up a little prayer for them as she picked up her cloak and set off to join Sir Lawrence downstairs.

The sun was high over head as they left the house.

'I am surprised you are willing to quit your new domain,' remarked Sir Lawrence as they set out across the courtyard.

'It is not my domain,' she told him. 'Evans is only too happy to sit in the kitchen, smoking his pipe and keeping the fire in. My presence is not required.'

They left the grounds by a little wicket gate that led directly to the lane. Rose walked behind Sir Lawrence, placing her boots in his footsteps, but still it was necessary to hold her cloak and skirts high to avoid them dragging in the snow. It was only one hundred yards to the end of the lane, but by the time they reached it she was breathing heavily, her boots and the hem of her skirts caked in snow. Sir Lawrence, she noted, in his country jacket, York tan gloves and stylish beaver hat, looked as fresh as the moment he had stepped out of the house. He had not put on his greatcoat and his only concession to the cold was a muffler wrapped about his neck.

She came to stand beside him and they gazed down upon an alien landscape, only the black outlines of the trees and bushes showing against the dazzling white of the lying snow.

'Evans is right,' said Sir Lawrence, shielding his eyes against the glare of sun on snow. 'It would be hard going for you to push your way through those deep drifts.'

'But how long must we wait for the packhorses to go through?'

He shrugged. 'A couple of days at the most.'

'Oh, no!'

He turned to smile down at her. 'You need not worry; livelihoods depend upon the business. They will be on the move as soon as they can.'

'Well, it cannot be soon enough for me.'

'Ungrateful woman! Is my house so lacking in hospitality?'

'Indeed it is,' she retorted, 'when I have been obliged to cook my food and to make my own bed!'

'Neither of which was necessary. Mrs Brendon left plenty of cold food and my bed was made; I would happily have shared both with you.'

Rose gasped.

'How…how dare you!' she stammered, her cheeks flaming.

'Oh, easily.' He grinned. 'I am quite notorious, you know.'

'Y-you are quite outrageous,' she retorted, trying not to laugh. 'You are trying to put me to the blush.'

'And succeeding!'

'Well, I wish you would not. It will make for a most uncomfortable time if I have to spend the rest of my stay in the kitchen with Evans.'

'It will, indeed, and I would not have you do that for the world. Shall we go back?'

The return journey was easier, for they had a beaten path to follow and Rose now found it possible to walk beside Sir Lawrence. His outrageous remarks had not disturbed her—quite the contrary, for there was understanding in his blue eyes and an invitation for her to share the joke. He was obviously in good spirits and she was a little surprised therefore, at the serious tone of his next remark.

'What you said to me last night,' he said, gazing up at the sun, 'do you think it true? That Annabelle never really wanted to marry me?'

'Sir—'

'No, tell me, if you please. I feel I have been surrounded by sycophants, people who only say what they think I want to hear.'

'Whereas I will tell you the truth as I see it.'

'Yes.'

Rose drew her breath, awed at the responsibility he was placing on her shoulders.

'I did not know your Annabelle. Perhaps she *was* a

saint, content to wait, but if she truly loved you, I wonder that she did not remonstrate with you.'

'She never did. Not one word. As I told you, she was an angel.'

'However much you might grieve for her, it will not bring her back. She is gone and the best you can do for her now is to make something of your life.'

He gave a mirthless bark of laughter.

'And just what am I good for? Spending money, charming women…'

She gripped his arm.

'You are young and strong. And rich! At the very least you should work to improve the lot of those you employ. And even if your land is in good heart and supporting you and your people, there are others who need help. For example, those poor wretches who fought at Waterloo. Soldiers, proud men who are now cast off, unnecessary to the government. One sees them sometimes, even in this out-of-the-way place, starving at the roadsides. They should be honoured, protected. If you have the means to help them, then you should do so.'

He stopped.

'Aha, so you *do* think a man can change?'

'No, sir.' She returned his look. It was easy to be brave when the winter world was so bright and fresh. 'But I do not think that *charming women* is all you need do with your life!'

The house was in sight, long and low, the leaded windows twinkling in the sun beneath the covering of snow on its gabled roof. All around them the drifts were piled against walls and hedges, turning everyday outlines into magical forms. Rose breathed deeply: the clear air was as heady as wine.

'It may interest you to know, madam, that my reputation is somewhat exaggerated. I do not go out of my way to attract females.'

'But you do not *go out of your way* to avoid them.'

'Well, no, but your sex can be quite…resolute.' He grinned. 'Especially when the prize is so worth the catching.'

When his blue eyes smiled in just that way Rose could understand why so many foolish women succumbed to his charms, but she was determined not to be one of their number. She said severely, 'You value yourself very highly, Sir Lawrence.'

Again he flashed that wicked smile.

'Who am I to dispute what the ladies say?'

They were approaching the wicket gate and he strode ahead of her so he did not hear her indignant gasp.

'Why, you…smug…arrogant…*conceited* man!'

She scooped up a handful of snow and squeezed it between her hands, taking aim as he applied himself to opening the gate.

Her snowball caught him only a glancing blow on the shoulder so she quickly formed another and hurled it after the first. Her aim was hurried and the snowball would have sailed harmlessly past his head, if Sir Lawrence had not turned back at that moment and taken the full force of her missile on his hat, which was knocked clean off his head.

'Well, that was most satisfactory.' Rose dusted her hands together, a grin tugging at her mouth, until she realised that Sir Lawrence was about to retaliate.

She turned away, uttering a small scream as his first attempt splashed on her neck, some of the snow finding its way onto her skin. She remembered the adage that the best form of defence was attack and fired off another couple of shots. However, she quickly realised that she was no match for Sir Lawrence's deadly aim.

'Enough!' she cried, laughing. 'Truce, sir, truce!'

'Oh, no, this is a duel to the death!'

Another well-aimed shot hit her shoulder and showered her face with icy flakes. Rose picked up her skirts and fled for the shelter of the hedge. Sir Lawrence followed and Rose set off across the field with its covering quilt of snow.

'Got you!'

The hand on her shoulder sent her tumbling, Sir Lawrence following as he lost his footing on the icy ground. They sprawled together, laughing and gasping for breath.

'Unfair, sir,' declared Rose, when she could at last speak. 'Do you know how difficult it is to move when one is hampered by skirts?'

'Hah! Who was it struck the first blow, when my back was turned?'

'That blow was well deserved!'

She was about to rise, but Sir Lawrence rolled over, pinning her down.

'Well deserved? What had I done?'

'It was punishment, for your arrogance!'

'My—' His black brows rose. 'Is it my fault if women find me irresistible?'

'You are incorrigible!' She was laughing up at him, finding it quite impossible to disagree and responding unselfconsciously to the humour in his eyes.

They continued thus, smiling at one another, blue eyes locked on blue-grey, for a long, long moment. Time stopped, everything around them was hushed and still, as if the world was holding its breath. Suddenly it occurred to Rose that she had never shared such a moment before, even with her husband.

She realised her situation: stretched out on the snow with Sir Lawrence almost lying on top of her, his lips only inches from her own, his breath feathering her cheek and the faint tang of eau de cologne filling her senses. In her imagination she reached out for him, pulling his face to hers and kissing him passionately. He would respond, of course, but it would not stop at kisses. Suddenly she knew why she had been feeling so restless… Panic filled her and she struggled to sit up. Immediately Lawrence rolled away.

'Very well, Mrs Westerhill, let us now agree to that truce!' He jumped up and held out his hand to her. 'Will you cry friends with me?' Even the touch of their gloved hands was unsettling. As soon as she was on her feet Rose pulled her fingers free and turned away, knowing she was blushing, but the thoughts of making love to him refused to leave her mind. He said quickly, 'I hope I did not hurt you?'

'N-no.' She concentrated on shaking out her skirts, speaking sharply to cover her discomfiture. 'But that was very irresponsible of us. Our clothes will be wet through.'

'Here, let me help you.' She started when he began to brush the snow off her back. 'There.' He turned her to face him. 'Forgive me,' he said gently, 'I did not mean to alarm you.'

Her eyes flew to his face. She was nervous, overset, but he had done nothing, save be there.

'Oh, no—that is, it was as much my fault as yours.' She struggled to smile. 'I fear the snow has made me a little light-headed.'

'It makes everything different,' he agreed, looking around them. 'It is like living in a fairy-tale world.' He held out his arm. 'Friends?'

She nodded.

'Friends.'

When they reached the kitchen garden Sir Lawrence stopped.

'It is Christmas Day and I have no present for you.' He reached across to a snow-covered bush and pulled off a small twig. 'Here. Rosemary, for remembrance.'

Rose took the spiky little branch and held it to her face, breathing in its scent. She never wanted to forget this day, however dull and respectable the rest of her life might be. The smell of rosemary would for ever remind her of Sir Lawrence.

'Thank you.' She tucked the stalk carefully into her pocket. 'But now I am in your debt.'

He put his fingers under her chin. She yielded to the pressure, tilting up her face, and he kissed her.

'Now we are equal.'

His kiss was brief, light as a feather, nothing like the impassioned, ravaging embrace of her imagination. It meant nothing, she kept telling herself. It was a friendly gesture, to reassure her that he had no designs upon her virtue. She was not sure she wanted to believe this argument, but as they walked back to the house she made a great effort to regain her composure. By the time they walked into the kitchen she had recovered sufficiently to smile at Evans's look of surprise.

'We have been very imprudent,' she told him, pulling off her cloak. 'Sir Lawrence will be able to change, but I shall have to rely upon a good blaze in the drawing room to dry my skirts.'

'Aye, well, I did build up the fire there for you and banked up the fires in the bedrooms, too, but you'll never sit around all day like that, Miss Rose,' declared her groom. 'Why, I can see from here that the back of your gown is soaked through!'

Sir Lawrence had been arranging their gloves on the mantelshelf, but now he turned, saying, 'If you would like to follow me, ma'am, perhaps we can find something for you to wear while we dry your clothes.'

Rose shook her head. 'I must put the chickens on the spit to roast—'

'I can do that for you, Miss Rose,' said Evans, waving her towards the door. 'You had best get out of those wet things before you catch your death.'

'That is the problem with servants one has known since a child,' she remarked, frowning at her groom, 'they tend to bully one.'

'But you know he is right,' replied Sir Lawrence. 'Come along, ma'am.'

There was nothing but friendliness to be read in his expression, so with a nod Rose followed him up the stairs, aware that her wet undergarments were becoming increasingly chilly against her skin.

'This is my bedroom,' he announced. 'You may come in or stay outside, but pray do not keep the door open, you are letting all the heat escape.'

Rose knew she should retreat and wait for him in the corridor, but the warmth of the fire was too tempting so she stepped into the room and closed the door. While Sir Lawrence delved into drawers and searched through a large linen press she looked about her. The painted walls glowed ruby red in the brilliant sunshine, matching the red-and-gold bed hangings. The ornately carved chimneypiece depicted hunting scenes that were repeated in the plaster frieze around the ceiling. In the daylight the chamber looked rich and warm; Rose imagined it at night, with the curtains pulled across the windows and the warm candlelight adding to the fire's glow. How much more comfortable to lie beside Sir Lawrence on that huge bed rather than in the cold snow…

Her body grew quite hot at the idea. Heavens, did merely being in the company of a rake make one prey to such dissolute thoughts? Rose quickly reached for the door handle.

'Perhaps I should wait in my own room…'

'No, no, I have found it now.'

Sir Lawrence came towards her, a floating confection of lace and ribbons in one hand. Despite her nerves Rose laughed.

'I cannot wear that,' she declared, gazing at the gossamer-thin nightgown. 'It would be most improper. And besides, it would afford me no warmth at all.'

Sir Lawrence grinned.

'One of my—er—guests left it here. And I cannot recall thinking it improper.'

Rose choked. She must not laugh at his outrageous comments. He continued as if he had not noticed. 'However, I agree it would not be very warm, but you might wear this over it.' He held up a grey woollen wrap. 'It is a banyan and a trifle small for me.' Rose hesitated and he added, 'Surely it would be better than risking your health by keeping on those wet clothes.'

'Very true.' She held out her hand. 'I will go and change.'

'Do you need help?' asked Sir Lawrence. 'I am not unfamiliar with…'

'No—thank you!'

Rose snatched the clothes from him and fled.

CHAPTER THREE

'WELL, it may not be stylish, but it is certainly respectable.'

Rose regarded her image in the mirror. Sir Lawrence's dressing gown almost wrapped around her twice, held in place by the belt which was knotted tightly at her waist. It covered her completely from her neck to her toes; if she had not folded back the sleeves, they would have hung down past her fingertips.

Thankfully her serviceable leather boots had been laced tightly at the ankle and not leaked, so she was able to put them on and protect her feet from the cold stone flags of the lower floors. When Rose left her chamber she was conscious of the soft silk and lace of the nightgown against her skin. Enveloped as she was in the dressing gown, no one could consider her dress immodest, but without her stays or chemise she felt decidedly underdressed.

The succulent smell of roasting chicken greeted her

as she entered the kitchen, making her realise how hungry she was. She reached for the cook's apron hanging behind the door and was tying it around her when Evans brought in a basket of vegetables from the cold room. If he noticed her unusual garb, he said nothing about it. Neither did Sir Lawrence, who came in shortly after, but she was aware of the way his eyes wandered over her and she had the uncomfortable feeling that he knew exactly what she was—or was not—wearing beneath the enveloping wrap.

'So you are going to cook Christmas dinner for us, ma'am?'

'I am.' She tried to keep her attention firmly fixed upon basting the chickens. 'I am quite adept at the art of cookery.'

'I am very glad to hear it.'

He sat down at the big table. Rose frowned.

'What are you doing?'

'Nothing. That is, I am watching you.'

She turned back to the fire.

'I wish you would not.'

'Why? I like watching you.'

Rose knew it was not just the fire that was heating her cheeks.

'Well, I do not want you to watch me,' she said crossly. 'It is very off-putting.'

He laughed. 'Very well. Is there anything you would like me to do?'

His good-humoured compliance disarmed her. She stood for a moment, wiping her hands on her apron.

'Well,' she said at last, 'the table will need to be prepared…'

'Then I shall do that,' he said promptly. 'If you are to be cook and serving maid, I will be footman—oh, and butler, of course. I will find a bottle of wine for us to drink!'

The drawing room looked very inviting. The heavy velvet curtains were pulled across the windows to shut out the cold night. On the table, candlelight twinkled on the array of glass and silver, and Sir Lawrence had even collected a few evergreens to decorate the table. A dish of steaming vegetables was placed in the centre and a chicken, golden and succulent, rested on a platter waiting for Sir Lawrence to carve.

'A simple meal,' declared Rose, surveying her handiwork as she took her place at the table, 'but I think it preferable to cold meat and cheese!'

'Infinitely so,' agreed Sir Lawrence. 'I congratulate you, madam. It looks, and smells, delicious.' He raised his glass. 'A toast. To the most resourceful woman of my acquaintance.'

Rose was thankful for the dim candlelight to hide her blushes.

'It is nothing. Any good housewife could do as much. And credit goes to you, too, sir, for the excellent smoke-jack in the kitchen; it turned the spit most successfully.'

'Ah. That was one of the conditions Mrs Brendon placed upon me when I purchased the place. She said she would not consent to work here unless I improved the kitchen.'

'When did you buy Knightscote?' she asked him. 'It is strange we heard nothing of it at Mersecombe.'

'I have owned it for a couple of years now, but I have seldom used it, so my coming made little noise.'

'What, was there no gossip?' she dared to tease him. 'Even when you brought your less-than-respectable guests here?'

He frowned at her, but she was not deceived, for she read the laughter in his eyes.

'Be thankful, Mrs Westerhill, that my disreputable guests *did* visit, else you would have nothing to wear.'

Instinctively her hand went up to the neck of the dressing gown.

'I had hoped my own clothes would have been dry by now…'

'I'm afraid we did too good a job of making them damp.'

Rose bit her lip and tried not to recall her wicked thoughts of that afternoon, but they were always there, in her head.

'At least you are most decorously attired,' he continued. 'You have only to cover your hair with that napkin and the result would be positively nun-like!'

She could not resist a retort.

'Some might suggest it is a necessary defence, sir, given your reputation.'

He bared his teeth.

'Put away your claws, vixen. I will not fight with you

on Christmas Day. Tell me instead about your life in Mersecombe. Do you have a large establishment?'

'No, a modest house with a couple of servants.'

'Yet you keep a groom.'

'Evans has been with me since I was a child. He came with me when I married, and when I sold the house at Exford he agreed to come with me to Mersecombe, although he is obliged to work in the house as well as look after the horses.' She smiled. 'They are my one luxury. I will buy a pony for little Sam, when the funds allow. Evans will teach him to ride—he put me on my first pony. I should like him to do the same for my son.'

'It must be hard, bringing up a boy on your own.'

'I have my mother to help me. But you are right, he misses his father. Sam was only four when I was widowed, so I am not sure how much he remembers of his papa.'

A good thing, perhaps, recalling the tears and the arguments.

'How did he die?'

Lost in the past, Rose looked at him, uncomprehending, and he said quickly, 'I beg your pardon, if you would rather not—'

'No, no. I have no objection to telling you. A riding accident. His horse slipped on the ice and threw him. He broke his neck.'

She did not add that he was returning from a tryst with his current mistress. Everyone in Exford might know the truth, but there was no reason she should admit it to this stranger.

'I am very sorry.'

She shrugged as if to evade his sympathy.

'It was four years ago. We have managed very well since then.' She added brightly, 'And now we have Magnus.'

'Magnus?'

'Magnus Emsleigh. He is a shipping merchant and owns a substantial property just outside Mersecombe. He is a pillar of the local society. An excellent example for my son to follow.'

'And does he wish to become Sam's father? Ah. I can see by your look that that is the case. Why have you not mentioned him before?'

Rose had wondered that herself. Surely to tell Sir Lawrence that she was betrothed to a wealthy, respected local gentleman would have added to her consequence. It was not a love match, but a prudent arrangement, designed to provide security for her and for Sam. It now occurred to Rose that she was reluctant to admit, even to herself, that she was soon to marry Magnus Emsleigh.

He spoke again, saying lightly, 'Have you set a date?'

'Lady Day.' She pushed a slice of chicken around on her plate. 'Magnus has no experience of children. Sometimes Sam can be...difficult.'

Lawrence sat back, his fingers playing with the stem of his wineglass. He remembered his own stepfather, a deeply religious man whose repressive regime of sermons and beatings had only made a spirited young boy even more determined to rebel.

'It can be hard for a young boy to accept another man in the house. It will take time and patience.'

'Yes,' she nodded eagerly. 'That is what I have told Magnus.'

Lawrence took a sip of his wine.

'But what is this pillar of society thinking of, to let you ride unattended in such weather?'

She put up her chin at that.

'He is not my keeper. I will not allow him to dictate to me.' Lawrence's brows went up and she added, 'Besides, he is in Bath at present and does not know what I am about.'

Rose turned her attention to her plate and Lawrence took the opportunity to study her. She looked absurdly young in her borrowed dressing gown, but it did nothing to hide her charms. The belt was pulled tight around her tiny waist and accentuated the full, rounded swell of her bosom. The ordered ringlets of yesterday had given way to more natural curls that she had caught back from her face with a wide ribbon, and her cheeks were still delicately flushed from her endeavours in the kitchen.

'I applaud your wish for independence, Mrs Westerhill, but I pity your suitor.'

He thought she might blush at that, but she surprised him by chuckling.

'Poor Magnus. He thinks I am not capable of managing my own affairs and he is eager to relieve me of all my burdens. As if I had any! My meagre savings require little effort and, no matter what I say, I cannot persuade him that Sam is *not* a burden! Magnus is a dear, but he is inclined to lecture me and I get quite cross with him sometimes—' She broke off. 'I beg your pardon. I should not be telling you all this.'

'You may tell me whatever you wish. In fact—' He stopped, slightly alarmed to discover that he wanted to know everything about her. He got up to throw more logs on the fire. He must be careful; this woman was getting under his skin. He enjoyed her company, enjoyed teasing her, watching the delicate colour mantle her cheek, but she was not of his world. The seduction of a respectable schoolteacher was not something he wanted on his conscience.

When he looked up again she had walked to the window and pushed apart the curtains.

'We have had more snow this evening. It has stopped now and the moon is rising. Do come and look, it is almost as bright as day.' She glanced over when he came to stand beside her. 'Is it not beautiful?'

Almost as beautiful as you.

The words were on the tip of his tongue, but he swallowed them, saying instead, 'If we have no more snow, then the packhorses should be able to get through tomorrow. You can be on your way.'

She looked a little startled at his harsh tone, then the lashes dropped, veiling her eyes.

'Yes, of course. And this little idyll will be over.' There was a hint of sadness in her voice that surprised him.

'An idyll? Is that how you have seen this?'

Her smile not only lit up her face, it illuminated the room.

'Stranded here, having to fend for ourselves—it has been so different from my everyday life.' She added shyly, 'Of course, I was a little frightened of you at first, but you have proved yourself to be most—'

'Be careful,' he warned her. 'Do not make a hero out of me!'

'—most *restrained*,' she ended, one corner of her mouth lifting a fraction. She looked back to the window. 'I wonder what might have happened if you had been less honourable.'

'I beg your pardon?' Surely he had misheard her? The faint blush on her cheek told him he had not.

'We have been given this opportunity to escape from our ordinary lives for a few days. Tomorrow, I will go back to Mersecombe and I assume you will soon return to London. It is unlikely that we shall ever meet again. I just wonder what it would have been like…'

For a long moment she held his eyes.

'Forgive me.' She looked away, giving her head a little shake. 'I think I have had too much wine. Please, ignore what I said.' She turned back to the table. 'I had best get these dishes to the kitchen. Evans will have finished his own meal by now and will be waiting to clear up.'

'Let me help you.'

She did not refuse and he followed her through to the kitchen, his mind buzzing with conjecture. Was she really regretting the fact that he had not tried to seduce her? He shook his head. No. She was far too respectable for that. His gaze was drawn to the proud line of her back, the narrow waist and the full hips that swayed so invitingly as she moved. It was unconsciously done and therefore all the more alluring.

Evans had already cleaned the spit and cooking pans and he would allow them to do no more than bring the dishes into the scullery.

'A kitchen's no place for the likes of you, Miss Rose,' he muttered, 'nor you, sir. If you will forgive me for saying so, I think you'd be more hindrance than help.'

Lawrence laughed at that. 'I fear you may be right. I'll go away.'

'Aye, do, and be so good as to take my mistress with you!'

'Really, Evans is growing quite autocratic,' grumbled Rose. She was kneeling before the drawing room fire, jabbing the poker between the logs. 'He knows I am more than capable of helping him!'

'Yes, but you should not have to.'

Sir Lawrence reached out and took the poker from her. She shook her head at him, smiling.

'I want to do *something*!'

He dropped down beside her and finished stirring the fire into a blaze.

'Then find something a little less harmful to your hands.' He took her fingers in a firm, warm clasp. 'Look how rough they are.'

Rose tried to pull away, embarrassed.

'That is not just from the last couple of days…'

He ignored her and continued to examine her hands. They were trapped in his gentle grasp. His intense scrutiny was unsettling; her heart was pounding, fluttering in her chest like a caged bird.

'You have even burned yourself.'

'A tiny mark!' She tried and failed to keep her voice steady, conscious of how near he was. The tug of attraction was almost palpable. He continued to study the small red weal on the edge of her palm. She swallowed. 'And one expects that in a kitchen…' Her words trailed off as he lifted her hand to his lips.

It was a gentle, intimate gesture and it took her breath away. Without thinking Rose tightened her fingers around his. She leaned closer and kissed him full on the mouth. His hands slid up her arms and rested lightly on her shoulders, holding her to him. Rose had closed her eyes, but the next instant they flew open and she drew back.

'Oh, my! I beg your pardon!'

'There is no need; I am not offended.' He was smiling at her in a way that made it difficult to think.

She knew she should get up off her knees, but his hands remained on her shoulders, the thumbs tracing the line of her collarbones through the wool of her wrap. She did not want him to stop.

'I—I do not know what came over me.'

'Curiosity, perhaps?' His smile grew and she felt her bones begin to melt.

'It…it is the snow,' she stammered. 'And the wine.

I am not normally so…wanton. What must you think of me?'

He skimmed one hand down her arm and even through the soft woollen sleeve her skin tingled beneath his touch.

'I think you are adorable.' He lifted her hand and began to kiss each of her fingers.

'Wh-what are you doing?'

'Trying to decide,' he murmured, between slow, deliberate kisses, 'if I most want to make love to you here on the rug in front of the fire, or in my bed, between silken sheets.'

The images conjured by his soft words made her tremble. If she had not already been kneeling, she thought she must have collapsed on the rug in a damp heap of desire and anticipation.

'Im-impossible,' she stammered. 'You will do neither of those things.'

'No?' He raised his eyes from the contemplation of her fingers, and what was left of her insides liquefied. 'It was *you* who kissed *me*. And you yourself questioned whether we were wasting this opportunity.'

She swallowed and ran her tongue nervously over her lips.

'Are…are you joking me, Sir Lawrence?' The look in his eyes told her he was in deadly earnest.

'One night,' he whispered. 'After that we will go back to our separate worlds and need never meet again. What do you say?'

It was the edge of a precipice. He was still holding

her hand, his thumb rubbing gently across the soft inner side of her wrist and sending arrows of heat through her body. They were still kneeling, and so close that she would only have to lean forwards a little to be in his arms.

Rose searched his eyes. Behind the intense blue was a shadow of sadness.

I could dispel that, she thought. *I could make him happy, at least for a while.*

'No.' Gently she disengaged her hands. 'I am very sorry if I led you to think—'

'You did, but I shall get over it.' He held out his hand to her. '"Since there's no help for it, come, let us kiss and part,"' he quoted, smiling.

Her throat swelled. Tears burned her eyes as he pulled her to her feet.

'Oh, *please* do not say such things to me!'

'Do you not like Drayton?'

'Too much!' She blinked. 'It—it has been a long day. I should retire now.'

He released her, and with another mumbled apology she ran out of the room.

Damnation!

Lawrence stared at the closed door. She had rejected him.

And quite right, too, argued the voice in his head. *She is too respectable for you, despite that unsolicited kiss.* But he had thought, for a while, that she might just count the world well lost. She had certainly considered it. He sighed. Such a heady mix of innocence and honesty. She had begged him to ignore her. How much better if he could have done so! Indeed, he had intended to keep his distance, until the moment he had taken her hands. The mere touch of her skin and all his honourable resolutions had fled. All he knew was that he wanted her in his arms. In his bed.

He had not felt such desire for months, possibly years. He was happy enough to attend the constant round of parties and balls that filled the London social calendar and was willing to indulge any of the ladies who threw themselves in his way in a little flirtation. Mostly it was no more than that, but he had only to escort a lady to her home for the gossips to claim she was his mistress. He had stopped trying to correct them, but the lies and intrigue of town life had begun to pall—society would be aghast if they knew how many nights he spent alone. He collected a glass of wine and threw himself down in a chair. Another lonely night would be nothing new. The rattling of the window reminded him of the weather. Pray heaven it did not snow again—he needed Rose out of the house. He was only flesh and blood, after all, and she was too damned desirable.

Rose shut and locked the door of the guest chamber. The room was warm and she sank down in front of the peat fire. What had she done? To kiss a rake, and so wantonly; she might as well have begged him to take her! It was to Sir Lawrence's credit that he had let her go so easily.

But you didn't want him to let you go.

The thought shocked her, but honesty compelled her to acknowledge it. Ever since she had arrived at Knightscote she had felt the tug of attraction. It was not just that he was wickedly handsome, it was the smile in his blue eyes, the way he made her laugh. She had not felt so alive since those early years with Harry, when he had courted her so assiduously. Her thoughts moved on from there to the marriage bed. Since Harry's death she had never craved another man's touch, until now. It was loneliness. She wrapped her arms about herself and inched even closer to the fire. That was the true reason for her restless state. She was lonely.

And she had read loneliness in Sir Lawrence's eyes, too. He had forsaken the world this Christmas to mourn his lost love. Rose's heart went out to him. He might be a rake, but he was sincerely grieving.

So why not comfort each other?

Rose shook off the insidious thought. It would not do, she was betrothed and she was a mother, although that life seemed a world away. She took off the wrap and slipped between the sheets. The bed was cold. She toyed with the idea of going downstairs in search of a warming pan, but abandoned it. She might see Sir Lawrence and then her noble resolve would crumble. It had been hard enough to walk out of the drawing room.

She shifted restlessly in the bed. Her body was on fire, aching for a man's touch, but not just any man. With a tiny cry of frustration she turned over.

'A rake makes the devil of a husband. You should know that by now.'

But her agitated mind would not be appeased. She was not looking for a husband, only a little comfort. An escape from her loneliness. A sweet memory to keep in her heart when she returned to her real world. Rose pummelled her pillow and lay down again, pulling the covers up to her cheek. She pictured Sir Lawrence in the drawing room, her stomach clenching as she imagined him smiling at her, felt again his gentle touch.

One night, then we need never meet again...

Lawrence remained in the drawing room, staring into the fire while the house grew silent around him. Evans would be snoring in his bed behind the kitchen, sleeping off the effects of the flagon of cider Lawrence had spotted on the floor beside his chair. Rose, too, would be asleep by now. The occasional creaking of the boards he put down to the wind, which was howling around the house.

He had risen to throw another log on the fire when he heard the rasp of the door hinges. He looked up, his eyes narrowing as he peered through the gloom.

'I thought...about what you said.' Rose moved across the room. She had left off the enveloping wrap, and the diaphanous folds of the nightgown glistened in the candlelight, outlining every curve of her body—she appeared to float towards him. 'One night. Then we will go our separate ways.'

Lawrence still could not believe it was not a dream,

until he reached out and felt her warm flesh beneath his hands.

'You are quite sure about this?'

A smile trembled on her lips.

'Quite sure.'

As he dragged her into his arms Rose tilted her face up, inviting his kiss. His mouth ground over hers, savage, possessive, and her mind reeled, but with excitement, not alarm. She threw her arms around his neck, her lips parting to allow his tongue to search her mouth, flickering and teasing. She leaned into him, revelling in the feel of his hard, aroused body pressing against her. There was too much cloth between them. She unwound her arms from around Lawrence's neck and began to unbutton his waistcoat. It was shed without a break in their deep, passionate kisses and she moved on to those tight buckskins.

Breathing heavily, Lawrence broke away, but only long enough to divest himself of his clothes. At last he stood before her, naked and golden in the firelight, his body as muscled and perfect as any Greek statue.

'Rose?'

She raised her eyes to his and slowly gathered up the gossamer folds of the nightgown, lifting them in one smooth movement. As the fine silk whispered over her head she heard another sigh, almost a groan, from Lawrence. Before the nightgown had left her hands and fluttered to the floor he had his arms around her, pulling her to him. He lowered her gently down onto the thick rug where the heat from the fire enveloped them. Her arms were still above her head and he reached out to catch her wrists, imprisoning them with one hand while the other explored her breasts. She writhed beneath his touch, uttering a little moan of pleasure when his circling fingers were replaced by his mouth. He gently teased and nibbled and sucked until she was gasping for breath, but even then he did not stop, but added to her exquisite torment by trailing his free hand down over the soft plain of her stomach, his fingers delving onwards, circling and stroking until her legs parted and her hips tilted invitingly. The long fingers continued to devastating effect; she groaned and twisted, pushed against his hand, crying out as wave after wave of pleasure burst over her. As the ecstatic spasms ceased Lawrence folded her in his arms and held her close.

'Oh.' She made her shuddering whisper into his shoulder. 'I had forgotten. *Thank* you.'

A soft laugh shook him. She felt it reverberate against her cheek.

'It was my pleasure.'

She struggled to sit up, smiling at him. She said, her voice warm and husky with passion, 'And this is mine.'

Gently she pushed him onto his back, smoothing her hands over his shoulders and across his chest. The dark smattering of hair caught at her fingers as she trailed them around the hard nipples. He reached up and removed the clips from her curls, so that when he pulled away the confining ribbon, her hair cascaded down to rest upon his naked body. Rose moved her head, dragging the silky tresses across the taut muscles of his stomach. He arched his back, eyes closed. Rose climbed over him, leaning forwards to kiss the fine line of his throat while the tips of her breasts rubbed against his skin and he groaned louder, his hands reaching for her, easing her into position so that he could thrust into her. It was Rose's turn to arch as she felt him inside her, sleek and hard. She moved against him, following the dictates of her body while his hands on her hips kept her firmly anchored over him. Excitement was building again, but this time it was centred on his pleasure. She held him deep and warm inside her, her body stroking and caressing until his grip tightened around her waist. He held her fast; she was powerless while he thrust into her hard and fast and she cried out, control swept away as he took her to new heights. One final thrust, a gasp, and they clung together until the last wonderful tremor shuddered through their bodies and they collapsed, sated, to lie in each other's arms before the dying embers.

Lawrence kissed her and carefully smoothed the damp tendrils of honey-brown hair back from her brow.

'Well, madam, was it as you expected?'

'Much, much better.' She snuggled deeper into his arms, smiling.

'And there's more.' He sat up and reached for his shirt. 'Put this on.'

'Why?' Obediently she allowed him to throw it over her head. She pushed her arms into the voluminous sleeves while he stepped into his buckskins. She watched him throw on his flowered waistcoat, marvelling at the way it accentuated the firm muscles of his stomach and arms. He reached down to pull her to her feet.

'I am taking you to bed, my love, but you will recall that the passages between here and the bedroom are unheated and I would not have you catch a chill.'

She could not resist reaching out and resting her hand against his naked chest.

'Will you not feel the cold?'

'No.' He swept her up into his arms. 'I shall have you next to my heart.'

He lowered his head to give her a fierce, savage kiss full of triumph and possession. Her body still glowing from their union, Rose wound her arms about his neck as he carried her to the bedroom.

A cold, rosy dawn illuminated the window. Rose stretched, feeling the warmth of Lawrence's sleeping form against her back. Her body felt wonderfully full, satisfied, and she could not help smiling into the semi-darkness. Their lovemaking in the bedroom had been even better than that first, astonishing coupling in front of the fire. Lawrence had proved himself an expert lover—she should not have been surprised, given his reputation, but his gentleness and the way he had sought to put her pleasure before his own had been a revelation.

It would make parting all the more difficult.

Rose eased herself away from his sleeping form and out of the bed. The discarded shirt and breeches on the floor brought back memories that sent a delightful shiver down her spine, but it also reminded her that they had left several telltale garments strewn across the drawing room. She reached for Sir Lawrence's brightly coloured dressing gown. She must go to her own room and dress. Then she could send Evans out to check on the state of the track.

When Lawrence awoke he was immediately aware of a feeling of well-being. The early-morning sun was pouring into the room, battering his eyelids. He did not want to open his eyes. He wanted to—

He turned over, but his hands found only cold empty sheets. Had he dreamed last night's events? His body told him not.

Lawrence sat up, blinking. His clothes were still on the floor, but his banyan was gone. Quickly he grabbed his clothes and scrambled into them, buttoning his coat even as he made his way to the guest room. It was empty. With a growing sense of unease he ran down the stairs to the drawing room.

Rose was standing by the window, fully dressed, her travelling cloak folded over a chair, gloves and bonnet resting neatly on the top. She turned as he came in, but the sunlight was behind her and he could not see her face.

'You are up betimes.' He crossed the room in a couple of strides and reached for her. She stepped away from him.

'I have a long ride ahead of me.'

'You are going, then.'

'Yes. Evans has already ventured out this morning and says the pack ponies have been on the move. We have only to make our way to the lane…'

She reached for her gloves, but Lawrence stepped in her way, catching her hands.

'Can we not talk, first? About last night…' She would not meet his eyes and he squeezed her fingers, saying sharply, 'It is customary to observe the civilities, you know, even with your lover.'

A faint shake of her head sent her curls dancing.

'We are not lovers. It was one night.'

'But a very special night, would you not agree?' The faint blush on her cheek gave him his answer. 'When will I see you again?'

'You will not.'

'But—'

She lifted one hand and placed her fingers against his mouth.

'It is better this way. I have to go back to Mersecombe, to my son. There is no place for you in my life.'

Lawrence frowned. Her words were calm, reasoned, but it made no sense to him.

'I want to be part of your life,' he said. 'After last night I want to know you better—'

'No!' She stepped away from him. 'There can only be pain that way.'

'Because of my past? Believe me, Rose—'

'Are you going to promise me you will change? It will not happen.'

'Hell and damnation, woman, how can you—?' Again that tiny shake of her head accompanied by such a sad smile that he bit back his fury. 'Tell me, Rose. Tell me why you are so sure.'

Her blue-grey eyes rested upon him for a long moment, then she turned and walked back to the window. Her eyes were fixed on the snowy scene, but her thoughts were very far away.

'Once a rake, always a rake. I was married to such a man. I met Harry when I was still at school in Barnstaple. He charmed me from the first. Everyone knew his reputation, but he told me it would be different when we were married. I believed him. I was just seventeen when I became his wife, Harry was five and twenty. For a few months I think, believe, he was faithful to me, but then I was with child and he…he began to stay away. Whenever I taxed him with it he would deny it; if I caught him out in his philandering then he would come back to me, repentant, promising he would reform. It was after one such incident that he bought the property at Exford. He said we would make a fresh start, but whenever there was a pretty woman…' She crossed her arms, hugging herself. 'His death was something of a relief. I could continue to love him, but he could no longer hurt me.' She turned back to look at him, her eyes bright with unshed tears. 'So you see why I will not allow that to happen to me again?'

'But I am not like your husband, Rose. I will prove it to you.'

She shook her head, taking out her handkerchief

to wipe her eyes. When she spoke again her tone was brisk.

'You can only prove it by living a respectable and chaste life for…I do not know…years. I can see by your horrified look that the idea does not appeal.'

Lawrence watched in silence as she put on her bonnet and gloves. She was going. If he could not come up with some argument within the next few minutes, she would walk out of his life for ever. He tried to think, but his brain refused to work. Mechanically he picked up her cloak and placed it around her. He noted the way her fingers paused in tying the strings when he allowed his hands to rest for a moment on her shoulders.

'So there is nothing I can say.'

'Nothing.'

'What if…' his hands tightened and he turned her to face him '…what if there is a child? I would have a right to know.'

She paled, her eyes dilating, and he braced himself to hold her, should she faint.

'You would, of course,' she murmured, her voice barely above a whisper. 'But there will be no child.'

'How can you be so sure?'

She gently pushed his hands away.

'I can be absolutely sure. That is all you need to know.'

With that she turned and swept out of the room.

Evans was waiting with the horses at the door. He stepped forwards to help Rose to mount, but a word from Lawrence forestalled him. She did not object as

Lawrence threw her up into the saddle. He checked the girth, made sure her foot was secure in the stirrup, anything to delay her departure.

'Goodbye.' She leaned down to him, holding out her hand. 'It was very good of you to take us in. I am very grateful. For everything.'

They might have been parting after an innocuous morning call, save for the haunted look in her eyes, from which all the blue had disappeared. He took her gloved fingers, felt them tremble in his grasp.

'If ever you need me—'

She nodded.

'That is kind, thank you, but I have everything I need at Mersecombe.'

'At least say I may call on you—'

'No.' Her fingers gripped his hand and she bent her serious gaze upon him. 'Promise me, promise me you will not come looking for me.' Her grip tightened. 'Please, Lawrence.'

Her eyes demanded an answer. He nodded.

'I give you my word.'

'Thank you.' She released his hand and straightened in the saddle.

It was a dismissal. There was nothing for it but to step back.

'Very well. I wish you Godspeed, madam.'

'And I wish you every happiness.'

A final smile, a final look from those slate-grey eyes, then she turned away, to ride out of his life for ever.

* * *

Lawrence knew that if the pack ponies were moving it would not be long before his servants returned to Knightscote. The scullery boy arrived first, followed by the stable lads. The short winter day was drawing to a close when his butler and housekeeper finally trooped into the house. By supper time the lodge had returned to normal, lights burning in the passages and servants on hand to attend to their master's slightest whim.

'Lord bless us, but why are you sitting in the dark, Sir Lawrence?' Mrs Brendon bustled in, carrying her master's supper on a tray. 'I do hope you haven't been too uncomfortable while we's been away, sir; I see you finished up all the ham, and someone's been using my kitchen, too…'

'Yes—how was your journey?' he asked the question to deflect her attention.

'Well, it could have been worse. Brendon and me got a ride on the carrier's cart as far as the crossroads, and the track was pretty well trodden from there on.' She put her tray down and began to go round the room, lighting candles from a taper. 'Now, sir, that's a game pie I brought back with me from Exford, so I hope it will do until I can get cooking again in the morning!'

'Excellent, thank you.'

'But there's hoof marks leading right up to the door, sir. Have you had visitors?'

'Yes. A traveller on the way to Mersecombe arrived here Christmas Eve. The weather was too bad to go further.'

'Ah, that explains the pots and pans that's been moved in my kitchen.' She nodded sagely. 'I was fair certain it weren't you that had taken to cooking!'

'No. Tell me, Mrs Brendon. You come from Exford way, do you not? Do you recall a gentleman who used to live there, name of Westerhill?'

'Harry Westerhill? Aye, I do. Gennleman, you say? Nothin' but a lecher I'd call 'n. The good Lord carried 'im off a few years back, and a good thing, too. No woman was safe!'

Lawrence pulled a chair to the table and sat down to his supper.

'He had a wife, I believe?' He hoped he sounded uninterested.

'Ah, that he did. Poor little thing. Led her a merry dance he did, what with his women and his gambling. And they say he used to beat her, when he was in his cups.'

Lawrence's hand tightened around his knife. 'Indeed?'

'Oh, he could charm the birds from the trees, could Harry Westerhill, but when he had had a few to drink…' She shook her head, tutting. 'Well, good riddance, that's what I'd say. The poor lady's better off without 'n. Better off without any man, if you ask me. Beggin yer pardon, sir!'

'No, you are right, Mrs Brendon.' Lawrence gazed down at the plate, his appetite quite gone. 'She is better off without any man.'

CHAPTER FOUR

'VERY well, children, that is all for today. Put your slates on the shelf, please, before you leave.'

A scraping of benches and sudden explosion of chatter announced the end of the school day. Rose began to tidy her desk while the room gradually emptied around her.

'Mama, Mama, Jem wants me to go to the farm with him, to see his pointer's new litter!'

Sam was tugging at her skirts, looking up at her with such a look of hope and trust in his eyes that her heart turned over. She put a hand on his unruly fair hair.

'I am not sure you should. Mrs Wooler will have chores for Jem to do…'

'Nothing very much tonight, Mrs Westerhill, and Sam can help me with those.' Jem twisted his cap between his hands and said haltingly, 'Me mam says she likes it when Sam comes to see us—she likes to hear us laughing…'

Rose imagined Mrs Wooler, only a few months widowed, and she nodded.

'Then of course Sam may go with you, as long as he is home before dark.' Sam's mouth opened to argue and she lifted her finger. 'Before dark, Sam. Promise me.'

With an audible sigh he nodded. The next moment the boys had disappeared and she heard them whooping and laughing as they ran down the steps and off through the village. She stood for a moment, enjoying the silence. She never worried when the two boys were together. Jem was a little older than Sam and built on sturdier lines. He had always protected Sam from the older boys in the village, who tended to bully him, and since Jem had lost his father the boys had become even closer, united in their common plight.

The little schoolroom was situated above the north porch of the parish church, and when Rose was alone the peace of the building settled around her like an old but comfortable cloak. However, it was not enough to keep out the cold and she shivered. With winter approaching it would soon be time to bring out the old brazier to heat the schoolroom. She must remember to speak to the churchwarden about it.

Rose locked the schoolroom door and descended the stone steps built at the side of the porch. She walked slowly through the graveyard, but at the gate she stopped. She should go home, Mama would be expecting her, but to her left the track wound upwards through the ancient woods and on to the moor. Surely there was time for a short walk? A carriage rattled along the high street, distracting her. She quickly turned back, but it was only Farmer Ansell's son in his new gig.

Who else should it be? Rose asked herself. Restlessly she set off up the hill into the woods. She declined to answer her own question. It was nearly ten months since she had seen Sir Lawrence Daunton, but there was not a day that she had not thought of him, nor a morning that she did not wake up and wonder if today he might travel to Mersecombe to find her.

Her short sojourn at Knightscote haunted her dreams. It did no good to tell herself that it was for the best. Upon her return to Mersecombe she had given her family and friends to understand that she had been stranded at some remote farmhouse. It had taken all her tact and skill to persuade Evans to corroborate her tale and for some time she had been torn between hope and dread that Sir Lawrence might turn up and give the lie to her story. When the snows had cleared two weeks later and Evans reassured her that he had made enquiries and learned that Knightscote was now cmpty once more, she was surprised at the depth of her disappointment. She tried to be glad there was now no possibility of meeting up with Sir Lawrence again, but sometimes, when the children were being particularly troublesome or she was yawning behind her fan at some tedious party, she longed for him to arrive and carry her off.

'Romantic nonsense!'

She uttered the words aloud as she strode along, her skirts dragging on the long grass. Sir Lawrence was not some fairy-tale prince who would carry her off to live happily ever after. He was a rake. A libertine. He might well run off with her; he might even make her forget the world for a short while, but then there would be nights of uncertainty when he did not come home, tears and recriminations and the certain knowledge that she would have to share him with every other female who caught his eye.

'Never!'

She stopped. She had reached the edge of the wood and she could see the moors ahead of her, the bracken glowing reddish-orange in the sunlight. She dared not go further. The sun was already low in the sky and her mother would be worried, just as she worried about little Sam.

Rose turned back.

By the time she reached the church again the sun had gone down and the air was filled with a faint haze and the scent of wood smoke. She saw a figure at the church gate, a stocky, thickset man in a brown riding jacket and tall hat. He was standing at the entrance to the churchyard, feet spread, hands behind him, as if waiting for someone.

Rose stifled a cowardly impulse to dive into the bushes and wait for him to go. Instead she fixed her smile and said brightly, 'Magnus! Have you been waiting for me?'

He swept off his hat, displaying ordered brown curls. 'I had business in Minehead which took longer than anticipated, so I was too late to catch you in the schoolroom, but since I had come from the high street I knew I could not have missed you. However, if you had not appeared in the next five minutes I would have gone home.'

If only she had walked a little further up the track! Rose chided herself for the thought and, to make up for her churlishness, tucked her hand into his arm.

'Well, I am here now, so you may walk me back to Bluebell Cottage.'

'Have you thought what you will wear for the Assembly?'

'Good heavens, Magnus, that is weeks away! I have not given it a thought.'

He gave a ponderous little laugh. 'I would like to be prepared; I want to present you with a corsage to match your gown and you know how difficult it is to find flowers in the dead of winter.'

She had a sudden unreasoning urge to announce she was going to wear the brightest, most vivid scarlet gown she could find. Instead she said, 'How kind you are, Magnus. It will most likely be my midnight blue.'

'What, are you not having a new gown? My sister Althea has ordered another, I saw it this morning. I thought it was the usual practice for all you ladies to have a new gown for every occasion.'

'I am sure it is, if one has unlimited funds!' She immediately regretted her snappish retort and squeezed his arm. 'I beg your pardon, Magnus. I know you were only funning.'

'And you know I would buy you a dozen gowns, if you would let me.' He stopped. 'Let us put an end to this dilly-dallying, Rose. Even without a special licence we could be wed before Christmas.'

'Magnus, I have explained to you why I cannot marry you yet.'

'You are concerned for young Samuel, I know that, and I understand why you cried off in the spring, but to postpone it for a whole year—'

'You have been very patient, Magnus. It is only a few more months.'

'Sometimes I wonder if you have changed your mind, what with the losses I suffered when the *Sealark* went down…'

'That is unjust,' she cried. 'My decision to postpone the wedding was taken months before you lost the *Sealark*. And besides, I would never allow such a misfortune to weigh with me!'

'Of course, and I beg your pardon.' He stopped to press a kiss upon her fingers. 'Forgive me, the whole affair is preying upon my mind—until the insurers pay out for the loss of the ship and the cargo I cannot honour my promissory notes to the crew!' He gave a rueful smile. 'I fear it is making me very bad company.'

'Not at all, I understand your concerns. I am only thankful that more lives were not lost in the accident. But that has nothing to do with my decision that we should delay our marriage.'

'Then it is solely to do with your son.'

'Yes.' Rose was relieved that he did not notice the heartbeat's hesitation before she responded.

He said heavily, 'In my opinion you refine too much upon the wishes of that young man! Once we are married he will soon learn to respect me.'

'But I do not want him to do so out of fear! Be patient, Magnus, please.'

'Well, if you will not agree to our marriage, then at least let me help you open up the mine at Hades Cove. I am sure it is not so unprofitable as you have been led to believe.'

She put up her hand.

'My dear, we have been over this before. My late husband poured a vast amount of our money into the mine. I will not allow you to do the same.'

'But once we are wed it will become my property.'

Rose smiled up at him mischievously. 'Ah, yes, well, *then* you will be master of everything and may do as you please!' She sighed. 'Let us not argue. Tell me instead about your sister's new gown. Is she having it made up in Minehead?'

'No, there is an excellent modiste in Dunster who has all the latest London pattern books. She showed me a drawing. Too many frills and flounces for my taste, but there you are, Althea says it is the latest thing. And you know Althea likes to keep up with fashion.' He chuckled. 'As my sister she knows she must set the standard, even at a little local gathering such as the Mersecombe Assembly!'

Rose smiled absently, her mind wandering to more anxious matters.

'I wonder if Sam is home yet,' she murmured, almost to herself. 'I gave him permission to go to the Woolers Farm, but told him he must come home before dark.'

They had reached the little bridge that led across the stream to Bluebell Cottage and Magnus stood back to allow Rose to precede him.

'Then I have no expectation of seeing the boy before midnight.'

She shook her head, saying over her shoulder, 'You know that generally he minds me very well, Magnus.'

She had reached the cottage, but stopped as she always did to admire the little rosemary bush growing beside the door before she stepped into the hall.

She allowed Magnus to take her cloak, then turned to smile at him. 'I hear voices. You see, he is home before me.'

Rose walked across and opened the sitting-room door, her smile freezing on her face when she found herself looking into the intensely blue eyes of Sir Lawrence Daunton.

'Sir Lawrence!' Magnus followed Rose into the room, his hearty tone quite at odds with the paralysing shock she was suffering. 'Good heavens, man, what are you doing here?'

'You know each other?' asked Mrs Molland, who was standing with her arm on Sam's shoulder and beaming at Sir Lawrence, delighted to have such a charming gentleman in her house.

'Aye, ma'am. We met at the Pullens' ball.'

Three weeks ago! Rose put a hand on the back of a nearby chair to steady herself. He had been at Knightscote for three weeks and she had not known!

Magnus turned to Rose, saying in a slightly aggrieved tone, 'You may recall, my dear, that upon my persuasion Lady Pullen sent you an invitation, but you chose not to go.'

'And *you* may recall that it fell upon a week-night and I was obliged to be up betimes to open the schoolhouse,' Rose answered coolly. 'If I had accompanied you, it would have meant you returning home at an unseasonably early hour and Althea would not have liked that.'

'No, no, you are right there,' he conceded, pursing his lips and looking a little thoughtful before turning back to Sir Lawrence. 'But what brings you to Mersecombe, sir?'

Rose was acutely conscious that Sir Lawrence's gaze had been fixed on her, but now he shifted his attention to the questioner.

'I heard about the pointer puppies for sale at Woolers Farm.' His eyes flickered across Rose again as he moved his gaze to Sam. 'This young man was there and helped me make my choice. Then, as it was growing dark, I asked him to show me the way back to the Ship.'

'Sir Lawrence allowed me to ride on his horse with him,' declared Sam, his eyes shining.

'It was the least I could do, since you were good

enough to guide me. And once we had stabled the horse I thought I should come along and explain why Sam was late…'

'You—you are staying in Mersecombe?' stuttered Rose.

The blue eyes once more rested on her face.

'Yes. I have more business here tomorrow, Mrs…'

'Oh, heavens, where are my wits?' cried Mrs Molland. 'This is my daughter, sir. Mrs Westerhill. Samuel's mother.'

Should she admit they had met before? Would he say anything? He was bowing, no sign of recognition in his face. Rose tried to think clearly. Perhaps it was coincidence. No. Even her befuddled brain could not believe that. He would not have forgotten her in ten months—would he?

'Sir Lawrence is having first pick of the litter,' Sam piped up. 'Of course they are too young yet and will not be taken from their mother until they are weaned, but Jem says they don't have buyers for them all. Could *we* have a puppy, Mama?'

Sam was looking up at her. She tried to concentrate on what he had said, tried to put out of her mind the fact that Lawrence was here, in her home, filling her sitting room and her senses with his presence.

'Please, Mama…it would be company for Grandmama!'

The childish logic caused a ripple of amusement.

'I have plenty to occupy me without adding a dog to the family, Sam,' laughed Mrs Molland, ruffling his hair.

'It is out of the question,' declared Magnus. 'If Mrs Molland truly requires a pet, she should consider a little lapdog. You do not have room here for a pointer.'

'We have plenty of room,' put in Rose, angered by his calm assumption of authority. 'But I'm afraid we cannot have a puppy just at the moment.'

The look of disappointment on Sam's face tugged at her heart and she dropped down beside him, putting her hands on his shoulders.

'This is a bad time of year to bring home a puppy that needs so much exercise, my dear,' she said gently. 'Perhaps next time, when the weather is a little better and you are older.'

His lip trembled, but before he could reply Mrs Molland held out her hand to him.

'We can talk about this more in the morning. Come along now, Sam; bid your mama and our guests goodnight and I will take you up to bed.'

Rose put her arms around him and kissed him, standing at his side as he made his bow.

'Do not forget to thank Sir Lawrence for seeing you home,' Magnus reminded him.

'No, no, you have that the wrong way round,' replied Lawrence seriously. 'Sam showed *me* the way.' He held out his hand. 'Goodnight, Master Westerhill. I am greatly indebted to you.'

'So, what business is it that keeps you in Mersecombe?' enquired Magnus, when Sam and his grandmother had left the room.

The gentlemen were settling into chairs close to the fire, but Rose moved to the window seat, still trying to collect her wits.

'Oh, this and that,' Sir Lawrence responded vaguely. 'I return to Knightscote tomorrow, but I shall have to come back again oncc Wooler sends word that the dog is weaned.'

Magnus leaned back in his chair. 'You could send your man to collect it.'

'I could, of course, but I enjoy finding my way about.' He added apologetically, 'I fear I have been far too reclusive during my previous visits to Exmoor.'

'I do not see what you need with a dog when you are here for only a few weeks each year.' Rose's statement brought both men's eyes upon her and Magnus was moved to protest. Lawrence held up his hand.

'No, no, Emsleigh, she has a point.' Again she was subjected to that intense gaze. 'I have brought my keeper with me. The dog will be put into his care to be trained up, for use on whichever of my estates we are visiting.'

'Do you plan a long stay at Knightscote, Sir Lawrence?' asked Magnus.

Rose looked down at her hands, desperate to hear his answer.

'That depends. I have made no firm plans yet.'

She dared not look up, afraid of what she might see in his eyes.

'Well, sir, if you are still here at the end of October you should come to the Mersecombe Assembly,' declared Magnus. 'I will be able to introduce you to everyone. Not the highest society, of course, as you are used to in London, but nevertheless it will give you an opportunity to meet your neighbours. It is held at the Ship, so before you leave tomorrow you could take a look at the Assembly Room—I think you will agree it is a fine space for dancing.'

'And will you be attending, Mrs Westerhill?'

Rose jumped as Sir Lawrence addressed her.

'Why…yes.'

'Then, if I am still at Knightscote, I shall look forward to seeing you there.' He picked up his hat. 'I must go.'

Rose jumped to her feet.

'I shall see you out.'

Magnus immediately sat up.

'My dear, you should ring for Janet—'

'She will be helping Mama put Sam to bed.' Rose went to the door. 'This way, sir, if you please.'

The hall was blessedly free of people, but suddenly all the questions that had been flying around in Rose's head disappeared. All she could think of was Lawrence standing at her shoulder.

'Do you know, I am not sure I can recall my way back to the inn?' His low voice provoked in Rose a shiver of aching memory.

'Nonsense,' she retorted. 'You walked here only a short while ago.'

'Ah, but I was distracted by my companion's non-stop chatter. Would you be good enough to walk a little way with me?'

Rose knew she should refuse, but she took up her cloak and threw it around her shoulders. As they stepped outside Sir Lawrence stopped and she saw that he was staring at the shrubs beside the door, illuminated by the lamp from the parlour window.

'Rosemary,' he muttered. 'For remembrance.'

Rose gave a little shrug, trying to ignore the sensation of his eyes boring into her.

'I planted it as soon as I got home. By some miracle it has survived.'

She turned away quickly, hurrying through the garden and across the stream. Once they were on the road Sir Lawrence held out his arm to her and she laid her fingers on his sleeve. Beneath the fine cloth the muscle felt reassuringly solid.

'So you did not marry him on Lady Day.'

'No.'

'Because of your visit to Knightscote?'

'Of course not.' The denial was far too quick, unconvincing even to her own ears. 'My son is not yet ready for a new father.' She added, so he should be in no doubt, 'My opinion of you is unchanged, Sir Lawrence. You should not have come in search of me.'

'I did not. I am here on business of my own.'

'Oh.' Rose bit her lip, trying not to dwell upon her sense of disappointment. 'Well, I am glad of it. I, um, I suppose I should thank you for not mentioning the fact that we have met before.'

'Your mother was clearly unaware of it and I doubted very much if you had told Emsleigh.'

'No indeed.'

'So what did you tell them?'

'They think I was stranded at one of the outlying farms.'

They had reached the crossroads and Rose stopped.

'There.' She pointed. 'The Ship is just around the corner; you can see the glow from the lighted windows on the road.'

'Ah, yes, of course.' He caught her outstretched hand. 'Thank you. And will you give me permission to call—?'

'No!' She stepped away from him, pulling her fingers free. 'No. We agreed.'

'We agreed nothing. Ten months ago I let you ride out of my life—'

'I told you then it was better if we did not meet again. Nothing has changed.'

'You do not know that.'

Rose desperately wanted to believe him, just as she had wanted to believe Harry every time he promised he would mend his ways. She took refuge in her bitterness.

'A rake reformed?' Her lip curled. 'An impossibility.' She shivered. 'I must go back.'

She pulled her cloak about her and began to retrace her steps.

'So you will not allow me to call upon you?'

Rose stopped.

'No.'

'But you will be at the Assembly?'

She shrugged.

'That is not until the end of the month. I cannot think you will want to stay at Knightscote for so long.'

'I shall be there.'

'I cannot prevent you from attending a public assembly, Sir Lawrence, although I think you will find it dull work.'

She saw the flash of his white teeth in the moonlight.

'We shall see!'

He strode away, whistling, and Rose hurried back to Bluebell Cottage. How dare he come back into her life? What was he doing in Mersecombe, if he had not come to find her? She had told him they should not meet again and she would hold to that. After all, it was not just her happiness that was at stake if she allowed herself to become entangled with a rake, but that of her son.

Rose returned to the house to find her mother and Magnus waiting for her in the sitting room. Mrs Molland looked up, relieved, as she walked in.

'My dear, we were about to send out a search party!'

'I beg your pardon. Sir Lawrence was unsure of the way, so I stepped outside to—er—point him in the right direction.'

Magnus frowned.

'That was imprudent, Rose. I would not advise you to step out into the dark with any man, but when it is someone of Sir Lawrence's reputation…'

Mrs Molland nodded.

'Mr Emsleigh has the right of it, my love. Sir Lawrence and his circle are constantly mentioned in the London news sheets. You may recall even your aunt has mentioned him in her letters. Rake Daunton! Why, his name is for ever being linked with some society hostess or another. They say he is never seen twice with the same woman on his arm.'

'There has been very little about him this year, Mama.' And she had searched the newspapers more carefully than usual, looking for his name. Rose told herself she was not defending Sir Lawrence, merely trying to be fair and just.

'Perhaps we missed it.' Mrs Molland laughed. 'Good heavens, Rose, Mr Emsleigh will think the society gossip is the only page we read!' She added soberly, 'For all that, I was most grateful to Sir Lawrence for seeing Sam home. That was very thoughtful. And I was most impressed that he should then sit and converse with Sam and me in a very civilised manner. He is most agreeable.'

'I would expect nothing less of the man,' put in Magnus, giving an indulgent little laugh. 'I noticed at the Pullens' ball that he is like a magnet to you ladies. Gambling and flirting is how he spends most of his time in town.'

'I wish he had stayed there,' muttered Rose.

Magnus smiled at her.

'I know. It is a pity that you should meet him, but you need not worry. It is most likely he will return to Knightscote in the morning and we shall hear no more of him. But if he *should* come to the Assembly, I shall make very sure he understands that we are to be married next Lady Day, and if he attempts to go beyond the line of what is pleasing, he will have to answer to *me*.'

Never had Rose known the weeks to drag by so slowly. Her work at the village school occupied her for four mornings of the week, but she spent the rest of the time thinking of Sir Lawrence and wondering if he was still at Knightscote. She had forbidden him to call upon her, but that did not stop the flutter of hope every time there was a knock at the door.

The day of the Mersecombe Assembly dawned cold and wet. Heavy rain fell all morning; although the weather became drier as the day went on the thick cloud shrouding the hills remained, bringing an early dusk. Despite the drear weather Rose experienced a little thrill of anticipation as she walked with her mother the short distance from Bluebell Cottage to the Ship Inn. She told herself it was merely the thought of dancing that excited her; she had no expectations that Sir Lawrence would attend a provincial ball. After all, she could not even be sure that he was at Knightscote—he had certainly made no attempt to see her again.

That was as it should be, she told herself as she followed Mrs Molland into the Ship, but she could not prevent the rough edge of disappointment chafing her spirits when she could not see his tall figure amongst the crowd in the Long Room. Magnus and his sister were already present and came up immediately.

'It is as I feared,' declared Magnus, kissing and retaining Rose's hand. 'A sad crush. All the village must be here, including those who can ill afford it!'

'Fie, sir, they are a very good sort of people, and why should they not enjoy themselves?' Mrs Molland responded, her eyes bright as she surveyed the company. 'I am sure we shall enjoy some lively dancing this evening. Miss Emsleigh—what a delightful gown.'

Althea spread her flounced skirts. 'This colour is called blushing rose. It is all the rage in London.'

'You are quite the most fashionable lady here this evening,' replied Rose diplomatically. Privately she thought the pink a little bright, for it clashed horribly with Althea's yellow hair and plump red cheeks. In her opinion the gown would also be better for a little less ribbon and lace, but Althea seemed delighted with it.

'You are very kind to say so,' she replied, simpering. 'Especially when it is you, Mrs Westerhill, who is always being held up to me as a model of elegance. Always so…neat.'

She means plain and drab, thought Rose, but she was not offended. Her midnight-blue silk was not new and had only a single row of silver lace around the hem, but it suited her and she had always liked its simplicity. She glanced down at her corsage: three large white camellias pinned to her shoulder. Magnus had delivered it to the cottage that morning and impressed upon her that he had ordered the flowers to be brought down from Bristol at great expense. Since he had gone to so much trouble Rose was obliged to wear it, although she felt it was a trifle ostentatious, more a badge of ownership than regard. She chided herself for her ungratefulness, but the impression remained.

'Of course,' Althea continued, 'as a widow, no one would expect you to wear a new gown on every occasion.'

Mrs Molland was quick to jump to her daughter's defence.

'When one has an excellent figure, like Rose, no one remembers the gown, only how lovely she looks.'

Althea gave a tinkling laugh. She smoothed her gloved hands over her skirts.

'I am sure you must think me very extravagant to buy another new gown. I know Magnus is always complaining that I cost him a fortune.' She giggled. 'My poor brother cannot wait to have me married and off his hands.'

'I do not deny it,' Magnus replied. 'But these things cannot be hurried and he must be a man of excellent birth and good fortune. I am seriously considering taking Althea to London next year.' He took a step closer to Rose. 'When I have a wife to escort her.'

'Oh, London,' sighed Althea, glassy-eyed. 'How I long to be away from the country! Just think of it, parties and balls every night. And we would be able to meet some *real* gentlemen—like the one standing in the doorway!'

The change in her tone coincided with a sudden lull in conversation. Nearly everyone in the room was looking towards the entrance and Rose suspected hers was not the only heart that leapt at the sight of Sir Lawrence Daunton as he walked in. His hair was brushed back from his brow and gleamed like a raven's wing in the candlelight. His black coat fitted so perfectly it might have been moulded to his form, and the pale waistcoat and breeches only added to the sophisticated elegance of the man. She heard Magnus harrumph and mutter, 'Bond Street Beau,' but there was nothing ostentatious about Lawrence's dress. It was simplicity itself and in Rose's opinion he looked magnificent.

'Is he not the most handsome man you have ever seen?' Althea gave an ecstatic sigh. 'We danced together at the Pullens' ball last month. So very much a gentleman—I told him we attend the Mersecombe Assembly, but I never thought he would remember! Magnus, we must go and greet him.'

Magnus nodded. 'If you wish. Rose?'

She stepped away, raising her hand.

'Please, take your sister. Mama and I will go and sit down.' She saw the concern in her mother's eyes and forced a tiny smile. 'It is the heat. It is a little oppressive and I need to save my energy for the dancing…'

Mrs Molland led her to the benches at the side of the room. Rose gave a sigh of relief, knowing that they were temporarily shielded from Sir Lawrence's gaze. Magnus returned shortly after to claim her hand for the first dance and when he led her out she noticed that Lawrence was standing a little way down the line, partnering Althea. She was a little surprised to find Magnus smiling happily upon the couple.

'You do not object to Sir Lawrence dancing with your sister?'

Magnus spread his hands.

'Whatever Sir Lawrence's reputation, he is unlikely to act with impropriety towards my sister. Or, for that matter, towards my fiancée.' He leaned closer and smiled complacently. 'You have been a widow too long, my dear. You have forgotten what it is to have a man's protection.'

Her response was little more than a murmur, lost as the music began. The dancing was lively, but Rose's enjoyment was tempered by the knowledge that the movement of the dance would soon bring her face to face with Lawrence, a moment she longed for and dreaded in equal measure. Magnus was left behind; she made her way through the line, partner by partner, ever closer to Lawrence. Her mouth dried when he held his hand out to her, a challenge in his eyes. But there was understanding, too. He knew how hard it was for her to smile politely and act as if they were mere acquaintances.

The brief, heady moment as he took her hands and led her through the line of dancers was everything Rose had anticipated. Despite her best efforts to remain impartial her heart was singing. She kept her eyes fixed upon the top button of his waistcoat, frowning a little as she tried to concentrate on the steps.

'Why, Rose, are you afraid of me?'

Her eyes flew to his face.

'No.' Her voice was little more than a croak and she was relieved that at that moment he had to release her and move on to the next partner. She whispered, to his departing back, 'I am afraid of me.'

She lost sight of Lawrence as she was swept up by her next partner and carried away, her smile bright, feet tripping lightly through the familiar steps. The dance continued until she was back with Magnus again. The world was righting itself, but her heart was still pounding far too heavily against her ribs. She scolded herself for allowing her peace to be overset so easily.

It would be best, she thought, *if I did not allow him near me again.*

She danced a few more times with older, safely married gentlemen who wanted nothing more than to enjoy a lively dance with a pretty woman, but at the end of each set she kept her attention firmly fixed upon her partner until she was engaged with the next, or she had been returned safely to her mother's side.

She was congratulating herself upon her tactics as she stood by the refreshment table, flanked by Magnus and her mother, when she heard Miss Emsleigh's grating laugh behind her.

'Here they are, sir. I told you we would find them!' Rose looked round to see Althea approaching on Lawrence's arm. He smiled across at her, his blue eyes glinting wickedly.

'At last I have caught up with you, Mrs Westerhill. Would you honour me with this next dance?'

Alarm bells began to clamour in her head.

'Thank you, sir, but I have danced enough tonight.'

She tucked her hand into Magnus's arm, indicating she was happy to remain with him.

Magnus beamed, but said magnanimously, 'I assure you I have no objection if you wish to dance one more measure.'

'Sadly, I do not.' Rose's smile took in them all. She said firmly, 'I am sure you will find other, more willing partners, Sir Lawrence.'

The sudden spark of anger in his eyes shook Rose. A tremor of unease ran through her, but she refused to succumb to it and held her smile. He must learn that she was not his for the asking. Lawrence gave a stiff little bow.

'As you wish, madam.'

Althea gave a loud sigh and watched him walk away.

'What a shame. If I had known you meant to refuse, I would not have told him that I was going to dance the next with Magnus.'

'What?' Magnus raised his quizzing glass. 'Oh, Lord, I had forgotten. Come along then, my dear, we had best take our places.' He gave his arm to Althea and led her away.

Rose heard a slight huff from Mrs Molland.

'What is it, Mama? Why do you look at me that way? I was not uncivil.'

'No-o, but I think you might have accepted Sir Lawrence. He is, after all, a visitor to Mersecombe.'

'But he has a fearsome reputation, Mama. You know what Aunt Jane says of him.'

Mrs Molland frowned.

'Your aunt enjoys gossip, my love. Entertaining as it is to read, it is often grossly exaggerated. We should take as we find. And Sir Lawrence was very kind to little Sam.'

Rose looked away, acknowledging her mother's gentle rebuke with a slight flutter of her hand.

'I…I did not want to encourage him, Mama.'

'One dance in a public assembly! What harm could that do?' Mrs Molland shook her head.

Rose did not reply. Everyone in the room was aware of the identity of the elegantly dressed gentleman and Rose knew that there were those present who loved gossip just as much as her Aunt Jane. If they had the slightest reason to connect her name with Sir Lawrence, then her reputation would be in jeopardy. She was the widow of one womaniser and any goodwill would quickly evaporate if she was seen to encourage the advances of another, far more notorious rake!

From then on the evening descended into a game of cat and mouse. Rose studiously avoided Sir Lawrence. When he drew near to the refreshment table she made sure she was at the far end of the room; later, when she was sitting with her mother and she saw him approaching, Rose quickly excused herself and slipped away into the crowd. Her behaviour was making him angry; he might continue to smile as he made his bow to this person or that, but the set of his jaw and the slight narrowing of his eyes told Rose that his temper was on a tight rein. It made her even more determined not to go near him again that evening.

The Assembly drew to a close. The musicians packed away their instruments and the crowd began to disperse. Rose collected her wrap and returned to the ballroom. There was no sign of Sir Lawrence.

'Mr Emsleigh has offered to take us up in his carriage, is that not kind of him?' Mrs Molland gave Rose a gentle nudge.

'Mmm? Oh, yes—yes indeed. Thank you, Magnus.'

He looked down at Rose, who had her sturdy leather half-boots in her hand. 'My dear, there is no need to put those on if I am taking you in the carriage.'

Rose hesitated. Her mother and Althea were already waiting by the door. She waved at them.

'It will not take me a moment. You may all go on; I shall join you as soon as I am done.'

She sat down and tugged off her dancing slippers. Really, Magnus was so irritating. All very well for him to declare that she only had to step into the carriage, but she knew full well that the stairs brought them down to the side door of the inn and the coach would only be able to pull into the yard or to wait in the street. Either way they would have to walk on the dirty cobbles and she had no intention of risking her last pair of good dancing slippers. Angrily she took her time over lacing her boots. They could easily have walked. It was only a step to Bluebell Cottage, but if Magnus was determined to coddle her then he must wait.

The rooms were almost empty when at last Rose made her way to the door. The servants were already blowing out the candles, filling the air with thick, pungent smoke that swirled like grey mist in the deepening shadows. Quickly she hurried down the wide staircase. Noise from the inn filtered up to her, but the stairs had been designed to carry those attending balls and routs directly to and from the Long Room, keeping them separate from customers drinking in the taproom.

She reached the door and stepped out. To her right the Emsleighs' carriage was waiting in the yard, but even as she looked that way a hand shot out and gripped her arm, jerking her roughly into the shadows. She found herself pinned against a hard, unyielding chest, her cheek rubbing against the fine wool of an evening coat. Rose raised her head to protest, but immediately a dark head swept down and her lips were captured in a savage, familiar kiss.

Rose went weak with relief as she recognised her attacker. How could she not know the feel of those strong arms around her, the arresting mouth that worked on hers in such a demanding way? She was in Lawrence's arms, where she had so often dreamed to be. For a few moments she clung to him, her body compliant, ready to surrender, then she recovered her senses and pushed against him. She was powerless to free herself, his arms were like iron bands holding her fast, but he released her mouth, moving his lips to her ear.

'I do believe you have been avoiding me, Rose.'

His voice was low and warm. Desire stirred. She closed her eyes, steeling herself to reply.

'Have you not been avoiding *me* these past weeks?'

'Ah. So you noticed that.' There was a purr of satisfaction in his voice. 'I had not meant to come here tonight, but the temptation to see you again was too strong. Why would you not dance with me?'

He was holding her very close, his cheek rubbing against her hair as her body leaned into him. Her heart was jumping in her throat, making speech difficult.

'I…I did not wish to dance. I did not want to be near you.'

'You enjoyed being near me last Christmas.' His teeth nibbled gently at her ear and she bit down hard on her bottom lip to counteract the pleasure curling and growing inside her. 'You called it an idyll.'

'We knew it would not work. We agreed…'

'We agreed that you were coming back here to marry Emsleigh. That has not happened.'

'Single or wed, it makes no difference.'

She put her hands against his chest, determined not to give in.

'No?' The single word was so low, so quiet, yet her body reacted; her breasts grew taut, almost painful as they pushed towards him, aching for his touch. He traced one finger down her cheek and drew it gently along the line of her jaw. Rose closed her eyes. She stopped trying to push him away and instead her fingers clutched at his jacket. This was madness. She could hear voices calling her. She looked up, trying to see his face; Lawrence had pulled her into a shallow alcove where the shadows were deep and black, adding to the unreality of the situation. The temptation to give in to him was almost irresistible. He was a devil to torment her so!

'No,' she managed at last. 'Go back to Knightscote, Sir Lawrence. Better still, go back to London. I'll have none of you.'

'Too late for that, Rose. What if I tell your friends how you came calling upon me last Christmas Eve?'

She caught her breath in dismay.

'You would not do that. I would be ruined!'

She felt the heartbeat's hesitation before he replied.

'No, I will say nothing, but if you continue to avoid me quite so blatantly people will begin to wonder why you shun me. It is only a matter of time before tongues begin to wag.'

'You expect us to meet as…as indifferent acquaintances?'

'We must, unless you wish to be something more…'

'No!' She hissed out the word, panic adding urgency. 'Oh, will you not go away and leave me in peace?'

His arms tightened. He said angrily, 'Do you think I like this situation any more than you?'

'Then leave, sir. My life is here. I cannot do so.'

'No more can I, at least not yet!'

It was as if the words had been forced out of him. Rose frowned.

'Why should that be—what keeps you here?'

He did not reply, and into the silence came the clatter of boots on the stair. She heard Magnus saying irritably, 'She is not upstairs, nor in the retiring room. Where can she be?'

Rose tensed. Any moment he might turn towards the shadows and discover her. The dark shape that was Lawrence drew her closer. He whispered in her ear.

'Your friends are looking for you. You must go.' His lips brushed her cheek. 'The next time we meet at least treat me with some semblance of civility. I am going to be around for a good while yet, Rose, so you had best get used to it!'

Lawrence gave Rose a little push and she stepped out of the shadows.

'Rose! What in heaven's name—!'

Magnus came hurrying towards her, his breath clouding on the frosty air.

Quickly she moved to meet him.

'I…I dropped my fan…' She waved her hand, implying that it had skittered into the darkness. A quick peep showed her that the alcove was empty.

'Well, never mind that now, let us get you home and out of this cold.'

He guided her to the carriage and she climbed in beside her mother.

'Goodness, you are shivering,' declared Mrs Molland. 'You should have left your fan, my love. We could have walked up and retrieved it in the morning.'

'Well, well, no harm done,' declared Althea, her hands tucked snugly inside her swansdown muff. 'Tell Lewis to drive on, Magnus. The sooner we have dropped Rose and Mrs Molland at Bluebell Cottage, the sooner we can be home.'

Magnus jumped into the carriage and almost fell into his seat as they pulled away, the lamps of the inn yard momentarily lighting up the carriage.

'My dear, whatever have you done to your corsage?'

Magnus's cry caused Rose to glance down. Her cloak had fallen open to reveal the neckline of her gown and on her shoulder were the sorry-looking remains of the three camellias, crushed flat against her gown.

Magnus was muttering about the inordinate cost of obtaining such delicate flowers and guiltily Rose pulled her cloak together to hide the damage.

'Oh, my,' giggled Althea. 'They look well and truly ravished!'

Rose sank her teeth into her bottom lip and stared miserably out into the night.

Ravished was exactly how she felt.

CHAPTER FIVE

FROM the deepest shadows Lawrence watched the Emsleigh carriage drive away, the horses' hooves ringing on the cobbles. Hell and damnation, he should never have come here tonight. He thought savagely that if George Craven had not been in such a fix he would never have come back to Exmoor at all.

Craven had come to him in London, when Lawrence was enjoying a solitary dinner at White's.

'Daunton, my friend. I have been looking for you all over.'

'Good evening, George. Come and join me,' Lawrence greeted him with the wave of his fork.

'Heard you were in town,' said Craven, sitting down at the table, 'but you have not shown your face in any of your usual haunts.'

'Turned over a new leaf, George.'

'Aye, so it would appear.' Craven grinned. 'The ladies are bemoaning the absence of Rake Daunton from their drawing rooms. What have you been doing with yourself in town?'

'Visiting my man of business.'

'Dull work!'

'Aye, but necessary. I spent the spring touring my estates in Surrey, and I have been in Hampshire for the past month, at Daunton, putting everything in order. Hadn't realised just how run-down the place had become. Once my business here is ended then I shall be going back. I dare say I shall make my home there.' He shot a sideways glance at his friend. 'Does it surprise you, George, that I can give up town life so easily?'

His friend shook his head.

'I always thought you would, one day.'

'The devil you did!'

'You forget, Lawrence, we've known each other for ever. You always loved Daunton, but you began to avoid it when it became linked with marriage to my late, lovely, lamented sister. Never could quite bring yourself to make that final commitment, could you, Lawrence?'

'Damn you, George, you know I always intended to go back.' He pushed his plate away, his appetite gone. 'We agreed we would wed when she was one and twenty, not before. But if she had only said the word I would have come back—'

'No need to blame yourself, old friend. Belle wanted the marriage even less than you.' He met Lawrence's amazed gaze with a rueful smile. 'I never thought much of it at the time, but she said to me once that she thought she would have liked to be a nun and dedicate her life to good works.'

'Well, if you think of the way she lived, in the end that is what she did.' Lawrence sighed, running a hand through his hair. 'What must she have thought of me? I positively flaunted my indiscretions—I never denied any scandal, no matter how outrageous or untrue.'

George shrugged.

'As for that, she knew better than to believe a half of what she read in the newspapers.'

Lawrence sighed.

'I still think I treated her abominably. I am surprised you did not call me out, George. I deserved it.'

'Devil a bit, I could hardly pull caps with you over your behaviour when I was kicking up every sort of lark myself!'

'No, it is good of you to say so, but I am ashamed of how I behaved towards your family. I wish I could make it up to you.'

'Perhaps you can.' George signalled to the waiter to bring them another bottle.

Lawrence frowned at him across the table. 'I heard you had some pretty bad losses recently. What was it, cards? Hazard?'

Craven shook his head, saying glumly, 'I wish it had been! No, I decided I should be doing something more prudent with my money. Prudent, hah!' Craven emptied his glass and refilled it. 'I underwrote a merchant ship, sailing out of Bristol. Hadn't even cleared the Channel before she foundered, ship and all the cargo lost.'

'A disaster, then.' Lawrence sat back. 'Many lives lost?'

'Only one. The bosun was lost overboard as the crew took to the boats. The rest were picked up by a passing vessel and brought safely ashore.'

'Fortunate that there were enough boats on board to take them all.'

'Aye, wasn't it,' muttered George Craven. He scowled. 'And how thoughtful of the owner to issue promissory notes to his crew, in case the ship should miscarry.'

'You suspect foul play?'

'Aye, and so do my fellow underwriters. We haven't paid out yet, and don't intend to do so until more investigations have taken place.' He leaned forwards. 'Which is why I have come to you, Daunton.'

'Me?' Lawrence laughed. 'I am no investigator!'

'We sent an agent to Bristol to talk to the crew, but very few of them were local, and those he did find would not talk to him. So he went to Somerset to find the captain, but he came up with nothing.'

'Then it seems a hopeless case. You will have to pay up.'

'But you do not understand!' George Craven banged his fist on the table, causing several of the other diners to look around. He chewed his lip for a moment. 'I was greedy, I admit it. I was convinced there could be no risk. It was high summer, the journey a routine sailing from Bristol to France, albeit with a bigger cargo than usual, a valuable one, too: the best English woollen cloth, fine linen, porcelain and pewter—' He gave a bitter laugh. 'What could possibly go wrong? I agreed to underwrite more than I could readily afford. If I have to pay out, I shall be ruined.' He looked up. 'I shall have to go to my father, and the only way he will be able to pay my debts will be to sell the Hampshire estate. It would kill my mother, I think, to leave the house she has lived in all her married life.'

'Do you want me to loan you the money?'

'No, no, I could not ask you for such a sum.'

Lawrence shook his head.

'Then I do not see how I can help you, my friend.'

Craven leaned closer.

'You have a property on Exmoor, do you not? The ship's owner has a house there and Captain Morris lives nearby. Why, man, they are practically your neighbours. It is possible they will let something slip to you.'

Lawrence shook his head.

'I'm sorry, my friend, this is not my line of work. I have no plans to go back there.'

'I'd go myself, but you know what it is like in these areas, any stranger is looked upon with suspicion. But if you were to go, well, no one would think anything of it.' George reached for the bottle and refilled their glasses. 'The bosun's family live on that coast, too, near a small village called Mersecombe. These are seafaring people, Lawrence; you could talk to them, see what they think of the ship foundering. If there is the least chance that this was no accident, I want to know about it!'

Lawrence lifted his glass, staring at the ruby-red contents.

'I haven't been to Knightscote this year,' he murmured, almost to himself.

'Then it is time you did, my friend,' declared Craven. 'What could be more natural than that you should visit the place now, with autumn coming on?'

Lawrence paid him no heed. He was picturing an exquisite little face with large blue-grey eyes that smiled up at him so trustingly. He had given his word to Rose that he would not seek her out and, despite the fact that she was constantly in his thoughts, he would abide by that. She would be married by now to her dull and upright tradesman. She might even be with child.

The idea wrenched at his gut, but suddenly he needed to know. To learn that Rose was happy and content in her new life would be painful, but nothing to the uncertainty that tortured him now. He sat very still, his hands clasped about his wineglass. What if he had business in Mersecombe, and they met by chance?

He raised his eyes to look at his friend.

'Very well, George. I make you no promises, but I will look into this case for you.'

How Lawrence regretted that momentary weakness. To return, to see Rose again and find her every bit as alluring as he remembered had only brought back the memories he had spent the summer trying to suppress. She wanted nothing to do with him and to observe her tricks and evasions at the Assembly only rubbed salt into the wound.

Lawrence had planned to stay at the Ship overnight,

but he now decided he would prefer to ride back to Knightscote. He strode into the inn and gave instructions for his horse to be saddled.

'You'll never be travelling at this time o'night, sir!' declared the landlord.

'Why not, there's a moon. You need not worry.' Lawrence reached into his pocket for his purse. 'I shall pay you for the bed, even though I won't be sleeping in it!'

Twenty minutes later he was trotting out of Mersecombe and making his way up over the moor towards Knightscote. The clouds had given way to a clear sky and a sharp frost now glittered in the moonlight, turning the world silver-grey. The bitter night air nipped at his cheeks, but he was glad of the icy chill; it cooled his anger and for the first time in hours he could think clearly.

He had been a fool to go to the Assembly. He was no further forwards with his investigations and he had suffered the humiliation of being snubbed. It was a novel experience. During his years in town he had never been rejected by any woman. The stricter chaperons might keep their innocent young charges away from him, but they could not prevent the young ladies from casting longing glances in his direction. He had been so sure that Rose would at least dance with him. He had anticipated the thrill of it; to anyone listening they would be talking upon unexceptional topics, but their carefully coded words would refer to their time together at

Knightscote. Even now he could imagine her eyes smiling into his, sharing the joke.

He shivered. She had spent the evening running away from him and when at last he cornered her she had refused to dance, had avoided all contact with him, until that last stolen kiss in the darkness. Then she had responded to him, albeit reluctantly.

For the first time in his adult life he doubted his ability to charm a woman. Perhaps Annabelle had never been as enamoured of him as he had believed: he remembered how incredulous he had been when Rose had suggested that his fiancée had preferred her single state. Perhaps she would have married him, to please her parents, to fulfil the contract that would combine two great estates. He would never know. He had never asked her, they had never *talked*. It was too late now to help Annabelle, but he would show Rose that there was more to him than smooth words and careless flirtations.

With a sigh he looked up at the cloudless night sky. The deep blue reminded him of Rose's gown. Heaven knew he had seen the back of her flowing skirts often enough as she spent the evening moving away from him.

'You are nothing but a fool,' he told himself angrily. 'She has told you she wants nothing more to do with you so you had best let be.'

He squared his shoulders and straightened in the saddle. Tonight had been a mistake. He would not go out of his way to see her again.

* * *

Rose huddled in her corner of the carriage, thankful that she was not expected to contribute to the discussion of the night's events. She was still shaken by being so roughly accosted by Sir Lawrence. That she had angered him was plain, but why did he not go away and leave her in peace? What reason could he have for lingering in Mersecombe, if he had not come to seek her out? She wondered if she had spoken this last thought aloud, for she heard Magnus say, 'Dashed if I know why the fellow showed up tonight. I know I told him of the Assembly, but I never really expected him to take me up on it. To my knowledge he has never before ventured away from Knightscote on his visits to Exmoor.'

'Well, I expect him to call upon me at Emsleigh House very soon,' replied Althea.

Magnus chuckled.

'I am not surprised, for you were making eyes at him all evening, you naughty puss. Well, if he calls, I suppose I shall have to invite him to dinner one night.'

'*You* are not deterred by his reputation with the ladies, sir?' asked Mrs Molland.

'Pho! I confess I was a little wary of the fellow to begin with, but I saw nothing in his manner to alarm me. He made no attempt to flirt with anyone tonight. I dare say his reputation is much exaggerated. Sir Lawrence is a rich man and as such his every move in town attracts attention. And if he wishes to fix his interest with my sister, well, his birth is impeccable and with his wealth I would have no hesitation in welcoming him as a brother-in-law!'

Rose shifted uncomfortably in her corner. She had seen Althea's attempts to capture Lawrence's interest and did not think they were successful, but what if she was wrong? In their last few moments together Lawrence had intimated that it would be necessary for them to meet. What if he was trying to fix his interest with Althea? Rose shivered. The idea was preposterous. Wasn't it?

Rose was glad to open up the little schoolroom the next morning. She needed to keep her mind away from the Assembly. To see Lawrence again had awoken all the memories she had tried so hard to bury, and when he had pulled her roughly into his arms and kissed her in the black shadows at the edge of the inn yard, her emotions had rioted out of control. She wanted him so badly that it hurt.

If she had been living in a fairy-tale world, she thought she would have given in to the demands of her body—and her heart. She could have danced with Lawrence, her infatuation clear for all the world to observe. The evening would have been one of unalloyed pleasure as they laughed and danced and talked together. But this was not a fairy tale. Any hint of impropriety and she would lose her position as teacher here in Mersecombe. Although it did not pay much, it provided a boost to her meagre savings and, more than that, the post carried with it the respect of the village. That meant a lot to her, not only for her own sake but for her mother's, and for Sam. It was very hard for him, growing up in Mersecombe without a father—he must not feel ashamed of his mother.

And what about marriage? Not that it had been mentioned, but nevertheless the question gnawed at her. Marriage to Sir Lawrence would give her respect, would it not? But only until some other pretty face lured him into infidelity.

'I do not know why you are even bothering to consider such things, Rose Westerhill,' she muttered savagely as she put out the slates ready for the morning lesson. 'You are not of his world. It is not marriage that he is likely to offer you!'

The door opened to admit the first of her pupils and she forced her mind back to the present. This was her world now, until she married Magnus in the spring. She found she was not looking forward to the event with any great enthusiasm, but Magnus represented security for her and for Sam. She would miss teaching, but she was sure she would find plenty of things to occupy her day as wife of one of the richest merchant traders in the area.

She looked up as Sam came in with Jem, chattering noisily. Rose frowned and gestured to them to sit down. In the schoolroom she tried to treat Sam like any other pupil, which was why she allowed him to wait at the cottage until Jem came by and the two of them could walk to school together rather than dragging him out of bed an hour earlier to accompany her.

Dear Sam. Everyone said he looked like her with his thatch of blond hair and blue-grey eyes, but she constantly saw his father in him, in the tilt of his head, his ready smile and charm of manner. As Magnus's wife she would be able to give Sam the education he deserved. He would grow up a gentleman, able to make his way in the world. She might not love Magnus, but she esteemed him. He would make a dull but faithful husband, she was sure, and that was all she required.

'Sir Lawrence. You've come to collect the puppy, I suppose.'

The woman holding the door open was no more than thirty, but a harsh life and her recent widowhood had etched lines in her face that made her look much older. Lawrence gave her his most charming smile.

'Good day to you, Mrs Wooler. I have indeed.' He held up the basket. 'And I thought you might find a use for these.' He was rewarded by the flush of pleasure on the woman's worn face.

'Oranges! That's very generous of you, Sir Lawrence.'

She stood back and signalled to him to enter, as he had known she would.

'They arrived yesterday from the hothouses on my Surrey estate, but I cannot use them all myself.'

A grey-haired lady was waiting for them in the sitting room, smoothing her gnarled hands over her apron.

'Here is Sir Lawrence, Mother Wooler, come to fetch the bitch he's chosen,' announced the younger woman. 'And look at what he has brought us.'

'I can see.' Old Mother Wooler smiled at him, gracious as a duchess. 'You will take a glass of fruit wine with us?' She indicated a chair at one side of the hearth and sat down opposite him. 'My husband is still out in the fields, sir, so you may have his place and welcome.'

The younger Mrs Wooler carried a glass of wine to them and stood, nervously clasping her hands together.

'I wonder—would ye mind waiting 'til our Jem has come in before you takes your pup, Sir Lawrence? He shouldn't be so very long…'

'Now, Maggie, Sir Lawrence is a busy man and can't linger on the whim of my grandson—'

'No, no, I should be delighted to wait,' put in Lawrence. He took the smallest sip of the overly sweet fruit wine. 'I take it Jem is still at the schoolroom?'

'Aye, learning his letters, good as gold,' replied the old lady proudly. 'Reads to me a passage from the Bible every night, he does. He'll not go to sea to earn his living, like his dad, God rest his soul.'

'You must miss your son a great deal, ma'am.'

'Aye, we do.' The old woman lifted the corner of her apron to wipe her eyes.

'He was on the *Sealark*, was he not?' said Lawrence gently.

'Aye, she sank out there in the Channel. Fire broke out, they said, and Ruben was lost in the confusion to get the men into the jolly boats.' She was silent for a moment, her thoughts far away, then with a visible effort she smoothed out her apron. 'Still, I'm thankful that we still have Abel. Losing two boys to the sea would have been too much to bear, although we wouldn't be the first around here to do so.' She reached out a hand to her daughter-in-law. 'But it was a good day when Ruben married his sweetheart and brought her here to live with us. We've been able to comfort each other, ain't that so, Maggie?'

'It is, truly, Mother Wooler. And it's good for Jem to be here, where he has his grandfather and uncle to teach him how to go on.' Maggie Wooler gave a tired little smile. 'It's a sad thing for a boy to lose his father.'

'Aye. I feel sorry for the poor little Westerhill boy, growing up with only his mother and grandma for company.'

'But that will change in the spring, Mother, when Mrs Westerhill marries Mr Emsleigh.'

Lawrence quickly brought the conversation back to its original course.

'So you intend to stay here with Jem, do you, Mrs Wooler?' The widow looked at him blankly. He added gently, 'Once the insurers pay out…'

'Oh, you mean the note that Mr Emsleigh gave us?' She shook her head. 'That money is going away for Jem.' She put the wine bottle on the hearth and hurried out of the room.

Her mother-in-law watched her go.

'Poor dear,' she muttered, shaking her head. 'Four months it's been and she still can't quite believe Ruben's not coming back. But at least Jem is provided for. It ain't as if we need the money, after all,' continued the old lady. 'The farm provides enough for us, and now we have Abel back working here we shall do very well.'

'I am still very new to this area,' remarked Lawrence.

'Is it common practice for shipowners to give these notes against the ship sinking?'

'Never happened before that I know of, but my son Abel might tell 'ee different. All I know is that when Ruben came in and told us that everyone sailing on the *Sealark* would get a payout if the ship miscarried I couldn't think but that it was a good thing. Not that we wouldn't rather have Ruben back with us, but forty-five guineas is a goodly sum. The note was left with Maggie, of course, to do with as she will, and it's her decision to put it aside for Jem.'

'Forty-five guineas?' Lawrence's brows went up. 'A good sum indeed.'

'Aye, Ruben was bosun, see, so gets more.' The old woman nodded. 'Abel only gets thirty, but that's not to be sniffed at. I'd wager 'tis more than the poor school-teacher gets in one year. Not that she ain't worth a great deal more, her being a lady born.'

Since the conversation had come back to Rose, Lawrence could not resist a question.

'Did you know her family, ma'am?'

'Nay, sir, she was from Barnstaple way, but I was born in Exford, where she and her husband lived, so I knows more than most.'

She sat back in her chair and drank her wine with every appearance of relish. She finished her wine and turned her bird-bright glance upon him.

'More wine, Sir Lawrence?'

He leaned down to pick up the bottle.

'Allow me, Mrs Wooler.'

As he had suspected, once she had a full glass she was ready to talk again.

'I don't say anything in front of the family,' she said. 'I wouldn't like the lady to think her business was common knowledge in Mersecombe, but you're a man of the world, sir, and I guess you've seen men like Westerhill before, them as can't resist both the bottle and a pretty face. He was a bad 'un.' She scowled, shaking her head. 'Me sister's midwife in Exford and she believes it was 'is doing that made Mrs Westerhill lose 'er baby. Poor dearie. Ill for weeks, she was, and the doctors said the damage was such that she would never have more children. She insisted that she lost her footing and fell down the stairs, but m'sister said she'd never seen such bruises, and she was with her when Westerhill came in, crying for forgiveness. Forgiveness—tch! I know what I'd have given 'im!'

Lawrence maintained a mask of polite interest as he listened to the old woman, but inside he was raging against Harry Westerhill. It was as much as he could do to prevent his hands clenching into fists at the thought of what he would like to do to such a man. He wanted to go and find Rose, hold her close and promise that he would never let anyone harm her again. A cold hand twisted at his stomach. She would refuse to listen to him, of course, especially after the way he had treated her at the Assembly. Was it any wonder that Rose did not believe he could change? The distant thud of a door and a sudden flurry of noise interrupted his thoughts. Old Mrs Wooler gave a dry chuckle.

'Ah, that's our Jem home now.'

It was not one boy but two that erupted into the room. Sam Westerhill stood expectantly beside his friend, cap in hand and looking so much like his mother that Lawrence had to clamp his jaw closed to prevent himself from remarking upon it.

'Just in time,' announced the old lady. 'Sir Lawrence is here to take his pup, so you had best go and say your goodbyes.'

'Yes, Grandma.'

Lawrence stood up.

'Come along then, Jem—show me the way!'

Lawrence and the boys crossed the yard to one of the smaller outhouses. Jem carried a lantern, for although the sun had not set, the shadows were lengthening and they would need its light once they entered the barn.

'How will you get her home?' asked Sam, skipping along beside Lawrence.

'I have a basket.' Lawrence sidestepped across to the gig and reached into the footwell. 'There, that will be more than sufficient, do you not think?'

'She'll be snug enough in there.' Jem nodded.

He unbolted the door to the outhouse and held up the lamp. The pointer bitch and her puppies were cosily tucked on to a pile of straw in one of the wooden stalls, sleeping peacefully. She raised her head as Jem moved forwards, alert for any danger to her offspring. Lawrence held Sam back.

'We had best wait until she knows we mean no harm.'

A board had been propped across the entrance to the stall to prevent the puppies from escaping; once Lawrence was confident that they would not alarm the mother he allowed Sam to step over. He followed, being careful not to tread on any of the small bundles of liver-and-white fur that were now moving around the floor. Lawrence identified the puppy he had chosen, a well-grown, healthy bitch with liver-coloured patches across her head.

'May I hold her?' asked Sam.

Lawrence glanced an enquiry at Jem, who nodded.

Sam picked up the wriggling, squirming bundle. The puppy lifted her head and licked at his nose.

'She is very lively.' Sam giggled. 'I hope you know how to look after her.'

'Well, I shall give her to my keeper to train,' said Lawrence apologetically. 'He is much the best person to do so.'

'She'll be a good gun dog, sir,' said Jem, kneeling beside the mother and tickling her ears. 'She comes from very good stock.'

Sam gave a very loud sigh.

'I wish I could have a dog. I would look after it and teach it to mind me, then when it was bigger it would come about with me and protect me from the bigger boys.'

'Oh, do they trouble you?' asked Lawrence.

Sam shrugged. 'Sometimes, if Jem is not with me.'

'They mean no harm,' said Jem. 'It is the way, to pick

on those of us who have no father.' He looked up. 'Abel is teaching us to box.'

'Very useful,' said Lawrence gravely.

'Jem is very handy with his fists,' added Sam, proud of his friend's achievement. 'But Abel says I'm too small yet to punch properly.'

Lawrence ruffled his hair.

'It is not always about your size, young man. There are few tricks you can use to give you the advantage.'

'Really?' Sam looked up, his eyes shining. 'Would you teach me?'

'Stow it,' muttered Jem, frowning. 'You can't ask Sir Lawrence that, he'll think you im…impertinent.'

Lawrence laughed.

'Do not look so anxious, Jem, I am not at all offended, and, yes, Sam, I would happily show you a few things you can do to protect yourself. But not tonight, for I must get my new puppy back to Knightscote.'

'I still wish I could take her home with me.' Sam hugged the puppy even closer.

'These are working dogs, Sam.' Lawrence scooped up another of the puppies that was trying to escape and put it back on the straw. 'I doubt if your mother or grandmother go out shooting.'

'No.' Sam sighed. 'But Mama does like to go for long walks!'

'Anyway, we have buyers for them all now,' said Jem. 'By this time next week they will all be gone.'

'Is your house very far away from here, Sir Lawrence?'

'It will take me the best part of an hour to get there.

Are you worried that the puppy will be cold? There's a folded cloth in the basket, you see, and I shall throw a rug over it while I am travelling.'

Sam giggled again as the puppy tried to bite his chin.

'I think she is my favourite,' he said.

Lawrence bent down until he was level with Sam and the puppy.

'And if she was yours, what would you call her?'

Sam frowned in concentration.

'I would call her… I would call her Bandit, because her markings look like a mask!'

'Then that shall be her name,' announced Lawrence with a smile.

Sam stared at him.

'Oh, that's…th-thank you, sir!'

As Sam stammered out his gratitude for this honour they heard footsteps on the cobbled yard.

'Sam, are you in there? Come along now, it is time we were going!'

Lawrence jumped to his feet and turned in time to see Rose enter the barn. In the dim lamplight the mulberry-coloured cloak and bonnet accentuated the delicate tone of her skin. Her cheeks were flushed and her eyes sparkled, as if she had relished the walk uphill to the farm.

'Oh, Sir Lawrence!' Instantly the sparkle was replaced by wariness. 'Mrs Wooler said I would find the boys here…'

'They are helping me collect my new acquisition.'

'This is Bandit.' Sam stepped forwards, holding up

the puppy for his mother to see. 'She is Sir Lawrence's new puppy and he let me give her a name!'

'He—he did? That was very good.' Rose was looking everywhere except at Lawrence. Who could blame her if she was uneasy in his company? He cursed himself for allowing his anger to get the better of him at the Assembly. She held her hand out to her son. 'Give Sir Lawrence back his puppy now, Sam. We must go home.'

'So you found them!' Old Mrs Wooler wheezed in, wrapped in a heavy shawl. 'Oh dear, oh dear, sir, you have straw all over your clothes. Will you step into the house again and I'll have Jem fetch a brush for you…?'

'No, no, ma'am, thank you. I must be going.' He carefully took Bandit from Sam and placed her in the basket. 'Thank you for your help, Master Westerhill.'

'Can I carry the basket to the carriage for you, sir?'

'Sam!' Rose reached out her hand again. 'Come along, young man. It is time we were going home.'

'Oh, but please!'

They were being shepherded out of the barn by Jem, who was anxious to settle the mother and her remaining puppies for the night.

'I have no objection to him carrying the basket,' said Lawrence mildly.

'Now, isn't it a fortunate thing that Sir Lawrence has his gig?' declared Mrs Wooler. 'I am sure he would be happy to drop you and your boy off at your cottage, Mrs Westerhill.'

'Ooh, yes! If you please, sir!' cried Sam.

'Oh, no, there is no need—'

Lawrence cut through Rose's protests.

'It is on my way, Mrs Westerhill. It would be very discourteous of me to drive past you.' Rose looked around, shifted from one foot to another and glanced down at Sam, who hovered expectantly. 'Young Sam may sit in between us and hold the basket,' murmured Lawrence helpfully.

'There now, Mrs Westerhill. What are you waiting for?' Mrs Wooler took Rose's arm and began to walk her back towards the gig. 'Let us get you up in that seat and Sir Lawrence will have you home in a twinkling.'

Rose capitulated, but she ignored Lawrence's hand and nimbly climbed up into the carriage. Lawrence lifted Sam onto the seat and placed the basket with its precious cargo in his lap. He pulled out the carriage rug.

'I think this is big enough to cover your legs, the basket and your mother—'

'I will do that.' Rose quickly batted away his hands as he tried to tuck the rug around her knees.

'As you wish.'

Once he had said all that was necessary to Mrs Wooler, Lawrence jumped up into the gig and set off down the winding lane.

'Are you warm enough, ma'am?'

'Perfectly, thank you.'

Sam was settled happily beside him, but Rose was sitting tense and rigid on the far side of the gig. Her silence weighed heavily between them.

He said abruptly, 'I am ashamed of my behaviour towards you last night.'

'I will not discuss this in front of my son!'

'I have no intention of *discussing* anything, but I must apologise and there is no reason why the boy should not hear me.' He glanced down at Sam. 'I was very uncivil to your mama, and I humbly beg her pardon, and yours. A gentleman should always respect and protect a lady, Sam, remember that.'

'Yes, sir.'

'Very well.' Even in the gloom he knew Rose was glaring at him over Sam's head. 'We will say no more about it, if you please.'

Lawrence wanted to say much more about it, but now was not the time. Instead he remarked, 'The Woolers are good people. They had only the two sons, I believe?'

'Yes, Ruben and Abel.'

'And both wanted to be sailors rather than follow their father on the farm?'

'Yes, but I think the death of his brother persuaded Abel to give up the sea.'

'Jem says Ruben was the best sailor ever,' put in Sam. 'He sailed across Mersecombe Bay to Sealham Point once, and put ashore there. He carved his name on the rocks. Jem's going to show me.'

'Oh, no,' said Rose quickly. 'You are not to go out sailing with Jem. You know his mama will not allow that.'

'I know *that*,' replied Sam. 'She is afraid he will

drown, like his poor papa. No, Jem says at low tide we can walk around the cliff to Sealham Point.'

'But not in winter,' Rose replied. 'It is not to be thought of until the weather improves.'

'But, Mama—'

'It would be a pretty miserable journey when it is this cold,' observed Lawrence.

'Oh, we would not mind that,' said Sam.

'But your mother would,' Lawrence replied quietly. 'You are the man of your household, Sam. She would worry for you and you would not want that, would you?'

'No, of course not.'

'And Jem, too, is needed on the farm. He will be expected to earn his keep, now his father is not there to provide for him.' Rose sighed. 'They must miss Ruben very much.'

'They do.' Sam nodded. 'Abel says that when he gets his money from Mr Emsleigh, he will have a stone carved with Ruben's name and put up in the church.'

'It is fortunate that Emsleigh gave them those promissory notes. Do you know why he did so, ma'am?'

'Why should you ask me that?' Rose sounded surprised. 'Magnus does not discuss his business with me, but it is the nature of the man to take care of those in his employ. That is why he took out the insurance.'

'If he is to pay the whole crew, it will amount to quite a sum.'

'That merely shows Magnus considered the risks so very slight.'

Lawrence said nothing, giving his attention to guiding his horse through the near-darkness. He had his own ideas about why Emsleigh had offered his crew that money, and why he had taken out such a high insurance on his cargo, but his suspicions were so far unproven. Should he share them with Rose and put her on her guard against Emsleigh? Would she believe him? He doubted it.

'I am surprised to find you driving a common gig, Sir Lawrence. A little beneath your touch, I would have thought.'

The gentle teasing in her voice decided it. She was thawing towards him and he would do nothing to jeopardise that.

'It is not my usual carriage, but perfect for these roads.' He grinned as they bounced over a particularly stony section and Rose grabbed the side-rail. 'I would not risk my racing curricle here.'

Sam looked up.

'You have a curricle? Ooh, I should like to see it.'

'Alas, it is in London.'

'Then how do you usually travel when you are here?' the boy asked.

'On horseback.'

'I like horses,' Sam declared. 'Evans is going to teach me to ride, one day, when I have a pony of my own. Then I shall ride up to Knightscote to see Bandit, if I may.'

'We must see what we can do about finding you a pony,' said Rose. She was smiling, and when Lawrence glanced at her she even met his eyes for a brief moment.

'*Pax*?' he murmured.

The dim light made it difficult to read her expression, but he was encouraged by the slight nod of her head. She turned away again, peering into the distance.

'Bluebell Cottage is just ahead of us, sir, and my mother is in the doorway, looking out for us.'

Lawrence drew up at the gate and Mrs Molland hurried to the little bridge to meet them.

'There you are at last, Rose. I was beginning to worry, with it growing so dark. Good evening, Sir Lawrence. How kind of you to bring Sam and my daughter home safely.'

'It was my pleasure, ma'am.' Lawrence handed the reins to Sam. 'Hold him steady for me, while I help your mother to get down.'

He smiled at the boy's obvious delight and left him concentrating hard on holding the reins, knowing all the time that nothing short of a pistol shot across its ears would make the nag between the shafts move an inch.

Watching such skilful handling of her son, it was only when Sir Lawrence stood at the side of the gig that Rose realised she should have climbed down earlier. Now she was obliged to put her hand in his. The memory evoked by his touch made her freeze and in that brief moment Lawrence took charge. Releasing her fingers, he put his hands firmly around her waist and lifted her out of the carriage. She expected him to prolong his hold and was prepared to protest, but as soon as her feet touched the ground he released her. Rose was obliged to grab hold of his coat as her knees gave way.

'Steady!'

He caught her again. There was something supremely comforting about the feel of his arms around her. The deep breath she took to calm herself had quite the opposite effect, for it carried with it the distinctive fragrance he wore and her wayward mind conjured up images of lying naked with Lawrence before a roaring fire. The shrieking of the hinges as Mrs Molland opened the gate was like a sharp rebuke for indulging in such memories. Rose quickly disengaged herself.

'I beg your pardon. I lost my balance. I must be a little cold from the journey.'

'Then let us get you indoors,' declared Mrs Molland. 'Samuel, come along, my dear.'

'A moment, Grandmama.' Sam secured the reins and scrambled down onto the road and made a very creditable bow. 'Goodnight, sir, and thank you for allowing me to name Bandit. Perhaps we might be able to come to Knightscote and see her one day?'

'Perhaps.' Sir Lawrence put a hand on his shoulder. 'Now, sir, take your mother indoors before she catches a chill!'

'Yes, come along, Sam.' Rose held out her hand to him.

'We did not have time to talk properly at the Assembly,' said Mrs Mollard, closing the gate. 'I wanted to invite you to come and take tea with us.'

Standing behind her mother, Rose shook her head vehemently, but Lawrence chose to ignore it.

'I would be delighted, Mrs Molland. I shall call the next time I am in Mersecombe.'

'Now you have your puppy I would have thought your business in the village was at an end,' said Rose, frowning at him.

'Oh, no, I expect to be riding this way often in the next few weeks.'

Rose detected a hint of laughter in his words and her eyes narrowed. Was he teasing her again? She said coolly, 'I am obliged to you, sir, for bringing Sam and me home, but we must not delay you any longer. You will not want to keep your horse standing in this chill wind. Samuel, come with me now.'

She caught Sam's hand and almost dragged him up the path.

'Well,' declared Mrs Molland, following behind, 'that is the second time Sir Lawrence has been of assistance to us. Did he come upon you in the lane, my love?'

'No, he was at the farm,' muttered Rose. 'Do hurry, Mama, it is far too cold to tarry out of doors.'

'Grandmama, he let me give his puppy a name,' cried Sam. 'And he let me carry her basket!'

'Did he now? Come inside and you can tell me all about it…'

The door closed firmly upon the little family and the voices were lost. Lawrence grinned to himself as he drove away. Rose was thawing towards him and now Mrs Molland had invited him to take tea. Mrs Rose

Westerhill might not like the idea, but he had been given another chance to show her he could behave like a gentleman and he was going to take it!

CHAPTER SIX

ROSE knew he would call. Much as she knew it would be better for her peace of mind if she never saw Sir Lawrence Daunton again, she could not deny she was curious to know just what was keeping him at Knightscote. That he had no intention of removing from the area in the near future she learned from Sam, who came home after spending the day with Jem to say that Sir Lawrence had been at Woolers Farm again.

'Oh? Is there something wrong with the puppy?'

'No, he said Bandit was very well and that his keeper is very pleased with her.'

'You spoke to him?'

'Of course. We are friends.'

He was smiling happily and Rose's heart ached with love for her son. Sam was a quiet boy who did not make friends easily and normally she would have been delighted to hear these words, but she could not help thinking that Sir Lawrence had won Sam's confidence after only a few meetings whereas Magnus, who had known Sam for more than two years now, was still treated with a grave reserve, despite his efforts to befriend the boy. Sam continued to chatter away, sublimely unaware of the heartache he was causing his mama.

'Sir Lawrence wanted to see Abel, but he wasn't there. Jem's mama told Sir Lawrence that Abel had gone to Minehead with old Mr Wooler—which was odd, because I thought I saw Abel in the barn when I arrived—but Sir Lawrence said it did not matter, and he took me up on his horse and we rode around the paddock. Sir Lawrence says I will be a—a bruising rider when I have my own pony!'

'I hope he has not been filling your head with extravagant nonsense,' declared Mrs Molland, coming into the room in time to hear this last remark. 'Evans has more than enough to do looking after two horses already—'

'Oh, no, Grandmama, I told Sir Lawrence that we cannot afford a pony for me until Mama marries Mr Emsleigh—' He broke off, frowning. 'What? Should I not have said that?'

'No, love.' Rose brushed his unruly hair back from his face. 'We should not tell strangers our business.'

Sam's brow cleared.

'Oh, if that is all—! I told you, Mama, Sir Lawrence is not a stranger, he is a *friend*! Oh, and, Grandmama, he said to tell you he would call upon you tomorrow!'

* * *

Rose would have delayed her return to Bluebell Cottage the following day, but Sam was determined that they should hurry home together and he tugged insistently at her hand all the way along the high street. He was a little disappointed not to see the gig or Sir Lawrence's bay mare standing outside the cottage when they arrived, but this was soon explained by Janet, the maid, who explained as she opened the door to them that Sir Lawrence was with the mistress, and that Evans had taken his horse to the stables out of the cold.

Thus prepared, Rose was able to greet Sir Lawrence with tolerable composure.

'Rose, my dear.' Mrs Molland came over to kiss her cheek. 'You will see that the kettle is filled and ready to set on the fire, and the tea tray has been set ready for you to begin as soon as you wish.'

'And how is Bandit, sir?' enquired Sam, making a hasty bow. 'Has she settled in, is she eating well? How—?'

'She is growing very fast.' Sir Lawrence threw up his hands to stem the flood of questions. 'She also has a predilection for chewing shoe leather, a habit that my man is even now trying to break.'

'How big is she?' demanded Sam. 'Up to my knees yet? I *wish* I could see her. If only she were not so far away. If only I had a pony I could ride there myself!'

Rose stiffened, but after a fleeting look towards her Sir Lawrence merely smiled and said, 'I shall be sure to give Bandit your regards when I get back.'

'Sam, my love, I do think you should go upstairs and

change your coat,' said Mrs Molland, shepherding her grandson towards the door. 'Janet will help you wash your face and hands, then you may come back and have a little cake with us.'

Rose gave her mother an anguished look, silently begging her not to leave them alone, but Mrs Molland appeared not to notice and she went out, closing the door behind her.

Almost a year ago they had been so easy together, but now an uncomfortable silence cloaked them. Rose's nerves were on edge. Even when he was sitting down Sir Lawrence dominated the room. It was as much as Rose could do to sit still, her hands clasped tightly in her lap. There was so much she wanted to say to him, so much that could never be spoken.

In an effort to break the tension Rose picked up the kettle and put it on the fire. She searched her mind for some innocuous remark.

'Is your business in the area completed now?'

'Business?'

'At the Assembly you said you could not leave.'

He looked surprised.

'I said that? I fear I misled you. I am here purely bent upon pleasure.'

'Not mine!' Rose uttered the retort unthinking and she quickly sat back down, blushing.

'No,' he said quietly, 'I am aware of that.'

He stood up and began to pace the little room, coming so close she could feel the air move as he passed her.

'However, there is a little…matter that I would like

to discuss with you, if I may. It concerns Sam. I would like to help him.'

'Why should you want to do that?'

'He is a delightful boy.' He could have said nothing more designed to please her, but his next words provoked panic. 'I would like to be better acquainted with him.'

'That is not possible. You—' She ran her tongue around her lips, forcing herself to speak. 'You are not a…a suitable person for him to know.'

He winced at that.

'Very well—but I should still like to help, and he does not need to know I had any hand in this.'

Immediately she was wary.

'Go on.'

'I was in Barnstaple the other day and happened to look in at the auction. I bought a pony.'

Rose jumped up.

'Sir Lawrence, I—'

'It is for my godson,' he continued, talking over her. 'I know the previous owner, a country gentleman whose own children have outgrown the animal. She is beautifully mannered and will suit my little godson perfectly when he is older. I did not want to miss the chance to obtain such a gift so…I bought her.' He turned his rueful smile upon Rose, who tried to ignore the tug of attraction it inspired. 'The only problem is what to do with her until then. She needs to be ridden or I fear she will soon forget her manners. I know it was your intention to find such a mount for Sam and I wondered if you could help me out. I need someone to make use of the pony until such time as my godson is old enough to ride her.'

'I cannot imagine any sensible person asking you to stand godparent to their child,' said Rose, momentarily distracted. 'Unless you have reformed.'

The disturbing twinkle appeared in his blue eyes. A familiar ache curled low in her belly. She swallowed hard. She wanted him now as much as ever.

'I *am* reformed. I told you I would do so, though you have yet to believe it. And my cousin is exceedingly sensible, although I cannot deny that she is very fond of me, which may have clouded her judgement when it came to choosing a godfather for her child. Well, Mrs Westerhill, will you help me out of my dilemma?'

She was not fooled by his innocent look.

'How old is your godson, Sir Lawrence?'

'Oh, he must be all of eighteen months, by now.'

Rose's lips twitched. She said gravely, 'It will be some years, then, before he will be able to appreciate your gift.'

'And until then I need someone to look after the mare. I will of course pay for her stabling.'

'That would not be necessary, I am not a pauper!'

His blue eyes captured her gaze and held it. At last she dragged her eyes away. She left her chair and walked towards the window.

'I cannot accept,' she said at last. 'I would be under such an obligation to you.'

'The obligation would be all mine.' He moved towards

her. Rose kept her eyes averted, but her spine tingled, knowing he was behind her. His breath was on her cheek as he murmured, 'Please, Rose, why should the animal be eating its head off in my stable when Sam could be learning to ride?'

She continued to stare out of the window, not daring to turn and face him. The air was charged with danger, like an electrical storm crackling about them. Rose tried to fight off the heady recklessness that was creeping under her skin. She should have nothing to do with Sir Lawrence if she truly wanted to forget him. And yet, how could she deny Sam this opportunity? A small voice of reason argued that it was madness. Magnus would certainly say so.

As if reading her mind, Lawrence murmured, 'Perhaps you should ask Emsleigh before you make a decision.'

Her chin went up.

'I do not need to consult him on such a matter!'

'No?'

The challenge was blatant.

'No.' She stifled the voice of reason and turned to face him. 'Very well, Sir Lawrence. We will look after this pony for you.' His lips curled in a slow smile that turned her insides to water. She struggled to continue. 'Your groom may bring the animal to the stables. If there is any communication regarding the arrangement, it is to be conducted through Evans. I want nothing more to do with the matter.'

'Nothing?'

'No. And…and I will explain the matter to Sam, if you please, but not today.'

'As you wish.'

He was still smiling at her and she turned away again, knowing that if he touched her the thin control she had over herself would slip away and she would melt into his arms, as she had dreamed of doing almost every night for the past year.

Sam saw nothing amiss in the idea of Sir Lawrence lending him a pony, but Rose was obliged to explain more fully to Mrs Molland, who was inclined to question Sir Lawrence's motive.

'I think it was an impetuous purchase,' said Rose, avoiding her eyes. 'Once he had bought the pony he had to do *something* with her until his godson is old enough to make use of her.'

'It does seem extremely generous of him, to loan the animal to us,' mused Mrs Molland. 'Forgive me, my love, but have you thought that he is perhaps trying to buy his way into your affections—as Aunt Jane might say, to have his evil way with you?'

Rose summoned up all her will-power to give a light-hearted laugh.

'Heavens, Mama, what a nonsensical notion!'

'No, it is not. You are young and pretty—'

'I am a widow and about to marry another man. Believe me, Mama, Sir Lawrence knows he would be wasting his time to set out lures to catch *me*!'

'Would he, though?' Rose found herself blushing at the knowing look in her mother's eye. 'The fact that you allowed the kettle to boil quite dry when I left you alone with him tells me you are not as immune to Sir Lawrence as you would have me believe.'

'We were discussing the pony, Mama, nothing more. And perhaps I should take *you* to task for leaving us alone in that shameful manner!'

'Well, I think Sir Lawrence is quite charming,' replied her mother, unabashed. 'If I was twenty years younger, I know I would enjoy being alone with him!'

'Mama! You are quite…quite outrageous. The more so when you know I am betrothed to Magnus, and very happily so,' she added defiantly.

'Then a few moments' *tête à tête* with Sir Lawrence Daunton should not have discomposed you.'

'It did not do so!' Rose felt the blood heating her cheeks and hurried on. 'Besides, I have already told him that he must deal with Evans—I will not have him use the animal as an excuse to call upon me. It…it is a perfectly sensible arrangement, to our mutual benefit. Nothing out of the ordinary at all.'

Mrs Molland looked sceptical.

'Well, whatever Magnus will say about it I don't know.'

Rose had wondered that herself, but when Magnus called at the cottage a few days later he said jovially, 'I have just bumped into Sam, who tells me he has a new pony. This is very sudden—you did not tell me you were going to buy him one?'

Rose said airily, 'No, it—it was rather sudden. I—er—had the opportunity to obtain the perfect mount for Sam.'

'Well, you know what you are about, my dear, but I would have thought keeping another animal would be too much of an expense for you.'

'Having two horses in livery already, we were able to negotiate a very good rate for a third,' put in Mrs Molland, with perfect truth.

She neatly turned the subject and exchanged a look with Rose that confirmed them as co-conspirators. There was a tacit understanding that Magnus need not be told.

Sam was delighted with his new pony and spent every spare moment at the stables. A period of clement weather enabled him to be out of doors every day and by the end of the first week the groom reported that Sam was making good progress, and showing an aptitude for riding. When Rose went to watch a lesson for herself, the happiness shining in her young son's face made her heart swell and she felt a wave of gratitude towards Lawrence.

She had seen nothing of him since his visit to Bluebell Cottage—it was as they had agreed: the loan of the pony was not to make any difference to their acquaintance. It was certainly much better for her peace of mind, yet she found herself wondering if he was still at Knightscote. Would he inform her if he went away? Her mind went round and round the question, but came up with no satisfactory answer; in the end she determined to put all thoughts of the dangerous rake out of her mind and concentrate upon her own life, and the forthcoming dinner at Emsleigh House.

It was a long-standing engagement; Mrs Molland had received the invitation from Althea Emsleigh several weeks ago and had told her daughter she was not at all deceived by its honeyed tones.

'The invitation really comes from Magnus. Althea considers us very poor company. You, a schoolteacher, and me, an ageing widow!'

'But she must be charming to us for her brother's sake.'

'And you should be charming to her,' retorted Mrs Molland. 'She will be your sister-in-law soon and you will have to share a house with her.'

'Heavens, yes,' replied Rose, much struck. 'She will not enjoy having to make way for me as mistress of Emsleigh.' A dimple appeared. She said mischievously, 'I wonder how quickly we can find her a husband?'

Magnus sent his carriage to Bluebell Cottage on the day of the dinner and the two ladies waved goodbye to Sam as they set off in style. That morning they had seen the first snowfall of the winter. It was very light, but it dusted the tops of the walls and the thatched roofs of the village and covered the surrounding hills with a blanket of white that glistened in the wintry sunset. They reached Emsleigh House just as the short winter's day was fading into night and thankfully hurried indoors.

They paused in the hall to divest themselves of their wraps. From her previous visits to the house, Rose knew that the drawing room lay at the top of the wide flight of stairs that swept upwards in front of them. She was surprised, therefore, to hear voices coming from Magnus's study, which was situated off the entrance hall. As she handed her cloak to the waiting footman the study door opened and a portly gentleman in a brown suit and bag-wig stepped out.

'I am very sorry to hear that your insurers have not yet paid up, Emsleigh,' he said, looking back into the room, 'but I have to tell you that unless I get my money soon I shall be forced to take action.'

The impassive butler was already shepherding Rose and her mother across the hall. Althea appeared at the top of the stairs to greet them, resplendent in blue shot silk decorated with pink ribbons.

Rose glanced back over her shoulder as she heard the front door bang.

'Who was that man?' asked Rose

'Oh, *him*.' Althea pouted and shook her head. 'Pray take no heed. He is merely one of Magnus's creditors. He rode all the way here from Minehead to dun us! Horrid little man. I do not think we should deal with him in future. Is that not so, Brother?'

Magnus had left the study and now ran lightly up the stairs to join them.

'Good evening, Mrs Molland, Rose. I am sorry you

had to witness that. A little untimely business.' He ushered them into the drawing room and closed the doors. 'But now we may be easy. You know everyone, I think?'

Rose regarded the assembled company. There were no surprises: the local magistrate, Sir Jonas Pullen, and his wife; the local vicar, Mr John Wilkins, and four other couples from Minehead thought worthy to dine at Emsleigh House.

'You will note, Mrs Westerhill, that we are at present an odd number.' Althea took Rose's arm and led her across to a sofa. 'But we are acquainted enough now for you to know I would never arrange anything so awkwardly! We have another gentleman coming to make up the numbers. We shall have eight couples sitting down to dinner. What do you say to that?'

'I wonder that you should put yourself to so much trouble when you have your Winter Ball in less than two weeks. I applaud your energy, Miss Emsleigh.'

Althea simpered and waved a hand.

'Oh, it is nothing. I have been my brother's hostess for so long now it is second nature to me to organise these things. But we digress. I was asking if you could guess who I had found to make up the numbers?'

Rose spread her hands.

'I have no idea, Miss Emsleigh… Mr Truelove, perhaps?'

'Truelove, the attorney?' Althea threw back her head and gave a little trill of laughter. 'Dear me, no. No one so provincial. It—but I do not need to tell you, because I think this is he!'

Rose's spirits fluttered erratically. Althea's words had aroused her suspicions and she was not surprised when she heard the butler's sonorous announcement.

'Sir Lawrence Daunton!'

Rose watched Althea fly across the room to greet him. Was it her imagination or did all the ladies in the room sit up a little straighter when he came in? Certainly he looked very elegant, his simply cut black coat moulded to his frame and his dark hair brushed back from his handsome face. Althea was guiding him around the room, ensuring he knew everyone, but keeping a proprietary hand on his arm. Rose knew they would have to speak and she drew herself up. She must not blush, or show any signs that they were other than the merest acquaintances.

I can do this, she told herself as Althea and Lawrence approached. *We mean nothing to each other.*

She schooled her features into a cool, distant smile.

'Mrs Westerhill.'

She tried not to be disappointed that he did not reach out for her hand and gave her only a slight nod of recognition, or to feel bereft when he turned away immediately. The greeting he gave Mrs Molland was much warmer. Quickly Rose moved across the room to join Magnus. There would be no sighs, no longing looks. She was no fainting schoolroom miss, but a grown woman. Not by the flicker of an eyelid would she betray how much Lawrence's presence affected her.

'Ah, Rose.' Magnus held out his hand to her. 'Mr Wilkins and I were agreeing that you are in high bloom tonight, my dear.'

'Why, thank you, sirs. And you, Mr Wilkins—how do you go on? You were suffering from a slight cough last Sunday.'

'I was. I hope it did not detract too much from my sermon. But it is quite cleared up now, ma'am, thank you.'

Rose smiled as she listened to him conversing with Magnus. She liked the Reverend John Wilkins. He was a mild-mannered man who worked hard for his parishioners and, despite a slightly distracted air, he managed the funds for the village school very efficiently.

'…and that is something I wanted to tell you, Mrs Westerhill.' He turned his kindly gaze back to Rose. 'I think I have found someone to replace you at the school.'

'So soon?' Rose was startled.

'I asked Mr Wilkins if he knew of anyone who could take over from you, my dear,' Magnus explained. 'There will be plenty to do before the wedding. You will not have time to be schoolmistress as well.'

'It is but a few mornings a week—'

'Mornings that you might be spending with me,' declared Magnus, squeezing her fingers. 'You must see why I am eager for your replacement to arrive.'

'The lady in question is a distant relative of mine, fallen upon hard times and in need of a position.' Mr Wilkins coughed, his eyes shifting to Magnus and back again. 'When Mr Emsleigh mentioned the matter to me…'

'Of course I do not expect you to give up your post

immediately,' said Magnus. 'I thought she might work with you for a little while, learn how you do things.'

Rose suspected he was trying to smooth her obviously ruffled feathers. She bit back a sharp retort and instead asked Mr Wilkins when his relative would be arriving.

'I expect her here any day now,' replied the vicar, patently relieved at her mild response.

'Then you must bring her to the schoolroom as soon as she is settled in. I look forward to meeting her.' She allowed Magnus to lead her away, saying quietly, as soon they were out of earshot, 'Really, Magnus, I do think you could have discussed this with me.'

'I beg your pardon, my dear, it quite slipped my mind.'

'Just as it slipped your mind to tell me you had been to Hades Cove.' It gave her some satisfaction to note his startled look. 'Mrs Ansell told me she had seen you riding there on Wednesday—you know full well the track down to the cove winds around the hill overlooking Mersecombe. You cannot expect to use it without someone seeing you.'

'Of course not. I had business in Lynton and decided to look at the mine on my way home. Surely you do not object.' He gave a soft laugh. 'I hope you do not plan to charge me with trespass.'

'Of course not, Magnus, but I would like to be kept informed of matters that concern me.'

He raised her hand to his lips.

'Neither the school nor the mine will be your concern

for much longer, my dear. When you are my wife all these little problems will be lifted from your shoulders. Now, shall we lead the way into dinner?'

The meal was long and protracted. Lawrence was seated at the far end of the table, next to Althea. Mrs Molland was also placed near him and both ladies seemed to be enjoying his company far too much. Rose had been given the place of honour next to Magnus, but although she conversed happily with those around her, she found herself wondering what Lawrence was saying to keep both ladies so well entertained. Her eyes strayed far too often to the far end of the table and it was an effort to attend to her neighbours. She could acquit Althea of malice—after all, she knew nothing of their previous acquaintance—but it was still painful for Rose to have to sit and watch her flirting with Lawrence.

'What an exciting few months lie ahead of us,' declared Lady Pullen. 'We have your ball here to look forward to, Mr Emsleigh, and then, in the spring, there will be the wedding.' She turned her gracious smile upon Rose. 'You must be looking forward to that, my dear. You can become a lady again.'

'I enjoy my work at the school,' replied Rose. 'I shall be sorry to give it up.'

'You will be far too busy to miss it,' Magnus assured her.

'Will I? What do you envisage me doing, Magnus?' Rose turned her direct gaze upon him, smiling to soften the challenge in her words.

'You will adorn my house and accompany me when I am obliged to make social calls.'

Rose wrinkled her nose.

'Really, Magnus, I think sometimes you want merely a pretty ornament to hang upon your arm.'

He reached across and pinched her cheek.

'A pretty, witty ornament, my dear!' Those around them laughed, but Rose found nothing to amuse her in the idea.

'I am sure, as my wife, there will be plenty of charitable work to amuse you,' offered Magnus.

'Talking of charity,' put in Mr Wilkins, 'I was in Minehead yesterday and bumped into a sailor there, from Bristol. He was one of the crew from the *Sealark*. He tells me he is still waiting for his money.'

Magnus frowned. He said shortly, 'He will get that as soon as the insurers send me payment for my losses.'

'They haven't paid out yet?' Sir Jonas leaned forwards, his voice carrying the length of the table. 'I thought it was as good as settled. They had the affidavit from every crew member months ago, attesting to it being an accident. What are they waiting for?'

'London investors,' declared his neighbour. 'You would have been better advised to use the insurers in Exeter, as I do.'

'Easy to say so now, Norris,' Magnus responded.

He tapped his glass and the butler rushed to refill it.

'But why do they delay?' asked Rose, frowning slightly. 'Surely there can be no question that it was an accident.'

'None at all, my love,' said Magnus. 'Pray, put it out of your mind. There is nothing for you to worry about.'

'Of course there is!' declared Mr Norris, who had imbibed rather freely and was now in a boisterous mood. 'Mrs Westerhill was expecting to marry a rich man, Emsleigh. If the insurers don't pay out, you'll have the creditors hammering on the door—'

He broke off as he received a hard jab in the ribs from his wife.

'Pray ignore my husband, Mrs Westerhill. His humour is sometimes quite out of place.' She glared at her husband, who returned his attention sheepishly to his dinner.

This altercation had claimed everyone's attention and an awkward silence had settled over the whole table. At the far end, Althea gave a little laugh.

'Well, I am sure I cannot wait for our Winter Ball. I do hope the weather will improve—what say you, Sir Lawrence, does this early snow mean we shall have a hard winter this year?'

Sir Lawrence was thoughtfully watching Magnus, and Althea had to repeat her question before he turned to answer her. The tension eased as a general murmur of conversation began again. Magnus addressed an innocuous comment to Mr Wilkins and good humour was restored.

'Whatever you say about Althea Emsleigh, she keeps a good table,' remarked Mrs Molland. 'Such a pity about Mr Norris! The man never could take his drink.'

The ladies had left the gentlemen to their wines and were gathered once more in the drawing room. Rose followed her mother to a sofa near the fire. She glanced around to make sure they were not overheard.

'But do you think he is correct, Mama? That Magnus will be ruined if the insurers do not pay out? After all, there was that man in the study when we arrived…'

'Good heavens, child, Magnus Emsleigh is one of the richest men in the county! No, no, I am sure there is nothing to worry about; it was merely Mr Norris joking at someone else's expense! Do not let him make you uncomfortable.'

The ladies settled down to while away the hour or so until the gentlemen joined them. Rose began to relax. She had been in Lawrence's company for several hours and survived. They had not been close enough during dinner to converse and she was hopeful that they could continue to avoid each other for the remainder of the evening, by which time she would be quite used to his company. That, of course, would stand her in good stead for their next meeting, when she did not doubt that they would be able to greet each other with polite indifference.

Her conviction was somewhat rocked when the gentlemen came in and she found her eyes immediately seeking out Lawrence, wanting him to look at her, yet such was her contrary nature, when he did so she immediately turned to join in an animated conversation with her neighbours.

Magnus pointed out that the pianoforte and harp stood ready, should any lady wish to entertain them.

'You are all so diffident,' declared Althea. 'I shall start, then!'

She sat down at the harp and began to pluck at the strings. A polite hush fell over the room. Lawrence moved silently towards Rose.

'Do you play, Mrs Westerhill?'

'The pianoforte, a little.'

'Do not be so modest, Rose,' said her mother in a loud whisper. 'She plays very well, Sir Lawrence.'

'Then I should very much like to hear her.'

Rose gave a little shake of her head. To sit at the pianoforte, inviting everyone to look at her—giving Lawrence every excuse to look at her—she could think of nothing worse.

'I do not intend to play tonight.'

She was immediately sorry for her sharp tone. Lawrence's brows went up, but it was impossible to apologise without drawing more attention to herself. She was on edge when he was so close and she could only begin to relax again when he moved away to sit beside Lady Pullen.

Althea's performance was warmly applauded and she crossed over to the pianoforte, calling to Lawrence to come and turn the pages for her. Rose watched him standing beside Althea, bending to catch something she said, sharing a smile with her. It took her a little while to realise that the hard, angry knot in her stomach was jealousy. She breathed deeply, her fingers clenching and unclenching in her lap. So much for her resolution!

'Bravo, my dear!'

Magnus's utterance caught her attention and with a little jolt of surprise she realised Althea had finished. She put her hands together in appreciation of the music, although she had not attended to a note.

'Now,' Magnus continued, looking about him, 'who will be next…Rose?'

'Thank you but, no, not tonight.'

'Pray show us what you can do,' he urged her. 'I know you play very prettily; I have heard you perform at Bluebell Cottage.'

Rose smiled and shook her head.

'Do not put her to the blush, Brother,' said Althea sweetly. 'To amuse oneself on the little box piano at home is all very well, but it is very different to playing *properly* on a Broadwood.'

Mrs Molland drew in a hissing breath. Rose put her hand on her mother's arm to prevent her from leaping to her defence.

'Of course it is,' she agreed cordially. 'However, now you mention it, I have been practising a rondo by Mr Mozart and confess I should like to know how it sounds on such a fine instrument.'

Rose walked across to the piano and sat down. Lawrence stepped closer.

'Do you have music, ma'am? May I turn the pages for you?'

She shook her head, the light of battle in her eyes.

'Thank you, I have no need of music for this piece.'

With that she spread her hands out over the keys and began to play with such gusto that an immediate silence descended over the room. It gave her immense satisfaction to see the shocked look upon Althea's features. Poor Miss Emsleigh, she rarely visited Bluebell Cottage so she was not to know that the piano was one of Rose's main pleasures, or that she spent many hours practising.

Rose ended her performance with a flourish and sat back. Magnus led the applause, beaming delightedly at her before looking around the room as if to invite his guests to appreciate just what an accomplished bride he had chosen.

'Exemplary,' murmured Sir Lawrence. 'I have rarely heard anything finer. I can think of no better set-down for our hostess.'

He had been standing by the piano, watching her, throughout her performance, but Rose had been so caught up in the music that she had barely noticed him. Now his words reminded her of her situation. With a strained smile she shook her head at him and slipped away.

The musical entertainment continued, but Rose could not enjoy it. She was angry that she had allowed her irritation to get the better of her. She had suffered Althea's barbed comments before and had always allowed them to pass unchallenged, but tonight was different. It had been Rose's intention to stay in the background and be nothing more than a spectator for the evening, but her display upon the pianoforte had drawn everyone's attention. With dismay she saw that both Althea and Lawrence were watching her, dark resentment in one glance, warm admiration in the other.

The evening dragged on. The tea tray was brought in and Althea dispensed cups of black Bohea to the guests who milled around the room, talking and laughing. Rose carried a cup of tea to her mother, but could not settle. She wanted to go home, but Magnus would not call the carriage for a good hour yet, and she did not wish to draw even more attention to herself by requesting to leave early. Instead she touched Magnus's arm and drew him aside.

'Is there somewhere I may sit quietly for a little while, Magnus?'

'What is it, my dear, are you unwell?'

'A severe headache, but I am sure it will ease presently, if I can only be alone.'

Immediately he guided her out of the room.

'There is a good fire in the library,' he said. 'Shall I send Althea to you, or your mother?'

'No, no, I would not upset your party, Magnus. I shall do very well alone, thank you.'

They slipped out of the room and Magnus led her away from the public rooms to the library. It was a large, imposing chamber, almost divided in two by the bookshelves that jutted out into the room. On this side of the divide a marble fireplace and two armchairs provided a degree of comfort. Beyond, a large mahogany desk filled the centre of the floor, its surface bare of any ornament.

Magnus used his study for working; this room was merely for show, neither the desk nor the leather-bound tomes, purchased by the yard from a Bristol bookseller, intended for anything more than ostentatious display.

Magnus settled her in one of the chairs beside the fire.

'No one will bother you here. I shall come back again in a little while—'

'No, there will be no need for that.' She gave him a weak smile. 'I have taken enough of your time. Go back to your guests, Magnus, and I will join you very soon, I promise.'

She watched him walk away, her smile fading as he left the room. Guilt ripped at her conscience; she was betrothed to Magnus, yet even here, in his house, her thoughts, her attention, constantly turned to Lawrence. Their brief liaison had lasted only two nights, but the pain of separation was as strong now as the day she had ridden away from Knightscote. It was like a raw, angry wound that would not heal.

'Oh, will it never end?' The words were dragged out of her and she dropped her head in her hands.

As if conjured by her own longing she heard his voice, full of concern.

'What is it, Rose? Are you ill?'

She lifted her head. Lawrence was standing with his back to the door, his blue eyes fixed upon her.

'How did you know where to find me?'

'I saw you leave—you did not look well. Then Magnus came back alone…'

She hunted frantically for her handkerchief.

'Please go.'

'I want to help.'

She wiped her eyes, ashamed that he should observe her weakness. Glancing up, she saw that he was still watching her.

'Talk to me,' he said quietly.

Rose jumped up and began to pace up and down. She sought around for some ladylike term to do justice to the pain inside. There was none.

'Damn you,' she uttered vehemently. '*Damn you*, Lawrence Daunton! You were not supposed to come back into my life. I was managing very well without you.'

This was not quite true, but Rose had no intention of admitting the gnawing loneliness she had felt during the spring months. Angrily she kneaded one fist into the palm of the other. 'I thought I could play this game. That we could meet as strangers, friends even, but it is not possible. I cannot relax in your company—you make me discontent with my lot in life!'

'This does not have to be your lot, Rose.'

She shook her head, hardly attending to him.

'I have worked *so hard* to forget you. My world was ordered and—and calm. My future was assured. Then you come striding back, overturning everything I have worked for, winning my son's regard—'

'I did not plan that.'

'No? And what about the pony?'

A sudden smile softened his features.

'Blame Sam for that! Little monkey, when he chattered away to me, saying you could not afford a mount for him, I could not help myself.'

'And thus he gave you a means to tempt me, to put myself into your debt.'

'No! I would never use Sam as a way into your affections!'

His vehemence surprised her.

'Nevertheless I am constrained to be obliged, when I would rather have nothing to do with you!'

'Do you think you are the only one suffering?' he flashed. 'To be near you, but unable to talk freely, unable to cherish and protect you—'

'We agreed it could never be—'

'No—*you* said it could not work. You had married one rake and would not risk your happiness with another. But I am no libertine, Rose. I was wild, yes, and I allowed rumours to circulate. But I am a changed man. Ask any of my friends in town—write to that wearisome aunt of yours who passes on to you all the gossip! They will all tell you I have not looked at a woman this year. My friends have waited in vain for me at the gaming tables. I have spent most of my time upon my estates, adding new buildings, improving the land—at first I did it out of anger, my only thought was that I would show you I was not the feckless character you thought me! Then, as the months went on, I found I enjoyed it, much more than the social round I had become locked into. I faced up to the truth that I had never wanted to marry Annabelle and had stayed in London merely to avoid the fateful day. I had misbehaved, flaunted my string of mistresses in front of her, hoping that she would realise I would not make a good husband and cry off. She never did. I was afraid to marry her; I did not want to be imprisoned in her world of dull domesticity.' He exhaled slowly. 'It was a dreadful thing to discover about myself, Rose, that I was too much of a coward to tell her the truth. I truly thought it would break her heart. Looking back now, I think she wanted the match as little as I. If only—! I bitterly regret it now, but there is nothing I can do to change the past. But *you* can change your future. You say you are not content with your life—then change it, Rose. Break off your engagement to Emsleigh!'

'You know I cannot.'

He grabbed her arms.

'Why not? Are you afraid of what everyone will say?'

'No!' She pushed her hands against the solid, unyielding wall of his chest. 'That is not the reason. I chose Magnus because he is everything you are not: correct, dependable, solidly upright. He will be a perfect father for Sam.'

'Are you sure, Rose? Are you sure Emsleigh is the upright, honest gentleman you think him?'

'Of course. He has never given me any reason to doubt that.'

'But you don't love him.'

Rose bit her lip.

'That is not a requirement of our marriage.'

'Then it is doomed to fail.' He pulled her closer, but as he went to kiss her she turned her head away. Her heart was pounding so hard it was a constant drumming in her ears. 'Your blood is on fire when I touch you,' he muttered, his lips grazing her neck and causing her to tremble. Her head went back as his kisses left a burning trail upon her skin. 'If you must marry, let it be me!'

'You—you are asking me to marry you?' she said raggedly. 'When you have just admitted you lived for years in London rather than succumb to—what did you call it?—dull domesticity?'

'There would be nothing dull about our marriage.' The dark desire in his eyes sent a shudder through her. 'I would be a good husband, Rose, if you will give me a chance to prove it.'

She closed her eyes, scalding tears welling up.

'Yes, you have behaved yourself for the past ten months, but that is not a lifetime!' She choked back a sob. 'Harry was a model husband for the first year, until Sam was born, but then he reverted to his old ways. I cannot—will not—risk that happening again.'

He sighed. 'One can never guarantee what life has in store. Sometimes you have to take a risk.' His grip tightened on her arms. 'Sometimes, you have to follow your heart. You have to trust me, Rose.'

With a tremendous effort she freed herself, shaking off his hands to say angrily, 'I do not *have* to do anything! You ask too much of me, sir, when all I ask of you is that you leave me alone!' She covered her face with her hands. 'Please,' she said softly, 'please, just go away.'

'Is there nothing I say will convince you that I have changed for good?'

She shook her head.

'Only time will tell us that, Lawrence, and that is something I do not have.' She drew a long, steadying breath and said resolutely, 'I am marrying Magnus in the spring.'

She spoke slowly, her words falling heavy as lead between them. Lawrence watched her, his face pale and impassive, but the muscle working in his jaw told her just how tense he was.

'So, I have my answer,' he said at last. 'This is goodbye.'

'Yes.' She put her hands to her cheeks. 'This year has been the most miserable I have ever spent. You c-cannot know how much I regret taking the wrong turning last winter.'

A wry smile twisted his lips.

'I am very sorry if you think that. I have come to believe your arriving at my door was the finest thing that ever happened in my life.'

With a final, clipped little bow he turned on his heel and walked out. In the silence she listened to his footsteps fading away. He would leave, she knew it. He would hurry down the stairs, there would be a flurry of activity as one footman hurried off to fetch his coat while another dashed to the stables to order his horse.

Go after him. Tell him you have changed your mind.

The insidious voice in her head teased her with views of a halcyon future where they would live in wedded bliss. She folded her arms across her stomach. Better to conjure the images of her marriage to Harry Westerhill: the arguments, the blows, the long waking nights knowing he was lying in another woman's bed. And even if she could endure all that, Lawrence would expect an heir. How was she to tell him that she could have no more children?

CHAPTER SEVEN

LAWRENCE groaned and turned carefully in his bed. His head hurt dreadfully, but he knew he could not blame Emsleigh's wine for that. He had returned to Knightscote in the early hours of the morning and settled down to contemplate his future with a bottle of brandy. To see Rose in such distress tore at his heart. When he had first learned that she had postponed her marriage to Emsleigh he had begun almost unconsciously to hope that she might have changed her mind about him, but that now seemed impossible. She was determined to marry Emsleigh, to provide Sam with a respectable father. Aye, that was the bitter irony—if Lawrence's suspicions were correct, then Magnus Emsleigh was anything but respectable: he was responsible for sinking the *Sealark* to claim the insurance and inadvertently responsible for Ruben Wooler's death. Lawrence could not ignore that, nor could he share his suspicions with Rose. But he could not let her marry Emsleigh while he suspected him of such villainy. He had to discover the truth.

A week later Lawrence was forced to admit that his investigations were not going well. He had sought out Captain Morris, but he had told him nothing more than the agent had already gleaned from the crew members: a fire had broken out in the hold and they had been forced to abandon ship. The accounts were all the same—too much so for Lawrence's liking—but since they all held notes of hand from Magnus Emsleigh, promising them various sums once the insurers had paid out, it was unlikely any one of them would admit to anything different. The only person who seemed troubled was Abel Wooler, brother of the drowned sailor. Lawrence had spoken to him on several occasions and had the distinct impression that he was hiding something.

Lawrence decided that he would go and see Abel once more. If he stuck to his story then there would be nothing for it but to return to London. He would have to tell George Craven that the insurance claim must stand.

And that would leave Rose free to marry Magnus Emsleigh. The thought irked him, but if he had nothing stronger than his own suspicions, what right had he to object to a marriage that would give Rose and Sam a secure and comfortable life?

Riding to Mersecombe did much to raise Lawrence's spirits. There were still signs of the early snow on the high ground and a biting wind cut at his cheeks as he galloped across the moor. It was a little warmer down in the valley, where the steeply wooded hills provided some shelter, and he slowed his hectic pace. Lawrence tried to convince himself that the sudden twisting in his gut as he rode past the church was due to the brandy and not the fact that Rose would be there, taking lessons in the little schoolroom.

'Good day, Sir Lawrence.'

The soft greeting interrupted his thoughts and he brought his horse to a stand. Mr Wilkins, the vicar, was standing at the edge of the road with a soberly clad woman at his side. He introduced her as Mrs Reed, a distant cousin.

'I am taking Mrs Reed to the schoolroom: she is to be Mrs Westerhill's replacement.'

'Ah, yes.' Lawrence nodded, said all that was proper and rode on.

Another reminder that Rose was to wed Magnus Emsleigh.

Lawrence clenched his teeth. Dear heaven, he would be glad to quit this place! As he rounded the bend in the road he spotted a figure on the road before him—it was Abel Wooler, heading for the Ship Inn. Well, perhaps fortune was favouring him at last.

He stabled his horse and entered the inn, pausing to allow his eyes to grow accustomed to the dim light. The inn was deserted and he soon spotted his quarry, sitting at a table near the fire.

'Good day to you, Wooler. Will you take a drink with me?'

The man looked up. His eyes were wary, but he nodded.

Lawrence called for ale and drew up a stool.

'How is the pointer bitch?'

'She is doing well,' Lawrence replied. 'Growing apace. You've sold all the other pups now?'

'Aye, they've all been taken.' Abel paused while the serving maid brought a heavy blackjack to the table and filled two tankards with frothy ale. Lawrence gave her a handful of coins and asked her to leave the black-jack on the table.

Abel raised his tankard to Lawrence, taking his time to savour the drink before saying in his slow drawl, 'Somehow I don't think 'tis dogs you wants to talk to me about.'

'No. I wanted to ask you again about the *Sealark*.'

'I've told you all I knows, Sir Lawrence.'

'But have you? Doesn't it seem odd to you that Emsleigh should entrust such a valuable cargo to his least seaworthy ship?'

Abel shrugged.

'Summer. He didn't expect it to suffer heavy weather.'

'And the fire? Tell me again how it broke out.'

'No one knows.' Abel took another long draught. 'There's a lot of tar on a ship, Sir Lawrence. Fires 'appen.'

'So everyone says. I've read the crew's accounts—those that could be collected. It took some time to gather them, with the crew scattered far and wide. Some have even set sail again.' Lawrence paused. 'Seems strange to me that Morris should sign up his crew in Bristol. He usually finds his crews locally, does he not? From Barnstaple or Minehead.'

Another shrug.

'So how did you and your brother come to sign up?'

'Cap'n Morris told Ruben about it. Ruben told me.'

'So Morris would not have taken you if your brother had not mentioned it?'

Abel said quickly, 'I never said that.'

Lawrence refilled the tankards.

'Some of the crew's accounts say the fire was the bosun's fault.' He saw the flash of anger in the other man's eyes, but it faded again and he merely shrugged.

'It's easy to blame the dead. They can't defend themselves.'

'But the fire could have been started deliberately.'

'To what end?'

'To scuttle the ship,' said Lawrence. 'After the cargo had been safely unloaded.' He paused, watching Abel closely. 'There would be a reward, you know, if the cargo was to be recovered.'

'You think if you get me drunk I will confess everything to you?' Abel's slow grin appeared. He shook his head. 'It will not happen. There's nothing to confess.'

'But you must admit it looks suspicious: Emsleigh has debts to pay, takes out a large insurance on his cargo—'

'Sir Lawrence, you are a gentleman, we've done business together. More than that, our Jem has taken a shine to 'ee, and you've paid for these drinks. All those things stop me from punching your daylights out for suggesting I might not be telling the truth!' Abel glowered at him. 'I have already signed to say we did all we could to save the ship. What would happen to me if I was to change my mind? My word against my fellows—that would do no good. Besides, if—and I'm not saying it was deliberate—*if* it was discovered that the *Sealark* was scuttled, then Jem would not get the money that was promised to his dad. I couldn't do that to the boy.'

Lawrence was about to argue more when a soft, distressed voice called from the doorway.

'Abel—Abel, are you there? Have you seen Jem?'

Both men swung round. Maggie Wooler was hurrying across the taproom with Rose close behind her. One look at Rose's face and Lawrence was on his feet.

'It's Jem,' said Maggie. 'He's not been to school.'

'Sam is missing, too,' added Rose. 'When they did not arrive at school I thought they had gone back to the farm. Mrs Reed was with me, so I left her in charge of the children and walked up to fetch them.'

'But they wasn't with me,' cried Maggie, wringing her hands. 'They've run away somewhere.'

Lawrence turned to Rose.

'What about the pony?'

She shook her head, eyes shadowed with worry.

'I checked the stables; Evans has not seen them.'

'Gone—?' Abel stopped. He slowly shook his head. 'Nay, he wouldn't.'

'What is it?' cried Maggie. 'What are you thinking, Abel?'

He rubbed his chin.

'Well, you know what today is, Maggie.'

'Aye, it's Ruben's birthday.'

'An' I remember, last time young Sam was up at the farm with us, he was telling Jem how on *his* father's birthday he and Mrs Westerhill went off to lay flowers on the grave in Exford.'

'But Ruben has no grave,' said Maggie.

'No,' muttered Abel. 'Just his initials carved at Sealham Point.'

Rose looked aghast. 'But they cannot have gone there. The tide…'

'Jem knows the tides; he'd reckon they could walk there and back before the tide came in and cut them off,' said Abel. 'But I'd wager it will have taken 'em longer than they thought to get to Sealham Point. The tide will have turned. They'll be stuck there now.'

'If they haven't been washed out to sea!' cried Mrs Wooler, lifting her apron to cover her face.

'Nonsense, Maggie, our Jem has more sense than that. He'll have seen that they can't get back and will be sitting it out on the rocks.'

'But it will be dark by the time the tide goes out again.' Rose tried to speak calmly, but could not prevent the quiver in her voice. 'They will not be able to see their way back. Th-that means they will have to wait until the morning…'

Abel stood up. 'I'll row across the bay and collect them. There'll be an onshore swell for an hour or so yet. It won't be too hard.'

'Let me come with you,' said Rose immediately.

'Nay, ma'am, I will not take thee, unless ye can row. An extra pair of oars would be useful, but everyone I know is already at sea, making the most of the daylight.'

'I'll go with you,' said Lawrence. His lips quirked at the incredulous look his words received. 'I suspect rowing on an English river is somewhat different to the open sea, but I'd like to help.'

Abel looked at him for a long moment, as if weighing him up.

'Very well. I'll be glad to have 'ee, sir.'

'What should we do?' asked Rose, following them to the door. 'Should we come down to the jetty…?'

'No,' said Lawrence, 'I suggest you both go to your homes. We could be wrong, you know, and the boys might already be home.' He watched the play of emotion on Rose's face. She wanted to argue, to do something more useful than sitting at home and waiting. He touched her arm. 'Don't worry, we'll bring them back safely.'

She swallowed. 'Very well.' She laid a hand on his sleeve as he turned to follow Abel out of the inn. 'Be careful.'

The soft words and the look that accompanied them cheered Lawrence as he followed Abel along the winding lane that led out of the village and through the fields to the shore. There were no signs of activity at the water's edge, only a few beached boats and the fishing nets spread out to dry. Abel headed for an upturned rowboat and with Lawrence's help it was soon on the water.

For a while they rowed in silence, the only sounds the scrape and splash of the oars, but Lawrence was aware that Abel's eyes were upon his back.

'Well,' he said over his shoulder, 'I am out of practice, but what do you think?'

He heard his companion chuckle.

'Aye,' said Abel in his deep, slow drawl, 'you'll do.'

They made good progress across the bay. Lawrence glanced over his shoulder at their destination, the ragged cliffs of Sealham Point, and his blood ran a little colder when he saw the white spume of the waves crashing against the rocks.

'I can't see them…'

'Jem'll know better than to stand on this side o' the Point,' said Abel. 'You can scramble up away from the waves on t'other side, and that's where we're going; we can bring the boat real close there.'

Lawrence put all his efforts into rowing as Abel guided them safely around the point to approach the shore from the south. At last his companion gave a grunt of satisfaction.

'There they are.'

Looking round, Lawrence saw two small figures waving from a rocky shelf some way up the cliff. They began to scramble down as the boat nosed its way towards them. He tried not to think of the jagged rocks just below the surface. Abel concentrated on keeping the boat steady while Lawrence reached out a hand to help first Sam and then Jem jump across.

'Little fools,' said Abel once both boys were safely on board. 'Forget the time, did you?'

'We was late settin' off,' stammered Jem, his teeth chattering. 'We never meant to—'

'We can discuss that later.' Lawrence shrugged himself out of his greatcoat. 'Put this around the both of you.'

'What about you, sir, won't you be c-cold?' asked Sam, his face pinched and white.

Lawrence grinned.

'I don't think so; I am working so hard at the rowing that it's keeping me warm.'

'Ah, an' it's time to be rowin' again, sir, if we're to get these nippers home!'

The two men pulled hard on the oars to bring the little boat away from the treacherous rocks and as they moved into clear water Lawrence had time to observe the rugged coastline with its towering cliffs. A little way south of Sealham Point was a cleft in the hills, a valley so deep and narrow that the shadowed woods looked almost black, save for a ragged clearing that ran like a scar along one side, a little way above the waterline.

'What is that?' He nodded towards the cliffs, his hands too busy with the oars to point.

'What? Oh, that's Hades Cove,' offered Jem, looking back.

'And the rocky outcrop? It does not look natural.'

'Tedn't natural,' Jem affirmed. 'It's the old drift-mine. They used to bring out the iron ore and load it onto the ships. You can still see the small jetty there, in the cove. No one uses it any more.'

'It belongs to Mama,' piped up Sam, buried deep in Lawrence's greatcoat.

'Really?' Lawrence rested on his oars and stared at the cove. 'But it's not used now, you say?'

'Tedn't been used for years.' Jem nodded. 'The ore ran out.'

'But ships could still get in there?' asked Lawrence.

'I suppose so.' Jem shrugged. 'As long as they had a pilot that knows the waters...'

'Stop yer gabbin', Jem!' Abel ordered him roughly. He leaned forwards to address Lawrence. 'I'd be obliged to 'ee, sir, if you'd give yer attention to getting us home. It'll be a lot harder to make progress once the tide turns!'

Lawrence swung round, but Abel had his head down, concentrating on rowing. With a shrug Lawrence accepted the rebuke and applied himself once more to the oars.

Rose quickly returned to the schoolroom where she found Mrs Reed had everything under control.

'You may safely leave me to finish up today,' she said, giving Rose's arm an understanding pat. 'The children are no trouble and I am sure you would prefer to be at home until you have news of your son. And if you need me to come in tomorrow, you only have to send word to the vicarage.'

So Rose made her way to the cottage, where she joined her mother in pacing up and down and staring out of the window at the deserted lane, knowing all the time there could be no news for hours yet. The short winter's day came to an end and Rose put a lighted lamp in the window. Janet prepared meals, but they were returned hardly touched.

'Surely they should be back by now,' she said, unable to settle. 'What if they cannot find them?' She shivered. 'What if they have capsized…?'

'Patience,' said Mrs Molland. 'The sea has not been particularly rough today and Abel Wooler is an experienced seaman. We will hear soon enough. The time would pass quicker for you if you had some occupation.'

An involuntary smile tugged at Rose's mouth. 'Like you, Mama? You have had your sewing on your lap for a good hour, but I have not seen you set a stitch. Besides, I have not been idle; I have built up the fire and brought down dry clothes and a blanket for Sam when he comes in. He is sure to be wet and cold.' She glanced at the clock again and exclaimed, 'Oh, what could have possessed them to go off like that? I shall give him *such* a scolding when he returns!'

Mrs Molland put up her hand, an expectant look upon her face. Voices could be heard in the hall and the next moment Sir Lawrence walked in with Sam in his arms.

'Here he is.' He handed the boy to Rose. 'Wet, cold and tired, but unharmed, I think.'

With a little cry Rose hugged her son tightly.

'It was as we thought,' he added, easing his shoulders.

'They had gone to Sealham Point to see where Jem's father had carved his name on the rock. It was some sort of tribute to him on his birthday, but they misjudged the tide.'

Rose nodded, distracted. She carried Sam over to the fire, where Mrs Molland was waiting to help her undress him.

'Thank heaven you are safe!' Rose's fingers trembled as she struggled with the buttons of his coat.

'I do beg your pardon, Mama,' muttered Sam. 'I never meant to be away so long. Jem said we'd be there and back before school ended.'

'And did you think I would not worry if you did not turn up at school?' demanded Rose. 'Naughty boy, I do not know what you deserve for such a trick—perhaps we should have left you on those horrid rocks all night!'

'Hush now, he has learned his lesson,' soothed Mrs Molland. 'And you are making a sad mull of undressing him, Rose. Give him to me.'

Realising she was far too tearful and shaken to be helpful, Rose left Sam to his grandmother's care. As she turned she saw Sir Lawrence heading for the door.

'Don't go!'

He stopped at her words. Rose went towards him, saying shyly, 'Will you not stay? I am sure Sam will want to thank you.'

He glanced across to make sure the others were not attending.

'I thought I was not a fit-and-proper person?'

She flushed. 'Did I say that? I beg your pardon!

Please, do not go just yet. I—we would like to hear what happened.'

It was not until he gave a little nod that she realised she had been holding her breath and, with some difficulty, she invited him to sit down.

Within the warm glow of the fire he briefly relayed the tale. Mrs Molland blanched as he described how Abel had guided the little boat into the shore, and Sam took her hand.

'Do not be afraid, Grandmama, Jem and I were safe enough up on the rocks.'

Rose smiled.

'You can see he has come to no harm, Mama. I have no doubt he will want to go out on his pony tomorrow, as usual.' She tried hard to look severe. 'Although I do not know whether we should allow him such a treat…'

'Mama, you would not stop me riding, would you?' Sam looked horrified. 'Not when I have told you how very sorry I am for making you worry?'

'No, not this time,' she relented, unable to withstand the pleading look in his eyes and her heart still full of relief that he was safe.

She turned to Lawrence. 'He is doing very well. Evans says he has a natural aptitude for riding.'

'I never doubted it.'

After a slight hesitation Rose said, 'You could come to the paddock tomorrow morning and watch him.'

'Better than that,' said Lawrence, 'if it is a fine morning, why do we not go up on the moor?'

'Ooh, yes, sir, if you please!' cried Sam, clapping his hands.

Rose shook her head. 'I do not think…'

'Oh, please, Mama,' Sam beseeched her, his eyes shining. He added, with a flash of inspiration, 'It will be Sir Lawrence's reward, for rescuing us!'

They all laughed at that.

Rose said slowly, 'I *should* like to go riding, I have not been out for over a week and my poor mare will be growing horribly restive.'

'You have not forgotten we attend the Emsleigh ball tomorrow night?' put in Mrs Molland.

'We shall be back in plenty of time for that,' said Rose, throwing caution to the winds. 'Very well, sir, Sam and I will ride out with you tomorrow!'

The assignation made, Sir Lawrence took his leave, but by the time the maid returned after showing him to the door Rose was having second thoughts about the morning. To ride out with him, even with Sam and Evans in attendance, would be sure to cause comment, and she was certain Magnus would not approve.

'I must catch him,' she muttered, snatching up her shawl. 'I must tell him I have changed my mind.'

Rose rushed out onto the path, but there was no sign of Lawrence, only the black outline of a lone rider clip-clopping up the lane towards her. She was about to make her way back indoors when she heard her name.

'Magnus.' She peered through the darkness at the rider.

'I heard from Wilkins that Samuel had run away so I came to see if there was any news.'

'He is here now, and safe.' She could not prevent herself giving him a wide, relieved smile. Rose waited for him to tie his horse to the gatepost and accompany her inside. 'He walked to Sealham Point with Jem Wooler and they found themselves stranded by the tide. Thankfully Jem's uncle guessed where they would be and rowed out to rescue them.'

'Indeed?'

He followed her into the sitting room. Sam was standing before the fire, concentrating on fastening the last buttons of his clean jacket.

'Well, young man, what do you have to say for yourself?' Sam jumped as Magnus addressed him sternly, but he was given no chance to speak as Magnus pressed on, hands clasped behind his back and glaring down at the little boy. 'You have given your mama a great deal of anxiety. What were you thinking of, to run off without a by your leave, to miss your schooling and take off on such a foolish venture? I am surprised your mother has not spanked you for your disobedience. You would have been well served if you had been left to shiver on the rocks all night!'

Rose had said very much the same thing, but to hear Magnus utter the words roused her in defence of her son. She stepped forwards, as if to shield Sam.

'Thank you, Magnus, he is well aware that he has done wrong and he has already begged my pardon.' She glanced down at her son, noting the mutinous look about his mouth. 'Mama, perhaps you will take Sam away. Janet can find him a little supper and then he should go to bed.' She bent to kiss him, murmuring, 'Run along. I will come up to tuck you in shortly.'

Rose waited until they had left the room and turned back to Magnus, who said heavily, 'You are too soft with the boy, Rose. I would thrash any son of mine who was so disobedient.'

Rose fought down a sharp retort. Instead she said quietly, 'In the main Sam minds me very well. He has had a fright, and that, I think, will do him good.'

'He should be at school.'

'And so he will be, when he is a little older.' She put out her hand. 'Please, Magnus, let us not fight. I have been in such a worry today. You cannot imagine how relieved I was when Sir Lawrence brought Sam back.'

'Oh?' Magnus's brows snapped together. 'What has Daunton to do with this?'

'He was with Abel in the Ship when Maggie Wooler and I called. He rowed across the bay with Abel to collect the boys.'

Magnus stroked his chin.

'I wonder what he was doing with Wooler?'

'I have no idea. All I know is that when he heard Sam was in trouble he offered to help.' Rose clasped her hands tightly together. And they were going riding tomorrow. To cry off would seem very churlish, when he had been such a good friend.

'So Daunton brought the boy back,' Magnus continued. 'Did he mention me, or ask you any questions about me?'

Roes blinked.

'No, why should he?'

'Oh, no reason.' He seemed to shake off his thoughtful mood and reached out for her hands, smiling. 'I am glad little Samuel is returned unharmed, and partly for my own very selfish reasons. If he was hurt, it might have prevented you from coming to the Emsleigh ball tomorrow night.' He squeezed her fingers. 'Are you sure I cannot persuade you to stay at Emsleigh House after? There is no school for you to teach the following day, and you know we have rooms and to spare.'

'Thank you, Magnus, but no. Mama and I will come home, as we agreed.'

'Perhaps it is for the best.' He drew her into his arms. 'If you were to stay under my roof, I might be tempted to pre-empt our wedding night!'

Rose stood passively while his lips met hers, waiting for the tremor of excitement, the unfurling of desire deep in her belly that she had experienced when Lawrence had kissed her, but there was nothing. In fact, she had to steel herself not to pull away. Magnus raised his head, a crease wrinkling his brow at her lack of response.

'I know what it is.' The frowning look vanished, replaced by a kindly smile. 'You are tired and distracted by Samuel's little escapade. I shall leave you to rest then, for I want you in your very best looks tomorrow night!'

* * *

Sam was up early the following morning, none the worse for his adventure. Rose was relieved and amused to see him so eager for his riding treat and she allowed him to go off to the stables with Evans to saddle up the horses, promising to join them once she and Mrs Molland had broken their fast. When she did at last reach the stable yard, Rose was surprised to find Lawrence had arrived before her. He was standing in one corner, showing Sam how to make his small hands into very serviceable fists. They looked up as she approached.

'I hope you are not teaching my son any bad habits, Sir Lawrence.'

'On the contrary, I have been showing him how to defend himself.'

Sam's face cleared when he saw that Rose was smiling.

'Sir Lawrence has been teaching me to box, Mama. Extra things to the punches Abel has been showing Jem.'

She raised her brows.

'Goodness, have I been so very long?'

'Not only this morning,' replied Sam in the tone of one explaining something to a simpleton. 'He showed Jem and me some moves the other day, up at the farm.'

Rose was not sure she was pleased to hear that, but Evans brought her mare out at that moment and she decided to let the matter drop.

'I hope you do not object,' said Lawrence, helping her to mount. 'When Sam mentioned to me that some of the bigger boys bully him, I thought it might help.'

Rose's doubts eased a little.

'If it gives him more confidence then I am very happy,' she replied. 'As long as it does not turn *him* into a bully.'

'Very little chance of that.' Lawrence looked across the yard to where Sam was scrambling up into the saddle. 'His manners do you credit.'

He could not have said anything better to Rose. Praise of her son always raised her spirits and she trotted out of the yard, convinced that they would spend a very agreeable morning.

A bright, wintry sun beamed down upon the little party as they rode through the village, Sam proudly putting his pony through its paces with Evans riding beside him.

'Playing chaperon?' queried Lawrence, nodding towards the groom.

'Yes, if you like.' An involuntary smile curved Rose's lips. Indeed, she felt she had not stopped smiling since rising from her bed that morning. This excursion in Sir Lawrence's company was not only a treat for Sam.

They rode up onto the moor. A chill wind was blowing in off the sea, scouring the hills and blowing away any warmth they might have gained from the bright winter sun.

'Bracing,' declared Rose, taking a deep breath.

They trotted along, taking care to keep Sam close, until they reached a stretch of open ground. After a nod from Rose, Sam allowed the little pony to dash off,

Evans following closely behind. Lawrence put his hand on Rose's bridle.

'Wait. Let them get ahead of us and we can enjoy a good gallop to catch up.' Rose tightened her grip as her mare snorted and sidled. 'She's eager to go,' observed Lawrence. 'Is she fast?'

'Yes, there's a touch of Arab in her.' She leaned forwards to pat the mare's glossy neck and added wistfully, 'I wish I had more time to ride her. I suppose I should not really keep the horses; they eat into my savings, but riding is my one indulgence.'

'Then why not,' said Lawrence, 'if it means so much to you?'

Rose was going to add that she could only afford to keep the mare because her circumstances would change when she married Magnus, but somehow she did not want to mention that. Instead she laughed and said teasingly, 'You speak as someone who has never had to go without.'

'That is not true. I have gone without a great deal this past year.'

Colour rushed to her cheeks. The serious look in his eyes stirred a fluttering panic in her chest. Swallowing hard, Rose gathered up her reins.

'I think Sam is far enough ahead now—shall we go?'

Thankfully Lawrence said no more, but set his horse to the gallop. Rose was left to follow on and the effort to keep pace with his sleek hunter over the uneven ground took all her concentration. When they caught up with Sam and Evans, Lawrence drew rein and addressed her in such a relaxed, matter-of-fact manner that it was easy for Rose to respond in kind, and to persuade herself that his earlier comments had not been a reference to his alleged reformation of character.

With everyone in good spirits the little party set off again.

'It is like riding on the top of the world,' cried Sam, sitting up in the saddle and gazing across the moor to the wooded hills beyond.

Lawrence laughed. His glance slid to Rose.

'Well, are you glad you came?'

Meeting his eyes, she could not help but return his smile.

'Very glad, thank you.'

'Mama, Evans says that path leads to the mine at Hades Cove.' Sam was pointing towards an overgrown track leading away to a wooded combe. 'Can we ride down there? Please.' He added the last word plaintively after reading a refusal on his mother's face.

Sir Lawrence consulted his watch.

'We *do* have time. And I, too, should like to go down there. We saw the mine when we were rowing back from Sealham Point.'

Rose demurred. 'I cannot think it would be of interest.'

'But, Mama!'

Lawrence put up his hand, saying quietly, 'We shall not go there if your mama objects, Sam.'

'I do not *object*, exactly,' said Rose, 'but there is nothing to see. I have not been there for years, but I believe it is boarded up now and wildly overgrown, with only ruined buildings, spoil heaps and the remains of a few rusted wagons to be seen.'

'I can think of nothing more likely to appeal to a child.'

Lawrence's boyish grin made her chuckle.

'Children of all ages, perhaps! Very well, if you wish to ride down to Hades Cove, let us do so!'

They wound their way down into the combe, leaving behind them the bracken and stunted gorse bushes and plunging into dense woodland, their path carpeted with fallen leaves. At one point the track took them through a wide clearing and they could look down on Mersecombe spread below them, before dropping down into the trees again.

'Someone has been this way recently,' observed Lawrence, who was following Evans along the narrow track. 'The grass has been trampled down in places.'

'That may have been Magnus; he visited the mine not long ago,' said Rose.

'Is he in the habit of coming here?'

'No, we rode here once, shortly after we met.' She added ruefully, 'I was out of reason cross with him when I learned of this last visit. It was very foolish of me; after all, it will all become his once we are married.'

'Did he say why he had come?'

She waved one hand in a dismissive gesture.

'He believes Hades Mine could still be profitable. I do not. When my husband was alive we paid for the best surveyors and engineers to report, but Magnus thinks he knows better.' She stopped. To air such opinions was disloyal to her future husband. With a faint, apologetic smile she relapsed into silence.

Finally they emerged from the trees and followed the path onto a windswept promontory. Rose brought her horse to a stand.

'Here we are. And, as you can see, it is nothing but a ruin.'

She looked about her sadly. They were on a narrow, grassy shelf of land near the bottom of a steep, wooded combe. Below them was nothing but bare grey rock leading down to an equally grey sea, which tossed and eddied in the narrow cove at the mouth of the combe. The small promontory had once been a hive of industry, but only a few bleak ruins remained. The walls of a small hut were still standing, but its roof and windows had long since disappeared. Spoil heaps were now green mounds and the entrance to the mine shaft was covered by heavy planks. An overgrown track ran down steeply to the cove, where an old jetty was still visible, but near the mine the track ran along the edge of the shelf with a sheer drop to the churning grey sea below. Rose called to Sam to be careful and Evans said gruffly, 'Don't 'ee worry, ma'am, I'll look after him.'

She watched for a moment as her groom followed Sam towards a wooden truck that lay at a drunken angle, one wheel broken off and the rails that had carried it lost beneath the weeds. The only sound was the cry of gulls overhead and the faint rush of the sea.

'A desolate place,' remarked Lawrence, dismounting and coming over to lift her down.

She dropped into his arms, trying not to think of his hands on her waist, the familiar fresh scent of his skin. Her heart thumped so loud and erratically she was sure he must hear it.

'And dangerous,' she said, referring not only to the physical hazards of the area. Flushing, she stepped out of his grasp, struggling to control her wayward thoughts. 'Thankfully it is some distance from all the main byways, and no one comes here. I should never forgive myself if a child should be injured in the mine.'

'Unlikely,' said Lawrence. 'It appears to be well boarded up.' He went across to the opening for a closer inspection. 'Yes, it is remarkably well secured.'

'I am pleased to hear it.'

'You say your husband bought the mine?'

Sir Lawrence came back and proffered his arm. With only a slight hesitation Rose placed her fingers on his sleeve.

'Harry could never resist a bargain. He thought Hades Mine would bring us wealth beyond our dreams. He won it from a man in Barnstaple. They had been playing at dice and his partner offered Harry the mine in lieu of the money he owed him. Harry was so pleased with himself when he came home with the deeds.'

'You were not so happy?'

Rose did not answer immediately, but at length she said in a low voice, 'I had only recently given birth to Sam; I knew very little about mines, but I thought it odd that a man should part with something supposedly worth a fortune for a gambling debt of a hundred pounds.' She turned her frank gaze upon him. 'What would you do if someone offered you such an exchange?'

'That depends upon who was offering it.'

'A fool, a spendthrift…almost as big a wastrel as my husband—I beg your pardon.' She began to hunt for her handkerchief. 'I should not have spoken so. I should be over this by now.'

Lawrence took her shoulders and turned her to him. Cupping her face in his hands, he smoothed his thumbs gently over her cheeks to wipe away the tears.

'You are angry and rightly so. From the little I have learned—not from you, you have been very discreet, but to be left thus, with a young son to raise—it must be very hard for you.'

'It is.' She moved away from him and finished wiping her eyes. 'I only want what is best for Sam.'

'And you think marrying Magnus Emsleigh is the best you can do?'

'He is a good man and will provide Sam with the father he needs.'

His blue eyes were fixed on her face, holding her gaze. Rose's pulse quickened; she felt again the strength of the bond between them. It was much more than the hot, urgent desire stirring inside her: it was a sense of meeting a kindred spirit, someone to share her hopes, her fears—someone to laugh with. If it were not for Sam, would she take a chance and throw in her lot with

Sir Lawrence Daunton? Would she give in to the temptation to enjoy his company and his lovemaking, until some other woman caught his attention? All this ran through her mind in the space of a moment, swiftly followed by the memory of the pain she had suffered with her husband. Not merely physical, that had been minor compared to the torture of knowing she was no longer first in his affections. Even in her company his mind had been elsewhere, longing to be back with the laughing beauties who would pander to his every whim and not burden him with the day-to-day responsibilities of looking after his family. That had been bad enough, but she was shocked now to find that the affection she had felt for her husband was nothing to the love she felt for the man now standing before her.

Lawrence watched the play of emotion crossing Rose's face. He guessed something of her confusion and was tempted to tell her his suspicions about Magnus Emsleigh, but he knew how it would sound. She would think it merely the accusations of a jealous rival. She still did not trust him. A shudder ran through her and she stepped away from him, dropping the lashes to veil her thoughts.

Stifling a sigh, he let her go; it seemed a year of living blamelessly was not enough to convince her that he was in earnest. She pulled up the collar of her riding jacket.

'It grows colder. I do not want to keep Sam out in this wind for too long.'

Confidences were at an end. Accepting that, Lawrence nodded.

'Very well. Stay here with the horses while I persuade Master Sam we have to go back. It may not be easy; he has found an exciting world to explore.'

He was rewarded with a faint smile; until he could prove that it was Emsleigh who was not the fit-and-proper person he appeared to be, Lawrence realised he would have to content himself with that.

Rose and Sam returned from their outing much refreshed, but although Sam was eager to recount everything to his grandmother, Rose was more reticent. She had seen the speculative look in her mother's eye when she had announced she was going riding with Sir Lawrence; she would not add to the conjecture by admitting how much she had enjoyed herself, and instead turned her mother's thoughts to what they should wear to Emsleigh House that evening.

As she made her preparations for the ball, Rose was increasingly thankful that she had refused to allow Magnus to send his carriage for them. She did not want to be under any more of an obligation to him and since her ride out that morning this feeling had intensified. On the journey back from the mine she and Lawrence had talked only of commonplace subjects, but she had rarely enjoyed herself more, and it was not until he had taken his leave of her that she realised she had never thanked him properly for bringing Sam back from

Sealham Point. She considered writing to him, then decided she would seek him out at the ball that evening. The little surge of pleasure she experienced at the thought gave her pause, and she began to question whether she could really marry Magnus, knowing she could never love him. If not, then she must tell him, and soon. And she thought it would be easier to make a decision if she was not enjoying the comfort of his elegant chaise.

In the end they were taken up by Farmer Finch and his wife in their ancient but stately carriage. The good-natured farmer and his lady were very vocal in their excitement at being invited to Emsleigh for the Winter Ball.

'Very good of Emsleigh, it is,' pronounced Mr Finch in his lazy, rolling drawl. 'Once a year he invites all his neighbours to Emsleigh House to eat, drink, dance and be merry until the morning!'

'Aye,' chuckled his wife. 'Not at all high in the instep is Mr Emsleigh, for all his money. And he dresses as fine as any London beau, don't you agree, Mrs Westerhill?' She gave Rose a playful dig in the ribs. 'He'll make you a fine husband, my dear, you mark my words. And don't you go putting him off for another year, else you might find some other lady will come along and snabble him up.'

'Just what I have been telling Rose myself, ma'am,' agreed Mrs Molland. 'She needs to make up her mind and stick to it.'

Rose peered through the darkness, trying to see her

mother's expression. The words were more than a casual remark, she was sure. Mrs Molland had never tried to influence Rose about her marriage, saying that she would be happy to have her daughter and grandson live with her for ever, but now Rose wondered if Mama was anxious to see her settled.

'Aye, and then p'raps you'll set yourself to finding a husband for that sister of his,' put in Mr Finch. 'Not that *that* will be so easy, since she thinks herself so far above her company.' He laughed. 'Lord, but this ball must be a sad trial for her, poor woman. She'll be worrying all evening that one of her brother's clodhopping guests will walk mud onto their carpets!'

They laughed at this, but Rose could not be comfortable at talking in such a way of Althea, even though she might share their opinions. She was relieved when her mother neatly turned the subject, asking Mrs Finch about the health of her latest grandchild, and they finished the journey listening to the harrowing story of little Jacob's continuing bouts of croup.

At Emsleigh House Rose and her mother alighted and followed the Finches into the hall, which was already crowded with laughing, chattering guests. They made their way up the wide curving stairs to the first landing, where the partition doors between the two reception rooms had been folded back to make one huge ballroom heated by roaring fires in the two hearths and hundreds of candles burning in the glittering chandeliers. Althea came up to greet them.

'So glad you are come,' she said, laying her hand on

Rose's arm. 'You are amongst the very few people here that I can bear to talk to!' She leaned closer. 'I really do not know why Magnus insists upon inviting so many *common* people—even his tenants!'

'But it has always been the custom for the foremost landowner in the area to hold the Winter Ball,' explained Mrs Molland. 'And who should do it, if not Mr Emsleigh?'

'Well, there is *that*,' agreed Althea, somewhat mollified, 'but why should we have them all in the house—could he not hold a dance in the barn?'

'That would avoid having clodhopping farmers in your house,' murmured Rose, sharing a mischievous look with her mother.

'Yes, it would,' agreed Althea. 'But there it is; Magnus wishes to be thought generous.' She added, brightening. 'At least we have more gentlemen here this year, including Captain Morris, who has just arrived.' She dropped her voice. 'He was captain of the *Sealark* on her last journey, you know, but such good manners, no one would think him a sailor!'

Althea tripped away as more guests arrived, leaving Mrs Molland to shake her head after her. Rose soon spotted Lawrence talking with a group of gentlemen in one far corner. She wanted to go immediately to speak to him, but the music started and Magnus came to claim her hand for the first dance.

No matter, she told herself. *Before the night is out I will thank him for rescuing Sam.*

And I will tell him I misjudged him.

Rose blinked. That had not been her original intention

at all, but suddenly it was important to set things right with Lawrence.

The ball was noisy but good-natured. Magnus strutted around the room full of cheerful goodwill, reminding Rose of a genial monarch with his subjects. Althea was more regal, but less genial, except when she stood up to dance with Lawrence. Then she was all smiles. Rose tried not to allow her eyes to follow them around the room. Her body was still singing from the morning ride. During the day she had relived every look, every word they had shared. She felt so alive, her skin tingling with the anticipation of being close to Lawrence again. However, as the evening wore on it became clear that Lawrence was not going to ask her to dance with him.

It is your own fault, she chided herself. *You asked him to leave you alone and that is what he is doing.*

Her spirits were dampened, but she was not wholly downcast. She herself did not lack partners and was content to bide her time until she could find the opportunity to speak to Lawrence. She was reluctant to approach with so many people around him, especially Althea, who was constantly at his side. Rose watched them dancing together and when the music ended he relinquished her hand to Captain Morris, one of the few gentlemen present that Althea thought sufficiently elevated to partner her. The two men exchanged a few words, then Lawrence bowed and moved towards the door.

Rose saw her chance. She casually walked into the card room and out again by another door that led onto the landing. As she had hoped, Lawrence was outside the supper room, talking to Mr Ansell. They broke off their conversation as Rose approached. She greeted them with a shy smile and turned to Lawrence. She was a little nervous now the moment had come—what if he should reject her?

'Sir Lawrence, I wonder if I might have a word with you?'

'Aye, take him, ma'am,' exclaimed Mr Ansell with a jovial laugh. 'I've just offered to buy his hunter and been refused, so I want nothing more to do with him. He is all yours, Mrs Westerhill!'

Lawrence smiled, but she detected a wary reserve in his eyes. She ran her tongue over her dry lips.

'Sir Lawrence, I wanted to say—'

A group of laughing young people came hurtling out of the supper room and Rose broke off. Sir Lawrence caught her arm and pulled her back out of the way.

'Perhaps we should find somewhere we may talk undisturbed.'

Rose nodded and led him away from the ballroom to an unlit corridor.

'The library is at the end of this passage, we will go there,' she murmured, blushing at her own temerity. She was glad he did not tease her. Instead he placed a hand beneath her elbow to guide her through the darkness. When they reached the library door she paused for a moment, listening. Reassured by the silence, she turned the handle.

The library was still and silent, illuminated only by

the pale light of a rising moon that shone in through the long, unshuttered windows. Rose slipped inside and Lawrence followed, softly closing the door behind him. She heard the click as he turned the key in the lock.

'There. Now we can be sure we will not be disturbed.'

What now? As they had progressed along the dark corridor, moving further from the noisy ballroom, Rose had been aware of a nervous excitement growing within her. Lawrence's hand on her arm had been warm, possessive. The heated blood pulsed around her body, heightening her senses. Alone with him in the darkness, all her wayward mind could think of was making love to him. That had not been her intention in bringing him here, but she acknowledged that she wanted him, with every fibre of her being. She remembered being here with him once before. Then he had pulled her into his arms. Now she wanted him to do the same, but instead he remained out of arms' reach, a still and silent shadow. With an effort she dragged her mind back to the original purpose of the meeting.

'I—I wanted to thank you.' Rose swallowed, trying to clear the nervous constriction in her throat. 'For rescuing Sam.'

Her voice sounded abnormally loud in the heavy silence. She moved away, hoping that by putting some distance between herself and Lawrence she could control her unruly desire. She heard Lawrence's voice behind her, deep and resonant in the darkness.

'It is Abel Wooler who deserves your thanks. He knew

where to find the boys and had the experience to row out to Sealham Point.'

She nodded. She had reached the desk and she stood before it, staring out of the window at the moonlit gardens.

'I realise that and spoke to him this afternoon. He knows how grateful I am. You l-left last night before I could thank you and this morning…' she faltered '…this morning I was very remiss in not telling you how much I am in your debt.' She clasped her hands together, determined to finish her confession. 'I—I wanted to say I may have been wrong. A-about you…'

Her heart was thudding so hard it was difficult to talk and her nerves were stretched to breaking. She heard no sound, but something made her turn around. Lawrence had come up behind her. He was standing so close she had to look up to see his face, but the shadows were too deep for her to read his expression. They were only inches apart and the sheer force of his presence enveloped her. Silence lay heavy around them; they were cocooned in their own little world.

Rose remained perfectly still. She knew she had reached some momentous point in her life: one false move, one wrong word, could mean disaster.

'You do not know how long I have wanted to hear you say that.'

The words were so soft that at first she thought she had imagined them. Lawrence reached out and ran the backs of his fingers over her cheek. She closed her eyes and leaned her head against his hand.

'You do not know how much I want it to be true.'

His fingers stroked across her chin and slipped around her neck. Obedient to the gentle pressure of his hand, she took the little step necessary to cover the distance between them, lifting her head for his kiss. The first touch of his lips was as gentle as a whisper, but it fanned the flames of the desire she had kept buried for so long. With a little cry Rose threw her arms around his neck, kissing him with a burning passion that was beyond all rational thought. He responded immediately. His arms tightened about her, lifting her off the floor as her mouth yielded to the demands of his kiss, their tongues tangling and exploring. She felt the hard edge of the desk behind her knees and Lawrence pushed her gently back onto its smooth surface. Aching desire pounded through her body, heating her blood, heightening all her senses. She arched against him as he trailed kisses down her neck and across the soft swell of her breasts, her skin burning wherever his lips touched it. Lawrence was leaning over her, pressing her down on the desk, his mouth seeking hers again for another bruising kiss. He gathered up her skirts and she felt his fingers on her thighs. Obedient to the pressure of his hands, she twined her legs about him, gasping as those wickedly long fingers played havoc with her senses, touching and caressing her until she was aching from the sweet torture he was inflicting. He continued to play her while his free hand opened the flap of his breeches. Excited anticipation ripped through her when she felt his flesh hard upon her own. She pushed against him, exultant, as he entered her. They moved together, harder, faster, until Rose lost control of her body while he worshipped her with his. She bucked and trembled as they shared a shattering climax, clinging tightly to Lawrence until the last, ecstatic spasm had finished and they were left gasping and exhausted.

Lawrence relaxed against her, but Rose held him close, savouring the wondrous, other-worldliness of their union. She was unwilling for it to end, reluctant to make the transition from carefree paradise to the reality of their situation. At length he eased himself away and Rose sat up. She reached for him, pulling him back so she could lean against his chest, feeling the thud of his heart against her cheek. After a few minutes she raised her head and turned to look out of the window.

'Rose? What is it, love?' He caught her face in his hands and she heard the concern in his voice.

'I would like to slip away from here now, just you and me.'

A gentle laugh rumbled in his chest.

'If we were not on the first floor we could climb out of the window and run off, but there is no help for it, we must go back to the ballroom. And I fear we must do so very soon.' He stepped away from her and straightened his clothing while Rose did the same, silently marvelling at the strength of passion that had overwhelmed them. This total loss of control had shaken her to her core. Never before had she felt so vulnerable: she had bared her soul and put herself completely at the mercy of one man. She needed to be alone, to examine her feelings and make sense of them. Her thoughts were still in turmoil and it was an effort to think rationally.

'I am not sure I can go back,' she whispered. 'Everyone will know...'

'I promise you they will not.' He pulled her to her feet and held her hand as they crossed to the door. Cautiously he looked out into the darkness beyond. 'Come, there is no one in sight.'

They slipped out of the library and made their way back towards the public rooms. Rose held Lawrence's hand, drawing comfort from those warm fingers wrapped around hers. She needed to think over what had happened to her in the library, to discuss it with Lawrence, but it was not possible, not yet. She must keep her newfound happiness hidden until she had found a way to explain everything to Magnus. Thoughts and emotions continued to crowd in upon her as she walked beside Lawrence. They had almost reached the lighted corridor leading to the ballroom when Rose spoke again.

'Do I look very dishevelled?'

'Not in the least. You look adorable.'

The glow in his eyes made her blush all over again, but she tried to ignore it and shook out her skirts before taking his arm to walk out into the light. They passed several couples making their way to the supper room and Rose was amazed that they did not stop to stare at her. She felt that she was somehow transformed into a completely different person. She stole a peep up at Lawrence. He looked perfectly at ease, although she thought his smile looked a little brighter and there was a definite glow in his eyes when he caught her glance.

'You must tell Emsleigh you cannot marry him,' he murmured as they reached the ballroom.

'Yes, but not tonight.'

'Of course not. We have much to talk about. I will call tomorrow.'

He squeezed her arm and Rose's heart gave a little flip of nervous excitement. Explaining to Magnus that she could not marry him would be painful, but once it was done she would be free…

'So there you are, Sir Lawrence!' Althea's high voice intruded. 'I have been looking everywhere for you, sir. I was hoping you would partner me for the next dance.'

'Alas, Miss Emsleigh, I cannot do that.'

She looked from Lawrence to Rose, whose new-found happiness was shining in her eyes.

'Have you been flirting with Mrs Westerhill?'

'I would never flirt with her.'

The warm smile he bestowed upon Rose was not lost on Althea, whose eyes now positively flashed.

'You have paid her far too much attention tonight.'

Lawrence shook his head.

'No, Miss Emsleigh, I—' He broke off as Magnus came up.

'Daunton, unhand my fiancée, if you please.' His curt, cold tone brought a guilty flush to Rose's cheeks. Had he guessed where they had been, what had occurred? She felt so changed, so altered, it seemed impossible that Magnus should not notice it. He ignored her and continued to stare at Lawrence, unsmiling.

'Captain Morris tells me you have been making enquiries about the *Sealark*.'

Lawrence made no move, his expression did not change, but he grew very still. Rose's initial relief was replaced by consternation. She did not understand the sudden tension that surrounded them. The air was thick with danger.

'Yes,' Lawrence said coolly, 'I spoke to him about it.'

'You are an agent for the insurers.'

Rose laughed.

'That is absurd, Magnus—'

'Yes, I am.'

Lawrence's answer cut across hers and at the same time he gently removed her hand from his arm. He was distancing himself from her and Rose did not know why.

Magnus drew himself up, eyes narrowing.

'You have inveigled your way into my house to spy on me!'

'By no means,' replied Lawrence evenly. 'You will recall that you invited *me*. Although I admit I am guilty of not telling you why I had come to Knightscote.'

Magnus glared at him. 'And have you discovered anything amiss, sir?'

There was a pause no longer than a heartbeat before Lawrence answered.

'No, I have not. As yet.'

'And nor will you. So you may go back to your

masters and tell them to pay me what is owed! And you will leave my house. This instant.'

'No!' cried Althea. 'Magnus, no harm has been done; he has found nothing to incriminate you. You cannot throw him out.'

Lawrence inclined his head.

'Perhaps it is best that I leave now.' He held out his hand to Rose, but Althea grabbed his sleeve.

'I will not let you go. You must stay!'

'Miss Emsleigh, please,' said Lawrence gently, 'this is not wise.'

He tried to remove her fingers from his coat, but she only clung tighter.

'No, you shall not walk out on me.'

'I'm afraid I must.'

'No! You cannot!' Her voice rose hysterically. 'I am carrying your child!'

Until that moment Rose had not been aware of the chatter around them, but she noticed immediately when it stopped, replaced by a shocked silence. Lawrence looked stunned.

'That is impossible,' he said quietly.

'What is this, Althea?' Magnus turned to his sister. 'What are you saying?'

'The first night we met, at the Pullens' ball. I w-was flattered by his attentions, s-swept away…' She was crying now, her hands twisting together. 'I allowed him to take me outside for a little air and…'

Lawrence shook his head. He disengaged himself and stepped away from her.

'You are mistaken, madam.'

Althea put up her chin.

'I will force you to marry me,' she said triumphantly. 'I will not let you abandon me!'

Magnus put his arm about her shoulders.

'Impossible. That such a man should be my brother—! No, no, my dear; were he as rich as Croesus I could not allow that.' He lifted a hand and summoned his footmen. 'You, sir, will leave my house immediately. And you will have nothing more to do with my sister.'

'I cannot leave with such a slur hanging over me!'

'A slur? Dear God, as if anyone would doubt it is true. You are well known for your rakish ways, sir, get out of my house.'

'No, Magnus!' Althea grabbed his coat. 'That is not what I want!'

Magnus patted her arm.

'You have nothing to fear, my dear, but whatever the shame, I will not allow you to marry this villain.'

Tight jawed, Lawrence shook his head.

'Rose, do not believe this. I swear I have not laid a hand on her or any woman since I met you.'

She tried to make herself think, but the high, joyous singing that had been resonating through her since they had come back into the ballroom was changed to an anguished scream inside her head. Hot tears burned her eyes, but she was too proud to let them fall. When Lawrence reached out for her, she backed away.

'Rose—it's a lie, I tell you!'

'Do not listen to him,' Magnus urged her. 'He is a libertine, a rogue, not to be trusted.' He raised his voice to address his servants. 'Escort Sir Lawrence from the premises.'

Lawrence gave a snarl of warning and the lackeys stopped, hovering uncertainly at his shoulder.

'Should you not be calling me out, Emsleigh? We could settle this at dawn with swords or pistols, whatever you chose.'

'Yes, that is the way of your sort, is it not?' Magnus curled his lip. 'That may be the custom in town, sir, but not here! Your name is disgraced here, sir, disgraced. You should quit Exmoor.'

'Not until I have proved you deliberately sank the *Sealark* to claim the insurance.'

Magnus laughed.

'Do you think anyone will help you after this? Captain Morris, assist my men to eject this, this *scoundrel*!'

Rose watched, transfixed, as the captain stepped up. Lawrence stiffened, his hands clenching into fists.

'Come, sir,' barked the captain, 'you cannot start a brawl in a gentleman's house.'

Lawrence hesitated, then turned to look at Rose. He was very pale and a muscle was working his cheek.

'Rose,' he said urgently, 'we must talk. You must let me explain—'

With a shudder she fluttered her hand in a small gesture of dismissal. Nothing made sense. The evening had taken on a nightmarish quality. She felt used, betrayed.

The servants and Captain Morris stepped closer to Lawrence, but he put up his hand.

'Very well, I will leave—for now.' With a final, blazing look at Rose he turned on his heel and strode out of the ballroom, the crowd hastily stepping back to clear a path to the door.

'Rose?'

Her mother's gentle hand was upon her arm. Magnus was escorting his sobbing sister from the room and Rose was aware of the eyes of the crowd turning upon her. Pride came to her aid. Her chin went up. Lawrence had gone and she wanted to throw herself into the soft, comforting warmth of her mother's embrace, but that must wait. She summoned every ounce of will to force out a few quiet words.

'Take me home, Mama.'

CHAPTER EIGHT

ROSE lay in her bed and watched the pinky-grey light of dawn creep into her tiny room. She had slept very little and cried even less, the pain in her heart too deep for tears. All night she had replayed the scene at Emsleigh House, trying to find some crumb of comfort, but there was none. Lawrence had not come to Knightscote for her sake; he had been investigating the sinking of the *Sealark*.

It did not explain his kindness to Sam, unless he thought to ingratiate himself with her and provide himself with a little amusement while he carried out his enquiries. If so, it had worked only too well; Rose had abandoned caution and thrown herself into his arms, prepared to count the world well lost. And it was. Her recklessness at Emsleigh House had cost her dear.

Her conscience had troubled her after those precious, snowbound days at Knightscote, but she had salved it by telling herself it had been an aberration caused by the exceptional circumstances. A chance meeting, a moment's happiness before they went their separate ways, never to meet again. Even so she had postponed her wedding for twelve months, unable to face marriage to another man while Lawrence's image was so fresh in her mind. Now she knew she could never marry Magnus Emsleigh, because despite her best intentions, for the second time in her life she had lost her heart to a rake—and how quickly, how cruelly she had been disillusioned.

Althea's outburst had been shocking and it *must* be true; Rose knew only too well Lawrence's impetuous nature—had he not accosted her outside the Ship after the Mersecombe Assembly? To say nothing of their passionate union last night. She had given herself to him, freely, lovingly, and she had been so sure he loved her in return, but she knew now that could not be true. With a groan she turned over and buried her face in her pillow. While her mind might dismiss Sir Lawrence Daunton as a rake and a libertine, her body still ached at the memory of his caresses. She did not know how she would survive without them.

But of course she would survive. She had Sam to think of, and her mother. She must go on, for their sake. Thus, when Janet brought her hot water, Rose dragged herself from her bed and forced herself into her clothes.

Her mother and Sam were already at the breakfast table, and Rose was thankful that, apart from subjecting her to a searching look, Mrs Molland made no mention of the events at Emsleigh House. After the morning pleasantries had been exchanged, Mrs Molland said brightly, 'Evans has hired the gig from Farmer Ansell and is driving me to Minehead today; there are several purchases I must make. Perhaps, Rose, you would like to come with me? You need do nothing but enjoy yourself—it would be purely a pleasure trip for you.'

Pleasure? Rose thought she would never know pleasure again. She shook her head.

'Thank you, Mama, but no. Mrs Reed has asked me to write down my observations upon how the school should be run. However, since there are no classes today, perhaps Sam might like to go with you…'

'No, no, Mama.' This was accompanied by a vigorous shaking of the head. 'You cannot have forgotten that once I have done my chores I am going to Woolers Farm to see Jem.'

Rose looked out of the window; there had been a light snowfall during the night, dusting everything with white, and the walls and roofs sparkled invitingly in the winter sunshine. A brisk walk might clear her head and help to shift the depression that enveloped her.

'Perhaps I shall come with you. I can postpone my writing for an hour or so.'

'An excellent idea,' agreed Mrs Molland. 'It is too lovely a day to stay indoors. And you can take with you the little note I have written for old Mrs Wooler. She suffers dreadfully in the winter months and I promised I would let her have the recipe for a tonic.' She rose from her chair as a movement outside the window caught her eye. 'Here is Evans now with the gig. Be good for your mama, Sam, and I shall bring you back a little present. Rose, is there anything I can get you?'

'Nothing, thank you, but I will walk with you to the gate and see you off.'

The two women went arm in arm out of the room and as they walked to the gig Mrs Molland cleared her throat.

'If you are writing up notes for Mrs Reed, does that mean you still intend to marry Magnus?' Her grip on Rose's arm tightened. 'You have no need to tell me that your affections are not engaged. Indeed, after last night I should think everyone—'

'Mama!'

She heeded the warning note in Rose's voice and said merely, 'So, are you going to cry off?'

'I think I must.' Rose bit her lip. 'Was…was it very apparent that—that Sir Lawrence and I had…formed an attachment?'

'Crystal clear,' replied Mrs Molland frankly. 'The only comfort is that his treatment of Althea Emsleigh has proved him to be a complete rogue and everyone will regard you with sympathy.'

Rose winced. Her mother patted her arm.

'You do not have to decide about your marriage immediately. When he took his leave of us last night, Magnus was most attentive. I do not believe he wishes to end your engagement. You must consider Sam's future as well, you know.'

'I do know it,' replied Rose, sighing. 'But whatever Magnus and I decide, I cannot continue at the school. I shall send a note to Mrs Reed today, explaining that I shall not be taking any more classes. Perhaps it would be best if I left Mersecombe.'

They had reached the gate and stopped for a moment.

'Consider carefully, my dear,' murmured Mrs Molland. 'You have many years ahead of you.'

Giving Rose a quick hug, she climbed up into the gig and Evans set off down the lane at a smart pace. Rose watched them go. The dark cloud descended even deeper into her soul. She wanted to do nothing except return to her bed, but that was impossible. She must find something to occupy her.

Indoors, Sam was helping Janet to clear the breakfast table, after which he would fill up the log basket in the sitting room. Small tasks, but Rose had insisted that he help out a little in the house and, since becoming friends with Jem and seeing how hard he had to work on the farm, Sam was keen to show that he, too, had a role to play.

Knowing it would be some little while yet before Sam was ready to go out, Rose carried her pens and paper to the little table in the sitting room. She must write letters to the vicar and to Mrs Reed, explaining that she would no longer be teaching at the school. After that, if there was time, she would make a start upon her notes. The letters were quickly dashed off, but when she pulled a clean sheet of paper towards her to write her notes the words would not come. Her mind kept wandering back to the ball.

She felt quite sick when she thought of Lawrence's betrayal—to be investigating Magnus was bad enough, but even that she could have borne, if he had not lied to her about Althea. She had begun to believe that he really had altered, that he was not the libertine she had thought him. Althea's announcement had shown her that her initial conviction had been true. A rake could not change his nature.

The faint sound of knocking at the front door brought her out of her reverie. A familiar deep voice sounded from the hall. With growing dismay she recognised the swift, booted tread outside the door. How foolish of her not to instruct Janet to deny him. Now it was too late to do anything other than rise from the table and school her features into a look of stony indifference.

Lawrence entered the little parlour and stopped just inside the door. The coldness of his reception was almost physical. It hit him like a blast of icy air. Rose stood on the opposite side of the room, rigidly aloof.

'I had to come,' he began. 'We need to talk—'

'There is nothing to be said. Please leave.' Her cold stare was fixed somewhere over his shoulder, her voice as hard as stone. He took a step towards her.

'Rose, please listen to me, I can expl—'

'Oh?' She curled her lip, the words dripping from her tongue like icy water. 'Will you deny that you came here to spy upon us?'

'Not upon you—never upon you!'

She continued as if he had not spoken.

'You sought to put the blame for the loss of the *Sealark* upon Magnus.'

'I did not *seek* to put the blame upon anyone. I merely came here looking for the truth.'

'You have the…the *gall* to talk of truth!'

'I never deceived you!'

'You deceived us all! If I had known you suspected Magnus—'

'You would never have let me near you,' he finished for her.

'What a blessing that would have been!'

'Not for me. I have been living for the moment I would see you again.'

'Do not say that!' She dashed a hand across her eyes. 'I will hear no more of your lies.'

'I have never lied to you, Rose.' He stopped and shook his head. He said slowly, 'Perhaps I did lie, by omission. But if you had asked me, I would have told you I was investigating the *Sealark*.' Lawrence moved a little closer. 'That was not my only reason for coming to Mersecombe.'

'Oh, of course. You wanted a pointer puppy.'

He smiled slightly.

'Puppy be damned. I wanted to see you.'

She ignored that.

'And was Althea Emsleigh one of your *lies by omission*?'

The smile disappeared. He said quietly, 'That is not

my lie. I have danced with Althea Emsleigh, but nothing more, I give you my word.'

She threw up her hand.

'Do not perjure yourself any further. I wish you would go now.'

She glared at him, full of righteous indignation. She was less than two strides away—Lawrence wanted to cross the space between them and take her in his arms, melting her icy rage with a passionate kiss. But something held him back, a thread as fine as silk, yet stronger than any chain: the fear that she would reject him.

Her eyes were dark and hard as slate, but he read in their depths such pain and rage that it cut like a knife. Unbidden, words rose to his lips. He said simply, 'I love you, Rose.'

She glared at him.

'How dare you talk to me of love?' Her voice shook with fury. 'I w-was silly enough to think— What a *fool* I have been!' She took a long, ragged breath, then said coldly, 'Enough of this. You will go now and never come here again.'

She fixed him with a look of such implacable loathing that further argument died on his lips.

'Very well,' he said at last, 'I will leave now, but whatever you think of me, Rose, you must not marry Emsleigh.'

'What we did last night has made it impossible for me to do so!' she flashed. Her spirits sagged. 'I have proved myself as false as you. I am ashamed.'

'You should not be. We cannot help our feelings for each other, Rose.'

'But what of Magnus? He deserves better—'

'No. He is not the upright gentleman he seems. He sank the *Sealark*—I have a witness who is prepared to tell the truth about that—'

Rose put her hands to her ears. 'Stop it! I will not listen to this. If *you* will not go away, then *I* shall—'

She went to run past him, but he grabbed her arm.

'You will listen to me, madam, or by God I will—'

'You will what?' She confronted him, brows raised, eyes stormy, challenging. 'You will beat me into submission? It would not be the first time I have suffered a man's blows.'

She had not meant to say that—Rose had never admitted it to anyone before and she berated herself as she saw the shock in his face.

'I am not such a monster.' The angry light faded from his eyes and she looked away, unwilling to bear his sympathy. 'Rose—'

'Sir Lawrence, Sir Lawrence, I saw your horse outside…'

They jumped apart as Sam burst into the room, his innocent face glowing with delight. He skidded to a halt before Lawrence, snatched off his cap and sketched a bow.

'Good day to you, sir. Mama and I are about walk to Woolers Farm—would you like to go with us?'

'Sam, you should not—'

Rose tried to protest, but she was shaking too much

to do more than murmur her remonstrance. Lawrence was faster to regain control.

'Alas, Sam, I am bound in the opposite direction.'

Rose said pointedly, 'Sir Lawrence is just leaving.'

Sam's face fell and Lawrence added quickly, 'My business may take some time. I should go now if I am to get back to Knightscote before dark.'

'Is that why you have a lantern strapped to your saddle, so you can find your way home?' asked Sam, wide-eyed.

Lawrence managed a smile and reached out to ruffle the boy's hair.

'No, you scapegrace, I am going exploring.'

'Oh, and what are you going to look for?' exclaimed Sam. 'Gold? Treasure?'

Lawrence's eyes flickered briefly to Rose.

'Something like that.'

'Can I come with you?'

'Not this time. Besides, your friend Jem will be waiting for you.'

'Indeed he will,' put in Rose. 'We must be going, too. Bid Sir Lawrence goodbye now.'

While Sam made his bow she forced herself to look at Lawrence, trying to memorise every detail of his face, while at the same time silently vowing never to see him again. He turned to take his leave of her, the unsmiling look in his eyes making it very plain he understood her thoughts. He made no attempt to take her hand.

'Goodbye, madam. I wish you well, now and always.'

She could not trust her voice to reply and merely

inclined her head, jaw clenched, lips firmly pressed together. Lawrence turned on his heel and walked out. The click of the door closing behind him echoed around the room with a sad finality.

'Mama? What did Sir Lawrence mean? Is he going away?'

'Yes, Sam, he is.'

'But he will not be gone for long, will he? We will see him again…'

'Heavens, is that the time? Poor Jem will think you have deserted him. Come along, Sam, put on your cap while I fetch my bonnet.'

With forced lightness Rose continued to chatter until she had hustled Sam out of the house, then she hurried him along the road at such a speed that he had no breath left to ask more awkward questions.

They had dropped the letters for Mrs Reed and Mr Wilkins at the vicarage and were hurrying along the high street when Magnus drove up.

'Good morning.' He stopped beside them. 'I have just called at your house and your maid told me where you are headed. Perhaps you will allow me to take you up?' He added, as she hesitated, 'There is room for three; neither you nor Samuel will take up much space.'

Rose would have preferred to continue walking, but as she could think of no excuse that would not require lengthy explanation, she merely uttered a quiet assent. She urged Sam to scramble up first and quickly climbed up after him. Magnus gave a little flick of his whip and the carriage pulled away.

'How is your sister?' asked Rose.

'Distraught, naturally, but I cannot wholly forgive her. To make such an announcement, when all the world was there to hear her. Pure folly!'

'Magnus!'

'I am aware I sound harsh and unfeeling, Rose, but however upset she may have been, I cannot condone such a lack of control. I shall send her away, of course—she has an aunt in the north country who will take care of her, but the damage is done: it cannot be hushed up now.'

Rose gripped her hands together so hard they shook. 'Are there no thoughts of…of marriage?'

'Out of the question. I cannot have my sister wed to a man who has shown himself so much my enemy.' He was silent for a moment. 'He tried to turn you against me, too.' She felt his eyes resting on her, but kept her own gaze lowered. He said quietly, 'I fear he insinuated himself into your affections.'

'Magnus, I—'

'Please, Rose, before you say anything more, let me assure you that despite the unfortunate events of last evening, I have not changed my mind: I still wish to make you my wife.'

Rose glanced down at Sam.

'Perhaps this is not the time…'

'Perhaps not, but I must take the opportunity while I can. We are so rarely alone.'

'We have been busy...'

'Not so busy that you could not go riding with Daunton yesterday morning. Oh, yes, my dear, I heard all about that.'

Rose flushed, but before she could respond Sam piped up, 'Sir Lawrence wanted to see how well I can ride his pony!'

'*His* pony?' Magnus raised his brows.

'It is on loan,' she said quickly. 'A gift for his godson. I am merely looking after it for a short while. It was a business arrangement.'

'And you believe that? You are far too trusting, Rose,' said Magnus heavily. 'I am glad you now know him for the scoundrel he really is.'

'I do,' she said bitterly. 'And can only be ashamed that I allowed myself to be so taken in.'

Sam's head came up.

'Sir Lawrence is not a scoundrel!'

'Hush, Sam.'

'But he's not—'

'That is enough, Samuel,' said Magnus sharply. 'Really, Rose, it is time your son learned his manners.'

'I beg your pardon, Magnus, but—'

'The management of the boy is obviously too much for you. Samuel has been without a father for too long, and you allowing him to be in the company of a villain like Daunton can only make matters worse. Once we are married I shall soon teach him—'

'Sir Lawrence says Mama should not marry you,'

exclaimed Sam, enraged by the criticism of his mother and his friend.

'Samuel, that is *enough*!' Rose put her hand on Sam's shoulder. 'One more word and I shall ask Mr Emsleigh to put us down here and I will take you home.' It was an empty threat, for they were already driving through the gate of Woolers Farm, but Sam firmly closed his lips, frowning with the effort to remain quiet. Magnus brought the carriage to a stand in the yard and a young farmhand came out from one of the barns and ran to the horses' heads. Rose waited for Magnus to come around and hand her down.

'Give my regards to your sister.' She smiled at him, trying to distract him from her son's incivility. 'I shall call upon her shortly.'

'You are very kind.' He raised his eyes to regard Sam, who was scrambling down from the carriage, and after a visible struggle he shook his head. 'I know he is your son, Rose, and your only link with your late beloved husband, but you are far too lenient with the boy. He should be at school, not mixing with the likes of Daunton—'

His words were very quiet, but Sam had excellent hearing. He turned and glared at Magnus.

'Sir Lawrence is my *friend*,' he said pugnaciously. 'He rescued Jem and me from Sealham Point.'

Magnus scowled.

'You will learn nothing from him but bad habits.'

'That is not true. *You* do not like him, but Mama does. He makes her laugh.'

'Sam!'

'It is true, Mama. When we went riding yesterday you laughed and smiled all the way to the mine.'

'The mine?' Magnus gripped Rose by the shoulders, subjecting her to a dark, searching look. 'You took him to Hades Cove yesterday?'

'Yes, I did.' She stepped away, disengaging herself. 'Sam has wanted to go there for a long time, so we rode that way. I think he was a little disappointed that we could not go inside the mine itself.'

'Thank heaven for that!' exclaimed Magnus. 'It was foolish in the extreme to go anywhere near it. Promise me you will not do so again. It is far too dangerous.'

'Sir Lawrence likes danger,' put in Sam, obviously unimpressed by this cautious attitude. 'In fact, he is going off adventuring today.'

'Nonsense,' said Magnus shortly.

'It is not nonsense,' cried Sam. 'He...he had a lamp, and...and a-a jemmy in his saddle bag!'

'A what?' exclaimed Magnus. 'You cannot possibly know what you are talking about.'

'I do.' Sam gave him a triumphant stare. 'It's an iron bar for opening boxes, trunks full of treasure and...and things. There's one at the stables, Evans showed me. And I saw the end of it sticking out of Sir Lawrence's saddle bag this morning. So you see, I am right. He is an adventurer and the bravest man I know.'

Flinging these words at them, Sam turned and dashed away. Magnus watched him go, a deep frown creasing his brow. Distressed, Rose laid her hand on his arm.

'Oh, Magnus, I do beg your pardon, he should not speak like that to you. Let me bring him back here and make him apologise.'

'What? Oh—no, my dear, let him go. We will take up the matter with him later. I must go.'

Rose watched in some surprise as he leapt back into his seat.

'Will you not come to the house with me? I only came to bring Sam and do not intend to stay long—you could drive me home.'

She had hoped to offer this as an olive branch, but Magnus merely shook his head.

'I have business requiring my attention. I shall call upon you tomorrow.'

With that he raised his whip in salute, turned the carriage and drove quickly away from the farm. Rose watched him go then walked towards the farmhouse. She found Maggie Wooler waiting for her at the door.

'Jem is feeding the cattle in the barn and I have sent little Sam to help him. I will make sure he sets off for home before it is too dark. I hope you will not object if he gets a little dirty?'

'Not at all. Dirt will wash off and a little hard work will make him sleep.' She reached into her reticule. 'I will not stop, but my mother promised old Mrs Wooler the recipe for a tisane she finds particularly useful against winter chills…'

'Thank you, but will you not step in and give it to her yourself? I know she would like to see you.' Mrs

Wooler opened the door wide. ‘Poor Mother Wooler has seen no one but me all morning, what with Jem having to do Abel’s work as well as his own.’

‘Oh, is Abel not well?’

Mrs Wooler shook her head as she led the way through the meandering passages of the farmhouse.

‘Nay, he left early this morning, soon after Sir Lawrence came to see him. Said he was off to see Sir Jonas, the magistrate. Wouldn’t say why, but I know summat’s been botherin’ him for a while now.’

‘Sir Lawrence was here?’

‘Aye.’ Maggie Wooler chuckled. ‘Gave me the shock of my life when I saw ’im in the yard at daybreak, talkin’ to Abel. He must have left his house afore dawn. Didn’t think gentlefolk could be about so early—!’

She broke off as they entered the parlour and Rose went forwards to greet the old lady sitting in a chair by the hearth. Once pleasantries had been exchanged and Rose had handed over the recipe, Mrs Wooler went off to bring in more wood for the fire.

‘A good girl, that,’ said old Mrs Wooler, as the door closed behind her daughter-in-law. ‘All the sorrow of losing Ruben, but she keeps so cheerful. ’Tis hard work for her, lookin’ after us all and running the household. But she never complains—even with Abel actin’ like the cares of the world are on his shoulders, mopin’ and grumbling. Like a bear with a sore head, he was. Then this mornin’ he ups and leaves, says there’s summat he’s got to put right.’

‘But he did not say what it was?’

The old woman shook her head.

'I wished he would, for he's not been happy ever since the *Sealark* went down. At first I thought it was the loss of his brother; heaven knows that's grief enough for a man to bear, but I do reckon 'twas more than that. But there, he likes to keep his own counsel, does Abel.' She wiped her eyes with the corner of her apron. 'But for all that he's a good boy. Came to my room this morning to say goodbye, he did. "Don't 'ee worry, Mother," he says to me. "I've a mind to see justice done, but there's those as have promised me our Jem won't lose out." Now what do you make o' that?'

'I am not sure,' said Rose slowly. 'Could it…?' She paused, not really wanting to ask the question. 'Could it be something to do with the insurance money Mr Emsleigh has promised those who sailed on the *Sealark*?'

The old lady sat forwards in her chair.

'Well, I was wondering that meself. Our Abel has always been reluctant to talk about it, apart from insisting that his share would pay for a memorial stone for his brother.' The old woman shook her head. 'Summat very havey-cavey about that whole business, if you was to ask me.'

Despite the roaring fire, Rose felt a chill run down her spine. What was it Lawrence had said? *I have a witness who is prepared to tell the truth about the sinking.* Had he meant Abel?

'Oh, dear God!'

Mother Wooler looked up.

'Is anything wrong, dear?'

Rose blinked. She had not realised she had spoken aloud.

'Y-yes,' she said, rising swiftly. 'I—I have remembered something. I must go home, immediately. Please, give my apologies to your daughter-in-law. I must go!'

With a hasty goodbye she almost ran from the room and out of the house, fastening her pelisse as she hurried through the yard towards the gate. A series of images flashed through her mind: Magnus wanting to open up the mine again; going to Hades Cove without telling her; his anger when he discovered she had taken Lawrence there.

Very soon I shall have proof.

Lawrence's words that morning came back to her, but more worrying, the thing that made her blood run cold, was the way Magnus had dashed away after Sam told him that Lawrence was going exploring with a lantern and an iron bar—the sort of bar one could use to lever nailed boards from the entrance to a mineshaft.

'No.' She stopped, panting. Magnus was no villain. He owned the largest house in the area, was welcomed everywhere. He was on the best of terms with all the local magistrates. He *could not* be involved in anything illegal.

She began to walk on again. Magnus might not have anything to hide, but he had no liking for Lawrence and would not want him breaking into his property.

'Hades Mine belongs to me, not Magnus.' She spoke aloud and immediately a voice in her head answered her. *But you are betrothed and he has long regarded the mine as his property. If he finds Lawrence trespassing there, he will think himself within his rights to kill him.*

CHAPTER NINE

THE boards were hard: bands of seasoned wood firmly fixed into place across the entrance to the mine. Lawrence set to work prising them away one by one. He made slow progress; each board had been secured with several long nails, designed to deter any curious passers-by. He wondered, not for the first time, if he should have brought someone to help him. Had the mine belonged to Emsleigh then he might have done so and risked the consequences, but Rose was involved and he was anxious to avoid casting any slur upon her good name. She was innocent, he would stake his life on it, but if his suspicions were correct and Magnus was using the mine to store the cargo from the *Sealark*, then he would have to persuade Rose to go with him to Sir Jonas. Anything less from her would look like collusion.

At last he had removed enough boards to give him access to the mine and he climbed through the opening.

He found himself in what looked like a large cavern. The ground dropped away gently in front of him and disappeared into darkness. He lit his lamp and set off into the gloom. As he moved deeper the salty fresh air was replaced with a damp mustiness. The tunnel curved, then made a sharp turn to the left, effectively blocking off the last of the natural light. The dim glow of his lamp showed a series of tunnels running off on each side of him, presumably where the miners had dug out the seams of iron ore until each one was exhausted. The first tunnel to his left was very short, barely six feet before the lantern's rays hit the jagged, uneven wall of rock at the end. Lawrence turned to his right and as he swung the lantern around he gave a low whistle. One side of the tunnel was lined with barrels and crates and various packages wrapped in oilcloth, everything neatly stacked against the wall and stretching away into the darkness beyond the lamp's reach. Enough goods, he estimated, to fill the hold of a ship.

Lawrence moved closer and inspected the nearest wooden crate. It bore the name of a Bristol ironmonger. Some of the packages had trade cards attached. It shouldn't be difficult to check back to find out if these goods tallied with those lost on the *Sealark*.

Quickly he strode back to the opening. The winter sun was already low in the sky; as it dipped towards the horizon it blazed into the mouth of the mine in a harsh, blinding glare. Lawrence extinguished his lantern and hooked one leg over the low boards he had left in place, ducking to avoid those above him. As he stepped out and straightened, some presentiment of danger came over him. He bunched his fists, but even as he began to turn a heavy blow caught him on the back of the head and he crumpled, lifeless, to the ground.

Rose went straight to the stables. The young lad looked startled to see her and explained that Evans had not yet returned from Minehead.

'No, and I do not expect him for some hours yet,' she replied, looking about her. 'Can you saddle my horse for me, now?'

The boy hurried to obey and ten minutes later she was trotting out of the village, the voluminous folds of her cloak covering the deficiencies of her walking dress, which was not cut quite so liberally as a riding habit and therefore exposed a rather immodest amount of leg and ankle.

Rose kept her horse to a sedate trot until the houses were left behind, then she dug in her heels and set off at a gallop. The snow lay thicker over the moor, but Rose kept up a fast but steady pace until she reached the track leading down to Hades Cove. She let her horse pick its way more slowly over the rocky path and down into the woods, where no sun had penetrated and the ground was iron hard beneath its white covering.

There were fresh tracks in the snow; one, possibly two riders had come this way. Squaring her shoulders, she moved on, impatient to reach the mine. At last the trees thinned and the little shelf of land was before her, but even before her horse had reached the clearing she saw Magnus dragging something dark and heavy through the snow towards the cliff edge. She jumped from her horse and ran forwards.

'Magnus, no! What are you doing?'

Her heart stopped as she approached and saw that he was pulling at Lawrence's unconscious form. She thought at first that Lawrence had a dark red ribbon twisted across his face, but as she drew closer she saw it was blood trickling from a head wound. It had reached his chin and was soaking into his neckcloth. She stared in horror.

'Have you killed him?'

'Not yet.'

Panic filled her.

'Let him go, Magnus. You cannot commit murder.'

Magnus straightened.

'What is this?' he exclaimed. 'I thought you would be glad to see him gone.'

'I want him out of my life, yes, but not like this.'

There was a groan. Lawrence stirred and began to push himself up onto one elbow.

'Oh, thank heaven!' she muttered.

Lawrence sat up, lifting one hand to his head. Rose dug her teeth into her lip to stop herself from crying when he lifted his fingers away, wet with blood. She dropped to her knees beside him.

'We must get you back—'

'You do not seem to understand, my dear,' drawled Magnus. 'Neither of you can leave this place now.'

He drew a wicked-looking pistol from his belt. Lawrence heaved himself onto one elbow.

'By God, Emsleigh—'

Magnus flourished the pistol.

'Now, now, Daunton, do not try anything heroic or I shall have to use this and at this range I am bound to kill one of you. Hush, now, while I think what I am to do with you.'

Rose frowned.

'What do you mean?'

'He intends to push us both over the cliff,' growled Lawrence, climbing unsteadily to his feet. 'But with only one pistol, one bullet, he cannot overpower us both.'

Magnus shrugged.

'I am an excellent shot, so one of you will die, and whoever is left…' His lips curved into a smile that sent a shiver through Rose. 'A woman or an injured man—either way, I do not see that I can lose.'

'Stop this, Magnus.' Rose put her arm around Lawrence as he swayed. 'He is no threat to you.' A flash of white sail caught her eye and she glanced quickly towards the grey sea. 'There is a ship just coming round the headland. They would hear you if you dared to fire.'

Magnus gave her a pitying look. 'The wind is blowing onshore. Any sound would be carried in the opposite direction. However, they may be watching and I would rather avoid witnesses. We will go back into the mine.'

'I would rather take my chances out here,' muttered Lawrence.

'But it is not your choice,' purred Magnus. He waved the pistol menacingly. 'Quickly now, or I may lose patience and risk shooting you here!'

'Please, Lawrence, let us do as he says,' Rose begged.

She pulled the fichu from her neck and gently held it against the cut on his head.

'Quite the ministering angel,' jeered Magnus.

Rose ignored him and began to half-drag, half-carry Lawrence towards the mine entrance.

'Why did you come?' In between his ragged breaths Lawrence muttered the question.

'Magnus guessed from something Sam said that you were going to explore the mine.'

'And you came to save me?'

'Yes—no!' She gave a little huff of exasperation. 'I did not want to believe he would hurt you.'

He started to laugh, but it ended in a gasp.

'Well, now you know differently.'

'I hope you are not hatching any plots between you!'

Magnus's sharp voice brought Rose's head up.

'I think you are the one hatching plots,' she retorted. 'Do I have to remind you that you are on my land?'

'No, my dear, but you will soon see that I have put it to good use. Now get into the mine or I will despatch one of you here and now!'

Her breath catching in her throat, she continued to help Lawrence across the uneven grass towards the mine. It was the longest few yards she had ever taken.

The knowledge that Magnus was following with a loaded pistol made her spine rigid with fear. The entrance yawned before her, a narrow black opening surrounded by bleached timbers. She helped Lawrence to climb in, wondering if it was possible to overpower Magnus when he followed them, but as if reading her mind he waved them away.

'Get over there by the wall, where I can see you.'

Once he had climbed through the gap into the shadowy chamber he ordered Rose to light the lantern, but elected to carry it himself in his left hand, while the right maintained a steady grip on the pistol.

Lawrence kept his arm about Rose, but he was no longer leaning heavily upon her and he was walking almost normally as they stumbled further on into complete darkness. He kept the folded muslin fichu to his head, lifting it away occasionally to check if the bleeding had stopped.

At last Magnus told them to halt. He hung the lantern from a hook high on one of the pit props and Rose had the opportunity to observe her surroundings. She had never been inside the mine before. The dim light from the lantern bounced back from the low roof and jagged walls. She found the still, musty air oppressive and fought against her rising panic. To distract herself she glanced at the tunnels on each side of her and suddenly became aware that one of them was far from empty. She moved a step closer. Just discernible on the edge of the lamp's glow were the outlines of the kegs, crates and bundles stacked high against the wall of the mine.

'Is—is this the cargo from the *Sealark*?'

'It is, my dear, thousands of pounds' worth, safely stowed.'

'But…you said it was lost.' She frowned. 'So you *did* scuttle her deliberately.'

'Yes,' said Magnus. 'But not until everything had been offloaded. I have been waiting for the chance to move it, but with the path visible to anyone who happens to be out of doors in Mersecombe I have had to wait—a trail of ponies coming to and from the mine would have caused comment. If only you had agreed to my plan to reopen the mine, my dear, then no one would have thought twice about the activity. It is so galling to have all this valuable cargo and not be able to sell it. And thanks to your friend here I still haven't received the insurance I am due.'

'But you are due nothing,' reasoned Rose. 'This…this is fraud.'

Again that sinister smile lifted his mouth.

'Only if we are caught.'

'We?' She looked at him scornfully. 'I am nothing to do with your schemes!'

'But this is your land,' he reminded her. 'And you are my fiancée.'

'No, that is over. Do you think I can condone what you have done? Have you forgotten that Ruben Wooler lost his life because of your wickedness?'

'That was an accident and his widow will get something.'

'Ah, yes,' said Lawrence. The cut on his head had

stopped bleeding and he discarded the bloody fichu. 'Your promissory notes. Very clever—you knew the crew would not speak against you, because if they did they would not get their money.'

'Yes, that's why I sent Captain Morris to Bristol to sign up a crew. I knew we could pick them from far and wide, and afterwards they would all go their separate ways. Pity was, Morris insisted we needed Ruben Wooler if we were to bring the *Sealark* safely into the jetty at Hades Cove. But Morris should have made some excuse to keep the brother out. I wanted a crew from as far afield as possible; I didn't want them sitting around here after and discussing what had happened.' Magnus turned his cold stare towards Lawrence. 'Don't think I don't know that you have been snooping around the farm, trying to persuade Wooler to testify against me, but he's a close one. He won't talk, because his brother's widow will be forty-five guineas the poorer if he does.'

Rose opened her mouth to speak, but Lawrence gripped her arm. Obediently she kept silent.

Lawrence said, 'He won't need to talk: this cargo is all the proof I need.'

Magnus curled his lip.

'My dear Daunton, surely you do not think I can let you go now?'

'This is the outside of enough, Magnus,' exclaimed Rose. 'You cannot think that I will let you do this!'

'Oh, but you will, my dear.'

'What do you mean?'

He smiled.

'You will marry me and share in the proceeds of my ill-gotten gains—'

'Never!'

'—or I shall have to kill you, too.'

The words were so matter-of-fact that she thought she had misheard him, but as understanding dawned she said slowly, 'You would really *kill* to protect your interests?'

'Of course, if I must.'

Lawrence gripped her wrist.

'You should save yourself, Rose.'

'No. I will stay with you.'

He gave her a little push and said roughly, 'Go on. To me you were nothing but a distraction.' He pinched her arm on the last word. 'Go.'

Rose took a step away from him. She looked at Magnus.

'You would still marry me? Knowing I could ruin you?'

'Oh, I don't think you would do that, my dear. The trappings of luxury are very hard to lay aside.' He held his hand out to her. 'Come, we will go back now and you can put it about that you have decided we will open the mine again. My people can be moving the goods out within the week. We won't attempt to sell anything in this area, of course, although I need to raise some money. I have been dipping far too deep recently, living on credit. I expected the insurers to pay up by now.'

Lawrence shook his head.

'If I do not make my report, I doubt they will ever pay up.'

'Nonsense. Once they are made aware of last night's little scene they will not think it odd that you have disappeared, gone to ground rather than face up to your responsibilities. Your reputation goes before you, Daunton. My sister is just the last in a long line of women you have seduced.'

'By God, Emsleigh, I'll make you pay for this!'

Magnus laughed, the sound magnified and monstrous as it bounced off the walls.

'Empty threats, Daunton.' He held out his hand. 'Come here, Rose, and let us end this—no, don't stand in front of him—!'

The brief moment of diversion was enough. Unsighted, Magnus lowered the pistol. Lawrence hurled himself at him and the two men fell to the ground. Lawrence grabbed his wrist, twisting viciously. The pistol dropped from his fingers and Rose swooped upon it, carrying it safely out of the way.

It was all over in a minute. Magnus was no match for Lawrence's superior strength and Rose heard him cry out, 'Enough, enough!'

Without taking his attention from Magnus, Lawrence jumped to his feet and took the pistol from Rose's shaking hands.

'Well, I think the tables are well and truly turned now,' he ground out. 'Get up, Emsleigh; it is time we took you to the magistrate.'

Magnus stood up, brushing the dust from his sleeve with rough, angry movements. He glared at Rose.

'So he has you in thrall, too. Just like my poor sister.'

'I am under no illusions about Sir Lawrence,' she retorted. 'But I would see justice done.'

'Justice!' Magnus gave a savage laugh. 'After all I have done for Mersecombe, providing alms for the poor, supporting your wretched school—'

'And bankrupting yourself with your excessive spending,' broke in Lawrence. 'Not that the people of Mersecombe know anything of that. You confined your gambling to your trips to Bristol and Bath; I made enquiries there before I came to Mersecombe and found you lost a small fortune in Bath last winter.'

'As did many others!' Magnus threw at him.

'Undoubtedly, but you have been obliged to live on credit since then, have you not? That is why you needed the insurance, to pay your debts.' Lawrence paused. 'I am surprised you did not get yourself a rich wife.'

'I tried,' he retorted bitterly. 'A rich widow, in charge of her own fortune, would have solved all my difficulties. There are any number of 'em in Bath, but they were all so damned cautious, wanting to know the state of my finances!'

'But you had asked me to marry you,' objected Rose. 'We were betrothed.'

His lip curled. 'And what did you have to offer me? A brat of your own and a worthless mine! If I could have secured a woman of sufficient means I would have found some way to break our engagement. But by the time I came back to Mersecombe I had already decided there was only one way to solve my problems. I could still raise enough funds for one last venture, so I loaded the *Sealark* with cargo and took out the insurance. But I needed somewhere to hide the cargo. Hades Mine was the obvious choice. It was an excellent plan.' His malevolent glance shifted to Rose. 'Then you decided to postpone our wedding. Not only that, you would not allow me to open up the mine. Damnation, if you had consented, then no one would have thought twice when they saw pack ponies on the road. I could have moved the cargo out months ago and sold it.'

'I am glad I thwarted you,' said Rose. 'Even if it was unwittingly done.' She shivered. 'Let us get out of this horrid place. We will take him to Sir Jonas Pullen. He will know what to do.'

Lawrence gestured to Magnus to go first, but even as they began to move, footsteps echoed through the tunnel. A high, nervous voice called out and Rose halted.

'Sam!' Her cry was shrill with alarm.

'Mama, Sir Lawrence? Are you here?'

'No, no, Sam, go back!'

'Sam, stop, don't come any further!'

Rose and Lawrence shouted at the same time, their voices bouncing off the walls, distorting into an unrecognisable cacophony of noise. It drowned out any further footsteps, but even as the echoes died away Sam hurtled around the corner, directly into Magnus's arms.

Rose watched in horror as Magnus gripped Sam's shoulders, pinning the boy in front of him like a shield.

'You should have shot me while you had the chance, Daunton.' He cursed as Sam squirmed and wriggled to free himself. 'Be still, Samuel, or it will be the worse for you! Well, Daunton, what do you say now? How good is your aim in this light, with a strange weapon? You have only my head and shoulders to aim for. Will you risk hitting the boy?'

'You know I won't,' said Lawrence, lowering the pistol.

'Very sensible.' Magnus began to back along the tunnel. 'You will both stay where you are. If I see you following us out of the mine, then I will break the boy's neck, do you understand?'

'Mama!'

Sam's distressed cry ripped at her heart

'It's all right, my love, I'm—'

'Get back,' snapped Magnus as Rose reached out for her son. 'He will be safe as long as you do as you are told.'

'Sam, remember what I taught you—about staying safe?' She heard Lawrence's voice beside her, calm and reassuring. Sam stopped wriggling. Lawrence said, 'Do it now, lad. Make it count.'

Sam's little hands clenched into fists and he jabbed his elbow with all his force into Magnus's groin. Magnus doubled up, shock and surprise loosening his grip, and Sam jumped away. Almost immediately a shot rang out and Magnus jerked back against the wall of the mine, clutching at his shoulder.

Lawrence gave a grunt of satisfaction. 'Not bad, even with a strange weapon. How is the boy?'

'Unharmed, thank heaven.' Rose had gathered Sam in her arms and was holding him tightly. 'I think,' she said unsteadily, 'I would like to go home now.'

Rose walked around the little sitting room at Bluebell Cottage, trying not to give in to the anxious thoughts and questions that threatened to overwhelm her. It was late, everyone else had gone to bed, but Lawrence had promised to come back once Magnus was safely locked up and she knew he would keep his word.

Before they left the mine, she had bound up Magnus's shoulder as best she could, then left Lawrence to take him to Sir Jonas Pullen while she took Sam home. Their arrival had coincided with Mrs Molland's return from Minehead and it was only to be expected that Sam would want to tell his grandmother all about his adventure.

The tale was recounted and revisited many times over dinner. Mrs Molland exclaimed over Magnus Emsleigh's villainy and praised Sir Lawrence's bravery, but she was mildly reproachful of her daughter and grandson for their foolishness in going to Hades Mine at all.

'But if Mama had not gone, then Sir Lawrence might well have been killed,' argued Sam, not at all chastened by the gentle rebuke.

Rose had been at pains to make light of her part in the proceedings and she was a little shocked at her young son's astute grasp of the situation. Her head was still buzzing with all that had occurred and she desperately wanted to be alone, so she was grateful when, soon after they had finished dinner, Mrs Molland declared that she would take Sam up to bed.

'He is far too excited to sleep,' she said when she rejoined Rose in the sitting room some time later. 'I have left Janet with him, and he is telling her of his adventure. He thinks of Sir Lawrence as quite the hero of the hour.' When Rose did not reply she added, 'I think we should invite him to call, that we may thank him properly.'

'We shall see.'

'You are not minded to receive him?'

'I do not deny that he was very brave, but it does not alter the fact that he is a libertine.'

'But perhaps it puts him in a slightly better light.'

'Mama, Althea Emsleigh is carrying his child!' Rose spread her hands. 'What would you have me do?'

Mrs Molland sighed.

'I do not know, but I admit I am seriously disappointed. I had begun to think that Sir Lawrence was just the man for you.'

She had risen then, and gone to bed, leaving Rose to pace up and down and wait for a knock on the door.

It came just after midnight.

'I saw your candle in your window.' Sir Lawrence stepped into the hall. It had started to snow and the shoulders of his jacket sparkled with a frosty dusting. 'How is Sam?'

'Sleeping peacefully. He is very resilient. He spotted me on the hill, riding down to Hades Cove, and decided to follow.'

'And how are you?'

Rose evaded his searching gaze.

'A little tired.'

She led him into the sitting room, where she had banked up the fire.

'I did not expect to be so late.'

He removed his hat and Rose looked intently at him for signs of injury. Apart from an angry graze on his temple there was no sign of the wound he had suffered; the cut itself was covered by his thick dark hair.

'Sir Jonas agreed to put Emsleigh in the lock-up, but insisted upon going back to the mine to see for himself. Abel Wooler was with him when I arrived. He had just finished making his deposition, so Sir Jonas already knew most of the story.' He held his hands out to the fire. 'We replaced the boards across the entrance and he has set a couple of stout fellows to guard it, until the goods can be moved.'

Rose watched him as he gazed silently into the fire. She was looking for similarities with her late husband. Harry had been floridly handsome; there was nothing florid about Lawrence. He was lean and dark with a slow smile that set her pulse racing in a way that Harry's boyish grin had never done. Harry had been incorrigible. Whenever she had confronted him with his latest transgression, be it heavy losses at the gaming table, or another woman, he would always react in the same way: first the denial, then the apology. Time and again he had promised her that this indiscretion would be his last; time and again she had believed him…

Lawrence straightened and turned to look at her, his eyes sombre.

'I am sorry, I should have trusted you. I should have told you I was investigating the loss of the *Sealark*.'

'I thought you had come to Mersecombe to find me.'

'I gave you my word I would not do that. An old friend asked me to investigate the loss of the *Sealark*, to find out if it really was an accident. He is one of those standing surety for the loss, and very reluctant to pay out if it was a fraud.' A wry smile twisted his lips. 'Knowing you were here made me keener to accept.'

'But for all you knew I might have been married!' she challenged him.

He shrugged.

'I knew that, but I needed to know. When I found you had postponed the wedding I thought…I hoped there might be a chance for us…'

Rose put up her hand. She did not want to hear any more of his hopes.

'That explains your frequent visits to the Woolers—you were questioning Abel.'

'Yes.'

'And you befriended Sam to get to me?'

'No—not exactly. If Sam had not been your son, I would have treated him just the same. He is a fine boy.' She turned away, unable to meet his gaze. He said quietly, 'I have changed, Rose. After you left me last Christmas I wanted to prove I could do so—to myself as well as to you. It was not hard to give up the rakehell lifestyle I had been living, but it was harder not to come and find you. When I had an excuse to come back I took it, but returning to Knightscote revived all the memories of those few precious days we shared. It was bad enough in London, constantly thinking of you, wondering what you were doing, if you were happy, but back at Knightscote—I kept opening doors and expecting to see you there. Even riding the moor I am reminded of you—I see your eyes in the blue-grey rocks, hear your laughter in the babbling of the stream.' He reached out for her. 'I cannot bear us to be apart any longer, Rose—'

'Impossible! Please, say no more!' Tears scalded her eyes, but she would not let them fall. She walked away so that he could not see her trembling lip.

'Impossible? No, why do you say that?'

Anger at his insouciance made her turn back.

'What about Althea? Will you still marry her?'

His black brows drew together.

'I have never had any intention of marrying her! If she expected that little outburst last night to persuade me, then I am sorry for it, but she has been deceiving herself.'

Just like Harry.

Hot, boiling fury erupted inside her. If there had been a knife to hand, she would have plunged it into him.

'A rake to the last,' she raged. 'Get out!'

'Rose, I have already sworn to you—I have had nothing to do with Althea Emsleigh.'

'And you expect me to believe that?'

'Yes! Do you think a woman cannot lie?'

'A woman could not lie about such a thing.'

'Perhaps *you* could not, but—'

'Get out! I never want to see you again. Ever.'

Lawrence stared at the rigid figure before him. She was shaking, her face paper white.

'Perhaps, in the morning…'

'No—never,' she spat at him. She put out her hand to clutch at the back of a nearby chair, breathing deeply so that when she spoke again her voice was low and held barely a quaver. 'You will not darken my door again and you will not see or speak to my son. We shall be leaving Mersecombe as soon as I can make arrangements, but until that time it shall be as if you never existed. Do you understand me?'

Lawrence straightened, overcome by a dark, despairing anger. It had been a very long day, his body ached from the blows he had sustained and the cut on his head throbbed painfully. He had successfully concluded his investigation and exposed Magnus Emsleigh for the villain he really was. He shook his head, saying angrily, 'I did not come here to be rewarded, but to be so summarily dismissed is harsh indeed!'

'You have brought it upon yourself.'

'You have made yourself both judge and jury and

have found me guilty without giving me any chance to defend myself!'

She shook her head, her hand coming up in a little gesture of denial. Lawrence fought down the angry words that crowded his head. In time she might know that she was wrong, but he had already spent a whole year trying to prove his worth to her. Enough was enough. He scooped up his hat.

'I cannot make you trust me,' he said quietly. 'You have made it perfectly clear tonight that you do not want to try. I know that you have had one bad husband and you came pretty close to taking a second. I understand that. It is enough to make anyone wary, so I shall not trouble you again. But I beg you will remember I am, always have been and always will be your humble servant.'

With a final stiff little bow he turned on his heel and walked out of the house.

CHAPTER TEN

ROSE heard the front door slam, then the silence of the sleeping house pressed in around her. She closed her eyes.

'I was right to send him away.'

She felt the hot tears squeezing out and running down her cheeks. Angrily she brushed them away. She must stop this, she had wasted tears enough. From now on the only man in her life would be her son.

Rose was determined to avoid Lawrence at all costs and when Sir Jonas called upon her the next day she cautiously enquired if she would have to give evidence.

'No, no, I will take statements from you and your boy and that should suffice. Sir Lawrence doesn't see any need for you to go all the way to London.'

'London!'

'Aye. Emsleigh's being taken there now. We arrested Captain Morris this morning, too, and put him in the same coach. Sir Lawrence is helping my men to escort the pair of them.' He shook his head. 'A bad business, this. When Abel Wooler came to see me yesterday I was much inclined to dismiss him—after all, it was his word against the captain and the rest of the crew. Not only that, but he was accusing Emsleigh of being behind it, one of our foremost citizens! But then Sir Lawrence turned up, and once I had seen for myself the cargo stashed away in Hades Mine I realised there would be a case to answer.'

'What will happen to Abel?' asked Rose, momentarily diverted from her own unhappiness. 'He signed the original affidavit, did he not, to say that the ship and cargo had been lost?'

Sir Jonas pursed his lips.

'Aye, he did, but as Sir Lawrence pointed out, Wooler had just lost his brother and was out of his mind with grief at that time. As soon as he came to his senses he realised the error of his ways and came to me to confess. I have been to see him this morning and told him he'd nothing to fear as long as he has told me the truth.'

Rose looked down at her hands.

'And…will Sir Lawrence be in London for long?' she asked casually.

'Oh, most likely. He told me he means to sell Knightscote—seems this business has given him a dislike for the place.'

'Well, then, that's settled,' she murmured, almost to herself.

* * *

Rose was slightly shocked to feel so bereft and sought for some occupation to fill her day. In the end she decided to accompany Sam to the stables, where he was to go riding with Evans. She changed into her riding habit and was just stepping out of the door with Sam when Janet returned from the market, her basket piled up with food.

'Well, here's a to-do and no mistake,' she announced as they stepped back to let her come in through the gate. 'All over the village, it is. Mr Emsleigh taken off to Lunnon to stand trial and Miss Emsleigh—'

'Yes, Janet, I know.' Rose hastily interrupted her. 'I am going to visit Miss Emsleigh now, to offer her any assistance I can.'

Janet stopped and stared at her, frowning.

'You never are. After what she said—'

'I was very nearly her sister,' Rose reminded her. 'I cannot abandon her in her hour of need.'

'*Her* need!' Janet snorted. 'Why, her maid's been tellin'—'

'I will not listen to gossip, Janet, and neither should you. Come along, Sam!'

Rose grabbed her son's hand and hurried him out into the lane.

'What is wrong with Miss Emsleigh, Mama?' Sam turned his innocent eyes up to her.

'She is being blamed for her brother's villainy,' Rose replied, her cheeks flushed with indignation. 'She has been cruelly used!'

She looked and sounded so fierce when she said this that Sam dared not say more, and they continued in silence to the stables.

'I beg your pardon, ma'am,' exclaimed Evans, surprised. 'I did not know you were planning to ride out with us and I have not saddled your mare…'

'I only decided this morning that I should like some exercise.' She made sure that Sam was out of earshot and continued quietly, 'I shall have to make arrangements for the pony to be returned to Sir Lawrence, and soon.'

'Will you, ma'am?' Evans looked surprised. 'That'll break the little man's heart.'

The knife inside Rose twisted a little further.

'It cannot be helped. We have imposed upon Sir Lawrence long enough.'

'But I hear Sir Lawrence is gone to London, ma'am. He won't be wantin' the pony sent there.'

'No, so you must write and ask for instructions.' She felt a little guilty about leaving such matters to her groom, but told herself it was best for her not to be involved.

'Very well, ma'am. But until then you'll let Master Sam ride as usual?'

'Yes…yes, I suppose so. And there is no need to say anything to Sam just yet,' she added, quelling another ripple of guilt. 'No point in making him unhappy for any longer than is necessary.'

She waited patiently for her mare to be saddled, but

then declined to ride with Sam and Evans up onto the moor—there was a visit she dreaded, but felt herself obliged to make.

She arrived at Emsleigh House to find the front windows shuttered and the door closed. There was only one nervous-looking groom in the stables and he suggested she should enter the house by the garden door. The butler met her in the hall with the air of one pushed to the limit of his endurance.

'I beg your pardon, ma'am, but we are constantly being pestered by tradesmen and the mistress insisted we should shut up the house.' He gestured towards the stairs. 'Miss Emsleigh is in her boudoir, ma'am. If you wait here, I will announce you—'

A loud hammering on the door interrupted him.

Rose's kind heart was touched at the thought of Althea's distress.

'No need, I will announce myself.'

She picked up the train of her riding habit and looped it over her arm before hurrying up the stairs. She had never been a close friend of Althea, but she recalled being taken to her dressing room on one occasion and hoped she could remember the way. There were signs of disorder everywhere: half-filled trunks stood in doorways, pictures had been removed from the walls and harassed-looking servants were hurrying back and forth.

Rose arrived at Althea's room and gave a soft knock.

A muffled sound that could have been 'come in' followed and she entered, closing the door quietly behind her. The room was quite as disordered as the rest of the house, but a number of smashed ornaments in the fireplace suggested that Althea was not in the sunniest of moods. She was pacing up and down, her blond curls jumping and her colour heightened to make her face an unattractive mottled red and white.

'Oh, it's you.' She barely glanced at Rose as she came in. 'Have you come to gloat?'

'Of course not. I came to see if you needed anything.'

'Nothing that you can provide—unless you have a spare fortune I may use to set myself up abroad?' Her lip curled. 'I thought not. I always said it was a mistake for Magnus to offer for you. He could have done much better for himself than an impoverished widow with a brat to look after.'

Rose fought down her anger. Althea was upset and quite possibly frightened.

'Well, it will not come to that now,' she said quietly. 'Will you remain here?'

'With tradesmen hammering on the door for payment day and night?' Althea picked up a teacup from her breakfast tray and hurled it at the fireplace. '*Damn* Magnus for leaving me in this mess!'

'Althea, please, this cannot be good for you—'

'You know nothing of the matter. Magnus has so many debts that everything in this house will have to be sold to pay them.' She began pacing the floor again. 'I have some money, but not enough to live in this style.

I shall be able to keep only two servants—three at the most. How could Magnus do this to me? I could *scream* with vexation!'

'My dear, you must try to stay calm,' Rose urged her. 'Think of your condition.'

Althea stopped pacing and stared at her.

'Condition? Oh, that—I am not really breeding.'

'You…you are not?'

'Of course not. It was an attempt to force Lawrence to marry me.' Althea scowled. 'I doubt he can be persuaded to do so now.'

The room started spinning and Rose put her hand on the wall to steady herself.

'Althea, I do not understand… You are *not* carrying his child?'

'No, of course not. Did you really think it was true?' She gave a scornful laugh. 'You must be the only one who believed it!'

'But how could you say such a thing, and say it so publicly?'

Althea shrugged her white shoulders.

'I never intended to do so, until I saw the way Lawrence looked at you. That put me in such a rage. He had never so much as squeezed my fingers, though I gave him every encouragement. La, I was quite disappointed, for he has such a reputation. I had planned to seduce him at the ball, but I soon realised that would not work, and when I saw he meant to leave I announced I was carrying his child. I thought it would be a sure way to give you a disgust of him and to force him into marriage. Only Magnus would not support me. That was a blow, I can tell you. I see why *now*, of course—Daunton was his enemy—but it put me in a damnable position. And I was so remiss I did not think to warn my maid, so when she went to market yesterday and heard them sniggering behind their hands she lost no time in telling everyone she could find that I could not be with child because my courses were as regular as a clock and I have never missed one. Heavens, was ever a woman cursed with such a well-meaning wretch.' She suddenly became aware of Rose's presence and rounded on her.

'Are you shocked? Well, Miss Propriety, if you had not been so caught up in your own petty concerns you would have snapped Magnus up last spring, then he would have been able to send all that cargo to market months ago, and none of this would have happened.'

'Surely you do not condone what he has done?' asked Rose, appalled. 'A sailor lost his life when they sunk that ship!'

'What do I care for that? With the insurance, and the profit from the cargo, we could have settled our accounts and lived very comfortably.'

She continued to rage, sending the saucer and teapot the same way as the cup, and ignoring Rose, who edged towards the door and made her escape. The butler suggested she should slip out through the kitchens to avoid the growing number of tradesman at the front of the house.

Rose followed his advice and collected her horse. She

trotted out of the yard and was cantering away down the drive before any of the irate crowd at the front door could accost her. Once out on the road she turned onto one of the many lanes that led up onto the hills, forcing herself to concentrate on pushing the mare on until she was at last on the moor with the icy wind whipping at her cheeks. The occasional drift of snow remained in a ditch or against a north-facing ridge, in stark contrast to the dull winter browns of the moor.

So, Lawrence had been telling the truth all the time. She turned her face up to the heavens. She had willingly given him her body, so why had she been so afraid to trust him, to believe him? Rose looked around, suddenly restless. She needed to see Lawrence, to beg him to forgive her, but that was impossible. He was miles away by now. But he would come back, wouldn't he? He would return and she would throw herself on his mercy. She remembered the stony, implacable look on his face when he had left her.

I shall not trouble you again.

The bleak wind cut through her cloak and she shivered. The moor stretched away on all sides, no sign of life in any direction. Even the stunted trees looked black and decayed. Lifeless. Perhaps it was already too late

She turned her horse and headed for home.

CHAPTER ELEVEN

'WELL, I am pleased that business is out of the way!' George Craven followed Lawrence out of the lawyer's office and into the waiting carriage. 'Can't tell you how grateful I am to you for sorting out that little matter, Daunton. With the cargo recovered, and the ship's captain making a full confession, we have a strong case against Emsleigh. And I've learned it is not the first time the man has come up against the law—it seems he's been sailing close to the wind for years, with his lawyers successfully defending him against several charges of smuggling. He's always escaped because there's never been enough evidence, but this time we've caught him fair and square. Well done, my friend.'

Lawrence settled himself into his seat.

'How soon will it come to court, do you think?'

'Oh, not 'til the spring,' replied Craven cheerfully. 'Until then Emsleigh is safe enough in Newgate; he seems to have enough funds for a few luxuries while he waits for his trial. Brrr!' He shivered. 'If I'm not mistaken we shall have snow before morning. The sooner we get out of the cold, the better. I'll drop you at your rooms and collect you again in, say, two hours. Will that be time enough for you to change? I am going to buy you the best dinner White's can provide!'

'Really, George, there is no need—'

'Nonsense, man, you have saved me from ruin. And you are in no rush to go to Hampshire?'

'None at all. In fact, I may well remain in town for Christmas.'

'What, you will stay away from Daunton House for another year? My family will be deeply disappointed. They hoped that after the amount of time you have spent there this year you would be making it your home.'

'And I probably shall—but not yet.'

'Ah, I understand.' George nodded and gave him a knowing wink. 'Christmas time. You would have that army of aunts, uncles and cousins descending upon you and they would be colluding with *my* family, doing their best to make you forget your grief over m'sister, but only making it worse with their dismal sighs and sympathetic looks.'

'Exactly.'

'No wonder, then, you would rather remain here! I'd stay with you, but—well—you know how it is. Having come so close to ruin this summer, I am minded to settle down. M'father is getting too old to manage the estate now, so I thought I would live at home and help him.'

'Very commendable,' said Lawrence gravely.

'Aye, I think so,' said George, pleased with himself. 'But I don't travel down until tomorrow, so tonight you and I will have one final spree!'

Lawrence frowned up at the imposing frontage of Samlesbury House as the carriage drew up before the door.

'Really, Craven, I am not sure I am in the mood to be sociable.'

'Nonsense, you are out of practice, having lived like a monk this past year! This isn't one of your starched-up *ton* parties—Nancy Samlesbury will have packed the place with dashing young matrons, every one of 'em eager for a little light-hearted dalliance.' George Craven jumped out of the carriage and held open the door. 'Come along, Daunton, I have already told our hostess I would be bringing you with me and I daren't disappoint her.'

Stifling a sigh, Lawrence followed him into the house and up the curving staircase towards the noisy ballroom. Lady Samlesbury swept across to them as they were announced.

'So you have brought him.' After flashing a smile at Craven, she turned her attention to Sir Lawrence, holding out her hand and fixing him with kohl-rimmed eyes that held more than a hint of an invitation. 'My dear Sir Lawrence, you have become a positive stranger at our little parties.' Her fingers tightened their grip as he bowed over her hand. She waited until George had moved away, then she lowered her voice to murmur in his ear, 'I was afraid you had forgotten me and our… time together.'

The corners of his mouth curved upwards.

'How could I ever forget such a pleasurable experience?'

She moved closer, peeping at him over the top of her fan.

'Perhaps we should try to recreate it…'

'Fie, Nancy, that was two years ago, before you married Samlesbury and became a respectable married woman. Would you make him jealous?'

'No, alas.' She sighed, fingering the exquisite diamonds at her neck. 'Not when he is so generous to me.' With a laugh she tucked her hand into his arm.

'No, Lawrence, you are right, I must behave myself now. But there are many ladies here who are eager to renew their acquaintance with you…'

By midnight Lawrence's cheeks ached from incessant smiling and his head was beginning to throb. It was not from the wine—he had drunk very little, needing to keep his wits about him to avoid the wiles of the numerous ladies who were intent upon flirting with him. He felt like a fox, being hunted at every turn. His first dance partner had twisted her ankle and needed to be helped to a secluded alcove; the next had felt a little faint and insisted he accompany her to a deserted balcony, where the arctic temperatures came to his aid in persuading her that dalliance in such circumstances would undoubtedly result in a severe inflammation of the lungs. Then there was the serious-looking matron who disputed with him over certain lines in 'The Lady of the Lake' and carried him off to the book room, where she threw herself against the door and refused to let him leave until he had kissed her.

A year ago Lawrence would have joined in their games, shrugged his broad shoulders and indulged these rapacious women with a fast, furious flirtation. One of them might even have ended up in his bed. Now there was only one woman he wanted in his arms, only one pair of eyes he wanted to find fixed upon him, and if he could not have Rose, he would have no one. These society ladies with their strong, cloying perfume and knowing smiles left him unmoved. It had taken rapid thinking and a great deal of tact and charm to avoid all the snares set for him, but somehow he had succeeded; so well, in fact, that when he dragged his friend out of the house in the early hours of the morning his hostess assured him that he was welcome at Samlesbury House at any time. And that he had secured his place as a firm favourite with her guests.

Unbelievably weary, Lawrence bundled George into a hired cab and gave the driver his instructions.

'Charming party,' declared George, slurring his words a little. 'Nancy always knows how to entertain her guests. Did you dance with that little redhead?'

'Yes, I danced with her,' said Lawrence, bringing to mind the freckle-faced matron who had pushed herself against him and told him the days he might find her at home alone.

'What a flirt. And with her husband standing by, too! By Gad, she was a tempting little thing.'

Lawrence turned his head to peer across the carriage. 'Tell me truthfully, George—did you really enjoy yourself tonight?'

'Why, yes, of course! Couldn't fail to enjoy myself with such a charming set. Did they not please you?'

'No, not really.'

'Extraordinary.' George sat up. 'Not coming down with something, are you, old boy? Touch of gout, perhaps?'

'I think not. Old age, perhaps.'

'Aye, could be,' came the serious reply. 'You are thirty now, after all. But if you no longer enjoy the society, there's precious little reason to stay in town for Christmas.'

'I know.'

'Dashed if I can understand you,' exclaimed Craven, shaking his head. 'You won't go to your family home, you dislike London—what *do* you want to do?'

Lawrence sighed and turned his head to look out at the night. The streets were still busy; lamps burned outside many of the houses, lighting the way for the non-stop procession of carriages that picked their way between the soil carts and the nightwatch, who cried the hour while keeping a wary eye upon the little groups of revellers making their way home. He had friends enough in town, but if he stayed they would be pressing him to join them—how could he explain that he wanted nothing more than to be alone, to ponder on his future?

As he watched, a few fat flakes of snow drifted past the carriage window.

'I don't know, George. I may go back to Knightscote.'

'Exmoor—in December?' Craven gave a crack of laughter. 'From what you've told me your lodge is in the middle of nowhere—you might not see anyone for weeks!'

Lawrence looked at him, a glimmer of a smile in his eyes.

'Perfect!'

Christmas Eve. A sharp icy wind had been scouring the moors for days and it howled around Knightscote Lodge, whispering under the doors and making the fires burn with an extra-bright glow. Lawrence pulled his chair closer to the hearth and sat down, stretching his long legs before him. He had arrived at the lodge at dusk that day, which had sent Mrs Brendon into a flurry of activity. She hurriedly despatched a man to Exford to buy more provisions and bustled about the house, muttering darkly about the difficulties of working for a man who says one minute he might never come back again and the next turns up without so much as a by your leave. The only one genuinely happy to see him was the pointer bitch, Bandit. Lawrence's keeper had gone off to visit his family for a few days and left the dog in the care of the stable boy. Thus, when Lawrence had arrived and ridden to the stables, Bandit had come running out, fawning around his legs and making it impossible for Lawrence to proceed until he had greeted her.

He had retreated to the drawing room while his housekeeper bustled about putting the house into what she considered a fit state for its master, but by the time he had complimented her upon a fine dinner and declared himself well satisfied with all her arrangements, harmony had been restored.

That had been some hours ago. Knowing the staff would be up early the following day to walk to church, Lawrence had sent them all to bed. He had fetched Bandit for company and a bottle of brandy for solace and was now settling down to while away the evening in front of the fire. He was in a reflective mood and his brandy glass remained untouched as he lounged in his chair, staring into the flames.

A year ago today it had all started. Rose Westerhill had burst into his life and changed it for ever. She had accused him of wallowing in self-pity and in his attempts to prove her wrong he had reformed his way of life. That had not been difficult, but making Rose believe that he was a changed man had proved impossible. A log shifted, sending a shower of sparks into the air and waking Bandit from her slumbers at her master's feet. Lawrence put out a hand and stroked the smooth head.

'Perhaps it's mere conceit,' he addressed the pointer, who was gazing up at him adoringly, 'but I thought she would know that I was different.'

Bandit merely licked his hand. Lawrence gave her a final pat and sank back in his chair. They remained thus, unmoving, until Lawrence heard the sound of hoofs clinking on the cobbles. In a flash he was at the window, throwing back the heavy curtains to peer out. A thin covering of snow lightened the darkness, but he could see nothing moving save the bushes at the edges of the drive, bending before the driving wind.

'There's no one there, you fool.' He returned to the chair and picked up his glass.

Wishful thinking. Perhaps it had been a mistake to return to Knightscote. The place held too many memories. He should sell it; there was nothing here for him any longer. As he leaned forwards to throw another log onto the fire a sudden gust of wind moaned through the house, rattling the door. Bandit was immediately on the alert.

'Easy, now. It's an old house, full of creaking boards and rattling windows.' Lawrence sipped at the brandy. 'Perhaps I will build myself a new hunting lodge in Leicestershire. What do you say to that?'

Bandit was not listening. She rose and padded towards the door, ears pricked.

Lawrence was about to order her back when the candlelight glinted on the turning handle. He put down his glass and rose to his feet.

'I am dreaming.'

Rose entered the drawing room and stood with her back pressed against the door, her powder-blue cloak glistening with melting snow. She remained there for a long moment, uncertain of her welcome, until Bandit's effusive greetings could no longer be ignored.

Lawrence watched, transfixed, as she bent down to make a fuss of the dog.

'How did you get in?'

'Through the kitchen. I could see no lights, so I rode round to the stables.' She gently pushed Bandit away and straightened. 'May I come in?'

Lawrence looked at the glass on the table beside him. It was almost full. So this was not a brandy-induced fantasy. His spirits lifted.

'Have you lost your way?'

'No.' A smile trembled on her lips. 'I think I may have found it.'

In two strides he crossed the room, reaching out for her. With a sob she fell into his arms, turning her face up to receive his kiss. He swooped, capturing her mouth, demanding a response that she was eager to give. Her arms crept up around his neck. He registered the damp leather of her gloves, felt the chill of her clothes as she pressed against him.

'You are like ice.' He led her towards the fire. 'Come and warm yourself.'

He unfastened her cloak and tossed it aside before pushing her down into the chair.

'If you are not lost, then what the devil are you doing abroad so late?'

His voice was rough with concern, but she did not appear to notice.

'I could not rest. I wondered—' A rueful smile played about her mouth. 'After my getting stranded last year, it was decided I should not go to Exford this Christmas. Indeed, my family have become so protective I have not been allowed to go anywhere alone. But I needed to know if—if you were here, so I waited until they retired, then slipped out and bribed a sleepy stable boy to saddle my mare.'

'And what would you have done if I had not been here?'

'"Made me a willow cabin at your gate,"' she quoted. '"And called upon my soul within the house."'

Lawrence wanted to be angry at such foolishness, but found he could not stop smiling.

'Ninnyhammer,' he murmured.

She blushed and looked away, suddenly shy. She stripped off her gloves and looked at her fingers. They were red and aching with the cold.

'Here, let me.' Lawrence knelt before her and took her hands between his own.

He pulled her fingers towards him and kissed first one pink tip, then the next, gently warming each one with his lips while his palms cradled her hands, infusing them with his own heat. When her skin had lost the raw redness, he pressed a kiss into one palm. Rose raised the other hand to cradle his cheek, slipping from the chair to kneel before him. He pulled her gently into his arms and began to kiss her face with the same slow care he had given to her fingers.

She gave a little murmur of disappointment when he

broke off. He pulled her to her feet and swept her up into his arms.

'We will continue with this in my bed.'

His low whisper sent a delicious shiver running through her. Rose twined her arms around his neck and laid her head on his shoulder.

With a muttered command to Bandit to go and lie down, Lawrence strode out of the room. Rose lay passive and silent in his arms, marvelling at the way he carried her, as if she weighed no more than a feather. He took the stairs two at a time and continued without pause until they reached his bedchamber, where he carried her over to the bed and laid her gently down upon the covers.

There was no light in the room save the flickering flames in the hearth, but Lawrence did not waste time lighting the candles. He lay down beside Rose and drew her into his arms, his mouth seeking her lips. The faint doubts that had begun to creep into her mind as they traversed the chill dark passages of the old house immediately fled. She sighed, closing her eyes and relishing the close attention he was giving to every inch of her skin. She breathed in the familiar scent of his cologne: the heady mix of lavender, rosemary and bergamot with a hint of bitter oranges. The fragrance awoke the most sensual memories of times shared, both here at Knightscote and the all-too-brief moments they had been together at Mersecombe. The last shreds of consciousness fled and Rose abandoned herself to the pleasures of his lovemaking. She tilted up her chin, allowing him access to the slender column of her throat. His lambent kisses sent waves of pleasure pulsing through her body and seemed to melt her very bones.

He began to unfasten her jacket, all the time anointing her neck and shoulders with tantalising kisses. She moaned as his hand slid over one breast. The chill in her limbs was replaced with burning desire. It was no longer enough to lie passively in his arms. Urgently she pulled his mouth to hers and began to kiss him. It was a deep, demanding kiss and he responded with equal energy. She tore at his clothes, desperate to feel his flesh pressed against hers. Hastily they undressed each other, pausing only to kiss and caress each newly exposed section of skin. Every touch, every kiss awoke a memory; they were joyfully rediscovering each other. As their clothes were discarded so the excitement grew. Blood pounded through their bodies; all sense of time and place was lost, nothing mattered but pleasuring each other until they reached the ultimate delight of their bodies uniting in a heady, exhilarating climax that left them both exhausted, their bodies entwined together, a tangle of limbs bathed in the red-gold glow of the dying fire.

Rose lay very still, eyes closed, arms wrapped tightly about Lawrence. He took her face between his hands and kissed her.

'Mmm.' She snuggled closer. 'I would like to stay like this for ever.'

He chuckled.

'Once the euphoria wears off, you will begin to feel the chill. We should get under the covers.'

They slipped between the sheets, their bodies fitting naturally together.

'What made you come here?' murmured Lawrence, nuzzling her ear. 'How could you risk riding out on such a night?'

She did not answer immediately.

'I had to come,' she said at last. 'I was wrong and I had to tell you. It seems everyone in Mersecombe knew the truth about Althea, except me. I should have been the first to know, not the last, because I should have listened to you.' She held him close, running her hands over his back as if to assure herself he was really there. 'I was afraid I would never see you again. There was no word from you; everyone thought you had left for good. Then Sir Jonas said he had heard from the lawyers that you had left London. He did not know where, but I hoped, prayed—so I came to find you.'

'Then thank heaven I was here.'

The warmth from his body was seeping into her own, driving away the aching cold, and when he raised his eyes to her face the message she read in them melted the icy fear that had numbed her heart.

'Yes.' She blinked back the tears that stung her eyes. 'Thank heaven.' She hugged him, burying her face in his shoulder. 'Oh, my love, I was such a fool not to trust you. Can you ever forgive me?'

'Never,' he muttered, covering her face and neck with hot, fervent kisses. 'You will have to make love to me for at least fifty years before I even begin to forgive you.'

Something between a sob and a chuckle escaped her. The familiar tug of desire was welling up inside and she measured the length of her body against his.

'Very well, then.' Her pulse leapt as she felt him pressing hard and aroused against her. 'Let us begin immediately.'

The fire had burned down to a faint glow, but moonlight shone in through the uncovered windows. Rose lay with her head resting on Lawrence's shoulder. Their love-making had continued long into the night. Sheets were tangled, covers had slipped to the floor and remained there, unregarded, until the icy night air began to bite and they gathered them up again, giggling like children. Then they had slept, locked in each other's arms.

Rose moved onto her back. Immediately Lawrence's hand closed on her fingers.

'What is it, my love?'

'Nothing. Only how wonderful this has been.'

He rolled over and gathered her against him.

'And it will continue to be. I do not intend to let you go again.'

'But you must,' she said gently. 'At least for a little while. I must go back to Mersecombe as soon as it is light. No one knows I am here—they will worry.'

'Then I shall come with you.'

'You do not have to do that.'

'I want to. I want to be part of your family from now on, Rose.'

His words made her heart soar.

'I would like that, Lawrence. Very much.'

'We need not wait for dawn.' He raised himself on one elbow, his face a shadowy blur hovering above her. 'There is moon enough. We will send for the gig and be back at Bluebell Cottage before your family has finished breakfast. And I will come to the church with you,' he added, his lips brushing hers. 'We can ask Mr Wilkins how soon we can be married.'

She put her hands against his chest.

'If we are to do all that, then ought we not to get ready?'

His voicc deepened and he slid his body closer.

'We should, of course. But not *quite* yet.'

'I have checked all her cupboards, ma'am, and she's not taken any of her clothes, but *her bed has not been slept in*!'

Mrs Molland put her hands to her cheeks as she heard Janet's anguished announcement. She glanced at the clock.

'We have a little time yet before we need to set off for church.' She tapped her foot, her brow furrowed, then shot another question at the maid. 'Does Sam know?'

'Not yet, ma'am, but—'

'Hush!' The hinges of the garden gate squeaked and Mrs Molland ran to the window in time to see Rose and Sir Lawrence walking up the path. 'Thank heavens!

She—I quite forgot that she has been out for an early-morning drive with Sir Lawrence.' Her eyes slid away from the maid's sceptical gaze. 'Go and let them in, Janet, if you please!'

If anything was needed to confirm Mrs Molland's suspicions, it was the glow of happiness in her daughter's eyes as she came into the room, followed by Sir Lawrence and a bouncing, liver-and-white pointer.

'Have I given you a fright, Mama? I beg your pardon.' Rose came forwards, happiness bubbling in her voice. 'I hope we are not too late for church?'

'Of course not, but where—?' Mrs Molland broke off as Sam came racing into the room. He pulled up quickly when he saw Sir Lawrence, but it was the sight of the puppy bounding up to him that caused him to cry out in delight.

'Bandit!'

Rose bit her lip to stop herself from laughing. Her mother was quite bursting with questions, none of which could be asked in front of Sam. That, of course, was a relief. She would have to explain everything at some stage, but she was quite happy to put it off for a little while.

'Sir Lawrence has come to spend the day with us,' she said, in answer to the unspoken question in Sam's round eyes. 'And he thought you might like to renew your acquaintance with Bandit.'

Sam was on his knees, happily allowing the dog to lick his face.

'I'm afraid we will have to lock her in the outhouse

while we go to church,' added Sir Lawrence, apologetically.

'And will you be coming to the Woolers' later, sir?' asked Sam, getting to his feet.

'I had forgotten,' uttered Rose, dismayed. 'Old Mrs Wooler invited us to join them for dinner this evening. We are the only guests. In light of their loss the family is observing a very quiet Christmas and as we were doing much the same thing—we will see them at the church, and I will ask them if they would object to you joining us.'

'Do say you will, sir,' cried Sam, his eyes shining. 'Jem has said there will not be any dancing, but there will be games, like snapdragon and forfeits, and bobbing for apples! Jem says they have decorated the house with garlands—and mistletoe.' He giggled and cast a mischievous look at Rose.

'Then I do hope they will allow me to come,' said Lawrence gravely.

A few minutes later the little party set off for the church. Rose was conscious of the curious stares as she walked in upon Sir Lawrence's arm, but she held her head high. She was encouraged by the vicar's kindly welcome, and by an approving nod and smile from old Mrs Wooler. That lady's keen eyes accurately assessed the situation and as soon as the service was finished she sent Jem over with an invitation for Sir Lawrence to join them for dinner.

'I think we may conclude that our marriage will generally be welcomed,' murmured Lawrence as he escorted Rose away from the church.

'I believe so.' Rose wondered how it was possible to feel so happy without bursting.

'It is starting to snow.' Lawrence turned up the collar of his greatcoat. 'I should have brought you in the gig.'

'No, it is only a few minutes' walk to get home. Besides, you have promised to use it to take us to the Woolers' later.' Mrs Molland and Sam were walking ahead of them and Rose could tell by her son's eager steps that he was keen to get back to the cottage. 'It was kind of you to bring Bandit; Sam is so excited to see her again.'

'Perhaps we should let him keep her, once we have decided where we are to live. It will be company for the boy.'

Rose hesitated.

'There is something I have not told you. I missed my monthly course.' Lawrence stopped immediately and she said quickly, 'It is early days, I know, but I went to see a doctor this week. A new man, just moved from Bath and said to be very experienced. He thinks there is no reason why I should not be able to have another child.'

Lawrence took her hands, giving her such a long, sober look that she began to panic.

'Of course it is not confirmed, and very likely it is not what I think—after all that has happened this year—'

Lawrence put his fingers to her lips, silencing her.

'If you are carrying my child, that would please me

more than I can say, but if our family is never more than you, me and Sam, I shall count myself the luckiest man alive.'

'Oh.' She blinked rapidly. 'Oh, what have I ever done to deserve you?'

His lips twitched.

'I cannot think.' The snow was falling heavily now, like a thick, white curtain, deadening all sound. 'You know,' he said, 'if this continues, I might not be able to get back to Knightscote this evening.'

'You should not even attempt it,' said Rose, trying to sound serious. 'We will put you up at the cottage.'

'What, you would risk sharing your house with one of the country's most notorious rakes?'

'Not at all.' She smiled up at him mistily. 'I would share it with my own, true love.'

* * * * *